Twenty-Two Essays of William Hazlitt

Selected by Arthur Beatty

Elibron Classics
www.elibron.com

Elibron Classics series.

© 2006 Adamant Media Corporation.

ISBN 0-543-85958-4 (paperback)
ISBN 0-543-85957-6 (hardcover)

This Elibron Classics Replica Edition is an unabridged facsimile
of the edition published by George G. Harrap & Co., Ltd., London.

THE HARRAP LIBRARY

Further volumes will be announced later

ESSAYS OF
WILLIAM HAZLITT

THE HARRAP LIBRARY

William Hazlitt

TWENTY-TWO ESSAYS OF WM. HAZLITT

Selected by ARTHUR BEATTY

LONDON: GEORGE
G. HARRAP & CO. LTD.
2-3 PORTSMOUTH ST. KINGSWAY

First published June 1920

Printed by THE BALLANTYNE PRESS
SPOTTISWOODE, BALLANTYNE & CO. LTD.
Colchester, London and Eton, England

CONTENTS

INTRODUCTION

I. PERSONALITY AND THEME

IT may be said that Hazlitt's peculiar bent in life can be explained by the fact that he came of a stock of Dissenters. Dissenters in England are mainly those who are opposed not only to the tenets of the Church of England, but also to the dominant policies of the ruling class, which the Church so largely represents. Hence they are led to oppose the existing order of things in religion, society, and thought, and thus it is that dissenters have always been in the vanguard of English development. In Hazlitt's case, this position as a dissenter caused him to take an attitude of criticism toward Tory politics, Tory journalism, and Tory literature, and, during the larger portion of his life, toward most of his fellow-workers in literature.

Moreover, Hazlitt was a man of a bad temper and cantankerous disposition. He quarrelled with both his wives, and with almost all his friends. He seemed to lack a saving realization of the necessity of certain social amenities which forbid the too-explosive expression of our opinions about the living; and as a result he had difficulties in getting on with other people in the rough round of daily life. He was somewhat distrustful of others; and this characteristic, with his retiring disposition, caused him to be regarded as a person rather impossible either as a friend or as an acquaintance. "Even in the common affairs of life," he once wrote in a mood not infrequently expressed in his essays, " in love, friendship and marriage, how little security we have when we trust our happiness into the hands of others! Most of the friends I have seen have turned out to be bitterest enemies, or cold, uncomfortable acquaintances. Old companions are like meats served up too often that lose their relish and their wholesomeness." [1]

[1] *On Living to One's-Self.*

vii

While this churlishness is an outstanding feature of Hazlitt's temper, too much has been made of it, largely because he has so freely confessed it; for after all it is on the surface, and is likely to conceal from us the love for simple honesty and downright truth which filled the central depths. Charles Lamb, who knew him better than any other soul, testified to Hazlitt in these noble terms, at a time when he could receive neither glory nor honor thereby:

"I should belie my own conscience, if I said less than that I think William Hazlitt to be, in his natural and healthy state, one of the wisest and finest spirits breathing. So far from being ashamed of that intimacy which was betwixt us, it is my boast that I was able for so many years to have preserved it entire, and I think I shall go to my grave without finding, or expecting to find, such another companion."

This deep-seated, congenital attitude of protest was emphasized and ennobled by a further, and in this case an external, complication. When he and his generation were in their formative years, the French Revolution burst upon an astonished world with cyclonic power, and was hailed by the youth of England as the dawn of a new day for the finest hopes and desires of humanity. Youth dated its day of birth from the Great Event, and all things were viewed only in connection with it. Coleridge gave memorable expression to the new hopes of the time in more than one poem, singing his worship of "the Spirit of divinest Liberty"; and Wordsworth summed up once and for all the universal feeling of the young:

"Bliss was it in that dawn to be alive,
But to be young was very Heaven."

Hazlitt was as deeply committed to the Revolution as any of his contemporaries and, unlike them, he remained faithful to it to his last day of life. In the following memorable passage he states what all Youth once believed, and what he never abandoned:

"For my part, I set out in life with the French Revolution, and that event had considerable influence on my early feelings, as on those of others. Youth was then doubly such. It was the dawn of a new

era, a new impulse had been given to men's minds, and the sun of
Liberty rose upon the sun of Life in the same day, and both were
proud to run their race together. Little did I dream, while my
first hopes and wishes went hand in hand with those of the human
race, that long before my eyes should close, that dawn should be
overcast, and set once more in the night of despotism — 'total eclipse!'
Happy that I did not. I felt for years, and during the best part of
my existence, *heart-whole* in that cause, and triumphed in the triumphs over the enemies of man! At that time, while the fairest
aspirations of the human mind seemed about to be realized, ere the
image of man was defaced and his breast mangled in scorn, philosophy
took a higher, poetry could afford a deeper range." [1]

Holding this faith as he did, it seemed to Hazlitt impossible
that anyone could have held it and become an apostate,
except from the basest motives. Hence his quarrel with
Wordsworth, Southey, Coleridge, Burke, and almost all the
other representative men of his time. In a day when Napoleon was hated and feared, Hazlitt remained faithful in
his admiration, for he maintained that Napoleon, being
opposed to kings, stood for democracy, and that kings are
the enemies of men:

"I knew all along there was but one alternative — the cause of
kings or of mankind. This I foresaw, this I feared; the world would
see it now, when it is too late. . . . There is but one question in the
heart of monarchs — whether mankind are their property or not." [2]

He passionately desired to make the world safe for democracy, and he believed Napoleon to be a main agency in that
laudable work; but in this belief and in his sarcastic attacks
on kings he stood alone on the farther side of a great gulf
which divided him from those who might have been his
companions.

Notwithstanding his differences with the representative
men of his time, it remains superlatively true that Hazlitt
gives us as complete a representation of the hopes and ideas
which animated those who furthered or fought the cause of
the Revolution, as any other prose writer. One might go
further and say that it is in his essays, rather than in the
prose of Wordsworth, Coleridge, Southey, and the rest of

[1] *The Feeling of Immortality in Youth.*
[2] *Whether Genius is Conscious of its Powers.*

the great poets, that we find the best commentary on the intellectual and emotional upheaval of that momentous period. *My First Acquaintance with Poets* is the most intimate view which we have into the psychology of Wordsworth and Coleridge in the very process of composing the epoch-making *Lyrical Ballads;* and the essay on *The Feeling of Immortality in Youth* and that on *Mr. Wordsworth* give the doctrine which underlies Wordsworth's poetry with a simplicity and accuracy which can come only from the insight of genius and the familiar knowledge of a friend.

But Hazlitt is no mere echo of any person or set of persons, however representative. In the final analysis, he is his own voice, speaking authentic words which reveal the truths which he has discovered for himself and which he expresses in his own individual manner. He was always free to say that before he knew Burke he did not know the true eloquence of a man pouring out his own mind on paper,[1] and that before he knew Coleridge he was "dumb, inarticulate, helpless, like a worm by the way-side, crushed, bleeding, lifeless," and that the reason why his understanding did not "remain dumb and brutish," or at length found a language to express itself, "he owed to Coleridge,"[2] who was the only person from whom he ever learned anything.[3]

But when his mind was awakened, it was to self-expression; and in these essays we have the words of a resilient, original mind which has been brought into fruitful contact with the realities of life in many of its aspects: with death, disagreeable people, the ignorance of the learned, the skill of jugglers and athletes, or the joy of going a journey.

Adopting the reminiscent, retrospective, and autobiographical method developed to its perfection by Wordsworth, Hazlitt poured forth his thoughts on life; and, guided in his structure by his emotional attitude, he moulded the loose essay into a rounded form with established bounds. In this new form which he developed he makes a distinct place for

[1] *On Reading Old Books.*
[2] *My First Acquaintance with Poets.*
[3] *Lectures on the English Poets, Last Lecture.*

himself as one of the greatest and most distinctive essayists in the great line of Temple, Selden, Steele, Addison, Johnson, and Goldsmith; and it might be said, without reflection on anyone, that he has had no successor.

II. STYLE

The most marked feature of Hazlitt's style is the lack of any eccentricity in his choice of words or in his sentence structure, and its prevailing qualities of straightforward simplicity and ever-present rhythm. In this respect Hazlitt's style may be regarded as characteristically English style of the more familiar and colloquial sort. This statement of the matter does not imply that this is a mean, or despicable, or easily-acquired style. Quite the opposite is meant, and on this point we had best consult Hazlitt himself, who has given a rather full exposition of his own ideals in English prose, which he endeavored to realize in his own practice. Speaking of the familiar style, he says:

"It is not easy to write a familiar style. Many people mistake a familiar for a vulgar style, and suppose that to write without affectation is to write at random. On the contrary, there is nothing that requires more precision, and, if I may so say, purity of expression, than the style I am speaking of. It utterly rejects not only all unmeaning pomp, but all low, cant phrases, and loose, unconnected, *slip-shod* allusions. It is not to take the first word that offers, but the best word in common use; it is not to throw words together in any combinations we please, but to follow and avail ourselves of the true idiom of the language. To write a genuine familiar or truly English style is to write as anyone would speak in common conversation, who had a thorough command and choice of words, or who could discourse with ease, force, and perspicuity, setting aside all pedantic and oratorical flourishes." [1]

With regard to vocabulary, he makes the following claim for himself:

"I conceive that words are like money, not the worse for being common, but that it is the stamp of custom alone that gives them circulation or value. I am fastidious in this respect, and would almost as soon coin the currency of the realm as counterfeit the King's English. I never invented or gave a new and unauthorized meaning to any word but a single one." [2]

[1] *On Familiar Style.* [2] *On Familiar Style.*

Even a brief examination of Hazlitt's vocabulary will bear out all these claims, and anyone who has even only a moderate knowledge of English prose knows that few authors show a finer choice of the fitting word on the colloquial level of dignified everyday intercourse.

Hazlitt's sentences, as has been said, follow the genius of the English idiom, that is, they are loose, not periodic or suspended. They conform to the general scheme of (1) the subject, (2) the verb, (3) the object, or complements; not only in the simpler, briefer sentences, but in the longer, more elaborated forms.

A few examples will suffice. First, the simple forms:

I can write fast enough now. **10**, 29.
I remember but one other topic of discourse in this walk. **11**, 1-2.
I cannot see the wit of walking and talking at the same time. **87**, 6.

To these simple forms as a basis Hazlitt frequently gives a suspended or periodic effect by the very simple, colloquial means of beginning the sentence with the representative "it," "there," or similar word. This method of sentence structure combines colloquial familiarity with the dignity of the periodic sentence.

Examples:

It was by this irresistible quality, and not by the force of his genius, that he vanquished. **130**, 8-9.
There is hardly anything that shows the short-sightedness or capriciousness of the imagination more than travelling does. **94**, 8-9.

Compound forms of the loose structure are illustrated by the following examples:

In the mean time I went to Llangollen Vale, by way of initiating myself in the mysteries of natural scenery; and I must say I was enchanted with it. **12**, 10-12.
We can never be satisfied with gazing; and nature will still want us to look and applaud. **166**, 3-5.
He was the son of Neptune; and having lost an eye in some affray between the gods and men, was told that if he would go to meet the rising sun, he would recover his sight. **223**, 3-5.

Elaborate examples of the multiplication of this simple structure to produce a magnificent harmony are to be

found in the passage describing Coleridge's influence on him
(**224,** 28–**225,** 28), and in the passage quoted in the introductory
note to the essay on Coleridge, which gives an account of
Coleridge's spiritual development.

Occasionally Hazlitt inverts the loose construction and
obtains a modified periodic effect, as in the great sentence
in *The Feeling of Immortality in Youth* (**166,** 17–**169,** 8), but
this construction is a departure from his usual practice and
is used only as an occasional grace.

These examples of the longer sentences illustrate very
clearly Hazlitt's love of balance and parallel construction;
but the shorter sentences also show that this is a constant
feature of his style. He has numerous sentences, short,
medium, and long, which are based on the parallel between
likenesses or contrasts.

Examples:

I can enjoy society in a room; but out of doors nature is company
enough for me. **87,** 2–3.

I am then never less alone than when alone. **87,** 4.

Give me the clear blue sky over my head, and the green turf beneath my feet, a winding road before me, and a three hours' march
to dinner — and then to thinking! **87,** 29–32.

I laugh, I run, I leap, I sing for joy. **88,** 1.

Burke has enunciated a canon of style that the master
sentence of every paragraph should involve, firstly, a thought,
secondly, an image, and, thirdly, a sentiment. This may be
fully applied to most of Hazlitt's sentences, for the thoughts
which he expounded are given flight and buoyancy by an
atmosphere of feeling, and continuity of progress by the
energy of images. This is the result of a full mind, which
brings to the subject a never-failing supply of supporting
images. Hazlitt's argument never becomes abstract, but
is always conducted in the concrete. Examples of this need
not be cited, for it would be impossible to open this volume
at any page which would not yield an abundance of instances
to establish this fact of his practice. It seemed to be an
impossibility with him to write in an empty manner; words,
illustrations, quotations, remembrances, images crowd in
upon him and vivify his pages. As Dryden says of Chaucer,

b

here is *God's plenty*, and the reader can glean in whichever
field he may desire, with the sober certainty of gathering a
generous sheaf.

To the fullness and riches of Hazlitt's mind we must add
the musical quality of his ear. Most of us write as deaf
men talk, — without life or rhythm. Hazlitt, on the contrary, writes a prose which seems to arise in speech; and he
seems to hear what he puts down on paper and to test it by
the standard of speech rhythm. It would be difficult indeed to
find in Hazlitt a sentence which is not instinct with the life
of the rhythm and cadence which is native to the English
tongue; and it is this constant quality which led Robert
Louis Stevenson to utter that famous ejaculation: "We are
mighty fine fellows, but we cannot write like William Hazlitt."

No one knew the sources of his style better than Hazlitt
himself, and nowhere has he indicated them more definitely
than in a passage in his *Letter to William Gifford, Esq.* This
passage we shall allow to stand as the final statement concerning Hazlitt's prose style:

"As to my style, I thought little about it. I only used the word
which seemed to me to signify the idea I wanted to convey, and
I did not rest till I had got it. In seeking for truth I sometimes
found beauty."

OUTLINE OF HAZLITT'S LIFE

1778. April 10. William Hazlitt was born at Maidstone, Kent. His father, John Hazlitt, was from Shronell, County Antrim, Ireland; his mother, Grace Loftus, was from Wisbeach, Cambridgeshire.

1780-1783. The Hazlitts were at Bandon, in the County of Cork, Ireland.

1783-1787. The Hazlitts were in America, residing in New York, Philadelphia, and Boston. William Hazlitt always remembered with pleasure some of his American experiences.

1787. The Hazlitts returned to England and took up their residence at Wem, an obscure and solitary village in Shropshire.

1791. Wrote a letter to the *Shrewsbury Chronicle* in defence of Dr. Priestley.

1793. Hazlitt entered the Unitarian College at Hackney, a borough of London.

1796. Hazlitt read Burke's "Letter to a Noble Lord," in the *St. James Chronicle*.

1798. Hazlitt met Coleridge and Wordsworth. This was the great event of Hazlitt's literary and intellectual life.

1802. Hazlitt went to Paris to study art in the Louvre.

1803. Hazlitt began a career as a portrait-painter.

1805. *Essay on the Principles of Human Action: Being an Argument in favour of the National Disinterestedness of the Human Mind.*

1806. *Free Thoughts on Public Affairs, or Advice to a Patriot.*

1807. *An Abridgement of the Light of Nature Pursued, by Abraham Tucker.*
Reply to the Essay on Population by Malthus.

1808. *The Eloquence of the British Senate.* 2 volumes.
Hazlitt married Sarah Stoddart, May 1, and settled at Winterslow, a village in Wiltshire.

1810. *A New and Improved Grammar of the English Tongue.*

1811. September 26. A son born, and christened William. This son became his father's literary executor.

1812. Removed to London, and became Parliamentary reporter for the *Morning Chronicle*. Lectured on "The Rise and Progress of Modern Philosophy."

1814. Became dramatic critic for the *Morning Chronicle*. Contributed to the *Edinburgh Review* and *The Examiner*.

1816. *Memoirs of the Late Thomas Holcroft, Written by Himself.*

1817. *The Round Table: a Collection of Essays on Literature, Men and Manners.* 2 volumes.

1818. *Lectures on the English Poets.* Delivered at the Surrey Institution. *A View of the English Stage, or A Series of Dramatic Criticisms.*

1819. *Lectures on the English Comic Writers.* Delivered at the Surrey Institution. *A Letter to William Gifford, Esq. Political Essays, with Sketches of Public Characters.*

1820. *Lectures on the Dramatic Literature of the Age of Elizabeth.* Delivered at the Surrey Institution.

1821. *Table-Talk, or Original Essays.* Vol. I.

1822. *Table-Talk, or Original Essays.* Vol. II.
Hazlitt was divorced from his wife at Edinburgh, in accordance with Scots law.

1823. *Liber Amoris, or the New Pygmalion.* This book is a record of his infatuation with Miss Sarah Walker.
Characteristics in the Manner of Rochefoucault's Maxims.

1824. *Sketches of the Principal Art Galleries in England.*
Contributed article on Fine Arts to the *Encyclopædia Britannica.*
Married Mrs. Bridgwater. She separated from him the following year.

1825. *The Spirit of the Age, or Contemporary Portraits.*
Select Poets of Great Britain, a revision of the *Select British Poets* published and suppressed in 1824.

1826. *The Plain Speaker: Opinions on Books, Men, and Things.*
Notes of a Journey through France and Italy.

1826–1827. *Boswell Redivivus,* published in the *New Monthly Magazine.* This is the first form of *Conversations of James Northcote, Esq., R. A.*

1828. *The Life of Napoleon Buonaparte,* Vols. I and II.

1830. *The Life of Napoleon Buonaparte,* Vols. III and IV.
The Conversations of James Northcote, Esq. R. A.

1830. September 18. Hazlitt died in London, aged 52 years.

1836. *Literary Remains of William Hazlitt;* with a Notice of his Life, by his son, and Thoughts on his Genius and Writings, by E. L. Bulwer and Mr. Serjeant Talfourd. 2 volumes.

1839. *Sketches and Essays,* by William Hazlitt. Now first collected by his son.

1850. *Winterslow;* Essays and Characters written there. By William Hazlitt. Collected by his son.

SELECTED BIBLIOGRAPHY

I. Editions and Selections

1. *The Collected Works of William Hazlitt, Edited by A. R. Waller and Arnold Glover*, London, 1902–1906. Twelve volumes, with introductions, bibliographical descriptions, and notes. The first volume contains an Introduction by William Ernest Henley. A thirteenth volume contains a full index to the Collected Works.
2. *Essays of William Hazlitt*, with Introduction by Frank Carr, London, 1889.
3. *Essays on Poetry*, Edited with Introduction and Notes by D. Nichol Smith, London, 1906.
4. *Selections from William Hazlitt*, Edited with Introduction and Notes by Will David Howe, Boston, 1913.

II. Biography

1. *Literary Remains of the Late William Hazlitt, with a Notice of his Life by his Son, and Thoughts on his Genius and Writings by E. L. Bulwer, Esq., M.P., and Mr. Serjeant Talfourd*. 2 vols. 1836.
2. *Memoirs of William Hazlitt*. William Carew Hazlitt. 2 vols. 1867.
3. *Four Generations of a Literary Family, the Hazlitts in England, Ireland, and America, their Friends and their Fortunes*. 1725–1896. William Carew Hazlitt. 2 vols. 1897.
4. *Lamb and Hazlitt*, Letters and Records. William Carew Hazlitt. 1899.
5. *William Hazlitt*. Augustine Birrell, English Men of Letters Series. 1902.
6. *Vie de William Hazlitt, L'Essayiste*. Jules Douady. Paris, 1907.
7. *Liste chronologique des Œuvres de William Hazlitt*. Jules Douady. Paris, 1906.

III. Criticism

1. De Quincey, Thomas. *Works*, V and VI (edited by Masson).
2. Elton, Oliver. *A Survey of English Literature* (1780–1830). 1912.
3. *Encyclopædia Britannica*, Vol. XIII.
4. Herford, C. H. *The Age of Wordsworth*. 1899.

5. Hunt, Leigh. *Autobiography.* 3 vols. 1850.
6. Hunt, Leigh. *Dramatic Essays* (edited by Archer and Lowe).
7. Saintsbury, George E. *Essays on English Literature* (1780–1860). 1891.
8. Saintsbury, George E. *History of Criticism.* 3 vols. 1900–1904.
9. Stephen, Leslie. *Hours in a Library.* Vol. II. 1874–1879.
10. Stephen, Leslie. *William Hazlitt* in *Dictionary of National Biography.*
11. Winchester, C. T. *A Group of English Essayists.* New York, 1910.

ESSAYS OF HAZLITT

MY FIRST ACQUAINTANCE WITH POETS

My father was a Dissenting Minister at W ——m in Shropshire; and in the year 1798 (the figures that compose that
date are to me like the "dreaded name of Demogorgon")
Mr. Coleridge came to Shrewsbury, to succeed Mr. Rowe in
the spiritual charge of a Unitarian congregation there. He
did not come till late on the Saturday afternoon before he
was to preach; and Mr. Rowe, who himself went down to
the coach in a state of anxiety and expectation, to look for the
arrival of his successor, could find no one at all answering the
description but a round-faced man in a short black coat (like
a shooting-jacket) which hardly seemed to have been made
for him, but who seemed to be talking at a great rate to his
fellow-passengers. Mr. Rowe had scarce returned to give
an account of his disappointment, when the round-faced man
in black entered, and dissipated all doubts on the subject,
by beginning to talk. He did not cease while he staid; nor
has he since, that I know of. He held the good town of
Shrewsbury in delightful suspense for three weeks that he
remained there, "fluttering the *proud Salopians* like an eagle
in a dove-cote;" and the Welsh mountains that skirt the
horizon with their tempestuous confusion, agree to have
heard no such mystic sounds since the days of

"High-born Hoel's harp or soft Llewellyn's lay!"

As we passed along between W——m and Shrewsbury, and
I eyed their blue tops seen through the wintry branches, or
the red rustling leaves of the sturdy oak-trees by the road-
side, a sound was in my ears as of a Siren's song; I was stunned,
startled with it, as from deep sleep; but I had no notion then
that I should ever be able to express my admiration to others
in motley imagery or quaint allusion, till the light of his genius

1

shone into my soul, like the sun's rays glittering in the puddles of the road.   I was at that time dumb, inarticulate, helpless, like a worm by the way-side, crushed, bleeding, lifeless; but now, bursting from the deadly bands that bound them,

"With Styx nine times round them,".

my ideas float on winged words, and as they expand their plumes, catch the golden light of other years.   My soul has indeed remained in its original bondage, dark, obscure, with longings infinite and unsatisfied; my heart, shut up in the prison-house of this rude clay, has never found, nor will it ever find, a heart to speak to; but that my understanding also did not remain dumb and brutish, or at length found a language to express itself, I owe to Coleridge.   But this is not to my purpose.

My father lived ten miles from Shrewsbury, and was in the habit of exchanging visits with Mr. Rowe, and with Mr. Jenkins of Whitchurch (nine miles farther on) according to the custom of Dissenting Ministers in each other's neighbourhood.   A line of communication is thus established, by which the flame of civil and religious liberty is kept alive, and nourishes its smouldering fire unquenchable, like the fires in the *Agamemnon* of Æschylus, placed at different stations, that waited for ten long years to announce with their blazing pyramids the destruction of Troy.   Coleridge had agreed to come over and see my father, according to the courtesy of the country, as Mr. Rowe's probable successor; but in the mean time I had gone to hear him preach the Sunday after his arrival.   A poet and a philosopher getting up into a Unitarian pulpit to preach the Gospel, was a romance in these degenerate days, a sort of revival of the primitive spirit of Christianity, which was not to be resisted.

It was in January, 1798, that I rose one morning before daylight, to walk ten miles in the mud, and went to hear this celebrated person preach.   Never, the longest day I have to live, shall I have such another walk as this cold, raw, comfortless one, in the winter of the year 1798.   *Il y a des impressions que ni le tems ni les circonstances peuvent effacer.   Dusse-je vivre des siècles entiers, le doux tems de ma jeunesse ne peut renaître pour moi, ni s'effacer jamais dans ma mémoire.* When I got there, the organ was playing the 100th psalm, and, when it was done, Mr. Coleridge rose and gave out his text, "And he went up into the mountain to pray, HIMSELF, ALONE." As he gave out this text, his voice "rose like a steam of rich distilled perfumes," and when he came to the two last words, which he pronounced loud, deep, and distinct, it seemed to me, who was then young, as if the sounds had echoed from the bottom of the human heart, and as if that prayer might have floated in solemn silence through the universe. The idea of St. John came into mind, "of one crying in the wilderness, who had his loins girt about, and whose food was locusts and wild honey." The preacher then launched into his subject, like an eagle dallying with the wind. The sermon was upon peace and war; upon church and state — not their alliance, but their separation — on the spirit of the world and the spirit of Christianity, not as the same, but as opposed to one another. He talked of those who had "inscribed the cross of Christ on banners dripping with human gore." He made a poetical and pastoral excursion, — and to shew the fatal effects of war, drew a striking contrast between the simple shepherd boy, driving his team afield, or sitting under the hawthorn, piping to his flock, "as though he should never be old," and the same poor country-lad, crimped, kidnapped, brought into town, made drunk at an alehouse, turned into a wretched drummerboy, with his hair sticking on end with powder and pomatum, a long cue at his back, and tricked out in the loathsome finery of the profession of blood.

"Such were the notes our once-lov'd poet sung."

And for myself, I could not have been more delighted if I had heard the music of the spheres. Poetry and Philosophy had met together, Truth and Genius had embraced, under the eye and with the sanction of Religion. This was even beyond my hopes. I returned home well satisfied. The sun that was still labouring pale and wan through the sky, obscured by

thick mists, seemed an emblem of the *good cause;* and the
cold dank drops of dew that hung half melted on the beard
of the thistle, had something genial and refreshing in them;
for there was a spirit of hope and youth in all nature, that
turned everything into good. The face of nature had not
then the brand of JUS DIVINUM on it:

> "Like to that sanguine flower inscrib'd with woe."

On the Tuesday following, the half-inspired speaker came.
I was called down into the room where he was, and went half-
hoping, half-afraid. He received me very graciously, and I
listened for a long time without uttering a word. I did not
suffer in his opinion by my silence. "For those two hours,"
he afterwards was pleased to say, "he was conversing with
W. H.'s forehead!" His appearance was different from what
I had anticipated from seeing him before. At a distance,
and in the dim light of the chapel, there was to me a strange
wildness in his aspect, a dusky obscurity, and I thought him
pitted with the small-pox. His complexion was at that
time clear, and even bright —

> "As are the children of yon azure sheen."

His forehead was broad and high, light as if built of ivory,
with large projecting eyebrows, and his eyes rolling beneath
them like a sea with darkened lustre. "A certain tender
bloom his face o'erspread," a purple tinge as we see it in the
pale thoughtful complexions of the Spanish portrait-painters,
Murillo and Velasquez. His mouth was gross, voluptuous,
open, eloquent; his chin good-humoured and round; but his
nose, the rudder of the face, the index of the will, was small,
feeble, nothing — like what he has done. It might seem that
the genius of his face as from a height surveyed and pro-
jected him (with sufficient capacity and huge aspiration) into
the world unknown of thought and imagination, with nothing
to support or guide his veering purpose, as if Columbus had
launched his adventurous course for the New World in a
scallop, without oars or compass. So at least I comment on
it after the event. Coleridge in his person was rather above
the common size, inclining to the corpulent, or like Lord

Hamlet, "somewhat fat and pursy." His hair (now, alas! grey) was then black and glossy as the raven's, and fell in smooth masses over his forehead. This long, pendulous hair is peculiar to enthusiasts, to those whose minds tend heavenward; and is traditionally inseparable (though of a different colour) from the pictures of Christ. It ought to belong, as a character, to all who preach *Christ crucified*, and Coleridge was at that time one of those!

It was curious to observe the contrast between him and my father, who was a veteran in the cause, and then declining into the vale of years. He had been a poor Irish lad, carefully brought up by his parents, and sent to the University of Glasgow (where he studied under Adam Smith) to prepare him for his future destination. It was his mother's proudest wish to see her son a Dissenting Minister. So if we look back to past generations (as far as eye can reach) we see the same hopes, fears, wishes, followed by the same disappointments, throbbing in the human heart; and so we may see them (if we look forward) rising up for ever, and disappearing, like vapourish bubbles, in the human breast! After being tossed about from congregation to congregation in the heats of the Unitarian controversy, and squabbles about the American war, he had been relegated to an obscure village, where he was to spend the last thirty years of his life, far from the only converse that he loved, the talk about disputed texts of Scripture and the cause of civil and religious liberty. Here he passed his days, repining but resigned, in the study of the Bible, and the perusal of the Commentators, — huge folios, not easily got through, one of which would outlast a winter! Why did he pore on these from morn to night (with the exception of a walk in the fields or a turn in the garden to gather broccoli-plants or kidney-beans of his own rearing, with no small degree of pride and pleasure)? Here were "no figures nor no fantasies," — neither poetry nor philosophy — nothing to dazzle, nothing to excite modern curiosity; but to his lack-lustre eyes there appeared, within the pages of the ponderous, unwieldy, neglected tomes, the sacred name of JEHOVAH in Hebrew Capitals: pressed down by the

weight of the style, worn to the last fading thinness of the
understanding, there were glimpses, glimmering notions of
the patriarchal wanderings, with palm-trees hovering in the
horizon, and processions of camels at the distance of three
thousand years; there was Moses with the Burning Bush,
the number of the Twelve Tribes, types, shadows, glosses
on the law and the prophets; there were discussions (dull
enough) on the age of Methuselah, a mighty speculation!
there were outlines, rude guesses at the shape of Noah's Ark
and of the riches of Solomon's Temple; questions as to the
date of the creation, predictions of the end of all things; the
great lapses of time, the strange mutations of the globe were
unfolded with the voluminous leaf, as it turned over; and
though the soul might slumber with an hieroglyphic veil of
inscrutable mysteries drawn over it, yet it was in a slumber
ill-exchanged for all the sharpened realities of sense, wit,
fancy, or reason. My father's life was comparatively a
dream; but it was a dream of infinity and eternity, of death,
the resurrection, and a judgment to come!

No two individuals were ever more unlike than were the
host and his guest. A poet was to my father a sort of nondescript: yet whatever added grace to the Unitarian cause
was to him welcome. He could hardly have been more surprised or pleased, if our visitor had worn wings. Indeed, his
thoughts had wings; and as the silken sounds rustled round
our little wainscoted parlour, my father threw back his
spectacles over his forehead, his white hairs mixing with its
sanguine hue; and a smile of delight beamed across his rugged
cordial face, to think that Truth had found a new ally in
Fancy![1] Besides, Coleridge seemed to take considerable
notice of me, and that of itself was enough. He talked very
familiarly, but agreeably, and glanced over a variety of subjects. At dinner-time he grew more animated, and dilated

---

[1] My father was one of those who mistook his talent after all. He
used to be very much dissatisfied that I preferred his Letters to his
Sermons. The last were forced and dry; the first came naturally
from him. For ease, half-plays on words, and a supine, monkish,
indolent pleasantry, I have never seen them equalled.

in a very edifying manner on Mary Wolstonecraft and Mackintosh. The last, he said, he considered (on my father's speaking of his *Vindiciæ Gallicæ* as a capital performance) as a clever, scholastic man — a master of the topics, — or as the ready warehouseman of letters, who knew exactly where to lay his hand on what he wanted, though the goods were not his own. He thought him no match for Burke, either in style or matter. Burke was a metaphysician, Mackintosh a mere logician. Burke was an orator (almost a poet) who reasoned in figures, because he had an eye for nature: Mackintosh, on the other hand, was a rhetorician, who had only an eye to commonplaces. On this I ventured to say that I had always entertained a great opinion of Burke, and that (as far as I could find) the speaking of him with contempt might be made the test of a vulgar, democratical mind. This was the first observation I ever made to Coleridge, and he said it was a very just and striking one. I remember the leg of Welsh mutton and the turnips on the table that day had the finest flavour imaginable. Coleridge added that Mackintosh and Tom Wedgwood (of whom, however, he spoke highly) had expressed a very indifferent opinion of his friend Mr. Wordsworth, on which he remarked to them — "He strides on so far before you, that he dwindles in the distance!" Godwin had once boasted to him of having carried on an argument with Mackintosh for three hours with dubious success; Coleridge told him — "If there had been a man of genius in the room, he would have settled the question in five minutes." He asked me if I had ever seen Mary Wolstonecraft, and I said, I had once for a few moments, and that she seemed to me to turn off Godwin's objections to something she advanced with quite a playful, easy air. He replied, that "this was only one instance of the ascendancy which people of imagination exercised over those of mere intellect." He did not rate Godwin very high [1] (this was caprice or prejudice, real or

[1] He complained in particular of the presumption of his attempting to establish the future immortality of man, "without" (as he said) "knowing what Death was or what Life was" — and the tone in which he pronounced these two words seemed to convey a complete image of both.

affected) but he had a great idea of Mrs. Wolstonecraft's powers of conversation, none at all of her talent for book-making. We talked a little about Holcroft. He had been asked if he was not much struck *with* him, and he said, he thought himself in more danger of being struck *by* him. I complained that he would not let me get on at all, for he required a definition of every the commonest word, exclaiming, "What do you mean by a *sensation*, Sir? What do you mean by an *idea?*" This, Coleridge said, was barricadoing the road to truth: — it was setting up a turnpike-gate at every step we took. I forget a great number of things, many more than I remember; but the day passed off pleasantly, and the next morning Mr. Coleridge was to return to Shrewsbury. When I came down to breakfast, I found that he had just received a letter from his friend, T. Wedgwood, making him an offer of £150 a-year if he chose to wave his present pursuit, and devote himself entirely to the study of poetry and philosophy. Coleridge seemed to make up his mind to close with this proposal in the act of tying on one of his shoes. It threw an additional damp on his departure. It took the wayward enthusiast quite from us to cast him into Deva's winding vales, or by the shores of old romance. Instead of living at ten miles distance, of being the pastor of a Dissenting congregation at Shrewsbury, he was henceforth to inhabit the Hill of Parnassus, to be a Shepherd on the Delectable Mountains. Alas! I knew not the way thither, and felt very little gratitude for Mr. Wedgwood's bounty. I was pleasantly relieved from this dilemma; for Mr. Coleridge, asking for a pen and ink, and going to a table to write something on a bit of card, advanced towards me with undulating step, and giving me the precious document, said that that was his address, *Mr. Coleridge, Nether Stowey, Somersetshire;* and that he should be glad to see me there in a few weeks' time, and, if I chose, would come half-way to meet me. I was not less surprised than the shepherd-boy (this simile is to be found in Cassandra) when he sees a thunder-bolt fall close at his feet. I stammered out my acknowledgments and acceptance of this offer (I thought Mr. Wedgwood's annuity a trifle to it) as well as I could; and this mighty business being settled, the poet-preacher took leave, and I accompanied him six miles on the road. It was a fine morning in the middle of winter, and he talked the whole way. The scholar in Chaucer is described as going

―― "sounding on his way."

So Coleridge went on his. In digressing, in dilating, in passing from subject to subject, he appeared to me to float in air, to slide on ice. He told me in confidence (going along) that he should have preached two sermons before he accepted the situation at Shrewsbury, one on Infant Baptism, the other on the Lord's Supper, shewing that he could not administer either, which would have effectually disqualified him for the object in view. I observed that he continually crossed me on the way by shifting from one side of the foot-path to the other. This struck me as an odd movement; but I did not at that time connect it with any instability of purpose or involuntary change of principle, as I have done since. He seemed unable to keep on in a straight line. He spoke slightingly of Hume (whose *Essays on Miracles* he said was stolen from an objection started in one of South's Sermons — *Credat Judæus Appella!*) I was not very much pleased at this account of Hume, for I had just been reading, with infinite relish, that completest of all metaphysical *choke-pears*, his *Treatise on Human Nature*, to which the *Essays*, in point of scholastic subtlety and close reasoning, are mere elegant trifling, light summer-reading. Coleridge even denied the excellence of Hume's general style, which I think betrayed a want of taste or candour. He however made me amends by the manner in which he spoke of Berkeley. He dwelt particularly on his *Essay on Vision* as a masterpiece of analytical reasoning. So it undoubtedly is. He was exceedingly angry with Dr. Johnson for striking the stone with his foot, in allusion to this author's *Theory of Matter and Spirit*, and saying, "Thus I confute him, Sir." Coleridge drew a parallel (I don't know how he brought about the connection) between Bishop Berkeley and Tom Paine. He said the one was an instance

of a subtle, the other of an acute mind, than which no two
things could be more distinct. The one was a shop-boy's
quality, the other the characteristic of a philosopher. He
considered Bishop Butler as a true philosopher, a profound
and conscientious thinker, a genuine reader of nature and his
own mind. He did not speak of his *Analogy*, but of his
Sermons at the Rolls' Chapel, of which I had never heard.
Coleridge somehow always contrived to prefer the *unknown*
to the *known*. In this instance he was right. The *Analogy*
is a tissue of sophistry, of wire-drawn, theological special-
pleading; the *Sermons* (with the Preface to them) are in a
fine vein of deep, matured reflection, a candid appeal to our
observation of human nature, without pedantry and without
bias. I told Coleridge I had written a few remarks, and was
sometimes foolish enough to believe that I had made a discovery on the same subject (the *Natural Disinterestedness of
the Human Mind*) — and I tried to explain my view of it to
Coleridge, who listened with great willingness, but I did not
succeed in making myself understood. I sat down to the
task shortly afterwards for the twentieth time, got new pens
and paper, determined to make clear work of it, wrote a few
meagre sentences in the skeleton-style of a mathematical
demonstration, stopped half way down the second page;
and, after trying in vain to pump up any words, images, notions, apprehensions, facts, or observations, from that gulf
of abstraction in which I had plunged myself for four or five
years preceding, gave up the attempt as labour in vain, and
shed tears of helpless despondency on the blank, unfinished
paper. I can write fast enough now. Am I better than I
was then? Oh, no! One truth discovered, one pang of regret
at not being able to express it, is better than all the fluency
and flippancy in the world. Would that I could go back to
what I then was! Why can we not revive past times as we
can revisit old places? If I had the quaint Muse of Sir
Philip Sidney to assist me, I would write a *Sonnet to the Road
between W——m and Shrewsbury*, and immortalise every step
of it by some fond enigmatical conceit. I would swear that
the very milestones had ears, and that Harmer-hill stooped

with all its pines, to listen to a poet, as he passed! I remember but one other topic of discourse in this walk. He mentioned Paley, praised the naturalness and clearness of his style, but condemned his sentiments, thought him a mere time-serving casuist, and said that "the fact of his work on *Moral and Political Philosophy* being made a text-book in our universities was a disgrace to the national character." We parted at the six-mile stone; and I returned homeward, pensive but much pleased. I had met with unexpected notice from a person whom I believed to have been prejudiced against me. "Kind and affable to me had been his condescension, and should be honoured ever with suitable regard." He was the first poet I had known, and he certainly answered to that inspired name. I had heard a great deal of his powers of conversation, and was not disappointed. In fact, I never met with anything at all like them, either before or since. I could easily credit the accounts which were circulated of his holding forth to a large party of ladies and gentlemen, an evening or two before, on the Berkeleian Theory, when he made the whole material universe look like a transparency of fine words; and another story (which I believe he has somewhere told himself) of his being asked to a party at Birmingham, of his smoking tobacco and going to sleep after dinner on a sofa, where the company found him to their no small surprise, which was increased to wonder when he started up of a sudden, and rubbing his eyes, looked about him, and launched into a three-hours' description of the third heaven, of which he had had a dream, very different from Mr. Southey's *Vision of Judgment*, and also from that other Vision of Judgment, which Mr. Murray, the Secretary of the Bridge-street Junto, has taken into his especial keeping!

On my way back, I had a sound in my ears, it was the voice of Fancy: I had a light before me, it was the face of Poetry. The one still lingers there, the other has not quitted my side! Coleridge in truth met me half-way on the ground of philosophy, or I should not have been won over to his imaginative creed. I had an uneasy, pleasurable sensation all the time, till I was to visit him. During those months the chill breath

C

of winter gave me a welcoming; the vernal air was balm and inspiration to me. The golden sunsets, the silver star of evening, lighted me on my way to new hopes and prospects. *I was to visit Coleridge in the Spring.* This circumstance was never absent from my thoughts, and mingled with all my feelings. I wrote to him at the time proposed, and received an answer postponing my intended visit for a week or two, but very cordially urging me to complete my promise then. This delay did not damp, but rather increased my ardour. In the mean time I went to Llangollen Vale, by way of initiating myself in the mysteries of natural scenery; and I must say I was enchanted with it. I had been reading Coleridge's description of England, in his fine *Ode on the Departing Year*, and I applied it, *con amore*, to the objects before me. That valley was to me (in a manner) the cradle of a new existence: in the river that winds through it, my spirit was baptised in the waters of Helicon!

I returned home, and soon after set out on my journey with unworn heart and untired feet. My way lay through Worcester and Gloucester, and by Upton, where I thought of Tom Jones and the adventure of the muff. I remember getting completely wet through one day, and stopping at an inn (I think it was at Tewkesbury) where I sat up all night to read *Paul and Virginia*. Sweet were the showers in early youth that drenched my body, and sweet the drops of pity that fell upon the books I read! I recollect a remark of Coleridge's upon this very book, that nothing could shew the gross indelicacy of French manners and the entire corruption of their imagination more strongly than the behaviour of the heroine in the last fatal scene, who turns away from a person on board the sinking vessel, that offers to save her life, because he has thrown off his clothes to assist him in swimming. Was this a time to think of such a circumstance? I once hinted to Wordsworth, as we were sailing in his boat on Grasmere Lake, that I thought he had borrowed the idea of his *Poems on the Naming of Places* from the local inscriptions of the same kind in *Paul and Virginia*. He did not own the obligation, and stated some distinction without a difference, in defense of his claim to originality. Any the slightest variation would be sufficient for this purpose in his mind; for whatever *he* added or omitted would inevitably be worth all that any one else had done, and contain the marrow of the sentiment. It was still two days before the time fixed for my arrival, for I had taken care to set out early enough. I stopped these two days at Bridgewater, and when I was tired of sauntering on the banks of its muddy river, returned to the inn, and read *Camilla*. So have I loitered my life away, reading books, looking at pictures, going to plays, hearing, thinking, writing on what pleased me best. I have wanted only one thing to make me happy; but wanting that, have wanted everything!

I arrived, and was well received. The country about Nether Stowey is beautiful, green and hilly, and near the seashore. I saw it but the other day, after an interval of twenty years, from a hill near Taunton. How was the map of my life spread out before me, as the map of the country lay at my feet! In the afternoon Coleridge took me over to All-Foxden, a romantic old family mansion of the St. Aubins, where Wordsworth lived. It was then in the possession of a friend of the poet's, who gave him the free use of it. Somehow that period (the time just after the French Revolution) was not a time when *nothing was given for nothing*. The mind opened, and a softness might be perceived coming over the heart of individuals, beneath "the scales that fence" our self-interest. Wordsworth himself was from home, but his sister kept house, and set before us a frugal repast; and we had free access to her brother's poems, the *Lyrical Ballads*, which were still in manuscript, or in the form of *Sybilline Leaves*. I dipped into a few of these with great satisfaction, and with the faith of a novice. I slept that night in an old room with blue hangings, and covered with the round-faced family portraits of the age of George I and II and from the wooded declivity of the adjoining park that overlooked my window, at the dawn of day, could

———"hear the loud stag speak."

In the outset of life (and particularly at this time I felt it so) our imagination has a body to it. We are in a state between sleeping and waking, and have indistinct but glorious glimpses of strange shapes, and there is always something to come better than what we see. As in our dreams the fulness of the blood gives warmth and reality to the coinage of the brain, so in youth our ideas are clothed, and fed, and pampered with our good spirits; we breathe thick with thoughtless happiness, the weight of future years presses on the strong pulses of the heart, and we repose with undisturbed faith in truth and good. As we advance, we exhaust our fund of enjoyment and of hope. We are no longer wrapped in *lamb's wool*, lulled in Elysium. As we taste the pleasures of life, their spirit evaporates, the sense palls; and nothing is left but the phantoms, the lifeless shadows of what *has been!*

That morning, as soon as breakfast was over, we strolled out into the park, and seating ourselves on the trunk of an old ash-tree that stretched along the ground, Coleridge read aloud with a sonorous and musical voice the ballad of *Betty Foy*. I was not critically or sceptically inclined. I saw touches of truth and nature, and took the rest for granted. But in the *Thorn*, the *Mad Mother*, and the *Complaint of the Poor Indian Woman*, I felt that deeper power and pathos which have been since acknowledged,

"In spite of pride, in erring reason's spite,"

as the characteristics of this author; and the sense of a new style and a new spirit in poetry came over me. It had to me something of the effect that arises from the turning up of the fresh soil, or of the first welcome breath of Spring:

"While yet the trembling year is unconfirmed."

Coleridge and myself walked back to Stowey that evening, and his voice sounded high

"Of Providence, foreknowledge, will, and fate,
    Fix'd fate, free-will, foreknowledge absolute,"

as we passed through echoing grove, by fairy stream or water-fall. gleaming in the summer moonlight! He lamented that

Wordsworth was not prone enough to believe in the traditional superstitions of the place, and that there was a something corporeal, a *matter-of-fact-ness*, a clinging to the palpable, or often to the petty, in his poetry, in consequence. His genius was not a spirit that descended to him through the air; it sprung out of the ground like a flower, or unfolded itself from a green spray, on which the gold-finch sang. He said, however (if I remember right) that this objection must be confined to his descriptive pieces, that his philosophic poetry had a grand and comprehensive spirit in it, so that his soul seemed to inhabit the universe like a palace, and to discover truth by intuition, rather than by deduction. The next day Wordsworth arrived from Bristol at Coleridge's cottage. I think I see him now. He answered in some degree to his friend's description of him, but was more gaunt and Don Quixote-like. He was quaintly dressed (according to the costume of that unconstrained period) in a brown fustian jacket and striped pantaloons. There was something of a roll, a lounge, in his gait, not unlike his own Peter Bell. There was a severe, worn pressure of thought about his temples, a fire in his eye (as if he saw something in objects more than the outward appearance), an intense, high, narrow forehead, a Roman nose, cheeks furrowed by strong purpose and feeling, and a convulsive inclination to laughter about the mouth, a good deal at variance with the solemn, stately expression of the rest of his face. Chantry's bust wants the marking traits; but he was teazed into making it regular and heavy; Haydon's head of him, introduced into the *Entrance of Christ into Jerusalem*, is the most like his drooping weight of thought and expression. He sat down and talked very naturally and freely, with a mixture of clear, gushing accents in his voice, a deep guttural intonation, and a strong tincture of the northern *burr*, like the crust on wine. He instantly began to make havoc of the half of a Cheshire cheese on the table, and said triumphantly that "his marriage with experience had not been so productive as Mr. Southey's in teaching him a knowledge of the good things of this life." He had been to see the *Castle Spectre*, by Monk Lewis, while at Bristol, and described it very well. He said "it fitted the taste of the audience like a glove." This *ad captandum* merit was however by no means a recommendation of it, according to the severe principles of the new school, which reject rather than court popular effect. Wordsworth, looking out of the low, latticed window, said, "How beautifully the sun sets on that yellow bank!" I thought within myself, "With what eyes these poets see nature!" and ever after, when I saw the sunset stream upon the objects facing it, conceived I had made a discovery, or thanked Mr. Wordsworth for having made one for me! We went over to All-Foxden again the day following, and Wordsworth read us the story of Peter Bell in the open air; and the comment made upon it by his face and voice was very different from that of some later critics! Whatever might be thought of the poem, "his face was as a book where men might read strange matters," and he announced the fate of his hero in prophetic tones. There is a *chaunt* in the recitation both of Coleridge and Wordsworth, which acts as a spell upon the hearer, and disarms the judgment. Perhaps they have deceived themselves by making habitual use of this ambiguous accompaniment. Coleridge's manner is more full, animated, and varied; Wordsworth's more equable, sustained, and internal. The one might be termed more *dramatic*, the other more *lyrical*. Coleridge has told me that he himself liked to compose in walking over uneven ground, or breaking through the straggling branches of a copsewood; whereas Wordsworth always wrote (if he could) walking up and down a straight gravel-walk, or in some spot where the continuity of his verse met with no collateral interruption. Returning that same evening, I got into a metaphysical argument with Wordsworth, while Coleridge was explaining the different notes of the nightingale to his sister, in which we neither of us succeeded in making ourselves perfectly clear and intelligible. Thus I passed three weeks at Nether Stowey and in the neighbourhood, generally devoting the afternoons to a delightful chat in an arbour made of bark by the poet's friend Tom Poole, sitting under two fine elm trees, and listening to the bees humming round us, while we quaffed our *flip*. It was agreed, among other things, that we should make a jaunt down the Bristol-Channel, as far as Linton. We set off together on foot, Coleridge, John Chester, and I. This Chester was a native of Nether Stowey, one of those who were attracted to Coleridge's discourse as flies are to honey, or bees in swarming-time to the sound of a brass pan. He "followed in the chase like a dog who hunts, not like one that made up the cry." He had on a brown cloth coat, boots, and corduroy breeches, was low in stature, bow-legged, had a drag in his walk like a drover, which he assisted by a hazel switch, and kept on a sort of trot by the side of Coleridge, like a running footman by a state coach, that he might not lose a syllable or sound that fell from Coleridge's lips. He told me his private opinion, that Coleridge was a wonderful man. He scarcely opened his lips, much less offered an opinion the whole way; yet of the three, had I to choose during the journey, I would be John Chester. He afterwards followed Coleridge into Germany, where the Kantean philosophers were puzzled how to bring him under any of their categories. When he sat down at table with his idol, John's felicity was complete; Sir Walter Scott's or Mr. Blackwood's, when they sat down at the same table with the King, was not more so. We passed Dunster on our right, a small town between the brow of a hill and the sea. I remember eyeing it wistfully as it lay below us; contrasted with the woody scene around, it looked as clear, as pure, as *embrowned* and ideal as any landscape I have seen since, of Gasper Poussin's or Domenichino's. We had a long day's march — (our feet kept time to the echoes of Coleridge's tongue) — through Minehead and by the Blue Anchor, and on to Linton, which we did not reach till near midnight, and where we had some difficulty in making a lodgment. We however knocked the people of the house up at last, and we were repaid for our apprehensions and fatigue by some excellent rashers of fried bacon and eggs. The view in coming along had been splendid. We walked for miles and miles on dark brown heaths overlooking the channel, with the Welsh hills beyond, and at times descended into little sheltered valleys close by the seaside, with a smuggler's face scowling by

us, and then had to ascend conical hills with a path winding up
through a coppice to a barren top, like a monk's shaven crown,
from one of which I pointed out to Coleridge's notice the bare
masts of a vessel on the very edge of the horizon and within
the red-orbed disk of the setting sun, like his own spectre-ship
in the *Ancient Mariner*. At Linton the character of the sea-
coast becomes more marked and rugged. There is a place
called the *Valley of Rocks* (I suspect this was only the poetical
name for it) bedded among precipices overhanging the sea,
with rocky caverns beneath, into which the waves dash, and
where the sea-gull forever wheels its screaming flight. On
the tops of these are huge stones thrown transverse, as if an
earthquake had tossed them there, and behind these is a fret-
work of perpendicular rocks, something like the *Giant's
Causeway*. A thunderstorm came on while we were at the
inn, and Coleridge was running out bareheaded to enjoy the
commotion of the elements in the *Valley of the Rocks*, but as if
in spite, the clouds only muttered a few angry sounds, and let
fall a few refreshing drops. Coleridge told me that he and
Wordsworth were to have made this place the scene of a
prose tale, which was to have been in the manner of, but far
superior to, the *Death of Abel*, but they had relinquished the
design. In the morning of the second day, we breakfasted
luxuriously in an old-fashioned parlour, on tea, toast, eggs,
and honey, in the very sight of the bee-hives from which it had
been taken, and a garden full of thyme and wild flowers that
had produced it. On this occasion Coleridge spoke of Virgil's
Georgics, but not well. I do not think he had much feeling
for the classical or elegant. It was in this room that we found
a little worn-out copy of the *Seasons*, lying in a window-seat,
on which Coleridge exclaimed, "*That* is true fame!" He said
Thomson was a great poet, rather than a good one; his style
was as meretricious as his thoughts were natural. He spoke
of Cowper as the best modern poet. He said the *Lyrical
Ballads* were an experiment about to be tried by him and
Wordsworth, to see how far the public taste would endure
poetry written in a more natural and simple style than had
hitherto been attempted; totally discarding the artifices of

poetical diction, and making use only of such words as had probably been common in the most ordinary language since the days of Henry II. Some comparison was introduced between Shakespeare and Milton. He said "he hardly knew which to prefer. Shakespeare appeared to him a mere stripling in the art; he was as tall and as strong, with infinitely more activity than Milton, but he never appeared to have come to man's estate; or if he had, he would not have been a man, but a monster." He spoke with contempt of Gray, and with intolerance of Pope. He did not like the versification of the latter. He observed that "the ears of these couplet-writers might be charged with having short memories that could not retain the harmony of whole passages." He thought little of Junius as a writer; he had a dislike of Dr. Johnson; and a much higher opinion of Burke as an orator and politician, than of Fox or Pitt. He however thought him very inferior in richness of style and imagery to some of our elder prose writers, particularly Jeremy Taylor. He liked Richardson, but not Fielding; nor could I get him to enter into the merits of *Caleb Williams*.[1]   In short, he was profound and discriminating with respect to those authors whom he liked, and where he gave his judgment fair play; capricious, perverse, and prejudiced in his antipathies and distastes. We loitered on the "ribbed sea-sands," in such talk as this, a whole morning, and I recollect met with a curious seaweed, of which John Chester told us the country name. A fisherman gave Coleridge an account of a boy that had been drowned the day before, and that they had tried to save him at the risk of their own lives. He said "he did not know how it was that they ventured, but, Sir, we have a *nature* towards one another." This expression, Coleridge remarked to me,

---

[1] He had no idea of pictures, of Claude or Raphael, and at this time I had as little as he. He sometimes gives a striking account at present of the cartoons at Pisa, by Buffamalco and others; of one in particular where Death is seen in the air brandishing his scythe, and the great and mighty of the earth shudder at his approach, while the beggars and the wretched kneel to him as their deliverer. He would of course understand so broad and fine a moral as this at any time.

was a fine illustration of that theory of disinterestedness which I (in common with Butler) had adopted. I broached to him an argument of mine to prove that *likeness* was not mere association of ideas. I said that the mark in the sand put one in mind of a man's foot, not because it was part of a former impression of a man's foot (for it was quite new) but because it was like the shape of a man's foot. He assented to the justness of this distinction (which I have explained at length elsewhere, for the benefit of the curious), and John Chester listened; not from any interest in the subject, but because he was astonished that I should be able to suggest anything to Coleridge that he did not already know. We returned on the third morning, and Coleridge remarked the silent cottage-smoke curling up the valleys where, a few evenings before, we had seen the lights gleaming through the dark.

In a day or two after we arrived at Stowey, we set out, I on my return home, and he for Germany. It was a Sunday morning, and he was to preach that day for Dr. Toulmin of Taunton. I asked him if he had prepared anything for the occasion? He said he had not even thought of the text, but should as soon as we parted. I did not go to hear him, — this was a fault, — but we met in the evening at Bridgewater. The next day we had a long day's walk to Bristol, and sat down, I recollect, by a well-side on the road, to cool ourselves and satisfy our thirst, when Coleridge repeated to me some descriptive lines of his tragedy of *Remorse*, which I must say became his mouth and that occasion better than they, some years after, did Mr. Elliston's and the Drury-lane boards, —

> "Oh! memory! shield me from the world's poor strife,
> And give those scenes thine everlasting life!"

I saw no more of him for a year or two, during which period he had been wandering in the Hartz Forest in Germany; and his return was cometary, meteorous, unlike his setting out. It was not till some time after that I knew his friends Lamb and Southey. The last always appears to me (as I first saw him) with a commonplace-book under his arm, and the first with a *bon-mot* in his mouth. It was at Godwin's that I met with Holcroft and Coleridge, where they were disputing fiercely which was the best — *Man as he was, or man as he is to be.* "Give me," says Lamb, "man as he is *not* to be." This saying was the beginning of a friendship between us, which I believe still continues. — Enough of this for the present.

> "But there is matter for another rhyme,
> And I to this may add a second tale."

ON READING OLD BOOKS

I hate to read new books. There are twenty or thirty volumes that I have read over and over again, and these are the only ones that I have any desire ever to read at all. It was a long time before I could bring myself to sit down to the *Tales of My Landlord*, but now that author's works have made a considerable addition to my scanty library. I am told that some of Lady Morgan's are good, and have been recommended to look into *Anastasius;* but I have not yet ventured upon that task. A lady, the other day, could not refrain from expressing her surprise to a friend who said he had been reading *Delphine;* — she asked, — If it had not been published some time back? Women judge of books as they do of fashions or complexions, which are admired only "in their newest gloss." That is not my way. I am not one of those who trouble the circulating libraries much, or pester the booksellers for mail-coach copies of standard periodical publications. I cannot say that I am greatly addicted to black-letter, but I profess myself well versed in the marble bindings of Andrew Millar, in the middle of the last century; nor does my taste revolt at Thurloe's *State Papers*, in Russia leather; or an ample impression of Sir William Temple's *Essays*, with a portrait after Sir Godfrey Kneller in front. I do not think altogether the worse of a book for having survived the author a generation or two. I have more confidence in the dead than the living. Contemporary writers may generally be divided into two classes — one's friends or one's foes. Of the first we are compelled to think too well, and of the last we are disposed to think too ill, to receive much genuine pleasure from the perusal, or to judge fairly of the merits of either. One candidate for literary fame, who happens to be of our acquaintance, writes finely, and like a man of genius; but

22

unfortunately has a foolish face, which spoils a delicate passage; — another inspires us with the highest respect for his personal talents and character, but does not quite come up to our expectations in print. All these contradictions and petty details interrupt the calm current of our reflections. If you want to know what any of the authors were who lived before our time, and are still objects of anxious inquiry, you have only to look into their works. But the dust and smoke and noise of modern literature have nothing in common with the pure, silent air of immortality.

When I take up a work that I have read before (the oftener the better) I know what I have to expect. The satisfaction is not lessened by being anticipated. When the entertainment is altogether new, I sit down to it as I should to a strange dish, — turn and pick out a bit here and there, and am in doubt what to think of the composition. There is a want of confidence and security to second appetite. New-fangled books are also like made-dishes in this respect, that they are generally little else than hashes and *rifaccimentos* of what has been served up entire and in a more natural state at other times. Besides, in thus turning to a well-known author, there is not only an assurance that my time will not be thrown away, or my palate nauseated with the most insipid or vilest trash, — but I shake hands with, and look an old, tried, and valued friend in the face, — compare notes, and chat the hours away. It is true, we form dear friendships with such ideal guests — dearer, alas! and more lasting, than those with our most intimate acquaintance. In reading a book which is an old favourite with me (say the first novel I ever read) I not only have the pleasure of imagination and of a critical relish of the work, but the pleasures of memory added to it. It recalls the same feelings and associations which I had in first reading it, and which I can never have again in any other way. Standard productions of this kind are links in the chain of our conscious being. They bind together the different scattered divisions of our personal identity. They are landmarks and guides in our journey through life. They are pegs and loops on which we can hang up, or from which we can take down, at pleasure, the wardrobe of a moral imagination, the relics of our best affections, the tokens and records of our happiest hours. They are "for thoughts and for remembrance." They are like Fortunatus's wishing-cap — they give us the best riches — those of Fancy; and transport us, not over half the globe, but (which is better) over half our lives, at a word's notice.

My father Shandy solaced himself with *Bruscambille*. Give me for this purpose a volume of *Peregrine Pickle* or *Tom Jones*. Open either of them anywhere — at the Memoirs of Lady Vane, or the adventures at the masquerade with Lady Bellaston, or the disputes between Thwackum and Square, or the escape of Molly Seagrim, or the incident of Sophia and her muff, or the edifying prolixity of her aunt's lecture — and there I find the same delightful, busy, bustling scene as ever, and feel myself the same as when I was first introduced into the midst of it. Nay, sometimes the sight of an odd volume of these good old English authors on a stall, or the name lettered on the back among others on the shelves of a library, answers the purpose, revives the whole train of ideas, and sets "the puppets dallying." Twenty years are struck off the list, and I am a child again. A sage philosopher, who was not a very wise man, said that he should like very well to be young again if he could take his experience along with him. This ingenious person did not seem to be aware, by the gravity of his remark, that the great advantage of being young is to be without this weight of experience, which he would fain place upon the shoulders of youth, and which never comes too late with years. Oh! what a privilege to be able to let this hump, like Christian's burthen, drop from off one's back, and transport oneself, by the help of a little musty duodecimo, to the time when "ignorance was bliss," and when we first got a peep at the raree-show of the world through the glass of fiction — gazing at mankind, as we do at wild beasts in a menagerie, through the bars of their cages, — or at curiosities in a museum, that we must not touch! For myself, not only are the old ideas of the contents of the work brought back to my mind in all their vividness, but the old associations of the faces and persons of those I then knew, as they were in their lifetime — the place where I sat to read the volume, the day when I got it, the feeling of the air, the fields, the sky — return, and all my early impressions with them. This is better to me — those places, those times, those persons, and those feelings that come across me as I retrace the story and devour the page, are to me better far than the wet sheets of the last new novel from the Ballantyne press, to say nothing of the Minerva press in Leadenhall-street. It is like visiting the scenes of early youth. I think of the time "when I was in my father's house, and my path ran down with butter and honey," — when I was a little, thoughtless child and had no other wish or care but to con my daily task and be happy! — *Tom Jones*, I remember, was the first work that broke the spell. It came down in numbers once a fortnight, in Cooke's pocket edition, embellished with cuts. I had hitherto read only in school-books, and a tiresome ecclesiastical history (with the exception of Mrs. Radcliffe's *Romance of the Forest*); but this had a different relish with it, — "sweet in the mouth," though not "bitter in the belly." It smacked of the world I lived in and in which I was to live — and showed me groups, "gay creatures" not "of the element," but of the earth; "living in the clouds," but travelling the same road that I did; — some that have passed on before me, and others that might soon overtake me. My heart had palpitated at the thoughts of a boarding-school ball, or gala-day at Midsummer or Christmas; but the world I had found out in Cooke's edition of the *British Novelists* was to me a dance through life, a perpetual gala-day. The six-penny numbers of this work regularly contrived to leave off just in the middle of a sentence, and in the nick of a story, where Tom Jones discovers Square behind the blanket; or where Parson Adams, in the inextricable confusion of events, very undesignedly gets to bed to Mrs. Slip-slop. Let me caution the reader against this impression of *Joseph Andrews;* for there is a picture of Fanny in it which he should not set his heart on, lest he should never meet with anything like it; or if he should, it would, perhaps, be better for him that he

had not. It was just like —— ——! With what eagerness I
used to look forward to the next number, and open the prints!
Ah! never again shall I feel the enthusiastic delight with which
I gazed at the figures, and anticipated the story and adventures of Major Bath and Commodore Trunnion, of Trim and
my Uncle Toby, of Don Quixote and Sancho and Dapple, of
Gil Blas and Dame Lorenza Sephora, of Laura and the fair
Lucretia, whose lips open and shut like buds of roses. To
what nameless ideas did they give rise, — with what airy
delights I filled up the outlines, as I hung in silence over the
page! — Let me still recall them, that they may breathe fresh
life into me, and that I may live that birthday of thought and
romantic pleasure over again! Talk of the *ideal!* This is the
only true ideal — the heavenly tints of Fancy reflected in the
bubbles that float upon the spring-tide of human life.

> O Memory! shield me from the world's poor strife,
> And give those scenes thine everlasting life!

The paradox with which I set out is, I hope, less startling
than it was; the reader will, by this time, have been let into
my secret. Much about the same time, or I believe rather
earlier, I took a particular satisfaction in reading Chubb's
Tracts, and I often think I will get them again to wade
through. There is a high gusto of polemical divinity in
them; and you fancy that you hear a club of shoemakers at
Salisbury, debating a disputable text from one of St. Paul's
Epistles in a workmanlike style, with equal shrewdness and
pertinacity. I cannot say much for my metaphysical studies,
into which I launched shortly after with great ardour, so as
to make a toil of a pleasure. I was presently entangled in
the briars and thorns of subtle distinctions, — of "fate, free-
will, foreknowledge absolute," though I cannot add that
"in their wandering mazes I found no end;" for I did arrive
at some very satisfactory and potent conclusions; nor will I
go so far, however ungrateful the subject might seem, as to
exclaim with Marlowe's Faustus — "Would I had never seen
Wittenberg, never read book" — that is, never studied such
authors as Hartley, Hume, Berkeley, etc. Locke's *Essay on*

the Human Understanding is, however, a work from which I never derived either pleasure or profit; and Hobbes, dry and powerful as he is, I did not read till long afterwards. I read a few poets, which did not much hit my taste, — for I would have the reader understand, I am deficient in the faculty of imagination; but I fell early upon French romances and philosophy, and devoured them tooth-and-nail. Many a dainty repast have I made of the *New Eloise;* — the description of the kiss; the excursion on the water; the letter of St. Preux, recalling the time of their first loves; and the account of Julia's death; these I read over and over again with unspeakable delight and wonder. Some years after, when I met with this work again, I found I had lost nearly my whole relish for it (except some few parts) and was, I remember, very much mortified with the change in my taste, which I sought to attribute to the smallness and gilt edges of the edition I had bought, and its being perfumed with rose-leaves. Nothing could exceed the gravity, the solemnity with which I carried home and read the Dedication to the *Social Contract*, with some other pieces of the same author, which I had picked up at a stall in a coarse leathern cover. Of the *Confessions* I have spoken elsewhere, and may repeat what I have said — "Sweet is the dew of their memory, and pleasant the balm of their recollection!" Their beauties are not "scattered like stray gifts o'er the earth," but sown thick on the page, rich and rare. I wish I had never read the *Emilius* or read it with less implicit faith. I had no occasion to pamper my natural aversion to affectation or pretence, by romantic and artificial means. I had better have formed myself on the model of Sir Fopling Flutter. There is a class of persons whose virtues and most shining qualities sink in, and are concealed by, an absorbent ground of modesty and reserve; and such a one I do, without vanity, profess myself.[1]

---

[1] Nearly the same sentiment was wittily and happily expressed by a friend, who had some lottery puffs, which he had been employed to write, returned on his hands for their too great severity of thought and classical terseness of style, and who observed on that occasion, that "Modest merit never can succeed!"

d

Now these are the very persons who are likely to attach themselves to the character of Emilius, and of whom it is sure to
be the bane. This dull, phlegmatic, retiring humour is not
in a fair way to be corrected, but confirmed and rendered
desperate, by being in that work held up as an object of
imitation, as an example of simplicity and magnanimity —
by coming upon us with all the recommendations of novelty,
surprise, and superiority to the prejudices of the world — by
being stuck upon a pedestal, made amiable, dazzling, a *leurre
de dupe!* The reliance on solid worth which it inculcates,
the preference of sober truth to gaudy tinsel, hangs like a
millstone round the neck of the imagination — "a load to
sink a navy" — impedes our progress, and blocks up every
prospect in life. A man, to get on, to be successful, conspicuous, applauded, should not retire upon the centre of his
conscious resources, but be always at the circumference of
appearances. He must envelop himself in a halo of mystery
— he must ride in an equipage of opinion — he must walk
with a train of self-conceit following him — he must not strip
himself to a buff-jerkin, to the doublet and hose of his real
merits, but must surround himself with a *cortége* of prejudices, like the signs of the Zodiac — he must seem anything
but what he is, and then he may pass for anything he pleases.
The world loves to be amused by hollow professions, to be
deceived by flattering appearances, to live in a state of hallucination; and can forgive everything but the plain, downright, simple, honest truth — such as we see it chalked out in
the character of Emilius. — To return from this digression,
which is a little out of place here.

Books have in a great measure lost their power over me;
nor can I revive the same interest in them as formerly. I perceive when a thing is good, rather than feel it. It is true,

Marcian Colonna is a dainty book;

and the reading of Mr. Keats's *Eve of St. Agnes* lately made
me regret that I was not young again. The beautiful and
tender images there conjured up, "come like shadows — so
depart." The "tiger-moth's wings," which he has spread

over his rich poetic blazonry, just flit across my fancy; the gorgeous twilight window which he has painted over again in his verse, to me "blushes" almost in vain "with blood of queens and kings." I know how I should have felt at one time in reading such passages; and that is all. The sharp, luscious flavour, the fine *aroma*, is fled, and nothing but the stalk, the bran, the husk of literature is left. If any one were to ask me what I read now, I might answer with my Lord Hamlet in the play — "Words, words, words." — "What is the matter?" — "*Nothing!*" — They have scarce a meaning. But it was not always so. There was a time when to my thinking, every word was a flower or a pearl, like those which dropped from the mouth of the little peasant-girl in the fairy tale, or like those that fall from the great preacher in the Caledonian Chapel! I drank of the stream of knowledge that tempted, but did not mock my lips, as of the river of life, freely. How eagerly I slaked my thirst of German sentiment, "as the hart that panteth for the water-springs;" how I bathed and revelled, and added my floods of tears to Goethe's *Sorrows of Werter*, and to Schiller's *Robbers* —

> Giving my stock of more to that which had too much!

I read, and assented with all my soul to Coleridge's fine sonnet, beginning —

> Schiller! that hour I would have wish'd to die,
> If through the shuddering midnight I had sent,
> From the dark dungeon of the tow'r time-rent,
> That fearful voice, a famish'd father's cry!

I believe I may date my insight into the mysteries of poetry from the commencement of my acquaintance with the authors of the *Lyrical Ballads;* at least, my discrimination of the higher sorts — not my predilection for such writers as Goldsmith or Pope: nor do I imagine they will say I got my liking for the novelists, or the comic writers, — for the characters of Valentine, Tattle, or Miss Prue, from them. If so, I must have got from them what they never had themselves. In points where poetic diction and conception are concerned, I may be at a loss, and liable to be imposed upon;

but in forming an estimate of passages relating to common
life and manners, I cannot think I am a plagiarist from any
man. I there "know my cue without a prompter." I may
say of such studies — *Intus et in cute.* I am just able to
admire those literal touches of observation and description
which persons of loftier pretensions overlook and despise.
I think I comprehend something of the characteristic part of
Shakspeare; and in him indeed, all is characteristic, even
the nonsense and poetry. I believe it was the celebrated Sir
Humphrey Davy who used to say, that Shakspeare was
rather a metaphysician than a poet. At any rate, it was not
ill said. I wish that I had sooner known the dramatic writers
contemporary with Shakspeare; for in looking them over
about a year ago, I almost revived my old passion for reading,
and my old delight in books, though they were very nearly
new to me. The periodical essayists I read long ago. The
Spectator I liked extremely: but the *Tatler* took my fancy
most. I read the others soon after, the *Rambler*, the *Ad-
venturer*, the *World*, the *Connoisseur*. I was not sorry to get
to the end of them, and have no desire to go regularly through
them again. I consider myself a thorough adept in Richardson. I like the longest of his novels best, and think no part
of them tedious; nor should I ask to have anything better
to do than to read them from beginning to end, to take them
up when I chose, and lay them down when I was tired, in
some old family mansion in the country, till every word and
syllable relating to the bright Clarissa, the divine Clementina,
the beautiful Pamela, "with every trick and line of their
sweet favour," were once more "graven in my heart's table." [1]
I have a sneaking kindness for Mackenzie's *Julia de Roubigné*

---

[1] During the peace of Amiens, a young English officer, of the name
of Lovelace, was presented at Buonaparte's levee. Instead of the
usual question, "Where have you served, Sir?" the First Consul
immediately addressed him, "I perceive your name, Sir, is the same
as that of the hero of Richardson's Romance!" Here was a Consul.
The young man's uncle, who was called Lovelace, told me this anecdote while we were stopping together at Calais. I had also been
thinking that his was the same name as that of the hero of Richardson's Romance. This is one of my reasons for liking Buonaparte.

— for the deserted mansion, and straggling gilliflowers on the mouldering garden wall; and still more for his *Man of Feeling;* not that it is better, nor so good; but at the time I read it, I sometimes thought of the heroine, Miss Walton, and of Miss —— together, and "that ligament, fine as it was, was never broken!" — One of the poets that I have always read with most pleasure, and can wander about in forever with a sort of voluptuous indolence, is Spenser; and I like Chaucer even better. The only writer among the Italians I can pretend to any knowledge of, is Boccaccio, and of him I cannot express half my admiration. His story of the hawk I could read and think of from day to day, just as I would look at a picture of Titian's!

I remember, as long ago as the year 1798, going to a neighbouring town (Shrewsbury, where Farquhar has laid the plot of his *Recruiting Officer*) and bringing home with me, "at one proud swoop," a copy of Milton's *Paradise Lost,* and another of Burke's *Reflections on the French Revolution* — both which I have still; and I still recollect, when I see the covers, the pleasure with which I dipped into them as I returned with my double prize. I was set up for one while. That time is past "with all its giddy raptures;" but I am still anxious to preserve its memory, "embalmed with odours." — With respect to the first of these works, I would be permitted to remark here in passing, that it is a sufficient answer to the German criticism which has since been started against the character of Satan (*viz.,* that it is not one of disgusting deformity, or pure, defecated malice) to say that Milton has there drawn, not the abstract principle of evil, not a devil incarnate, but a fallen angel. This is the scriptural account, and the poet has followed it. We may safely retain such passages as that well-known one —

> —— " His form had not yet lost
> All her original brightness; nor appear'd
> Less than archangel ruin'd, and the excess
> Of glory obscur'd " —

for the theory, which is opposed to them, "falls flat upon the grunsel edge, and shames its worshippers." Let us hear no

more then of this monkish cant and bigoted outcry for the
restoration of the horns and tail of the devil! — Again, as to
the other work, Burke's *Reflections*, I took a particular pride
and pleasure in it, and read it to myself and others for months
afterwards.   I had reason for my prejudice in favour of this
author.   To understand an adversary is some praise; to admire him is more.   I thought I did both; I knew I did one.
From the first time I ever cast my eyes on anything of
Burke's (which was an extract from his *Letter to a Noble
Lord* in a three-times a week paper, *The St. James's Chronicle*, in 1796), I said to myself, "This is true eloquence:
this is a man pouring out his mind on paper."   All other
style seemed to me pedantic and impertinent.   Dr. Johnson's was walking on stilts; and even Junius's (who was at
that time a favourite with me) with all his terseness, shrunk
up into little antithetic points and well-trimmed sentences.
But Burke's style was forked and playful as the lightning,
crested like the serpent.   He delivered plain things on a
plain ground; but when he rose, there was no end of his
flights and circumgyrations — and in this very *Letter*, "he,
like an eagle in a dove-cot, fluttered *his* Volscians" (the Duke
of Bedford and the Earl of Lauderdale) [1] "in Corioli."   I
did not care for his doctrines.   I was then, and am still, proof
against their contagion; but I admired the author, and was
considered as not a very staunch partisan of the opposite side,
though I thought myself that an abstract proposition was one
thing — a masterly transition, a brilliant metaphor, another.
I conceived too that he might be wrong in his main argument,
and yet deliver fifty truths in arriving at a false conclusion.   I
remember Coleridge assuring me, as a poetical and political
set-off to my sceptical admiration, that Wordsworth had
written an *Essay on Marriage*, which, for manly thought and
nervous expression, he deemed incomparably superior.   As I
had not, at that time, seen any specimens of Mr. Wordsworth's prose style, I could not express my doubts on the
subject.   If there are greater prose-writers than Burke, they

---

[1] He is there called "Citizen Lauderdale."   Is this the present Earl?

either lie out of my course of study, or are beyond my sphere
of comprehension. I am too old to be a convert to a new
mythology of genius. The niches are occupied, the tables are
full. If such is still my admiration of this man's misapplied
powers, what must it have been at a time when I myself was
in vain trying, year after year, to write a single essay, nay,
a single page or sentence; when I regarded the wonders of
his pen with the longing eyes of one who was dumb and a
changeling; and when, to be able to convey the slightest
conception of my meaning to others in words, was the height
of an almost hopeless ambition! But I never measured others'
excellences by my own defects; though a sense of my own
incapacity, and of the steep, impassable ascent from me to
them, made me regard them with greater awe and fondness.
I have thus run through most of my early studies and favourite
authors, some of whom I have since criticised more at large.
Whether those observations will survive me, I neither know
nor do I much care; but to the works themselves, "worthy of
all acceptation," and to the feelings they have always excited
in me since I could distinguish a meaning in language, nothing
shall ever prevent me from looking back with gratitude and
triumph. To have lived in the cultivation of an intimacy
with such works, and to have familiarly relished such names,
is not to have lived quite in vain.

There are other authors whom I have never read, and yet
whom I have frequently had a great desire to read, from some
circumstance relating to them. Among these is Lord Clarendon's *History of the Grand Rebellion*, after which I have a
hankering, from hearing it spoken of by good judges — from
my interest in the events, and knowledge of the characters
from other sources, and from having seen fine portraits of most
of them. I like to read a well-penned character, and Clarendon is said to have been a master in this way. I should like
to read Froissart's *Chronicles*, Holinshed and Stowe, and
Fuller's *Worthies*. I intend, whenever I can, to read Beaumont and Fletcher all through. There are fifty-two of their
plays, and I have only read a dozen or fourteen of them. *A
Wife for a Month* and *Thierry and Theodoret* are, I am told,

delicious, and I can believe it.   I should like to read the
speeches in Thucydides, and Guicciardini's *History of Florence*,
and *Don Quixote* in the original.   I have often thought of
reading the *Loves of Persiles and Sigismunda*, and the *Galatea*
of the same author.   But I somehow reserve them like
"another Yarrow."   I should also like to read the last new
novel (if I could be sure it was so) of the author of *Waverley;*—
no one would be more glad than I to find it the best!

WHETHER GENIUS IS CONSCIOUS OF ITS POWERS?

No really great man ever thought himself so. The idea of greatness in the mind answers but ill to our knowledge — or to our ignorance of ourselves. What living prose-writer, for instance, would think of comparing himself with Burke? Yet would it not have been equal presumption or egotism in him to fancy himself equal to those who had gone before him — Bolingbroke or Johnson, or Sir William Temple? Because his rank in letters is become a settled point with us, we conclude that it must have been quite as self-evident to him, and that he must have been perfectly conscious of his vast superiority to the rest of the world. Alas! not so. No man is truly himself, but in the idea which others entertain of him. The mind, as well as the eye, "sees not itself, but by reflection from some other thing." What parity can there be between the effect of habitual composition on the mind of the individual, and the surprise occasioned by first reading a fine passage in an admired author; between what we do with ease, and what we thought it next to impossible ever to be done; between the reverential awe we have for years encouraged, without seeing reason to alter it, for distinguished genius, and the slow, reluctant, unwelcome conviction that after infinite toil and repeated disappointments, and when it is too late and to little purpose, we have ourselves at length accomplished what we at first proposed; between the insignificance of our petty, personal pretensions, and the vastness and splendour which the atmosphere of imagination lends to an illustrious name? He who comes up to his own idea of greatness must always have had a very low standard of it in his mind. "What a pity," said some one, "that Milton had not the pleasure of reading *Paradise Lost!*" He could not read it as we do, with the weight of impression that a hundred years of admiration have added to it — "a phœnix gazed by

35

all" — with the sense of the number of editions it has passed
through with still increasing reputation, with the tone of
solidity, time-proof, which it has received from the breath of
cold, envious maligners, with the sound which the voice of
Fame has lent to every line of it! The writer of an ephemeral
production may be as much dazzled with it as the public:
it may sparkle in his own eyes for a moment, and be soon
forgotten by every one else. But no one can anticipate the
suffrages of posterity. Every man, in judging of himself,
is his own contemporary. He may feel the gale of popularity,
but he cannot tell how long it will last. His opinion of himself wants distance, wants time, wants numbers, to set it
off and confirm it. He must be indifferent to his own merits
before he can feel a confidence in them. Besides, everyone
must be sensible of a thousand weaknesses and deficiencies in
himself; whereas Genius only leaves behind it the monuments
of its strength. A great name is an abstraction of some one
excellence; but whoever fancies himself an abstraction of
excellence; so far from being great, may be sure that he is a
blockhead, equally ignorant of excellence or defect, of himself
or others. Mr. Burke, besides being the author of the *Reflections* and the *Letter to a Noble Lord*, had a wife and son;
and had to think as much about them as we do about him.
The imagination gains nothing by the minute details of personal knowledge.

On the other hand, it may be said that no man knows so
well as the author of any performance what it has cost him,
and the length of time and study devoted to it. This is one,
among other reasons, why no man can pronounce an opinion
upon himself. The happiness of the result bears no proportion to the difficulties overcome or the pains taken. *Materiam superabat opus* (the workmanship surpasses the materials) is an old and fatal complaint. The definition of
genius is that it acts unconsciously; and those who have
produced immortal works have done so without knowing how
or why. The greatest power operates unseen, and executes
its appointed task with as little ostentation as difficulty.
Whatever is done best is done from the natural bent and dis-

position of the mind. It is only where our incapacity begins that we begin to feel the obstacles, and to set an undue value on our triumph over them. Correggio, Michael Angelo, Rembrandt, did what they did without premeditation or effort — their works came from their minds as a natural birth — if you had asked them why they adopted this or that style, they would have answered, *because they could not help it*, and because they knew of no other. So Shakespeare says: —

> "Our poesy is as a gum which oozes
> From whence 'tis nourished: the fire i' the flint
> Shows not till it be struck: our gentle flame
> Provokes itself; and, like the current, flies
> Each bound it chafes."

Shakespeare himself was an example of his own rule, and appears to have owed almost everything to industry or design. His poetry flashes from him like the lightning from the summer cloud, or the stroke from the sun-flower. When we look at the admirable comic designs of Hogarth, they seem from the unfinished state in which they are left, and from the freedom of the pencilling, to have cost him little trouble; whereas the *Sigismunda* is a very laboured and comparatively feeble performance, and he accordingly set great store by it. He also thought highly of his portraits, and boasted that "he could paint equal to Vandyke, give him his time, and let him choose his subject." This was the very reason why he could not. Vandyke's excellence consisted in this, that he could paint a fine portrait of anyone at sight; let him take ever so much pains or choose ever so bad a subject, he could not help making something of it. His eye, his mind, his hand was cast in the mould of grace and delicacy. Milton, again, is understood to have preferred *Paradise Regained* to his other works. This, if so, was either because he himself was conscious of having failed in it, or because others thought he had. We are willing to think well of that which we know wants our favourable opinion, and to prop the rickety bantling. Every step taken, *invitâ Minervâ*, costs us something, and is set down to account; whereas we are borne on the full tide of genius and success into the very haven of our desires almost imperceptibly. The strength of the impulse by which we are carried along prevents the sense of difficulty or resistance; the true inspiration of the Muse is soft and balmy as the air we breathe; and indeed leaves us little to boast of, for the effect hardly seems to be our own.

There are two persons who always appear to me to have worked under this involuntary, silent impulse more than any others; I mean Rembrandt and Correggio. It is not known that Correggio ever saw a picture of any great master. He lived and died obscurely in an obscure village. We have few of his works, but they are all perfect. What truth, what grace, what angelic sweetness are there! Not one line or tone that is not divinely soft or exquisitely fair; the painter's mind rejecting, by a natural process, all that is discordant, coarse, or unpleasing. The whole is an emanation of pure thought. The work grew under his hand as if of itself, and came out without a flaw, like the diamond from the rock. He knew not what he did; and looked at each modest grace as it stole from the canvas with anxious delight and wonder. Ah! gracious God! not he alone; how many more in all time have looked at their works with the same feelings, not knowing but they too may have done something divine, immortal, and finding in that sole doubt ample amends for pining solitude, for want, neglect, and an untimely fate. Oh! for one hour of that uneasy rapture, when the mind first thinks that it has struck out something that may last for ever; when the germ of excellence burst from nothing on the startled sight! Take, take away the gaudy triumphs of the world, the long deathless shout of fame, and give back that heartfelt sigh with which the youthful enthusiast first weds immortality as his secret bride! And thou too, Rembrandt! Thou wert a man of genius if ever painter was a man of genius! — did this dream hang over you as you painted that strange picture of *Jacob's Ladder?* Did your eye strain over those gradual dusky clouds into futurity, or did those white-vested, beaked figures babble to you of fame as they approached? Did you know what you were about, or did you not paint much as it happened? Oh! if you had thought once about yourself, or anything but the subject, it would have been all over with "the glory, the intuition, the amenity," the dream had fled, the spell had been broken. The hills would not have looked like those we see in sleep — that tatterdemalion figure of Jacob, thrown on one side, would not have slept as if the breath was fairly taken out of his body. So much do Rembrandt's pictures savour of the soul and body of reality, that the thoughts seem identical with the objects — if there had been the least question what he should have done, or how he should do it, or how far he had succeeded, it would have spoiled everything. Lumps of light hung upon his pencil and fell upon his canvas like dewdrops; the shadowy veil was drawn over his backgrounds by the dull, obtuse finger of night, making darkness visible by still greater darkness that could only be felt!

Cervantes is another instance of a man of genius, whose work may be said to have sprung from his mind, like Minerva from the head of Jupiter. Don Quixote and Sancho were a kind of twins; and the jests of the latter, as he says, fell from him like drops of rain when he least thought of it. Shakespeare's creations were more multiform, but equally natural and unstudied. Raphael and Milton seem partial exceptions to this rule. Their productions were the *composite order;* and those of the latter sometimes even amount to centos. Accordingly, we find Milton quoted among those authors who have left proofs of their entertaining a high opinion of themselves, and of cherishing a strong aspiration after fame. Some of Shakespeare's sonnets have been also cited to the same purpose; but they seem rather to convey wayward and dissatisfied complaints of his untoward fortune than anything like a triumphant and confident reliance on his future renown. He appears to have stood more alone and to have thought less about himself than any living being. One reason for this indifference may have been, that as a writer he was tolerably successful in his lifetime, and no doubt produced his works with very great facility.

I hardly know whether to class Claude Lorraine as among those who succeeded most "through happiness or pains." It is certain that he imitated no one, and has had no successful imitator. The perfection of his landscapes seems to have been owing to an inherent quality of harmony, to an exquisite sense of delicacy in his mind. His monotony has been complained of, which is apparently produced from a preconceived idea in his mind; and not long ago I heard a person, not more distinguished for the subtilty than the *naïveté* of his sarcasms, remark, "Oh! I never look at Claude: if one has seen one of his pictures, one has seen them all; they are every one alike: there is the same sky, the same climate, the same time of day, the same tree, and that tree is like a cabbage. To be sure, they say he did pretty well; but when a man is always doing one thing, he ought to do it pretty well." There is no occasion to write the name under this criticism, and the best answer to it is that it is true — his pictures always are the same, but we never wish them to be otherwise. Perfection is one thing. I confess I think that Claude knew this, and felt that his were the finest landscapes in the world — that ever had been, or would ever be.

I am not in the humour to pursue this argument any farther at present, but to write a digression. If the reader is not already apprised of it, he will please to take notice that I write this at Winterslow. My style there is apt to be redundant and excursive. At other times it may be cramped, dry, abrupt; but here it flows like a river, and overspreads its banks. I have not to seek for thoughts or hunt for images: they come of themselves, I inhale them with the breeze, and the silent groves are vocal with a thousand recollections —

> "And visions, as poetic eyes avow,
> Hang on each leaf, and cling to ev'ry bough."

Here I came fifteen years ago, a willing exile; and as I trod the lengthened greensward by the low woodside, repeated the old line,

> "My mind to me a kingdom is!"

I found it so then, before, and since; and shall I faint, now that I have poured out the spirit of that mind to the world, and treated many subjects with truth, with freedom, and power, because I have been followed with one cry of abuse ever since *for not being a Government tool?* Here I returned a few years after to finish some works I had undertaken, doubtful of the event, but determined to do my best; and wrote that character of Millimant which was once transcribed by fingers fairer than Aurora's, but no notice was taken of it, because I was not a Government tool, and must be supposed devoid of taste and elegance by all who aspired to these qualities in their own persons. Here I sketched my account of that old honest Signior Orlando Friscobaldo, which with its fine, racy, acrid tone that old crab-apple, G . ff . . d, would have relished or pretended to relish, had I been a Government tool! Here, too, I have written *Table-Talks* without number, and as yet without a falling-off, till now that they are nearly done, or I should not make this boast. I could swear (were they not mine) the thoughts in many of them are founded as the rock, free as air, the tone like an Italian picture. What then? Had the style been like polished steel, as firm and as bright, it would have availed me nothing, for I am not a Government tool! I had endeavoured to guide the taste of the English people to the best old English writers; but I had said that English kings did not reign by right divine, and that his present Majesty was descended from an Elector of Hanover in a right line; and no loyal subject would after this look into Webster or Dekker because I had pointed them out. I had done something (more than anyone except Schlegel) to vindicate the *Characters of Shakespeare's Plays* from the stigma of French criticism; but our Anti-Jacobin and Anti-Gallican writers soon found out that I had said and written that Frenchmen, Englishmen, men were not slaves by birthright. This was enough to *damn* the work. Such has been the head and front of my offending. While my friend, Leigh Hunt, was writing the *Descent of Liberty*, and strewing the march of the Allied Sovereigns with flowers, I sat by the waters of Babylon and hung my harp upon the willows. I knew all along there was but one alternative — the cause of kings or of mankind. This I foresaw, this I feared; the world would see it now, when it is too late. Therefore I lamented, and would take no comfort when the Mighty fell, because we, all men, fell with him, like lightning from heaven,

to grovel in the grave of Liberty, in the stye of Legitimacy!
There is but one question in the hearts of monarchs — whether
mankind are their property or not. There was but this one
question in mine. I had made an abstract, metaphysical
principle of this question. I was not the dupe of the voice of
the charmers. By my hatred of tyrants I knew what their
hatred of the freeborn spirit of man must be, of the semblance,
of the very name of Liberty and Humanity. And while others
bowed their heads to the image of the BEAST, I spat upon it
and buffeted it, and made mouths at it, and pointed at it, and
drew aside the veil that then half concealed it but has been
since thrown off, and named it by its right name; and it is not
to be supposed that my having penetrated their mystery
would go unrequited by those whose darling and whose delight the idol, half-brute, half-demon, was, and who were
ashamed to acknowledge the image and superscription as
their own!

Two half-friends of mine, who would not make a whole
one between them, agreed the other day that the indiscriminate, incessant abuse of what I write was mere prejudice and party spirit, and that what I do in periodicals and
without a name does well, pays well, and is "cried out upon
in the top of the compass." It is this indeed that has saved
my shallow skiff from quite foundering on Tory spite and
rancour; for when people have been reading and approving
an article in a miscellaneous journal, it does not do to say
when they discover the author afterwards (whatever might
have been the case before) it is written by a blockhead; and
even Mr. Jerdan recommends the volume of *Characteristics* as
an excellent little work, because it has no cabalistic name in
the title-page, and swears "there is a first-rate article of forty
pages in the last number of the *Edinburgh* from Jeffrey's own
hand," though when he learns against his will that it is mine,
he devotes three successive numbers of the *Literary Gazette* to
abuse "that *strange* article in the last number of the *Edinburgh Review*." Others who had not this advantage have
fallen a sacrifice to the obloquy attached to the suspicion of
doubting, or of being acquainted with anyone who is known

to doubt, the divinity of kings. Poor Keats paid the forfeit
of this *lezè majesté* with his health and life. What, though his
verses were like the breath of spring, and many of his thoughts
like flowers — would this, with the circle of critics that beset
a throne, lessen the crime of their having been praised in the
Examiner? The lively and most agreeable editor of that
paper has in like manner been driven from his country and his
friends who delighted in him, for no other reason than having
written the *Story of Rimini*, and asserted ten years ago, "that
the most accomplished prince in Europe was an Adonis of
fifty!"

> "Return, Alpheus, the dread voice is past
> That shrunk thy streams; return Sicilian Muse!"

I look out of my window and see that a shower has just fallen:
the fields look green after it, and a rosy cloud hangs over the
brow of the hill; a lily expands its petals in the moisture,
dressed in its lovely green and white; a shepherd boy has just
brought some pieces of turf with daisies and grass for his young
mistress to make a bed for her skylark, not doomed to dip his
wings in the dappled dawn — my cloudy thoughts draw off,
the storm of angry politics has blown over — Mr. Blackwood,
I am yours — Mr. Croker, my service to you — Mr. T. Moore,
I am alive and well — really, it is wonderful how little the
worse I am for fifteen years' wear and tear, how I came upon
my legs again on the ground of truth and nature, and "look
abroad into universality," forgetting that there is any such
person as myself in the world!

I have let this passage stand (however critical) because it
may serve as a practical illustration to show what authors
really think of themselves when put upon the defensive —
(I confess, the subject has nothing to do with the title at the
head of the Essay!) — and as a warning to those who may
reckon upon their fair portion of popularity, as the reward of
the exercise of an independent spirit and such talents as they
possess. It sometimes seems at first sight as if the low scur-
rility and jargon of abuse by which it is attempted to overlay
all common sense and decency by the tissue of lies and nicknames everlastingly repeated and applied indiscriminately

to all those who are not of the regular Government party,
was peculiar to the present time, and the anomalous growth
of modern criticism; but if we look back, we shall find the same
system acted upon as often as power, prejudice, dullness, and
spite found their account in playing the game into one another's hands — in decrying popular efforts, and in giving
currency to every species of base metal that had their own
conventional stamp upon it.   The names of Pope and Dryden
were assailed with daily and unsparing abuse; the epithet
A. P. E. was levelled at the sacred head of the former; and if
even men like these, having to deal with the consciousness of
their own infirmities and the insolence and spurns of wanton
enmity, must have found it hard to possess their souls in
patience, any living writer amidst such contradictory evidence
can scarcely expect to retain much calm, steady conviction
of his own merits, or build himself a secure reversion in immortality.

However one may in a fit of spleen and impatience turn
round and assert one's claims in the face of low-bred, hireling
malice, I will here repeat what I set out with saying, that there
never yet was a man of sense and proper spirit who would not
decline rather than court a comparison with any of those
names whose reputation he really emulates — who would not
be sorry to suppose that any of the great heirs of memory had
as many foibles as he knows himself to possess — and who
would not shrink from including himself or being included by
others in the same praise that was offered to long-established
and universally acknowledged merits, as a kind of profanation.   Those who are ready to fancy themselves Raphaels
and Homers are very inferior men indeed — they have not
even an idea of the mighty names that "they take in vain."
They are as deficient in pride as in modesty, and have not so
much as served an apprenticeship to a true and honourable
ambition.   They mistake a momentary popularity for lasting
renown, and a sanguine temperament for the inspirations of
genius.   The love of fame is too high and delicate a feeling
in the mind to be mixed up with realities — it is a solitary
abstraction, the secret sigh of the soul —

> "It is all one as we should love
> A bright particular star, and think to wed it."

A name "fast-anchored in the deep abyss of time" is like a star twinkling in the firmanent, cold, silent, distant, but eternal and sublime; and our transmitting one to posterity is as if we should contemplate our translation to the skies. If we are not contented with this feeling on the subject, we shall never sit in Cassiopeia's chair, nor will our names, studding Ariadne's crown or streaming with Berenice's locks, ever make

> "the face of heaven so bright,
> That birds shall sing, and think it were not night."

Those who are in love only with noise and show, instead of devoting themselves to a life of study, had better hire a booth at Bartlemy Fair, or march at the head of a recruiting regiment with drums beating and colours flying!

It has been urged that however little we may be disposed to indulge the reflection at other times or out of mere self-complacency, yet the mind cannot help being conscious of the effort required for any great work while it is about it, of

> "The high endeavour and the glad success."

I grant that there is a sense of power in such cases, with the exception before stated; but then this very effort and state of excitement engrosses the mind at the time, and leaves it listless and exhausted afterwards. The energy we exert, or the high state of enjoyment we feel, puts us out of conceit with ourselves at other times; compared to what we are in the act of composition, we seem dull, commonplace people, generally speaking; and what we have been able to perform is rather matter of wonder than of self-congratulation to us. The stimulus of writing is like the stimulus of intoxication, with which we can hardly sympathise in our sober moments, when we are no longer under the inspiration of the demon, or when the virtue is gone out of us. While we are engaged in any work, we are thinking of the subject, and cannot stop to admire ourselves; and when it is done, we look at it with comparative indifference. I will venture to say that no one but a pedant ever read his own works regularly through. They are not *his* — they are become mere words, waste paper, and have none of the glow, the creative enthusiasm, the vehemence, and natural spirit with which he wrote them. When we have once committed our thoughts to paper, written them fairly out, and seen that they are right in the printing, if we are in our right wits, we have done with them forever. I sometimes try to read an article I have written in some magazine or review — (for when they are bound up in a volume, I dread the very sight of them) — but stop after a sentence or two, and never recur to the task. I know pretty well what I have to say on the subject, and do not want to go to school to myself. It is the worst instance of the *bis repetita crambe* in the world. I do not think that even painters have much delight in looking at their works after they are done. While they are in progress, there is a great degree of satisfaction in considering what has been done, or what is still to do — but this is hope, is reverie, and ceases with the completion of our efforts. I should not imagine Raphael or Correggio would have much pleasure in looking at their former works, though they might recollect the pleasure they had had in painting them; they might spy defects in them (for the idea of unattainable perfection still keeps pace with our actual approaches to it), and fancy that they were not worthy of immortality. The greatest portrait painter the world ever saw used to write under his pictures, "*Titianus faciebat,*" signifying that they were imperfect; and in his letter to Charles V accompanying one of his most admired works, he only spoke of the time he had been about it. Annibal Caracci boasted that he could do like Titian and Correggio, and, like most boasters, was wrong. (See his spirited letter to his cousin Ludovico, on seeing the pictures at Parma.)

The greatest pleasure in life is that of reading, while we are young. I have had as much of this pleasure as perhaps anyone. As I grow older, it fades; or else, the stronger stimulus of writing takes off the edge of it. At present, I have neither time nor inclination for it; yet I should like to devote a year's entire leisure to a course of the English novelists; and perhaps clap on that sly old knave, Sir Walter, to the end of the list. It is astonishing how I used formerly to relish the style of certain authors, at a time when I myself despaired of ever writing a single line. Probably this was the reason. It is not in mental as in natural ascent — intellectual objects seem higher when we survey them from below, than when we look down from any given elevation above the common level. My three favourite writers about the time I speak of were Burke, Junius, and Rousseau. I was never weary of admiring and wondering at the felicities of the style, the turns of expression, the refinements of thought and sentiment. I laid the book down to find out the secret of so much strength and beauty, and I took it up again in despair, to read on and admire. So I passed whole days, months, and I may add, years; and have only this to say now, that as my life began, so I could wish that it may end. The last time I tasted this luxury in its full perfection was one day after a sultry day's walk in summer between Farnham and Alton. I was fairly tired out; I walked into an inn-yard (I think at the latter place); I was shown by the waiter to what looked at first like common out-houses at the other end of it, but they turned out to be a suite of rooms, probably a hundred years old — the one I entered opened into an old-fashioned garden, embellished with beds of larkspur and a leaden Mercury; it was wain-scotted, and there was a grave-looking, dark-coloured portrait of Charles II hanging over the tiled chimney-piece. I had *Love for Love* in my pocket, and began to read; coffee was brought in in a silver coffee-pot; the cream, the bread and butter, everything was excellent, and the flavour of Congreve's style prevailed over all. I prolonged the entertainment till a late hour, and relished this divine comedy better even than when I used to see it played by Miss Mellon, as Miss Lrue; Bob Palmer, as Tattle; and Bannister, as honest Ben. This circumstance happened just five years ago, and it seems like yesterday. If I count my life so by lustres, it will soon glide away; yet I shall not have to repine, if, while it lasts, it is enriched with a few such recollections!

A FAREWELL TO ESSAY-WRITING

"This life is best, if quiet life is best."

Food, warmth, sleep, and a book; these are all I at present ask — the *ultima thule* of my wandering desires. Do you not then wish for

"A friend in your retreat,
Whom you may whisper, solitude is sweet?"

Expected, well enough:— gone, still better. Such attractions are strengthened by distance. Nor a mistress? "Beautiful mask! I know thee!" When I can judge of the heart from the face, of the thoughts from the lips, I may again trust myself. Instead of these, give me the robin red-breast, pecking the crumbs at the door, or warbling on the leafless spray, the same glancing form that has followed me wherever I have been, and "done its spiriting gently;" or the rich notes of the thrush that startle the ear of winter, and seem to have drunk up the full draught of joy from the very sense of contrast. To these I adhere and am faithful, for they are true to me; and, dear in themselves, are dearer for the sake of what is departed, leading me back (by the hand) to that dreaming world, in the innocence of which they sat and made sweet music, waking the promise of future years, and answered by the eager throbbings of my own breast. But now "the credulous hope of mutual minds is o'er," and I turn back from the world that has deceived me, to nature that lent it a false beauty and that keeps up the illusion of the past. As I quaff my libations of tea in a morning, I love to watch the clouds sailing from the west, and fancy that "the spring comes slowly up this way." In this hope, while "fields are dank and ways are mire," I follow the same direction to a neighbouring wood, where, having gained the dry, level greensward, I can see my way for a mile before me, closed in on each side by copsewood, and ending in a point of light more or

48

less brilliant, as the day is bright or cloudy. What a walk is this to me! I have no need of book or companion — the days, the hours, the thoughts of my youth are at my side and blend with the air that fans my cheek. Here I can saunter for hours, bending my eye forward, stopping and turning to look back, thinking to strike off into some less trodden path, yet hesitating to quit the one I am in, afraid to snap the brittle threads of memory. I remark the shining trunks and slender branches of the birch trees, waving in the idle breeze; or a pheasant springs up on whirring wing; or I recall the spot where I once found a wood-pigeon at the foot of a tree, weltering in its gore, and think how many seasons have flown since "it left its little life in air." Dates, names, faces come back — to what purpose? Or why think of them now? Or rather, why not think of them oftener? We walk through life, as through a narrow path, with a thin curtain drawn around it; behind are ranged rich portraits, airy harps are strung — yet we will not stretch forth our hands and lift aside the veil, to catch glimpses of the one, or sweep the chords of the other. As in a theatre, when the old-fashioned green curtain drew up, groups of figures, fantastic dresses, laughing faces, rich banquets, stately columns, gleaming vistas appeared beyond; so we have only at any time to "peep through the blanket of the past," to possess ourselves at once of all that has regaled our senses, that is stored up in our memory, that has struck our fancy, that has pierced our hearts; — yet to all this we are indifferent, insensible, and seem intent only on the present vexation, the future disappointment. If there is a Titian hanging up in the room with me, I scarcely regard it; how then should I be expected to strain the mental eye so far, or to throw down, by the magic spells of the will, the stone walls that enclose it in the Louvre? There is one head there of which I have often thought, when looking at it, that nothing should ever disturb me again, and I would become the character it represents — such perfect calmness and self-possession reigns in it! Why do I not hang an image of this in some dusky corner of my brain and turn an eye upon it ever and anon, as I have need of some such talis-

man to calm my troubled thoughts? The attempt is fruit-
less, if not natural; or, like that of the French, to hang gar-
lands on the grave, and to conjure back the dead by miniature
pictures of them while living! It is only some actual coincidence or local association that tends, without violence, to
"open all the cells where memory slept." I can easily, by
stooping over the long-sprent grass and clay-cold clod, recall
the tufts of primroses, or purple hyacinths, that formerly grew
on the same spot, and cover the bushes with leaves and singing birds, as they were eighteen summers ago; or prolonging
my walk and hearing the sighing gale rustle through a tall,
straight wood at the end of it, can fancy that I distinguish the
cry of hounds, and the fatal group issuing from it, as in the
tale of *Theodore and Honoria.* A moaning gust of wind aids
the belief; I look once more to see whether the trees before me
answer to the idea of the horror-stricken grove, and an air-
built city towers over their grey tops.

> "Of all the cities in Romanian lands,
> The chief and most renown'd Ravenna stands."

I return home resolved to read the entire poem through, and,
after dinner, drawing my chair to the fire, and holding a small
print close to my eyes, launch into the full tide of Dryden's
couplets (a stream of sound), comparing his didactic and descriptive pomp with the simple pathos and picturesque truth
of Boccaccio's story, and tasting with a pleasure, which none
but an habitual reader can feel, some quaint examples of
pronunciation in this accomplished versifier.

> "Which when Honoria view'd,
> The fresh *impulse* her former fright renew'd."
> *Theodore and Honoria*

> "And made th' *insult*, which in his grief appears,
> The means to mourn thee with my pious tears."
> *Sigismonda and Guiscardo*

These trifling instances of the wavering and unsettled state of
the language give double effect to the firm and stately march
of the verse, and make me dwell with a sort of tender interest
on the difficulties and doubts of an earlier period of literature.
They pronounced words then in a manner which we should

laugh at now; and they wrote verse in a manner which we can do anything but laugh at. The pride of a new acquisition seems to give fresh confidence to it; to impel the rolling syllables through the moulds provided for them, and to overflow the envious bounds of rhyme into time-honoured triplets. I am much pleased with Leigh Hunt's mention of Moore's involuntary admiration of Dryden's free, unshackled verse, and of his repeating *con amore*, and with an Irish spirit and accent, the fine lines —

> "Let honour and preferment go for gold,
> But glorious beauty isn't to be sold."

What sometimes surprises me in looking back to the past, is, with the exception already stated, to find myself so little changed in the time. The same images and trains of thought stick by me; I have the same tastes, likings, sentiments, and wishes that I had then. One great ground of confidence and support has, indeed, been struck from under my feet; but I have made it up to myself by proportionable pertinacity of opinion. The success of the great cause, to which I had vowed myself, was to me more than all the world; I had a strength in its strength, a resource which I knew not of, till it failed me for the second time.

> "Fall'n was Glenartny's stately tree!
> Oh! ne'er to see Lord Ronald more!"

It was not till I saw the axe laid to the root, that I found the full extent of what I had to lose and suffer. But my conviction of the right was only established by the triumph of the wrong; and my earliest hopes will be my last regrets. One source of this unbendingness (which some may call obstinacy), is that, though living much alone, I have never worshipped the echo. I see plainly enough that black is not white, that the grass is green, that kings are not their subjects; and, in such self-evident cases, do not think it necessary to collate my opinions with the received prejudices. In subtler questions, and matters that admit of doubt, as I do not impose my opinion on others without a reason, so I will not give up mine to them without a better reason; and a person calling me names, or giving himself airs of authority, does not convince me of his having taken more pains to find out the truth than I have, but the contrary. Mr. Gifford once said, that "while I was sitting over my gin and tobacco pipes, I fancied myself a Leibnitz." He did not so much as know that I had ever read a metaphysical book: — was I therefore, out of complaisance or deference to him, to forget whether I had or not? I am rather disappointed, both on my own account and his, that Mr. Hunt has missed the opportunity of explaining the character of a friend as clearly as he might have done. He is puzzled to reconcile the shyness of my pretensions with the inveteracy and sturdiness of my principles. I should have thought they were nearly the same thing. Both from disposition and habit, I can *assume* nothing in word, look, or manner. I cannot steal a march upon public opinion in any way. My standing upright, speaking loud, entering a room gracefully, proves nothing; therefore I neglect these ordinary means of recommending myself to the good graces and admiration of strangers (and, as it appears, even of philosophers and friends). Why? Because I have other resources, or, at least, am absorbed in other studies and pursuits. Suppose this absorption to be extreme, and even morbid — that I have brooded over an idea till it has become a kind of substance in my brain, that I have reasons for a thing which I have found out with much labour and pains, and to which I can scarcely do justice without the utmost violence of exertion (and that only to a few persons) — is this a reason for my playing off my out-of-the-way notions in all companies, wearing a prim and self-complacent air, as if I were "the admired of all observers"? or is it not rather an argument (together with a want of animal spirits), why I should retire into myself, and perhaps acquire a nervous and uneasy look, from a consciousness of the disproportion between the interest and conviction I feel on certain subjects, and my ability to communicate what weighs upon my own mind to others? If my ideas, which I do not avouch, but suppose, lie below the surface, why am I to be always attempting to dazzle superficial people with them, or smiling, delighted, at my own want of success?

What I have here stated is only the excess of the common and well-known English and scholastic character. I am neither a buffoon, a fop, nor a Frenchman, which Mr. Hunt would have me to be. He finds it odd that I am a close reasoner and a loose dresser. I have been (among other follies) a hard liver as well as a hard thinker; and the consequences of that will not allow me to dress as I please. People in real life are not like players on a stage, who put on a certain look or costume, merely for effect. I am aware, indeed, that the gay and airy pen of the author does not seriously probe the errors or misfortunes of his friends — he only glances at their seeming peculiarities, so as to make them odd and ridiculous; for which forbearance few of them will thank him. Why does he assert that I was vain of my hair when it was black, and am equally vain of it now it is grey, when this is true in neither case? This transposition of motives makes me almost doubt whether Lord Byron was thinking so much of the rings on his fingers as his biographer was. These sort of criticisms should be left to women. I am made to wear a little hat, stuck on the top of my head the wrong way. Nay, I commonly wear a large slouching hat over my eyebrows; and if ever I had another, I must have twisted it about in any shape to get rid of the annoyance. This probably tickled Mr. Hunt's fancy and retains possession of it, to the exclusion of the obvious truism that I naturally wear "a melancholy hat."

I am charged with using strange gestures and contortions of features in argument, in order to "look energetic." One would rather suppose that the heat of the argument produced the extravagance of the gestures, as I am said to be calm at other times. It is like saying that a man in a passion clenches his teeth, not because he is, but in order to seem, angry. Why should everything be construed into air and affectation? With Hamlet, I may say, "I know not *seems*."

Again, my old friend and pleasant "Companion" remarks it, as an anomaly in my character, that I crawl about the fives-court like a cripple till I get the racket in my hand, when I start up as if I was possessed with a devil. I have

then a motive for exertion; I lie by for difficulties and extreme cases. *Aut Cæsar aut nullus.* I have no notion of
doing nothing with an air of importance, nor should I ever
take a liking to the game of battledoor and shuttlecock. I
have only seen by accident a page of the unpublished manuscript relating to the present subject, which I dare say is, on
the whole, friendly and just, and which has been suppressed
as being too favourable, considering certain prejudices against
me.

In matters of taste and feeling, one proof that my conclusions have not been quite shallow or hasty, is the circumstance of their having been lasting. I have the same favourite books, pictures, passages that I ever had; I may therefore
presume that they will last me my life — nay, I may indulge
a hope that my thoughts will survive me. This continuity
of impression is the only thing on which I pride myself.
Even L——, whose relish on certain things is as keen and
earnest as possible, takes a surfeit of admiration, and I
should be afraid to ask about his select authors or particular
friends, after a lapse of ten years. As to myself, anyone
knows where to have me. What I have once made up my
mind to, I abide by to the end of the chapter. One cause of
my independence of opinion is, I believe, the liberty I give
to others, or the very diffidence and distrust of making converts. I should be an excellent man on a jury: I might say
little, but should starve "the other eleven obstinate fellows"
out. I remember Mr. Godwin writing to Mr. Wordsworth
that "his tragedy of *Antonio* could not fail of success." It
was damned past all redemption. I said to Mr. Wordsworth
that I thought this a natural consequence; for how could any
one have a dramatic turn of mind who judged entirely of
others from himself? Mr. Godwin might be convinced of the
excellence of his work; but how could he know that others
would be convinced of it, unless by supposing that they were
as wise as himself, and as infallible critics of dramatic poetry
— so many Aristotles sitting in judgment on Euripides!
This shows why pride is connected with shyness and reserve;
for the really proud have not so high an opinion of the gener-

ality as to suppose that they can understand them, or that there is any common measure between them. So Dryden exclaims of his opponents with bitter disdain —

"Nor can I think what thoughts they can conceive."

I have not sought to make partisans, still less did I dream of making enemies; and have therefore kept my opinions myself, whether they were currently adopted or not. To get others to come into our ways of thinking, we must go over to theirs; and it is necessary to follow, in order to lead. At the time I lived here formerly, I had no suspicion that I should ever become a voluminous writer; yet I had just the same confidence in my feelings before I had ventured to air them in public as I have now. Neither the outcry *for* or *against* moves me a jot; I do not say that the one is not more agreeable than the other.

Not far from the spot where I write, I first read Chaucer's *Flower and Leaf*, and was charmed with that young beauty, shrouded in her bower, and listening with ever-fresh delight to the repeated song of the nightingale close by her — the impression of the scene, the vernal landscape, the cool of the · morning, the gushing notes of the songstress,

"And ayen, methought she sung close by mine ear,"

is as vivid as if it had been of yesterday; and nothing can persuade me that that is not a fine poem. I do not find this impression conveyed in Dryden's version, and therefore nothing can persuade me that that is as fine. I used to walk out at this time with Mr. and Miss L —— of an evening to look at the Claude Lorraine skies over our heads, melting from azure into purple and gold, and to gather mushrooms, that sprung up at our feet, to throw into our hashed mutton at supper. I was at that time an enthusiastic admirer of Claude, and could dwell forever on one or two of the finest prints from him hung round my little room: the fleecy flocks, the bending trees, the winding streams, the groves, the nodding temples, the air-wove hills, and distant sunny vales; and tried to translate them into their lovely living hues,

People then told me that Wilson was much superior to Claude. I did not believe them. Their pictures have since been seen together at the British Institution, and all the world have come into my opinion. I have not, on that account, given it up. I will not compare our hashed mutton with Amelia's; but it put us in mind of it, and led to a discussion, sharply seasoned and well sustained, till midnight, the result of which appeared some years after in the *Edinburgh Review*. Have I a better opinion of those criticisms on that account, or should I therefore maintain them with greater vehemence and tenaciousness? Oh, no! Both rather with less, now that they are before the public, and it is for them to make their election.

It is in looking back to such scenes that I draw my best consolation for the future. Later impressions come and go, and serve to fill up the intervals; but these are my standing resource, my true classics. If I have had few real pleasures or advantages, my ideas, from their sinewy texture, have been to me in the nature of realities; and if I should not be able to add to the stock, I can live by husbanding the interest. As to my speculations, there is little to admire in them but my admiration of others; and whether they have an echo in time to come or not, I have learned to set a grateful value on the past, and am content to wind up the account of what is personal only to myself and the immediate circle of objects in which I have moved, with an act of easy oblivion,

"And curtain close such scene from every future view."

ON CLASSICAL EDUCATION

THE study of the classics is less to be regarded as an exercise of the intellect, than as a "discipline of humanity." The peculiar advantage of this mode of education consists not so much in strengthening the understanding, as in softening and refining the taste. It gives men liberal views; it accustoms the mind to take an interest in things foreign to itself; to love virtue for its own sake; to prefer fame to life, glory to riches; and to fix our thoughts on the remote and permanent, instead of narrow and fleeting objects. It teaches us to believe that there is something really great and excellent in the world, surviving all the shocks of accident and fluctuations of opinion, and raises us above that low and servile fear which bows only to present power and upstart authority. Rome and Athens filled a place in the history of mankind, which can never be occupied again. They were two cities set on a hill, which could not be hid; all eyes have seen them, and their light shines like a mighty sea-mark into the abyss of time.

> "Still green with bays each ancient altar stands,
> Above the reach of sacrilegious hands;
> Secure from flames, from envy's fiercest rage,
> Destructive war, and all-involving age.
> Hail, bards triumphant, born in happier days,
> Immortal heirs of universal praise!
> Whose honours with increasing ages, grow,
> As streams roll down, enlarging as they flow!"

It is this feeling, more than anything else, which produces a marked difference between the study of the ancient and modern languages, and which, from the weight and importance of the consequences attached to the former, stamps every word with a monumental firmness. By conversing with the *mighty dead*, we imbibe sentiment with knowledge; we become strongly attached to those who can no longer hurt or serve us, except through the influence which they exert over the

mind. We feel the presence of that power which gives immortality to human thoughts and actions, and catch the
flame of enthusiasm from all nations and ages.

It is hard to find in minds otherwise formed, either a real
love of excellence, or a belief that any excellence exists
superior to their own. Everything is brought down to the
vulgar level of their own ideas and pursuits. Persons without education certainly do not want either acuteness or
strength of mind in what concerns themselves or in things
immediately within their observation; but they have no
power of abstraction, no general standard of taste or scale
of opinion. They see their objects always near, and never
in the horizon. Hence arises that egotism which has been
remarked as the characteristic of self-taught men, and which
degenerates into obstinate prejudice or petulant fickleness of
opinion, according to the natural sluggishness or activity of
their minds. For they either become blindly bigoted to the
first opinions they have struck out for themselves, and in-
accessible to conviction; or else (the dupes of their own vanity and shrewdness) are everlasting converts to every crude
suggestion that presents itself, and the last opinion is always the true one. Each successive discovery flashes upon
them with equal light and evidence, and every new fact
overturns their whole system. It is among this class of
persons, whose ideas never extend beyond the feeling of the
moment, that we find partisans, who are very honest men,
with a total want of principle, and who unite the most hard-
ened effrontery and intolerance of opinion, to endless inconsistency and self-contradiction.

A celebrated political writer of the present day, who is a
great enemy to classical education, is a remarkable instance
both of what can and what cannot be done without it.

It has been attempted of late to set up a distinction between
the education *of words*, and the education *of things*, and to
give the preference in all cases to the latter. But, in the
first place, the knowledge of things, or of the realities of life,
is not easily to be taught except by things themselves, and,
even if it were, it is not so absolutely indispensable as it has

been supposed. "The world is too much with us, early and late"; and the fine dream of our youth is best prolonged among the visionary objects of antiquity. We owe many of our most amiable delusions, and some of our superiority, to the grossness of mere physical existence, to the strength of our associations with words. Language, if it throws a veil over our ideas, adds a softness and refinement to them, like that which the atmosphere gives to naked objects. There can be no true elegance without taste in style. In the next place, we mean absolutely to deny the application of the principle of utility to the present question. By an obvious transposition of ideas, some persons have confounded a knowledge of useful things with useful knowledge. Knowledge is only useful in itself as it exercises or gives pleasure to the mind: the only knowledge that is of use in a practical sense, is professional knowledge. But knowledge, considered as a branch of general education, can be of use only to the mind of the person acquiring it. If the knowledge of language produces pedants, the other kind of knowledge (which is supposed to be substituted for it) can only produce quacks. There is no question but that the knowledge of astronomy, of chemistry, and of agriculture, is highly useful to the world, and absolutely necessary to be acquired by persons carrying on certain professions; but the practical utility of a knowledge of these subjects ends there. For example, it is of the utmost importance to the navigator to know exactly in what degree of longitude and latitude such a rock lies; but to us, sitting here about our Round Table, it is not of the smallest consequence whatever, whether the map-maker has placed it an inch to the right or to the left; we are in no danger of running against it. So the art of making shoes is a highly useful art, and very proper to be known and practised by somebody: that is, by the shoemaker. But to pretend that everyone else should be thoroughly acquainted with the whole process of this ingenious handicraft, as one branch of useful knowledge, would be preposterous. It is sometimes asked, what is the use of poetry, and we have heard the argument carried on almost like a parody of *Falstaff's* reasoning about Honour.

f

"Can it set a leg? No. Or an arm? No. Or take away the grief of a wound? No. Poetry hath no skill in surgery then? No." It is likely that the most enthusiastic lover of poetry would so far agree to the truth of this statement, that if he had just broken a leg, he would send for a surgeon, instead of a volume of poems from a library. But, "they that are whole need not a physician." The reasoning would be well founded if we lived in a hospital and not in the world.

ON THE IGNORANCE OF THE LEARNED

"For the more languages a man can speak,
His talent has but sprung the greater leak;
And, for the industry he has spent upon 't,
Must full as much some other way discount.
The Hebrew, Chaldee, and the Syriac
Do, like their letters, set men's reason back,
And turn their wits that strive to understand it
(Like those that write the characters) left-handed.
Yet he that is but able to express
No sense at all in several languages,
Will pass for learneder than he that's known
To speak the strongest reason in his own."

THE description of persons who have the fewest ideas of all others are mere authors and readers. It is better to be able neither to read nor write than to be able to do nothing else. A lounger who is ordinarily seen with a book in his hand is (we may be almost sure) equally without the power or inclination to attend either to what passes around him or in his own mind. Such a one may be said to carry his understanding about with him in his pocket, or to leave it at home on his library shelves. He is afraid of venturing on any train of reasoning, or of striking out any observation that is not mechanically suggested to him by passing his eyes over certain legible characters; shrinks from the fatigue of thought, which, for want of practice, becomes insupportable to him; and sits down contented with an endless wearisome succession of words and half-formed images which fill the void of the mind and continually efface one another. Learning is, in too many cases, but a foil to common sense; a substitute for true knowledge. Books are less often made use of as "spectacles" to look at nature with, than as blinds to keep out its strong light and shifting scenery from weak eyes and indolent dispositions. The book-worm wraps himself up in his web of verbal generalities, and sees only the glimmering shadows of things reflected from the minds of others. Nature *puts him*

61

out. The impressions of real objects, stripped of the disguises of words and voluminous roundabout descriptions, are
blows that stagger him; their variety distracts, their rapidity
exhausts him; and he turns from the bustle, the noise, and
glare, and whirling motion of the world about him (which he
has not an eye to follow in its fantastic changes, nor an understanding to reduce to fixed principles), to the quiet monotony
of the dead languages, and the less startling and more intelligible combinations of the letters of the alphabet. It is
well, it is perfectly well. "Leave me to my repose," is the
motto of the sleeping and the dead. You might as well ask
the paralytic to leap from his chair and throw away his
crutch, or, without a miracle, to "take up his bed and walk,"
as expect the learned reader to throw down his book and think
for himself. He clings to it for his intellectual support;
and his dread of being left to himself is like the horror of a
vacuum. He can only breathe a learned atmosphere, as
other men breathe common air. He is a borrower of sense.
He has no ideas of his own, and must live on those of other
people. The habit of supplying our ideas from foreign
sources "enfeebles all internal strength of thought," as a
course of dram-drinking destroys the tone of the stomach.
The faculties of the mind, when not exerted, or when cramped
by custom and authority, become listless, torpid, and unfit
for the purposes of thought or action. Can we wonder at
the languor and lassitude which is thus produced by a life of
learned sloth and ignorance; by poring over lines and syllables that excite little more idea or interest than if they were
the characters of an unknown tongue, till the eye closes on
vacancy, and the book drops from the feeble hand! I would
rather be a wood-cutter, or the meanest hind, that all day
"sweats in the eye of Phœbus, and at night sleeps in Elysium," than wear out my life so, 'twixt dreaming and awake.
The learned author differs from the learned student in this,
that the one transcribes what the other reads. The learned
are mere literary drudges. If you set them upon original
composition, their heads turn; they don't know where they
are. The indefatigable readers of books are like the ever-

lasting copiers of pictures, who, when they attempt to do anything of their own, find they want an eye quick enough, a hand steady enough, and colours bright enough, to trace the living forms of nature.

Anyone who has passed through the regular gradations of a classical education, and is not made a fool by it, may consider himself as having had a very narrow escape. It is an old remark, that boys who shine at school do not make the greatest figure when they grow up and come out into the world. The things, in fact, which a boy is set to learn at school, and on which his success depends, are things which do not require the exercise either of the highest or the most useful faculties of the mind. Memory (and that of the lowest kind) is the chief faculty called into play in conning over and repeating lessons by rote in grammar, in languages, in geography, arithmetic, etc., so that he who has the most of this technical memory, with the least turn for other things which have a stronger and more natural claim upon his childish attention, will make the most forward school-boy. The jargon containing the definitions of the parts of speech, the rules for casting up an account, or the inflections of a Greek verb can have no attraction to the tyro of ten years old, except as they are imposed as a task upon him by others, or from his feeling the want of sufficient relish or amusement in other things. A lad with a sickly constitution, and no very active mind, who can just retain what is pointed out to him, and has neither sagacity to distinguish nor spirit to enjoy for himself, will generally be at the head of his form. An idler at school, on the other hand, is one who has high health and spirits, who has the free use of his limbs, with all his wits about him, who feels the circulation of his blood and the motion of his heart, who is ready to laugh and cry in a breath, and who had rather chase a ball or a butterfly, feel the open air in his face, look at the fields or the sky, follow a winding path, or enter with eagerness into all the little conflicts and interests of his acquaintances and friends, than doze over a musty spelling-book, repeat barbarous distichs after his master, sit so many hours pinioned to a writing desk, and receive his reward for the loss of time and pleasure in paltry prize medals at Christmas and Midsummer. There is indeed a degree of stupidity which prevents children from learning the usual lessons, or ever arriving at these puny academic honours. But what passes for stupidity is much oftener a want of interest, of a sufficient motive to fix the attention and force a reluctant application to the dry and unmeaning pursuits of school-learning. The best capacities are as much above this drudgery, as the dullest are beneath it. Our men of the greatest genius have not been most distinguished for their acquirements at school or at the university.

> "Th' enthusiast Fancy was a truant ever.",

Gray and Collins were among the instances of this wayward disposition. Such persons do not think so highly of the advantages, nor can they submit their imaginations so servilely to the trammels of strict scholastic discipline. There is a certain kind and degree of intellect in which words take root, but into which things have not power to penetrate. A mediocrity of talent, with a certain slenderness of moral constitution, is the soil that produces the most brilliant specimens of successful prize-essayists and Greek epigrammatists. It should not be forgotten, that the least respectable character among modern politicians was the cleverest boy at Eton.

Learning is the knowledge of that which is not generally known to others, and which we can only derive at second-hand from books or other artificial sources. The knowledge of that which is before us, or about us, which appeals to our experience, passions, and pursuits, to the bosoms and businesses of men, is not learning. Learning is the knowledge of that which none but the learned know. He is the most learned man who knows the most of what is farthest removed from common life and actual observation, that is of the least practical utility, and least liable to be brought to the test of experience, and that, having been handed down through the greatest number of intermediate stages, is the most full of uncertainty, difficulties, and contradictions. It is seeing with the eyes of others, hearing with their ears, and pinning our faith on their understandings. The learned man prides himself in the knowledge of names, and dates, not of men or things. He thinks and cares nothing about his next-door neighbours, but he is deeply read in the tribes and casts of the Hindoos and Calmuc Tartars. He can hardly find his way into the next street, though he is acquainted with the exact dimensions of Constantinople and Pekin. He does not know whether his oldest acquaintance is a knave or a fool, but he can pronounce a pompous lecture on all the principal characters in history. He cannot tell whether an object is black or white, round or square, and yet he is a professed master of the laws of optics and the rules of perspective. He knows as much of what he talks about as a blind man does of colours. He cannot give a satisfactory answer to the plainest question, nor is he ever in the right in any one of his opinions, upon any one matter of fact that really comes before him, and yet he gives himself out for an infallible judge on all those points of which it is impossible that he or any other person living should know anything but by conjecture. He is expert in all the dead and in most of the living languages; but he can neither speak his own fluently, nor write it correctly. A person of this class, the second Greek scholar of his day, undertook to point out several solecisms in Milton's Latin style; and in his own performance there is hardly a sentence of common English. Such was Dr. ——. Such is Dr. ——. Such was not Porson. He was an exception that confirmed the general rule — a man that, by uniting talents and knowledge with learning, made the distinction between them more striking and palpable.

A mere scholar, who knows nothing but books, must be ignorant even of them. "Books do not teach the use of books." How should he know anything of a work, who knows nothing of the subject of it? The learned pedant is conversant with books only as they are made of other books, and those again of others, without end. He parrots those who have parroted others. He can translate the same word into ten different languages, but he knows nothing of the

thing which it means in any one of them. He stuffs his head
with authorities built on authorities, with quotations quoted
from quotations, while he locks up his senses, his understanding, and his heart. He is unacquainted with the maxims and
manners of the world; he is to seek in the characters of individuals. He sees no beauty in the face of nature or of art.
To him "the mighty world of eye and ear" is hid; and
"knowledge," except at one entrance, "quite shut out."
His pride takes part with his ignorance; and his self-impor-
tance rises with the number of things of which he does not
know the value, and which he therefore despises as unworthy
of his notice. He knows nothing of pictures;—"of the colouring of Titian, the grace of Raphael, the purity of Domenichino,
the *corregiescity* of Corregio, the learning of Poussin, the airs
of Guido, the taste of the Caracci, or the grand contour of
Michael Angelo,"— of all those glories of the Italian and
miracles of the Flemish school, which have filled the eyes of
mankind with delight, and to the study and imitation of
which thousands have in vain devoted their lives. These
are to him as if they had never been, a mere dead letter,
a byword; and no wonder: for he neither sees nor under-
stands their prototypes in nature. A print of Rubens's
Watering-place, or Claude's Enchanted Castle, may be hanging on the walls of his room for months without his once per-
ceiving them; and if you point them out to him, he will turn
away from them. The language of nature, or of art (which is
another nature), is one that he does not understand. He
repeats indeed the names of Apelles and Phidias, because they
are to be found in classic authors, and boasts of their works
as prodigies, because they no longer exist; or, when he sees
the finest remains of Grecian art actually before him in
the Elgin marbles, takes no other interest in them than as
they lead to a learned dispute, and (which is the same thing)
a quarrel about the meaning of a Greek particle. He is
equally ignorant of music; he "knows no touch of it," from
the strains of the all-accomplished Mozart to the shepherd's
pipe upon the mountain. His ears are nailed to his books;
and deadened with the sound of the Greek and Latin tongues,

and the din and smithery of school-learning. Does he know anything more of poetry? He knows the number of feet in a verse, and of acts in a play; but of the soul or spirit he knows nothing. He can turn a Greek ode into English, or a Latin epigram into Greek verse, but whether either is worth the trouble, he leaves to the critics. Does he understand "the act and practique part of life" better than "the theorique?" No. He knows no liberal or mechanic art; no trade or occupation; no game of skill or chance. Learning "has no skill in surgery," in agriculture, in building, in working in wood or in iron; it cannot make any instrument of labour, or use it when made; it cannot handle the plough or the spade, or the chisel or the hammer; it knows nothing of hunting or hawking, fishing or shooting, of horses or dogs, of fencing or dancing, or cudgel-playing, or bowls, or cards, or tennis, or anything else. The learned professor of all arts and sciences cannot reduce any one of them to practice, though he may contribute an account of them to an Encyclopædia. He has not the use of his hands or of his feet; he can neither run, nor walk, nor swim; and he considers all those who actually understand and can exercise any of these arts of body or mind, as vulgar and mechanical men; —though to know almost any one of them in perfection requires long time and practice, with powers originally fitted, and a turn of mind particularly devoted to them. It does not require more than this to enable the learned candidate to arrive, by painful study, at a doctor's degree and a fellowship, and to eat, drink, and sleep, the rest of his life!

The thing is plain. All that men really understand, is confined to a very small compass: to their daily affairs and experience; to what they have an opportunity to know, and motives to study or practise. The rest is affectation and imposture. The common people have the use of their limbs; for they live by their labour or skill. They understand their own business and the characters of those they have to deal with; for it is necessary that they should. They have eloquence to express their passions, and wit at will to express their contempt and provoke laughter. Their natural use of speech is not hung up in monumental mockery, in an obsolete language; nor is their sense of what is ludicrous, or readiness at finding out allusions to express it, buried in collections of *Anas*. You will hear more good things on the outside of a stagecoach from London to Oxford, than if you were to pass a twelvemonth with the undergraduates, or heads of colleges, of that famous university; and more *home* truths are to be learnt from listening to a noisy debate in an alehouse, than from attending to a formal one in the House of Commons. An elderly country gentlewoman will often know more of character, and be able to illustrate it by more amusing anecdotes taken from the history of what has been said, done, and gossiped in a country town for the last fifty years, than the best blue-stocking of the age will be able to glean from that sort of learning which consists in an acquaintance with all the novels and satirical poems published in the same period. People in towns, indeed, are woefully deficient in a knowledge of character, which they see only *in the bust*, not as a whole-length. People in the country not only know all that has happened to a man, but trace his virtues or vices, as they do his features, in their descent through several generations, and solve some contradiction in his behaviour by a cross in the breed, half a century ago   The learned know nothing of the matter, either in town or country. Above all, the mass of society have common sense, which the learned in all ages want. The vulgar are in the right when they judge for themselves; they are wrong when they trust to their blind guides. The celebrated nonconformist divine, Baxter, was almost stoned to death by the good women of Kidderminster, for asserting from the pulpit that ."hell was paved with infants' skulls"; but, by the force of argument and of learned quotations from the Fathers, the reverend preacher at length prevailed over the scruples of his congregation, and over reason and humanity.

Such is the use which has been made of human learning. The labourers in this vineyard seem as if it was their object to confound all common sense, and the distinctions of good and evil, by means of traditional maxims and preconceived notions, taken upon trust, and increasing in absurdity with increase of age. They pile hypothesis on hypothesis, mountain high, till it is impossible to come at the plain truth on any question. They see things, not as they are, but as they find them in books; and "wink and shut their apprehensions up," in order that they may discover nothing to interfere with their prejudices or convince them of their absurdity. It might be supposed that the height of human wisdom consisted in maintaining contradictions and rendering nonsense sacred. There is no dogma, however fierce or foolish, to which these persons have not set their seals and tried to impose on the understandings of their followers, as the will of Heaven, clothed with all the terrors and sanctions of religion. How little has the human understanding been directed to find out the true and useful! How much ingenuity has been thrown away in the defense of creeds and systems! How much time and talents have been wasted in theological controversy, in law, in politics, in verbal criticism, in judicial astrology, and in finding out the art of making gold! What actual benefit do we reap from the writings of a Laud or a Whitgift, or of Bishop Bull or Bishop Waterland, or Prideaux' *Connections*, or Beausobre, or Calmet, or St. Augustine, or Puffendorf, or Vattel, or from the more literal but equally learned and unprofitable labours of Scaliger, Cardan, and Scioppius? How many grains of sense are there in their thousand folio or quarto volumes? What would the world lose if they were committed to the flames to-morrow? Or are they not already "gone to the vault of all the Capulets?" Yet all these were oracles in their time, and would have scoffed at you or me, at common sense and human nature, for differing with them. It is our turn to laugh now.

To conclude this subject. The most sensible people to be met with in society are men of business and of the world, who argue from what they see and know, instead of spinning cobweb distinctions of what things ought to be. Women have often more of what is called *good sense* than men. They have fewer pretensions; are less implicated in theories; and judge of objects more from their immediate and involuntary impression on the mind; and, therefore, more truly and naturally. They cannot reason wrong; for they do not reason at all. They do not think or speak by rule; and they have in general more eloquence and wit, as well as sense, on that account. By their wit, sense, and eloquence together, they generally contrive to govern their husbands. Their style, when they write to their friends (not for the booksellers) is better than that of most authors. — Uneducated people have most exuberance of invention and the greatest freedom from prejudice. Shakespeare's was evidently an uneducated mind, both in the freshness of his imagination and in the variety of his views; as Milton's was scholastic in the texture both of his thoughts and feelings. Shakespeare had not been accustomed to write themes at school in favour of virtue or against vice. To this we owe the unaffected but healthy tone of his dramatic morality. If we wish to know the force of human genius, we should read Shakespeare. If we wish to see the insignificance of human learning, we may study his commentators.

THE INDIAN JUGGLERS

COMING forward and seating himself on the ground in his white dress and tightened turban, the chief of the Indian Jugglers begins with tossing up two brass balls, which is what any of us could do, and concludes with keeping up four at the same time, which is what none of us could do to save our lives, nor if we were to take our whole lives to do it in. Is it then a trifling power we see at work, or is it not something next to miraculous? It is the utmost stretch of human ingenuity, which nothing but the bending the faculties of body and mind to it from the tenderest infancy with incessant, ever-anxious application up to manhood, can accomplish or make even a slight approach to. Man, thou art a wonderful animal and thy ways past finding out! Thou canst do strange things, but thou turnest them to little account! — To conceive of this effort of extraordinary dexterity distracts the imagination and makes admiration breathless. Yet it costs nothing to the performer, any more than if it were a mere mechanical deception with which he had nothing to do but to watch and laugh at the astonishment of the spectators. A single error of a hair's-breadth, of the smallest conceivable portion of time, would be fatal: the precision of the movements must be like a mathematical truth, their rapidity is like lightning. To catch four balls in succession in less than a second of time, and deliver them back so as to return with seeming consciousness to the hand again, to make them revolve round him at certain intervals, like the planets in their spheres, to make them chase one another like sparkles of fire, or shoot up like flowers or meteors, to throw them behind his back and twine them round his neck like ribbons or like serpents, to do what appears an impossibility, and to do it with all the ease, the grace, the carelessness imaginable, to laugh at, to play with the glittering mockeries, to follow them with his eye as if he could fascinate them with its lambent fire, or

71

as if he had only to see that they kept time with the music on
the stage — there is something in all this which he who does
not admire may be quite sure he never really admired anything in the whole course of his life. It is skill surmounting
difficulty, and beauty triumphing over skill. It seems as if the
difficulty once mastered naturally resolved itself into ease
and grace, and as if to be overcome at all, it must be overcome without an effort. The smallest awkwardness or want
of pliancy or self-possession would stop the whole process.
It is the work of witchcraft, and yet sport for children. Some
of the other feats are quite as curious and wonderful, such as
the balancing the artificial tree and shooting a bird from each
branch through a quill; though none of them have the elegance or facility of the keeping up of the brass balls. You
are in pain for the result, and glad when the experiment is
over; they are not accompanied with the same unmixed,
unchecked delight as the former; and I would not give much
to be merely astonished without being pleased at the same
time. As to the swallowing of the sword, the police ought to
interfere to prevent it. When I saw the Indian Juggler do
the same things before, his feet were bare, and he had large
rings on the toes, which kept turning round all the time of the
performance, as if they moved of themselves. — The hearing
a speech in Parliament, drawled or stammered out by the
Honourable Member or the Noble Lord, the ringing the
changes on their common-places, which anyone could repeat
after them as well as they, stirs me not a jot, shakes not my
good opinion of myself: but the seeing the Indian Jugglers
does. It makes me ashamed of myself. I ask what there
is that I can do as well as this? Nothing. What have I
been doing all my life? Have I been idle, or have I nothing
to shew for all my labour and pains? Or have I passed my
time in pouring words like water into empty sieves, rolling a
stone up a hill and then down again, trying to prove an argument in the teeth of facts, and looking for causes in the
dark, and not finding them? Is there no one thing in which
I can challenge competition, that I can bring as an instance
of exact perfection, in which others cannot find a flaw? The

utmost I can pretend to is to write a description of what this fellow can do. I can write a book; so can many others who have not even learned to spell. What abortions are these Essays! What errors, what ill-pieced transitions, what crooked reasons, what lame conclusions! How little is made out, and that little how ill! Yet they are the best I can do. I endeavour to recollect all I have ever observed or thought upon a subject, and to express it as nearly as I can. Instead of writing on four subjects at a time, it is as much as I can manage to keep the thread of one discourse clear and un-entangled. I have also time on my hands to correct my opinions, and polish my periods: but the one I cannot, and the other I will not do. I am fond of arguing; yet with a good deal of pains and practice it is often as much as I can do to beat my man; though he may be a very indifferent hand. A common fencer would disarm his adversary in the twink-ling of an eye, unless he were a professor like himself. A stroke of wit will sometimes produce this effect, but there is no such power or superiority in sense or reasoning. There is no complete mastery of execution to be shown there; and you hardly know the professor from the impudent pretender or the mere clown.[1]

I have always had this feeling of the inefficacy and slow progress of intellectual compared to mechanical excellence, and it has always made me somewhat dissatisfied. It is a great many years since I saw Richer, the famous rope-dancer, perform at Sadler's Wells. He was matchless in his art, and

---

[1] The celebrated Peter Pindar (Dr. Wolcot) first discovered and brought out the talents of the late Mr. Opie, the painter. He was a poor Cornish boy, and was out at work in the fields, when the poet went in search of him. "Well, my lad, can you go and bring me your very best picture?" The other flew like lightning, and soon came back with what he considered as his masterpiece. The stranger looked at it, and the young artist, after waiting for some time with-out his giving any opinion, at length exclaimed eagerly, "Well, what do you think of it?" "Think of it?" said Wolcot, "why, I think you ought to be ashamed of it — that you who might do so well, do no better!" The same answer would have applied to this artist's latest performances, that had been suggested by one of his earliest efforts.

added to his extraordinary skill exquisite ease and unaffected natural grace. I was at that time employed in copying a half-length picture of Sir Joshua Reynolds's; and it put me out of conceit with it. How ill this part was made out in the drawing! How heavy, how slovenly this other was painted! I could not help saying to myself, "If the rope-dancer had performed his task in this manner, leaving so many gaps and botches in his work, he would have broke his neck long ago; I should never have seen that vigorous elasticity of nerve and precision of movement!" — Is it then so easy an undertaking (comparatively) to dance on a tight-rope? Let anyone who thinks so get up and try. There is the thing. It is that which at first we cannot do at all, which in the end is done to such perfection. To account for this in some degree, I might observe that mechanical dexterity is confined to doing some one particular thing, which you can repeat as often as you please, in which you know whether you succeed or fail, and where the point of perfection consists in succeeding in a given undertaking. In mechanical efforts, you improve by perpetual practice, and you do so infallibly, because the object to be attained is not a matter of taste or fancy or opinion, but of actual experiment, in which you must either do the thing or not do it. If a man is put to aim at a mark with a bow and arrow, he must hit it or miss it, that's certain. He cannot deceive himself, and go on shooting wide or falling short, and still fancy that he is making progress. The distinction between right and wrong, between true and false, is here palpable; and he must either correct his aim or persevere in his error with his eyes open, for which there is neither excuse nor temptation. If a man is learning to dance on a rope, if he does not mind what he is about, he will break his neck. After that, it will be in vain for him to argue that he did not make a false step. His situation is not like that of Goldsmith's pedagogue.

> "In argument they own'd his wondrous skill,
> And e'en though vanquish'd, he could argue still."

Danger is a good teacher and makes apt scholars. So are disgrace, defeat, exposure to immediate scorn and laughter.

There is no opportunity in such cases for self-delusion, no idling time away, no being off your guard (or you must take the consequences) — neither is there any room for humour or caprice or prejudice. If the Indian Juggler were to play tricks in throwing up the three case-knives, which keep their positions like the leaves of a crocus in the air, he would cut his fingers. I can make a very bad antithesis without cutting my fingers. The tact of style is more ambiguous than that of double-edged instruments. If the Juggler were told that by flinging himself under the wheels of the Jaggernaut, when the idol issues forth on a gaudy day, he would immediately be transported into Paradise, he might believe it, and nobody could disprove it. So the Brahmins may say what they please on that subject, may build up dogmas and mysteries without end, and not be detected; but their ingenious countryman cannot persuade the frequenters of the Olympic Theatre that he performs a number of astonishing feats without actually giving proofs of what he says. — There is then in this sort of manual dexterity, first a gradual aptitude acquired to a given exertion of muscular power, from constant repetition, and in the next place, an exact knowledge how much is still wanting and necessary to be supplied. The obvious test is to increase the effort or nicety of the operation, and still to find it come true. The muscles ply instinctively to the dictates of habit. Certain movements and impressions of the hand and eye, having been repeated together an infinite number of times, are unconsciously but unavoidably cemented into closer and closer union; the limbs require little more than to be put in motion for them to follow a regular track with ease and certainty; so that the mere intention of the will acts mathematically, like touching the spring of a machine, and you come with Locksley in *Ivanhoe*, in shooting at a mark, "to allow for the wind."

Farther, what is meant by perfection in mechanical exercise is the performing certain feats to a uniform nicety, that is, in fact, undertaking no more than you can perform. You task yourself, the limit you fix is optional, and no more than human industry and skill can attain to; but you have no abstract,

independent standard of difficulty or excellence (other than
the extent of your own powers). Thus he who can keep up
four brass balls does this *to perfection;* but he cannot keep
up five at the same instant, and would fail every time he attempted it. That is, the mechanical performer undertakes to
emulate himself, not to equal another.[1] But the artist undertakes to imitate another, or to do what nature has done, and
this it appears is more difficult, *viz.* to copy what she has set
before us in the face of nature or "human face divine," entire
and without a blemish, than to keep up four brass balls at
the same instant; for the one is done by the power of human
skill and industry, and the other never was nor will be. Upon
the whole, therefore, I have more respect for Reynolds, than
I have for Richer; for, happen how it will, there have been
more people in the world who could dance on a rope like the
one than who could paint like Sir Joshua. The latter was
but a bungler in his profession to the other, it is true; but
then he had a harder task-master to obey, whose will was
more wayward and obscure, and whose instructions it was
more difficult to practise. You can put a child apprentice
to a tumbler or rope-dancer with a comfortable prospect of
success, if they are but sound of wind and limb; but you cannot do the same thing in painting. The odds are a million
to one. You may make indeed as many H——s and H——s
as you put into that sort of machine, but not one Reynolds
amongst them all, with his grace, his grandeur, his bland-
ness of *gusto,* "in tones and gestures hit," unless you could
make the man over again. To snatch this grace beyond the
reach of art is then the height of art — where fine art begins,
and where mechanical skill ends. The soft suffusion of
the soul, the speechless breathing eloquence, the looks "commercing with the skies," the ever-shifting forms of an eternal
principle, that which is seen but for a moment, but dwells
in the heart always, and is only seized as it passes by strong
and secret sympathy, must be taught by nature and genius,
not by rules or study. It is suggested by feeling, not by

---

[1] If two persons play against each other at any game, one of them
necessarily fails.

laborious microscopic inspection; in seeking for it without, we lose the harmonious clue to it within; and in aiming to grasp the substance, we let the very spirit of art evaporate. In a word, the objects of fine art are not the objects of sight but as these last are the objects of taste and imagination, that is, as they appeal to the sense of beauty, of pleasure, and of power in the human breast, and are explained by that finer sense and revealed in their inner structure to the eye in return. Nature is also a language. Objects, like words, have a meaning; and the true artist is the interpreter of this language, which he can only do by knowing its application to a thousand other objects in a thousand other situations. Thus the eye is too blind a guide of itself to distinguish between the warm or cold tone of a deep blue sky, but another sense acts as a monitor to it and does not err. The colour of the leaves in autumn would be nothing without the feeling that accompanies it; but it is that feeling that stamps them on the canvas, faded, seared, blighted, shrinking from the winter's flaw, and makes the sight as true as touch —

> "And visions, as poetic eyes avow,
> Cling to each leaf and hang on every bough."

The more ethereal, evanescent, more refined and sublime part of art is the seeing nature through the medium of sentiment and passion, as each object is a symbol of the affections and a link in the chain of our endless being. But the unravelling this mysterious web of thought and feeling is alone in the Muse's gift, namely, in the power of that trembling sensibility which is awake to every change and every modification of its ever-varying impressions, that

> "Thrills in each nerve, and lives along the line."

This power is indifferently called genius, imagination, feeling, taste; but the manner in which it acts upon the mind can neither be defined by abstract rules, as is the case in science, nor verified by continual unvarying experiments, as is the case in mechanical performances. The mechanical excellence of the Dutch painters in colouring and handling is that which comes the nearest in fine art to the perfection of certain manual exhibitions of skill. The truth of the effect and the facility with which it is produced are equally admirable. Up to a certain point, everything is faultless. The hand and eye have done their part. There is only a want of taste and genius. It is after we enter upon that enchanted ground that the human mind begins to droop and flag as in a strange road, or in a thick mist, benighted and making little way with many attempts and many failures, and that the best of us only escape with half a triumph. The undefined and the imaginary are the regions that we must pass like Satan, difficult and doubtful, "half flying, half on foot." The object in sense is a positive thing, and execution comes with practice.

Cleverness is a certain *knack* or aptitude at doing certain things which depend more on a particular adroitness and off-hand readiness than on force or perseverance, such as making puns, making epigrams, making extempore verses, mimicking the company, mimicking a style, etc. Cleverness is either liveliness and smartness, or something answering to *sleight of hand*, like letting a glass fall sideways off a table, or else a trick, like knowing the secret spring of a watch. Accomplishments are certain external graces, which are to be learnt from others and which are easily displayed to the admiration of the beholder, *viz.* dancing, riding, fencing, music, and so on. These ornamental acquirements are only proper to those who are at ease in mind and fortune. I know an individual who if he had been born to an estate of five thousand a year, would have been the most accomplished gentleman of the age. He would have been the delight and envy of the circle in which he moved — would have graced by his manners the liberality flowing from the openness of his heart, would have laughed with the women, have argued with the men, have said good things and written agreeable ones, have taken a hand at piquet or the lead at the harpsichord, and have set and sung his own verses — *nugæ canoræ* — with tenderness and spirit; a Rochester without the vice, a modern Surrey! As it is, all these capabilities of excellence stand in his way. He is too versatile for a professional man, not dull enough for a political drudge, too gay to be happy, too thoughtless to be rich. He wants the enthusiasm of the poet, the severity of the prose writer, and the application of the man of business. — Talent is the capacity of doing anything that depends on application and industry, such as writing a criticism, making a speech, studying the law. Talent differs from genius, as voluntary differs from involuntary power. Ingenuity is genius in trifles, greatness is genius in undertakings of much pith and moment. A clever or ingenious man is one who can do anything well, whether it is worth doing or not: a great man is one who can do that which when done is of the highest importance. Themistocles said he could not play on the flute, but that he could make of a small city a great one. This gives one a pretty good idea of the distinction in question.

Greatness is great power, producing great effects. It is not enough that a man has great power in himself, he must show it to all the world in a way that cannot be hid or gainsaid. He must fill up a certain idea in the public mind. I have no other notion of greatness than this two-fold definition, great results springing from great inherent energy. The great in visible objects has relation to that which extends over space: the great in mental ones has to do with space and time. No man is truly great who is great only in his lifetime. The test of greatness is the page of history. Nothing can be said to be great that has a distinct limit, or that borders on something evidently greater than itself. Besides, what is short-lived and pampered into mere notoriety is of a gross and vulgar quality in itself. A Lord Mayor is hardly a great man. A city orator or patriot of the day only show, by reaching the height of their wishes, the distance they are at from any true ambition. Popularity is neither fame nor greatness. A king (as such) is not a great man. He has great power, but it is not his own. He merely wields the lever of the state, which a child, an idiot, or a madman can do. It is the office, not the man, we gaze at. Anyone else in the same situation would be just as much an object of abject curiosity. We laugh at the country girl who having seen a king, expressed her disappointment by saying, "Why, he is only a man!" Yet, knowing this, we run to see a king as if he was something more than a man. — To display the greatest powers, unless they are applied to great purposes, makes nothing for the character of greatness. To throw a barley-corn through the eye of a needle, to multiply nine figures by nine in the memory, argues infinite dexterity of body and capacity of mind, but nothing comes of either. There is a surprising power at work, but the effects are not proportionate, or such as take hold of the imagination. To impress the idea of power on others, they must be made in some way to feel it. It must be communicated to their understandings in the shape of an increase of knowledge, or it must subdue and overawe them by subjecting their wills. Admiration, to be solid and lasting, must be founded on proofs from which we have no means of escaping; it is neither a slight nor a voluntary gift. A mathematician who solves a profound problem, a poet who creates an image of beauty in the mind that was not there before, imparts knowledge and power to others, in which his greatness and his fame consists and on which it reposes. Jedediah Buxton will be forgotten; but Napier's bones will live. Lawgivers, philosophers, founders of religion, conquerors and heroes, inventors, and great geniuses in arts and sciences, are great men; for they are great public benefactors, or formidable scourges to mankind. Among ourselves, Shakespeare, Newton, Bacon, Milton, Cromwell, were great men; for they showed great power by acts and thoughts which have not yet been consigned to oblivion. They must needs be men of lofty stature, whose shadows lengthen out to remote posterity. A great farce-writer may be a great man; for Molière was but a great farce-writer. In my mind, the author of *Don Quixote* was a great man. So have there been many others. A great chess-player is not a great man, for he leaves the world as he found it. No act terminating in itself constitutes greatness. This will apply to all displays of power or trials of skill which are confined to the momentary, individual effort, and construct no permanent image or trophy of themselves without them. Is not an actor then a great

man, because "he dies and leaves the world no copy"? I
must make an exception for Mrs. Siddons, or else give up my
definition of greatness for her sake. A man at the top of
his profession is not therefore a great man. He is great in
his way, but that is all, unless he shews the marks of a great
moving intellect, so that we trace the master-mind, and can
sympathise with the springs that urge him on. The rest is
but a craft or *mystery*. John Hunter was a great man —
that anyone might see without the smallest skill in surgery.
His style and manner showed the man. He would set about
cutting up the carcass of a whale with the same greatness of
gusto that Michael Angelo would have hewn a block of marble.
Lord Nelson was a great naval commander; but for myself,
I have not much opinion of a sea-faring life. Sir Humphry
Davy is a great chemist, but I am not sure that he is a great
man. I am not a bit the wiser for any of his discoveries, nor
I never met with anyone that was. But it is in the nature
of greatness to propagate an idea of itself, as wave impels
wave, circle without circle. It is a contradiction in terms for
a coxcomb to be a great man. A really great man has always an idea of something greater than himself. I have
observed that certain sectaries and polemical writers have no
higher compliments to pay their most shining lights than to
say that "Such a one was a considerable man in his day."
Some new elucidation of a text sets aside the authority of the
old interpretation, and a "great scholar's memory outlives
him half a century," at the utmost. A rich man is not a
great man, except to his dependants and his steward. A
lord is a great man in the idea we have of his ancestry, and
probably of himself, if we know nothing of him but his title.
I have heard a story of two bishops, one of whom said (speaking of St. Peter's at Rome) that when he first entered it he
was rather awe-struck, but that as he walked up it, his mind
seemed to swell and dilate with it and at last to fill the whole
building — the other said that as he saw more of it, he appeared to himself to grow less and less every step he took,
and in the end to dwindle into nothing. This was in some
respects a striking picture of a great and little mind — for

greatness sympathises with greatness, and littleness shrinks into itself. The one might have become a Wolsey; the other was only fit to become a Mendicant Friar — or there might have been court-reasons for making him a bishop. The French have to me a character of littleness in all about them; but they have produced three great men that belong to every country, Molière, Rabelais, and Montaigne.

To return from this digression and conclude the Essay. A singular instance of manual dexterity was shewn in the person of the late John Cavanagh, whom I have several times seen. His death was celebrated at the time in an article in the *Examiner* newspaper (Feb. 7, 1819), written apparently between jest and earnest; but as it is *pat* to our purpose, and falls in with my own way of considering such subjects, I shall here take leave to quote it.

"Died at his house in Burbage-street, St. Giles's, John Cavanagh, the famous hand fives-player. When a person dies, who does any one thing better than anyone else in the world, which so many others are trying to do well, it leaves a gap in society. It is not likely that anyone will now see the game of fives played in its perfection for many years to come — for Cavanagh is dead and has not left his peer behind him. It may be said that there are things of more importance than striking a ball against a wall — there are things indeed which make more noise and do as little good, such as making war and peace, making speeches and answering them, making verses and blotting them; making money and throwing it away. But the game of fives is what no one despises who has ever played at it. It is the finest exercise for the body and the best relaxation for the mind. The Roman poet said that 'Care mounted behind the horseman and stuck to his skirts.' But this remark would not have applied to the fives-player. He who takes to playing at fives is twice young. He feels neither the past nor future 'in the instant.' Debts, taxes, 'domestic treason, foreign levy, nothing can touch him further.' He has no other wish, no other thought, from the moment the game begins, but that of striking the ball, of placing it, of *making* it! This Cavanagh was sure to do.

Whenever he touched the ball, there was an end of the chase.
His eye was certain, his hand fatal, his presence of mind complete. He could do what he pleased, and he always knew
exactly what to do. He saw the whole game, and played
it; took instant advantage of his adversary's weakness, and
recovered balls, as if by a miracle and from sudden thought,
that everyone gave for lost. He had equal power and skill,
quickness, and judgment. He could either out-wit his antagonist by finesse, or beat him by main strength. Sometimes, when he seemed preparing to send the ball with the
full swing of his arm, he would by a slight turn of his wrist
drop it within an inch of the line. In general, the ball came
from his hand, as if from a racket, in a straight horizontal
line; so that it was in vain to attempt to overtake or stop it.
As it was said of a great orator that he never was at a loss for
a word, and for the properest word, so Cavanagh always could
tell the degree of force necessary to be given to a ball, and the
precise direction in which it should be sent. He did his work
with the greatest ease; never took more pains than was
necessary; and while others were fagging themselves to
death, was as cool and collected as if he had just entered the
court. His style of play was as remarkable as his power of
execution. He had no affectation, no trifling. He did not
throw away the game to show off an attitude or try an experiment. He was a fine, sensible, manly player, who did
what he could, but that was more than anyone else could
even affect to do. His blows were not undecided and in-
effectual — lumbering like Mr. Wordsworth's epic poetry,
nor wavering like Mr. Coleridge's lyric prose, nor short of the
mark like Mr. Brougham's speeches, nor wide of it like Mr.
Canning's wit, nor foul like the *Quarterly*, not *let* balls like
the *Edinburgh Review*. Cobbett and Junius together would
have made a Cavanagh. He was the best *up-hill* player in
the world; even when his adversary was fourteen, he would
play on the same or better, and as he never flung away the
game through carelessness and conceit, he never gave it up
through laziness or want of heart. The only peculiarity of
his play was that he never *volleyed*, but let the balls hop; but

if they rose an inch from the ground, he never missed having
them. There was not only nobody equal, but nobody second
to him. It is supposed that he could give any other player
half the game, or beat him with his left hand. His service
was tremendous. He once played Woodward and Meredith
together (two of the best players in England) in the Fives-
court, St. Martin's-street, and made seven and twenty aces
following by services alone — a thing unheard of. He another time played Peru, who was considered a first-rate fives-
player, a match of the best out of five games, and in the three
first games, which of course decided the match, Peru got only
one ace. Cavanagh was an Irishman by birth and a house-
painter by profession. He had once laid aside his working-
dress and walked up, in his smartest clothes, to the Rosemary
Branch to have an afternoon's pleasure. A person accosted
him and asked him if he would have a game. So they agreed
to play for half-a-crown a game, and a bottle of cider. The
first game began — it was seven, eight, ten, thirteen, fourteen, all. Cavanagh won it. The next was the same.
They played on, and each game was hardly contested.
'There,' said the unconscious fives-player, there was a
stroke that Cavanagh could not take; I never played better
in my life, and yet I can't win a game. I don't know how it
is.' However, they played on, Cavanagh winning every
game, and the by-standers drinking the cider and laughing
all the time. In the twelfth game, when Cavanagh was only
four, and the stranger thirteen, a person came in and said,
'What! are you here, Cavanagh?' The words were no
sooner pronounced than the astonished player let the ball drop
from his hand, and saying, 'What! have I been breaking my
heart all this time to beat Cavanagh?' refused to make another effort. 'And yet, I give you my word,' said Cavanagh,
telling the story with some triumph, 'I played all the while
with my clenched fist.' — He used frequently to play matches
at Copenhagen-house for wagers and dinners. The wall
against which they play is the same that supports the kitchen-
chimney, and when the wall resounded louder than usual,
the cooks exclaimed, 'Those are the Irishman's balls,' and

the joints trembled on the spit! — Goldsmith consoled himself that there were places where he too was admired; and
Cavanagh was the admiration of all the fives-courts where he
ever played. Mr. Powell, when he played matches in the
Court in St. Martin's-street, used to fill his gallery at half a
crown a head with amateurs and admirers of talent in whatever department it is shown. He could not have shown himself in any ground in England but he would have been immediately surrounded with inquisitive gazers, trying to find
out in what part of his frame his unrivalled skill lay, as
politicians wonder to see the balance of Europe suspended in
Lord Castlereagh's face, and admire the trophies of the
British Navy lurking under Mr. Croker's hanging brow.
Now Cavanagh was as good-looking a man as the Noble
Lord, and much better looking than the Right Hon. Secretary.
He had a clear, open countenance, and did not look sideways
or down, like Mr. Murray, the bookseller. He was a young
fellow of sense, humour, and courage. He once had a quarrel
with a waterman at Hungerford-stairs, and, they say, served
him out in great style. In a word, there are hundreds at this
day who cannot mention his name without admiration as the
best fives-player that perhaps ever lived (the greatest excellence of which they have any notion) — and the noisy
shout of the ring happily stood him in stead of the unheard
voice of posterity! — The only person who seems to have
excelled as much in another way as Cavanagh did in his, was
the late John Davies, the racket-player. It was remarked
of him that he did not seem to follow the ball, but the ball
seemed to follow him. Give him a foot of wall, and he was
sure to make the ball. The four best racket-players of that
day were Jack Spines, Jem. Harding, Armitage, and Church.
Davies could give any one of these two hands a time, that is,
half the game, and each of these, at their best, could give the
best player now in London the same odds. Such are the
gradations in all exertions of human skill and art. He once
played four capital players together, and beat them. He was
also a first-rate tennis-player, and an excellent fives-player.
In the Fleet or King's Bench, he would have stood against

Powell, who was reckoned the best open-ground player of his time. This last-mentioned player is at present the keeper of the Fives-court, and we might recommend to him for a motto over his door — 'Who enters here, forgets himself, his country, and his friends.' And the best of it is, that by the calculation of the odds, none of the three are worth remembering! — Cavanagh died from the bursting of a blood-vessel, which prevented him from playing for the last two or three years. This, he was often heard to say, he thought hard upon him. He was fast recovering, however, when he was suddenly carried off, to the regret of all who knew him. As Mr. Peel made it a qualification of the present Speaker, Mr. Manners Sutton, that he was an excellent moral character, so Jack Cavanagh was a zealous Catholic, and could not be persuaded to eat meat on a Friday, the day on which he died. We have paid this willing tribute to his memory.

> 'Let no rude hand deface it,
> And his forlorn "*Hic jacet.*"' "

ON GOING A JOURNEY

ONE of the pleasantest things in the world is going a journey; but I like to go by myself. I can enjoy society in a room; but out of doors, nature is company enough for me. I am then never less alone than when alone.

"The fields his study, nature was his book."

I cannot see the wit of walking and talking at the same time. When I am in the country, I wish to vegetate like the country. I am not for criticising hedge-rows and black cattle. I go out of town in order to forget the town and all that is in it. There are those who for this purpose go to watering-places and carry the metropolis with them. I like more elbow-room and fewer incumbrances. I like solitude, when I give myself up to it, for the sake of solitude; nor do I ask for

" —— a friend in my retreat,
Whom I may whisper, solitude is sweet."

The soul of a journey is liberty, perfect liberty, to think, feel, do, just as one pleases. We go a journey chiefly to be free of all impediments and of all inconveniences; to leave ourselves behind, much more to get rid of others. It is because I want a little breathing-space to muse on indifferent matters, where Contemplation

"May plume her feathers and let grow her wings,
That in the various bustle of resort
Were all too ruffled, and sometimes impair'd,"

that I absent myself from the town for awhile, without feeling at a loss the moment I am left by myself. Instead of a friend in a post-chaise or in a Tilbury, to exchange good things with and vary the same stale topics over again, for once let me have a truce with impertinence. Give me the clear blue sky over my head, and the green turf beneath my feet, a winding road before me, and a three hours' march to dinner — and then to thinking! It is hard if I cannot start some game on these lone heaths. I laugh, I run, I leap, I sing for joy. From the point of yonder rolling cloud, I plunge into my past being and revel there, as the sun-burnt Indian plunges headlong into the wave that wafts him to his native shore. Then long-forgotten things, like "sunken wrack and sumless treasuries," burst upon my eager sight, and I begin to feel, think, and be myself again. Instead of an awkward silence, broken by attempts at wit or dull common-places, mine is that undisturbed silence of the heart which alone is perfect eloquence. No one likes puns, alliterations, antitheses, argument, and analysis better than I do; but I sometimes had rather be without them. "Leave, oh, leave me to my repose!" I have just now other business in hand, which would seem idle to you, but is with me "very stuff of the conscience." Is not this wild rose sweet without a comment? Does not this daisy leap to my heart set in its coat of emerald? Yet if I were to explain to you the circumstance that has so endeared it to me, you would only smile. Had I not better then keep it to myself, and let it serve me to brood over, from here to yonder craggy point, and from thence onward to the far-distant horizon? I should be but bad company all that way, and therefore prefer being alone. I have heard it said that you may, when the moody fit comes on, walk or ride on by yourself and indulge your reveries. But this looks like a breach of manners, a neglect of others, and you are thinking all the time that you ought to rejoin your party. "Out upon such half-faced fellowship," say I. I like to be either entirely to myself, or entirely at the disposal of others; to talk or be silent, to walk or sit still, to be sociable or solitary. I was pleased with an observation of Mr. Cobbett's, that "he thought it a bad French custom to drink our wine with our meals, and that an Englishman ought to do only one thing at a time." So I cannot talk and think, or indulge in melancholy musing and lively conversation by fits and starts. "Let me have a companion of my way," says Sterne, "were it but to remark how the shadows lengthen as the sun declines." It is beautifully said; but in my opinion, this continual comparing of notes interferes with the involuntary impression of things upon the mind and hurts the sentiment. If you only hint what you feel in a kind of dumb show, it is insipid; if you have to explain it, it is making a toil of a pleasure. You cannot read the book of nature without being perpetually put to the trouble of translating it for the benefit of others. I am for the synthetical method on a journey, in preference to the analytical. I am content to lay in a stock of ideas then, and to examine and anatomise them afterwards. I want to see my vague notions float like the down of the thistle before the breeze, and not to have them entangled in the briars and thorns of controversy. For once, I like to have it all my own way; and this is impossible unless you are alone, or in such company as I do not covet. I have no objection to argue a point with any one for twenty miles of measured road, but not for pleasure. If you remark the scent of a bean-field crossing the road, perhaps your fellow-traveller has no smell. If you point to a distant object, perhaps he is short-sighted, and has to take out his glass to look at it. There is a feeling in the air, a tone in the colour of a cloud which hits your fancy, but the effect of which you are unable to account for. There is then no sympathy, but an uneasy craving after it, and a dissatisfaction which pursues you on the way, and in the end probably produces ill humour. Now I never quarrel with myself, and take all my own conclusions for granted till I find it necessary to defend them against objections. It is not merely that you may not be of accord on the objects and circumstances that present themselves before you — these may recall a number of objects and lead to associations too delicate and refined to be possibly communicated to others. Yet these I love to cherish, and sometimes still fondly clutch them, when I can escape from the throng to do so. To give way to our feelings before company, seems extravagance or affectation; and, on the other hand, to have to unravel this mystery of our being at every turn, and to make others take an equal interest in it (otherwise the end is not answered) is a task to which few are competent. We must "give it an understanding, but no tongue." My old friend C ——, however, could do both.

He could go on in the most delightful explanatory way over hill and dale, a summer's day, and convert a landscape into a didactic poem or a Pindaric ode. "He talked far above singing." If I could so clothe my ideas in sounding and flowing words, I might perhaps wish to have someone with me to admire the swelling theme; or I could be more content, were it possible for me still to hear his echoing voice in the woods of All-Foxden. They had "that fine madness in them which our first poets had;" and if they could have been caught by some rare instrument, would have breathed such strains as the following.

> " —— Here be woods as green
> As any, air likewise as fresh and sweet
> As when smooth Zephyrus plays on the fleet
> Face of the curled streams, with flow'rs as many
> As the young spring gives, and as choice as any;
> Here be all new delights, cool streams and wells,
> Arbours o'ergrown with woodbines, caves and dells;
> Choose where thou wilt, whilst I sit by and sing,
> Or gather rushes, to make many a ring
> For thy long fingers; tell thee tales of love;
> How the pale Phœbe, hunting in a grove,
> First saw the boy Endymion, from whose eyes
> She took eternal fire that never dies;
> How she convey'd him softly in a sleep,
> His temples bound with poppy, to the steep
> Head of old Latmos, where she stoops each night,
> Gilding the mountain with her brother's light,
> To kiss her sweetest." — *Faithful Shepherdess*.

Had I words and images at command like these, I would attempt to wake the thoughts that lie slumbering on golden ridges in the evening clouds; but at the sight of nature my fancy, poor as it is, droops and closes up its leaves, like flowers at sunset. I can make nothing out on the spot: — I must have time to collect myself.

In general, a good thing spoils out-of-door prospects; it should be reserved for table-talk. L —— is for this reason, I take it, the worst company in the world out of doors; because he is the best within. I grant, there is one subject on which it is pleasant to talk on a journey; and that is, what one shall have for supper when we get to our inn at night.

The open air improves this sort of conversation or friendly altercation by setting a keener edge on appetite. Every mile of the road heightens the flavour of the viands we expect at the end of it. How fine is it to enter some old town, walled and turreted, just at approach of night-fall, or to come to some straggling village, with the lights streaming through the surrounding gloom; and then after inquiring for the best entertainment that the place affords, to "take one's ease at one's inn!" These eventful moments in our lives' history are too precious, too full of solid, heart-felt happiness to be frittered and dribbled away in imperfect sympathy. I would have them all to myself, and drain them to the last drop; they will do to talk of or to write about afterwards. What a delicate speculation it is, after drinking whole goblets of tea,

"The cups that cheer, but not inebriate,"

and letting the fumes ascend into the brain, to sit considering what we shall have for supper — eggs and a rasher, a rabbit smothered in onions, or an excellent veal-cutlet! Sancho in such a situation once fixed on cow-heel; and his choice, though he could not help it, is not to be disparaged. Then, in the intervals of pictured scenery and Shandean contemplation, to catch the preparation and the stir in the kitchen — *Procul, O procul este profani!* These hours are sacred to silence and to musing, to be treasured up in the memory, and to feed the source of smiling thoughts hereafter. I would not waste them in idle talk; or if I must have the integrity of fancy broken in upon, I would rather it were by a stranger than a friend. A stranger takes his hue and character from the time and place; he is a part of the furniture and costume of an inn. If he is a Quaker, or from the West Riding of Yorkshire, so much the better. I do not even try to sympathise with him, and he breaks no squares. I associate nothing with my travelling companion but present objects and passing events. In his ignorance of me and my affairs, I in a manner forget myself. But a friend reminds one of other things, rips up old grievances, and destroys the abstraction of the scene. He comes in ungraciously between us and our imagi-

h

nary character. Something is dropped in the course of
conversation that gives a hint of your profession and pursuits; or from having someone with you that knows the less
sublime portions of your history, it seems that other people do.
You are no longer a citizen of the world: but your "unhoused
free condition is put into circumspection and confine." The
incognito of an inn is one of its striking privileges — "Lord
of one's self, uncumber'd with a name." Oh! it is great to
shake off the trammels of the world and of public opinion —
to lose our importunate, tormenting, everlasting personal
identity in the elements of nature, and become the creature
of the moment, clear of all ties — to hold to the universe
only by a dish of sweet-breads, and to owe nothing but the
score of the evening — and no longer seeking for applause and
meeting with contempt, to be known by no other title than
the Gentleman in the parlour! One may take one's choice of
all characters in this romantic state of uncertainty as to one's
real pretensions, and become indefinitely respectable and
negatively right-worshipful. We baffle prejudice and disappoint conjecture; and from being so to others, begin to be objects of curiosity and wonder even to ourselves. We are no
more those hackneyed common-places that we appear in the
world; an inn restores us to the level of nature and quits
scores with society! I have certainly spent some enviable
hours at inns — sometimes when I have been left entirely to
myself and have tried to solve some metaphysical problem, as
once at Witham-common, where I found out the proof that
likeness is not a case of the association of ideas — at other
times, when there have been pictures in the room, as at St.
Neot's (I think it was), where I first met with Gribelin's
engravings of the Cartoons, into which I entered at once,
and at a little inn on the borders of Wales, where there happened to be hanging some of Westall's drawings, which I
compared triumphantly (for a theory that I had, not for the
admired artist) with the figure of a girl who had ferried me
over the Severn, standing up in a boat between me and the
twilight — at other times I might mention luxuriating in
books, with a peculiar interest in this way, as I remember

sitting up half the night to read *Paul and Virginia*, which I
picked up at an inn at Bridgewater, after being drenched in
the rain all day; and at the same place I got through two
volumes of Madame D'Arblay's *Camilla*. It was on the
10th of April, 1798, that I sat down to a volume of the *New
Eloise*, at the inn at Llangollen, over a bottle of sherry and
a cold chicken. The letter I chose was that in which St.
Preux describes his feelings as he first caught a glimpse from
the heights of the Jura of the Pays de Vaud, which I had
brought with me as a *bon bouche* to crown the evening with.
It was my birthday, and I had for the first time come from a
place in the neighborhood to visit this delightful spot. The
road to Llangollen turns off between Chirk and Wrexham;
and on passing a certain point, you come all at once upon the
valley, which opens like an amphitheatre, broad, barren hills
rising in majestic state on either side, with "green upland
swells that echo to the bleat of flocks" below, and the river
Dee babbling over its stony bed in the midst of them. The
valley at this time "glittered green with sunny showers,"
and a budding ash-tree dipped its tender branches in the
chiding stream. How proud, how glad I was to walk along
the high road that overlooks the delicious prospect, repeating
the lines which I have just quoted from Mr. Coleridge's
poems! But besides the prospect which opened beneath my
feet, another also opened to my inward sight, a heavenly
vision, on which were written, in letters large as Hope could
make them, these four words, LIBERTY, GENIUS, LOVE,
VIRTUE; which have since faded into the light of common day,
or mock my idle gaze.

" The beautiful is vanished, and returns not."

Still I would return some time or other to this enchanted spot;
but I would return to it alone. What other self could I find to
share that influx of thoughts, of regret and delight, the fragments of which I could hardly conjure up to myself, so much
have they been broken and defaced! I could stand on some
tall rock and overlook the precipice of years that separates
me from what I then was. I was at that time going shortly

to visit the poet whom I have above named. Where is he now? Not only I myself have changed; the world, which was then new to me, has become old and incorrigible. Yet will I turn to thee in thought, O sylvan Dee, in joy, in youth and gladness as thou then wert; and thou shalt always be to me the river of Paradise, where I will drink of the waters of life freely!

There is hardly anything that shows the short-sightedness or capriciousness of the imagination more than travelling does. With change of place we change our ideas; nay, our opinions and feelings. We can by an effort indeed transport ourselves to old and long-forgotten scenes, and then the picture of the mind revives again; but we forget those that we have just left. It seems that we can think but of one place at a time. The canvas of the fancy is but of a certain extent, and if we paint one set of objects upon it, they immediately efface every other. We cannot enlarge our conceptions, we only shift our point of view. The landscape bares its bosom to the enraptured eye, we take our fill of it and seem as if we could form no other image of beauty or grandeur. We pass on and think no more of it; the horizon that shuts it from our sight, also blots it from our memory like a dream. In travelling through a wild, barren country, I can form no idea of a woody and cultivated one. It appears to me that all the world must be barren, like what I see of it. In the country we forget the town, and in town we despise the country. "Beyond Hyde Park," says Sir Fopling Flutter, "all is a desert." All that part of the map that we do not see before us is a blank. The world in our conceit of it is not much bigger than a nutshell. It is not one prospect expanded into another, county joined to county, kingdom to kingdom, land to seas, making an image voluminous and vast; — the mind can form no larger idea of space than the eye can take in at a single glance. The rest is a name written in a map, a calculation of arithmetic. For instance, what is the true signification of that immense mass of territory and population, known by the name of China to us? An inch of pasteboard on a wooden globe, of no more account than a China orange! Things near us are seen of the size of life: things at a distance are diminished to the size of the understanding. We measure the universe by ourselves, and even comprehend the texture of our own being only piece-meal. In this way, however, we remember an infinity of things and places. The mind is like a mechanical instrument that plays a great variety of tunes, but it must play them in succession. One idea recalls another, but it at the same time excludes all others. In trying to renew old recollections, we cannot as it were unfold the whole web of our existence; we must pick out the single threads. So in coming to a place where we have formerly lived and with which we have intimate associations, everyone must have found that the feeling grows more vivid the nearer we approach the spot, from the mere anticipation of the actual impression: we remember circumstances, feelings, persons, faces, names that we had not thought of for years; but for the time all the rest of the world is forgotten! — To return to the question I have quitted above.

I have no objection to go to see ruins, aqueducts, pictures, in company with a friend or a party, but rather the contrary, for the former reason reversed. They are intelligible matters and will bear talking about. The sentiment here is not tacit, but communicable and overt. Salisbury Plain is barren of criticism, but Stonehenge will bear a discussion antiquarian, picturesque, and philosophical. In setting out on a party of pleasure, the first consideration always is where we shall go to; in taking a solitary ramble, the question is what we shall meet with by the way. "The mind is its own place;" nor are we anxious to arrive at the end of our journey. I can myself do the honours indifferently well to works of art and curiosity. I once took a party to Oxford with no mean *eclat* — showed them that seat of the Muses at a distance,

"The glistering spires and pinnacles adorn'd" —

descanted on the learned air that breathes from the grassy quadrangles and stone walls of halls and colleges — was at home in the Bodleian; and at Blenheim quite superseded the powdered ciceroni that attended us, and that pointed in vain

with his wand to common-place beauties in matchless pictures.
— As another exception to the above reasoning, I should not
feel confident in venturing on a journey in a foreign country
without a companion. I should want at intervals to hear
the sound of my own language. There is an involuntary
antipathy in the mind of an Englishman to foreign manners
and notions that requires the assistance of social sympathy
to carry it off. As the distance from home increases, this
relief, which was at first a luxury, becomes a passion and an
appetite. A person would almost feel stifled to find himself
in the deserts of Arabia without friends and countrymen;
there must be allowed to be something in the view of Athens
or old Rome that claims the utterance of speech; and I own
that the Pyramids are too mighty for any single contemplation. In such situations, so opposite to all one's ordinary
train of ideas, one seems a species by one's-self, a limb torn
off from society, unless one can meet with instant fellowship
and support. — Yet I did not feel this want or craving very
pressing once, when I first set my foot on the laughing shores
of France. Calais was peopled with novelty and delight.
The confused, busy murmur of the place was like oil and wine
poured into my ears; nor did the mariners' hymn, which was
sung from the top of an old crazy vessel in the harbour, as the
sun went down, send an alien sound into my soul. I only
breathed the air of general humanity. I walked over "the
vine-covered hills and gay regions of France," erect and
satisfied; for the image of man was not cast down and chained
to the foot of arbitrary thrones; I was at no loss for language,
for that of all the great schools of painting was open to me.
The whole is vanished like a shade. Pictures, heroes, glory,
freedom, all are fled: nothing remains but the Bourbons and
the French people! — There is undoubtedly a sensation in
travelling into foreign parts that is to be had nowhere else;
but it is more pleasing at the time than lasting. It is too
remote from our habitual associations to be a common topic
of discourse or reference, and, like a dream or another state of
existence, does not piece into our daily modes of life. It is an
animated but a momentary hallucination. It demands an

effort to exchange our actual for our ideal identity; and to feel the pulse of our old transports revive very keenly, we must "jump" all our present comforts and connexions. Our romantic and itinerant character is not to be domesticated. Dr. Johnson remarked how little foreign travel added to the facilities of conversation in those who had been abroad. In fact, the time we have spent there is both delightful and in one sense instructive; but it appears to be cut out of our substantial, downright existence, and never to join kindly on to it. We are not the same, but another, and perhaps more enviable individual, all the time we are out of our own country. We are lost to ourselves, as well as our friends. So the poet somewhat quaintly sings,

"Out of my country and myself I go.".

Those who wish to forget painful thoughts, do well to absent themselves for a while from the ties and objects that recall them; but we can be said only to fulfil our destiny in the place that gave us birth. I should on this account like well enough to spend the whole of my life in travelling abroad, if I could anywhere borrow another life to spend afterwards at home!

WHY DISTANT OBJECTS PLEASE

DISTANT objects please, because, in the first place, they imply an idea of space and magnitude, and because, not being obtruded too close upon the eye, we clothe them with the indistinct and airy colours of fancy. In looking at the misty mountain-tops that bound the horizon, the mind is as it were conscious of all the conceivable objects and interests that lie between; we imagine all sorts of adventures in the interim; strain our hopes and wishes to reach the air-drawn circle, or to "descry new lands, rivers, and mountains," stretching far beyond it, our feelings carried out of themselves lose their grossness and their husk, are rarefied, expanded, melt into softness and brighten into beauty, turning to ethereal mould, sky-tinctured. We drink the air before us, and borrow a more refined existence from objects that hover on the brink of nothing. Where the landscape fades from the dull sight, we fill the thin, viewless space with shapes of unknown good, and tinge the hazy prospect with hopes and wishes and more charming fears.

> "But thou, oh Hope! with eyes so fair,
> What was thy delighted measure?
> Still it whisper'd promised pleasure,
> And bade the lovely scenes at distance hail!"

Whatever is placed beyond the reach of sense and knowledge, whatever is imperfectly discerned, the fancy pieces out at its leisure; and all but the present moment, but the present spot, passion claims for its own, and brooding over it with wings outspread, stamps it with an image of itself. Passion is lord of infinite space, and distant objects please because they border on its confines, and are moulded by its touch. When I was a boy, I lived within sight of a range of lofty hills, whose blue tops blending with the setting sun had often tempted my longing eyes and wandering feet. At last I put my project in execution, and on a nearer approach, instead of glimmering air woven into fantastic shapes, found them huge, lumpish heaps of discoloured earth. I learnt from this (in part) to leave "Yarrow unvisited," and not idly to disturb a dream of good! Distance of time has much the same effect as distance of place. It is not surprising that fancy colours the prospect of the future as it thinks good, when it even effaces the forms of memory. Time takes out the sting of pain; our sorrows after a certain period have been so often steeped in a medium of thought and passion, that they "unmould their essence"; and all that remains of our original impressions is what we would wish them to have been. Not only the untried steep ascent before us, but the rude, unsightly masses of our past experience presently resume their power of deception over the eye: the golden cloud soon rests upon their heads, and the purple light of fancy clothes their barren sides! Thus we pass on, while both ends of our existence touch upon Heaven! — There is (so to speak) "a mighty stream of tendency" to good in the human mind, upon which all objects float and are imperceptibly borne along; and though in the voyage of life we meet with strong rebuffs, with rocks and quicksands, yet there is "a tide in the affairs of men," a heaving and a restless aspiration of the soul, by means of which, "with sails and tackle torn," the wreck and scattered fragments of our entire being drift into the port and haven of our desires! In all that relates to the affections, we put the will for the deed; so that the instant the pressure of unwelcome circumstances is removed, the mind recoils from their hold, recovers its elasticity, and re-unites itself to that image of good, which is but a reflection and configuration of its own nature. Seen in the distance, in the long perspective of waning years, the meanest incidents, enlarged and enriched by countless recollections, become interesting; the most painful, broken and softened by time, soothe. How any object that unexpectedly brings back to us old scenes and associations, startles the mind! What a yearning it creates within us; what a longing to leap the intermediate space! How fondly we cling to, and try to revive the impression of all that we then were!

"Such tricks hath strong imagination!"

In truth, we impose upon ourselves, and know not what we wish. It is a cunning artifice, a quaint delusion, by which, in pretending to be what we were at a particular moment of time, we would fain be all that we have since been, and have our lives to come over again. It is not the little, glimmering, almost annihilated speck in the distance, that rivets our attention and "hangs upon the beatings of our hearts": it is the interval that separates us from it, and of which it is the trembling boundary, that excites all this coil and mighty pudder in the breast. Into that great gap in our being "come thronging soft desires" and infinite regrets. It is the contrast, the change from what we then were, that arms the half-extinguished recollection with its giant-strength, and lifts the fabric of the affections from its shadowy base. In contemplating its utmost verge, we overlook the map of our existence, and re-tread, in apprehension, the journey of life. So it is that in early youth we strain our eager sight after the pursuits of manhood; and, as we are sliding off the stage, strive to gather up the toys and flowers that pleased our thoughtless childhood.

When I was quite a boy, my father used to take me to the Montpelier Tea-gardens at Walworth. Do I go there now? No; the place is deserted, and its borders and its beds o'erturned. Is there, then, nothing that can

"bring back the hour
Of glory in the grass, of splendour in the flower?",

Oh! yes. I unlock the casket of memory, and draw back the warders of the brain; and there this scene of my infant wanderings still lives unfaded, or with fresher dyes. A new sense comes upon me, as in a dream; a richer perfume, brighter colours start out; my eyes dazzle; my heart heaves with its new load of bliss, and I am a child again. My sensations are all glossy, spruce, voluptuous, and fine: they wear a candied coat, and are in holiday trim. I see the beds of larkspur with purple eyes; tall holy-oaks, red and yellow; the broad sunflowers, caked in gold, with bees buzzing round them; wildernesses of pinks, and hot-glowing peonies; poppies run to seed;

the sugared lily, and faint mignionette, all ranged in order, and as thick as they can grow; the box-tree borders; the gravel-walks, the painted alcove, the confectionary, the clotted cream: — I think I see them now with sparkling looks; or have they vanished while I have been writing this description of them? No matter; they will return again when I least think of them. All that I have observed since, of flowers and plants, and grass-plots, and of suburb delights, seems, to me, borrowed from "that first garden of my innocence" — to be slips and scions stolen from that bed of memory. In this manner the darlings of our childhood burnish out in the eye of after-years, and derive their sweetest perfume from the first heartfelt sigh of pleasure breathed upon them,

> ——"like the sweet south,
> That breathes upon a bank of violets,
> Stealing and giving odour!"

If I have pleasure in a flower-garden, I have in a kitchen-garden too, and for the same reason. If I see a row of cabbage plants or of peas or beans coming up, I immediately think of those which I used so carefully to water of an evening at W—m, when my day's tasks were done, and of the pain with which I saw them droop and hang down their leaves in the morning's sun. Again, I never see a child's kite in the air, but it seems to pull at my heart. It is to me a "thing of life." I feel the twinge at my elbow, the flutter and palpitation, with which I used to let go the string of my own, as it rose in the air and towered among the clouds. My little cargo of hopes and fears ascended with it; and as it made a part of my own consciousness then, it does so still, and appears "like some gay creature of the element," my playmate when life was young, and twin-born with my earliest recollections. I could enlarge on this subject of childish amusements, but Mr. Leigh Hunt has treated it so well, in a paper in the *Indicator*, on the productions of the toy-shops of the metropolis, that if I were to insist more on it, I should only pass for an imitator of that ingenious and agreeable writer, *and for an indifferent one into the bargain.*

Sounds, smells, and sometimes tastes, are remembered longer than visible objects, and serve, perhaps, better for links in the chain of association. The reason seems to be this: they are in their nature intermittent and comparatively rare; whereas objects of sight are always before us, and, by their continuous succession, drive one another out. The eye is always open; and between any given impression and its recurrence a second time, fifty thousand other impressions have, in all likelihood, been stamped upon the sense and on the brain. The other senses are not so active or vigilant. They are but seldom called into play. The ear, for example, is oftener courted by silence than noise; and the sounds that break that silence sink deeper and more durably into the mind. I have a more present and lively recollection of certain scents, tastes, and sounds, for this reason, than I have of mere visible images, because they are more original, and less worn by frequent repetition. Where there is nothing interposed between any two impressions, whatever the distance of time that parts them, they naturally seem to touch; and the renewed impression recalls the former one in full force, without distraction or competitor. The taste of barberries which have hung out in the snow during the severity of a North American winter, I have in my mouth still, after an interval of thirty years; for I have met with no other taste, in all that time, at all like it. It remains by itself, almost like the impression of a sixth sense. But the colour is mixed up indiscriminately with the colours of many other berries, nor should I be able to distinguish it among them. The smell of a brick-kiln carries the evidence of its own identity with it; neither is it to me (from peculiar associations) unpleasant. The colour of brick-dust, on the contrary, is more common, and easily confounded with other colours. Raphael did not keep it quite distinct from his flesh colour. I will not say that we have a more perfect recollection of the human voice than of that complex picture the human face, but I think the sudden hearing of a well-known voice has something in it more affecting and striking than the sudden meeting with the face; perhaps, indeed, this may be because we have a more familiar remembrance of the one than the other, and the voice takes us more by surprise on that account. I am by no means certain (generally speaking) that we have the ideas of the other senses so accurate and well made out as those of visible form: what I chiefly mean is, that the feelings belonging to the sensations of our other organs, when accidentally recalled, are kept more separate and pure. Musical sounds, probably, owe a good deal of their interest and romantic effect to the principle here spoken of. Were they constant, they would become indifferent, as we may find with respect to disagreeable noises, which we do not hear after a time. I know no situation more pitiable than that of a blind fiddler, who has but one sense left (if we except the sense of snuff-taking[1]) and who has that stunned or deafened by his own villainous noises. Shakespeare says,

"How silver-sweet sound lovers' tongues by night!"

It has been observed, in explanation of this passage, that it is because in the daytime lovers are occupied with one another's faces, but that at night they can only distinguish the sound of each other's voices. I know not how this may be; but I have, ere now, heard a voice break so upon the silence,

"To angels 'twas most like,"

and charm the moonlight air with its balmy essence, that the budding leaves trembled to its accents. Would I might have heard it once more whisper peace and hope (as erst when it was mingled with the breath of spring), and with its soft pulsations lift winged fancy to heaven! But it has ceased, or turned where I no more shall hear it! Hence, also, we see what is the charm of the shepherd's pastoral reed; and why we hear him, as it were, piping to his flock, even in a picture. Our ears are fancy-stung! I remember once strolling along the margin of a stream, skirted with willows and plashy sedges, in one of those low, sheltered valleys on Salisbury Plain, where the monks of former ages had planted chapels and built hermits' cells. There was a little parish church near, but

[1] See Wilkie's *Blind Fiddler*.

tall elms and quivering alders hid it from my sight, when, all of a sudden, I was startled by the sound of the full organ pealing on the ear, accompanied by rustic voices and the willing quire of village maids and children. It rose, indeed, "like an exhalation of rich distilled perfumes." The dew from a thousand pastures was gathered in its softness; the silence of a thousand years spoke in it. It came upon the heart like the calm beauty of death; fancy caught the sound, and faith mounted on it to the skies. It filled the valley like a mist, and still poured out its endless chant, and still it swells upon the ear, and wraps me in a golden trance, drowning the noisy tumult of the world!

There is a curious and interesting discussion, on the comparative distinctness of our visual and other external impressions, in Mr. Fearn's *Essay on Consciousness*, with which I shall try to descend from this rhapsody to the ground of common sense and plain reasoning again. After observing, a little before, that "nothing is more untrue than that sensations of vision do necessarily leave more vivid and durable ideas than those of grosser senses," he proceeds to give a number of illustrations in support of this position. "Notwithstanding," he says, "the advantages here enumerated in favour of sight, I think there is no doubt that a man will come to forget acquaintance, and many other visible objects noticed in mature age, before he will in the least forget tastes and smells of only moderate interest, encountered either in his childhood or at any time since.

"In the course of voyaging to various distant regions, it has several times happened that I have eaten once or twice of different things that never came in my way before nor since. Some of these have been pleasant, and some scarce better than insipid; but I have no reason to think I have forgot or much altered the ideas left by those single impulses of taste; though here the memory of them certainly has not been preserved by repetition. It is clear I must have seen as well as tasted those things; and I am decided that I remember the tastes with more precision than I do the visual sensations.

"I remember having once, and only once, eat kangaroo

in New Holland; and having once smelled a baker's shop, having a peculiar odour, in the city of Bassorah. Now both these gross ideas remain with me quite as vivid as any visual ideas of those places; and this could not be from repetition, but really from interest in the sensation.

"Twenty-eight years ago, in the island of Jamaica, I partook (perhaps twice) of a certain fruit, of the taste of which I have now a very fresh idea; and I could add other instances of that period.

"I have had repeated proofs of having lost retention of visual objects, at various distances of time, though they had once been familiar. I have not, during thirty years, forgot the delicate, and in itself most trifling sensation, that the palm of my hand used to convey, when I was a boy, trying the different effects of what boys call *light* and *heavy* tops; but I cannot remember within several shades of the brown coat which I left off a week ago. If any man thinks he can do better, let him take an ideal survey of his wardrobe, and then actually refer to it for proof.

"After retention of such ideas, it certainly would be very difficult to persuade me that feeling, taste, and smell can scarce be said to leave ideas, unless indistinct and obscure ones. . . .

"Shew a Londoner correct models of   London churches, and, at the same time, a model of each, which differs in several considerable features from the truth, and I venture to say he shall not tell you, in any instance, which is the correct one, except by mere chance.

"If he is an architect, he may be much more correct than any ordinary person; and this obviously is, because he has felt an interest in viewing these structures, which an ordinary person does not feel; and here interest is the sole reason of his remembering more correctly than his neighbour.

"I once heard a person quaintly ask another, How many trees there are in St. Paul's churchyard? The question itself indicates that many cannot answer it; and this is found to be the case with those who have passed the church an hundred times; whilst the cause is, that every individual in the busy stream which glides past St. Paul's is engrossed in various other interests.

"How often does it happen that we enter a well-known apartment, or meet a well-known friend, and receive some vague idea of visible difference, but cannot possibly find out *what* it is; until at length we come to perceive (or perhaps must be told) that some ornament or furniture is removed, altered, or added in the apartment; or that our friend has cut his hair, taken a wig, or has made any of twenty considerable alterations in his appearance. At other times, we have no perception of alteration whatever, though the like has taken place.

"It is, however, certain, that sight, apposited with interest, can retain tolerably exact copies of sensations, especially if not too complex; such as of the human countenance and figure. Yet the voice will convince us, when the countenance will not; and he is reckoned an excellent painter, and no ordinary genius, who can make a tolerable likeness from memory. Nay, more, it is a conspicuous proof of the inaccuracy of visual ideas, that it is an effort to consummate art, attained by many years' practice, to take a strict likeness of the human countenance, even when the object is present; and among those cases where the wilful cheat of flattery has been avoided, we still find in haw very few instances the best painters produce a likeness up to the life, though practice and interest join in the attempt.

"I imagine an ordinary person would find it very difficult, supposing he had some knowledge of drawing, to afford, from memory, a tolerable sketch of such a familiar object as his curtain, his carpet, or his dressing-gown, if the pattern of either be at all various or irregular; yet he will instantly tell, with precision, either if his snuff or his wine has not the same character it had yesterday, though both these are compounds.

"Beyond all this I may observe, that a draper, who is in the daily habit of such comparisons, cannot carry in his mind the particular shade of a colour during a second of time; and has no certainty of tolerably matching two simple colours except by placing the patterns in contact." — *Essay on Consciousness*, p. 303.

I will conclude the subject of this Essay with observing, that (as it appears to me) a nearer and more familiar acquaintance with persons has a different and more favourable effect than that with places or things. The latter improve (as an almost universal rule) by being removed to a distance; the former, generally at least, gain by being brought nearer and more home to us. Report or imagination seldom raises any individual so high in our estimation as to disappoint us greatly when we are introduced to him; prejudice and malice constantly exaggerate defects beyond the reality. Ignorance alone makes monsters or bugbears; our actual acquaintances are all very common-place people. The thing is, that as a matter of hearsay or conjecture, we make abstractions of particular vices, and irritate ourselves against some particular quality or action of the person we dislike; — whereas, individuals are concrete existences, not arbitrary denominations or nicknames; and have innumerable other qualities, good, bad, and indifferent, besides the damning feature with which we fill up the portrait or caricature, in our previous fancies. We can scarcely hate anyone that we know. An acute observer complained, that if there was anyone to whom he had a particular spite and a wish to let him see it, the moment he came to sit down with him his enmity was disarmed by some unforeseen circumstance. If it was a Quarterly Reviewer, he was in other respects like any other man. Suppose, again, your adversary turns out a very ugly man, or wants an eye, you are balked in that way; — he is not what you expected, the object of your abstract hatred and implacable disgust. He may be a very disagreeable person, but he is no longer the same. If you come into a room where a man is, you find, in general, that he has a nose upon his face. "There's, sympathy!" This alone is a diversion to your unqualified contempt. He is stupid and says nothing, but he seems to have something in him when he laughs. You had conceived of him as a rank Whig or Tory — yet he talks upon other subjects. You knew that he was a virulent party-writer;

i

but you find that the man himself is a tame sort of animal enough. He does not bite. That's something. In short, you can make nothing of it. Even opposite vices balance one another. A man may be pert in company, but he is also dull; so that you cannot, though you try, hate him cordially, merely for the wish to be offensive. He is a knave. Granted. You learn, on a nearer acquaintance, what you did not know before — that he is a fool as well; so you forgive him. On the other hand, he may be a profligate public character, and may make no secret of it; but he gives you a hearty shake by the hand, speaks kindly to servants, and supports an aged father and mother. Politics apart, he is a very honest fellow. You are told that a person has carbuncles on his face; but you have ocular proofs that he is sallow, and pale as a ghost. This does not much mend the matter; but it blunts the edge of the ridicule, and turns your indignation against the inventor of the lie; but he is ——, the editor of a Scotch magazine; so you are just where you were. I am not very fond of anonymous criticism; I want to know who the author can be: but the moment I learn this, I am satisfied. Even —— would do well to come out of his disguise. It is the mask only that we dread and hate: the man may have something human about him! The notions, in short, which we entertain of people at a distance, or from partial representations, or from guess-work, are simple, uncompounded ideas, which answer to nothing in reality: those which we derive from experiences are mixed modes, the only true, and, in general, the most favourable ones. Instead of naked deformity, or abstract perfection —

"Those faultless monsters which the world ne'er saw," —

"the web of our lives is of a mingled yarn, good and ill together; our virtues would be proud, if our faults whipt them not; and our vices would despair, if they were not encouraged by our virtues." This was truly and finely said long ago by one who knew the strong and weak points of human nature; but it is what sects, and parties, and those philosophers whose pride and boast it is to classify by nicknames, have yet to learn the meaning of!

ON THE DISADVANTAGES OF INTEL-
LECTUAL SUPERIORITY

THE chief disadvantage of knowing more and seeing farther than others, is not to be generally understood. A man is, in consequence of this, liable to start paradoxes, which immediately transport him beyond the reach of the commonplace reader. A person speaking once in a slighting manner of a very original-minded man, received for answer — "He strides on so far before you, that he dwindles in the distance!"

Petrarch complains, that "Nature had made him different from other people" — *singular d'altra genti*. The great happiness of life is, to be neither better nor worse than the general run of those you meet with. If you are beneath them, you are trampled upon; if you are above them, you soon find a mortifying level in their indifference to what you particularly pique yourself upon. What is the use of being moral in a night-cellar, or wise in Bedlam? "To be honest, as this world goes, is to be one man picked out of ten thousand." So says Shakespear; and the commentators have not added that, under these circumstances, a man is more likely to become the butt of slander than the mark of admiration for being so. "How now, thou particular fellow[1]?" is the common answer to all such out-of-the-way pretensions. By not doing as those at Rome do, we cut ourselves off from good-fellowship and society. We speak another language, have notions of our own, and are treated as of a different species. Nothing can be more awkward than to intrude with any such far-fetched ideas among the common herd, who will be sure to

[1] Jack Cade's salutation to one who tries to recommend himself by saying he can write and read. — See *Henry VI*. Part Second.

—— "Stand all astonied, like a sort of steers,
'Mongst whom some beast of strange and foreign race
Unwares is chanced, far straying from his peers:
So will their ghastly gaze betray their hidden fears.".

Ignorance of another's meaning is a sufficient cause of fear, and fear produces hatred: hence the suspicion and rancour entertained against all those who set up for greater refinement and wisdom than their neighbours. It is in vain to think of softening down this spirit of hostility by simplicity of manners, or by condescending to persons of low estate. The more you condescend, the more they will presume upon it; they will fear you less, but hate you more; and will be the more determined to take their revenge on you for a superiority as to which they are entirely in the dark, and of which you yourself seem to entertain considerable doubts. All the humility in the world will only pass for weakness and folly. They have no notion of such a thing. They always put their best foot forward; and argue that you would do the same if you had any such wonderful talents as people say. You had better, therefore, play off the great man at once — hector, swagger, talk big, and ride the high horse over them: you may by this means extort outward respect or common civility; but you will get nothing (with low people) by forbearance and good-nature but open insult or silent contempt. C—— always talks to people about what they don't understand: I, for one, endeavour to talk to them about what they do understand, and find I only get the more ill-will by it. They conceive I do not think them capable of any thing better; that I do not think it worth while, as the vulgar saying is, to *throw a word to a dog*. I once complained of this to C——, thinking it hard I should be sent to Coventry for not making a prodigious display. He said, "As you assume a certain character, you ought to produce your credentials. It is a tax upon people's goodnature to admit superiority of any kind, even where there is the most evident proof of it: but it is too hard a task for the imagination to admit it without any apparent ground at all."

There is not a greater error than to suppose that you avoid

the envy, malice, and uncharitableness, so common in the
world, by going among people without pretensions. There
are no people who have no pretensions; or the fewer their
pretensions, the less they can afford to acknowledge yours
without some sort of value received. The more information
individuals possess, or the more they have refined upon any
subject, the more readily can they conceive and admit the
same kind of superiority to themselves that they feel over
others. But from the low, dull, level sink of ignorance and
vulgarity, no idea or love of excellence can arise. You think
you are doing mighty well with them; that you are laying
aside the buckram of pedantry and pretence, and getting the
character of a plain, unassuming, good sort of fellow. It will
not do. All the while that you are making these familiar
advances, and wanting to be at your ease, they are trying to
recover the wind of you. You may forget that you are an
author, an artist, or what not — they do not forget that they
are nothing, nor bate one jot of their desire to prove you in
the same predicament. They take hold of some circumstance
in your dress; your manner of entering a room is different
from that of other people; you do not eat vegetables — that's
odd; you have a particular phrase, which they repeat, and
this becomes a sort of standing joke; you look grave, or ill;
you talk, or are more silent than usual; you are in or out of
pocket: all these petty, inconsiderable circumstances, in
which you resemble, or are unlike other people, form so many
counts in the indictment which is going on in their imaginations against you, and are so many contradictions in your
character. In anyone else they would pass unnoticed, but in
a person of whom they had heard so much, they cannot make
them out at all. Meanwhile, those things in which you may
really excel, go for nothing, because they cannot judge of
them. They speak highly of some book which you do not
like, and therefore you make no answer. You recommend
them to go and see some picture, in which they do not find
much to admire. How are you to convince them that you
are right? Can you make them perceive that the fault is in
them, and not in the picture, unless you could give them your

knowledge? They hardly distinguish the difference between a Correggio and a common daub. Does this bring you any nearer to an understanding? The more you know of the difference, the more deeply you feel it, or the more earnestly you wish to convey it, the farther do you find yourself removed to an immeasurable distance from the possibility of making them enter into views and feelings of which they have not even the first rudiments. You cannot make them see with your eyes, and they must judge for themselves.

Intellectual is not like bodily strength. You have no hold of the understanding of others but by their sympathy. Your knowing, in fact, so much more about a subject does not give you a superiority, that is, a power over them, but only renders it the more impossible for you to make the least impression on them. Is it then an advantage to you? It may be, as it relates to your own private satisfaction, but it places a greater gulf between you and society. It throws stumbling blocks in your way at every turn. All that you take most pride and pleasure in is lost upon the vulgar eye. What they are pleased with is a matter of indifference or of distaste to you. In seeing a number of persons turn over a portfolio of prints from different masters, what a trial it is to the patience, how it jars the nerves to hear them fall into raptures at some commonplace, flimsy thing, and pass over some divine expression of countenance without notice, or with a remark that it is very singular-looking? How useless is it in such cases to fret or argue, or remonstrate? Is it not quite as well to be without all this hypercritical, fastidious knowledge, and to be pleased or displeased as it happens, or struck with the first fault or beauty that is pointed out by others? I would be glad almost to change my acquaintance with pictures, with books, and certainly, what I know of mankind, for anybody's ignorance of them!

It is recorded in the life of some worthy (whose name I forget) that he was one of those "who loved hospitality and respect;" and I profess to belong to the same classification of mankind. Civility is with me a jewel. I like a little comfortable cheer, and careless, indolent chat. I hate to be always wise, or aiming at wisdom. I have enough to do with literary cabals, questions, critics, actors, essay writing, without taking them out with me for recreation, and into all companies. I wish at these times to pass for a good-humoured fellow; and good will is all I ask in return to make good company. I do not desire to be always posing myself or others with the questions of fate, free-will, foreknowledge absolute, etc. I must unbend sometimes. I must occasionally lie fallow. The kind of conversation that I affect most is what sort of a day it is, and whether it is likely to rain or hold up fine for to-morrow. This I consider as enjoying the *otium cum dignitate*, as the end and privilege of a life of study. I would resign myself to this state of easy indifference, but I find I cannot. I must maintain a certain pretension, which is far enough from my wish. I must be put on my defense, I must take up the gauntlet continually, or I find I lose ground. "I am nothing, if not critical." While I am thinking what o'clock it is, or how I came to blunder in quoting a well-known passage, as if I had done it on purpose, others are thinking whether I am not really as dull a fellow as I am sometimes said to be. If a drizzling shower patters against the windows, it puts me in mind of a mild spring rain from which I retired twenty years ago into a little public house near Wem in Shropshire, and while I saw the plants and shrubs before the door imbibe the dewy moisture, quaffed a glass of sparkling ale, and walked home in the dusk of evening, brighter to me than noon-day suns at present are! Would I indulge this feeling? In vain. They ask me what news there is, and stare if I say I don't know. If a new actress has come out, why must I have seen her? If a new novel has appeared, why must I have read it? I, at one time, used to go and take a hand at cribbage with a friend, and afterwards discuss a cold sirloin of beef, and throw out a few lack-a-daisical remarks, in a way to please myself, but it would not do long. I set up little pretension, and therefore the little that I did set up was taken from me. As I said nothing on that subject myself, it was continually thrown in my teeth that I was *an author*. From having me at this disadvantage, my

friend wanted to peg on a hole or two in the game, and was
displeased if I would not let him. If I won of him, it was hard
he should be beat by an author. If he won, it would be
strange if he did not understand the game better than I did.
If I mentioned my favourite game of rackets, there was a
general silence, as if this was my weak point. If I complained
of being ill, it was asked why I made myself so? If I said such
an actor had played a part well, the answer was, there was a
different account in one of the newspapers. If any allusion
was made to men of letters, there was a suppressed smile.
If I told a humorous story, it was difficult to say whether the
laugh was at me or at the narrative. The wife hated me
for my ugly face; the servants because I could not always get
them tickets for the play, and because they could not tell
exactly what an author meant. If a paragraph appeared
against anything I had written, I found it was ready there
before me, and I was to undergo a regular *roasting*. I submitted to all this till I was tired, and then I gave it up.

One of the miseries of intellectual pretensions is, that nine-
tenths of those you come in contact with do not know whether
you are an impostor or not. I dread that certain anonymous
criticisms should get into the hands of servants where I go, or
that my hatter or shoemaker should happen to read them, who
cannot possibly tell whether they are well or ill founded.
The ignorance of the world leaves one at the mercy of its
malice. There are people whose good opinion or good will
you want, setting aside all literary pretensions; and it is hard
to lose by an ill report (which you have no means of rectifying)
what you cannot gain by a good one. After a *diatribe* in the
——, (which is taken in by a gentleman who occupies my old
apartments on the first floor) my landlord brings me up his
bill (of some standing), and on my offering to give him so much
in money, and a note of hand for the rest, shakes his head, and
says, he is afraid he could make no use of it. Soon after,
the daughter comes in, and on my mentioning the circumstance carelessly to her, replies gravely, "that indeed her
father has been almost ruined by bills." *This is the unkindest cut of all.* It is vain for me to endeavour to explain

that the publication in which I am abused is a mere government engine — an organ of a political faction. They know nothing about that. They only know such and such imputations are thrown out; and the more I try to remove them, the more they think there is some truth in them. Perhaps the people of the house are strong Tories — government agents of some sort. Is it for me to enlighten their ignorance? If I say, I once wrote a thing called *Prince Maurice's Parrot*, and an *Essay on the Regal Character*, in the former of which allusion is made to a noble marquis, and in the latter to a great personage (so at least, I am told, it has been construed), and that Mr. Croker has peremptory instructions to retaliate; they cannot conceive what connection there can be between me and such distinguished characters. I can get no farther. Such is the misery of pretensions beyond your situation, and which are not backed by any external symbols of wealth or rank, intelligible to all mankind!

The impertinence of admiration is scarcely more tolerable than the demonstrations of contempt. I have known a person, whom I had never seen before, besiege me all dinner-time with asking what articles I had written in the *Edinburgh Review?* I was at last ashamed to answer to my splendid sins in that way. Others will pick out something not yours, and say, they are sure no one else could write it. By the first sentence they can always tell your style. Now I hate my style to be known; as I hate all *idiosyncracy*. These obsequious flatterers could not pay me a worse compliment. Then there are those who make a point of reading everything you write (which is fulsome); while others, more provoking, regularly lend your works to a friend as soon as they receive them. They pretty well know your notions on the different subjects, from having heard you talk about them. Besides, they have a greater value for your personal character than they have for your writings. You explain things better in a common way, when you are not aiming at effect. Others tell you of the faults they have heard found with your last book, and that they defend your style in general from a charge of obscurity. A friend once told me of a quarrel he

had with a near relation, who denied that I knew how to
spell the commonest words. These are comfortable, con-
fidential communications, to which authors, who have their
friends and excusers, are subject. A gentleman told me that
a lady had objected to my use of the word *learneder*, as bad
grammar. He said that he thought it a pity that I did not
take more care, but that the lady was perhaps prejudiced, as
her husband held a government office. I looked for the word,
and found it in a motto from Butler. I was piqued, and desired him to tell the fair critic that the fault was not in me,
but in one who had far more wit, more learning, and loyalty
than I could pretend to. Then, again, some will pick out
the flattest thing of yours they can find, to load it with pane-
gyrics; and others tell you (by the way of letting you see how
high they rank your capacity), that your best passages are
failures. L —— has a knack of tasting (or as he would say,
palating) the insipid; L. H. has a trick of turning away from
the relishing morsels you put on his plate. There is no getting
the start of some people. Do what you will, they can do it
better; meet with what success you may, their own good
opinion stands them in better stead, and runs before the
applause of the world. I once shewed a person of this overweening turn (with no small triumph, I confess) a letter of a
very flattering description I had received from the celebrated
Count Stendhal, dated Rome. He returned it with a smile
of indifference, and said he had had a letter from Rome
himself the day before, from his friend S ——! I did not
think this "germane to the matter." G — dw —n pretends
I never wrote anything worth a farthing but my answers to
Vetus, and that I fail altogether when I attempt to write an
essay, or anything in a short compass.

What can one do in such cases? Shall I confess a weakness? The only set-off I know to these rebuffs and morti-
fications, is sometimes in an accidental notice or involuntary
mark of distinction from a stranger. I feel the force of Horace's *digito monstrari* — I like to be pointed out in the street,
or to hear people ask in Mr. Powell's court, *which is Mr. H. —*?
This is to me a pleasing extension of one's personal identity.

Your name so repeated leaves an echo like music on the ear; it stirs the blood like the sound of a trumpet. It shews that other people are curious to see you; that they think of you, and feel an interest in you without your knowing it. This is a bolster to lean upon; a lining to your poor, shivering, threadbare opinion of yourself. You want some such cordial to exhausted spirits, and relief to the dreariness of abstract speculation. You are something; and, from occupying a place in the thoughts of others, think less contemptuously of yourself. You are the better able to run the gauntlet of prejudice and vulgar abuse. It is pleasant in this way to have your opinion quoted against yourself, and your own sayings repeated to you as good things. I was once talking with an intelligent man in the pit, and criticising Mr. Knight's performance of Filch. "Ah!" he said, "little Simmons was the fellow to play that character." He added, "There was a most excellent remark made upon his acting it in the *Examiner* (I think it was) — *That he looked as if he had the gallows in one eye and a pretty girl in the other.*" I said nothing, but was in remarkably good humour the rest of the evening. I have seldom been in a company where fives-playing has been talked of, but some one has asked, in the course of it, "Pray did anyone ever see an account of one Cavanagh, that appeared some time back in most of the papers? Is it known who wrote it?" These are trying moments. I had a triumph over a person, whose name I will not mention, on the following occasion. I happened to be saying something about Burke, and was expressing my opinion of his talents in no measured terms, when this gentleman interrupted me by saying, he thought, for his part, that Burke had been greatly over-rated, and then added, in a careless way, "Pray did you read a character of him in the last number of the ———?" "I wrote it!" — I could not resist the antithesis, but was afterwards ashamed of my momentary petulance. Yet no one that I find ever spares me.

Some persons seek out and obtrude themselves on public characters, in order, as it might seem, to pick out their failings, and afterwards betray them. Appearances are for it, but truth and a better knowledge of nature are against this interpretation of the matter. Sycophants and flatterers are undesignedly treacherous and fickle. They are prone to admire inordinately at first, and not finding a constant supply of food for this kind of sickly appetite, take a distaste to the object of their idolatry. To be even with themselves for their credulity, they sharpen their wits to spy out faults, and are delighted to find that this answers better than their first employment. It is a course of study, "lively, audible, and full of vent." They have the organ of wonder and the organ of fear in a prominent degree. The first requires new objects of admiration to satisfy its uneasy cravings; the second makes them crouch to power wherever its shifting standard appears, and willing to curry favour with all parties, and ready to betray any out of sheer weakness and servility. I do not think they mean any harm. At least, I can look at this obliquity with indifference in my own particular case. I have been more disposed to resent it as I have seen it practised upon others, where I have been better able to judge of the extent of the mischief, and the heartlessness and idiot folly it discovered.

I do not think great intellectual attainments are any recommendation to the women. They puzzle them, and are a diversion to the main question. If scholars talk to ladies of what they understand, their hearers are none the wiser; if they talk of other things, they only prove themselves fools. The conversation between Angelica and Foresight, in *Love for Love*, is a receipt in full for all such overstrained nonsense: while he is wandering among the signs of the zodiac, she is standing a tip-toe on the earth. It has been remarked that poets do not choose mistresses very wisely. I believe it is not choice, but necessity. If they could throw the handkerchief like the Grand Turk, I imagine we should see scarce mortals, but rather goddesses, surrounding their steps, and each exclaiming, with Lord Byron's own Ionian maid —

"So shalt thou find me ever at thy side,
Here and hereafter, if the last may be!'

Ah! no, these are bespoke, carried off by men of mortal, not ethereal mould, and thenceforth the poet, from whose mind the ideas of love and beauty are inseparable as dreams from sleep, goes on the forlorn hope of the passion, and dresses up the first Dulcinea that will take compassion on him, in all the colours of fancy. What boots it to complain if the delusion lasts for life, and the rainbow still paints its form in the cloud?

There is one mistake I would wish, if possible, to correct. Men of letters, artists, and others, not succeeding with women in a certain rank of life, think the objection is to their want of fortune, and that they shall stand a better chance by descending lower, where only their good qualities or talents will be thought of. Oh! worse and worse. The objection is to themselves, not to their fortune — to their abstraction, to their absence of mind, to their unintelligible and romantic notions. Women of education may have a glimpse of their meaning, may get a clue to their character, but to all others they are thick darkness. If the mistress smiles at their *ideal* advances, the maid will laugh outright; she will throw water over you, get her little sister to listen, send her sweetheart to ask you what you mean, will set the village or the house upon your back; it will be a farce, a comedy, a standing jest for a year, and then the murder will out. Scholars should be sworn at Highgate. They are no match for chamber maids, or wenches at lodging-houses. They had better try their hands on heiresses or ladies of quality. These last have high notions of themselves that may fit some of your epithets! They are above mortality, so are your thoughts! But with low life, trick, ignorance, and cunning, you have nothing in common. Whoever you are, that think you can make a compromise or a conquest there by good nature, or good sense, be warned by a friendly voice, and retreat in time from the unequal contest.

If, as I have said above, scholars are no match for chamber-maids, on the other hand, gentlemen are no match for black-guards. The former are on their honour, act on the square; the latter take all advantages, and have no idea of any other principle. It is astonishing how soon a fellow without education will learn to cheat. He is impervious to any ray of liberal knowledge; his understanding is

"Not pierceable by power of any star" —

but it is porous to all sorts of tricks, chicanery, stratagems, and knavery, by which anything is to be got. Mrs. Peachum, indeed, says, that "to succeed at the gaming-table, the candidate should have the education of a nobleman." I do not know how far this example contradicts my theory. I think it is a rule that men in business should not be taught other things. Anyone will be almost sure to make money who has no other idea in his head. A college education, or intense study of abstract truth, will not enable a man to drive a bargain, to over-reach another, or even to guard himself from being over-reached. As Shakespeare says, that "to have a good face is the effect of study, but reading and writing come by nature:" so it might be argued, that to be a knave is the gift of fortune, but to play the fool to advantage it is necessary to be a learned man. The best politicians are not those who are deeply grounded in mathematical or in ethical science. Rules stand in the way of expediency. Many a man has been hindered from pushing his fortune in the world by an early cultivation of his moral sense, and has repented of it at leisure during the rest of his life. A shrewd man said of my father, that he would not send a son of his to school to him on any account, for that by teaching him to speak the truth, he would disqualify him from getting his living in the world!

It is hardly necessary to add any illustration to prove that the most original and profound thinkers are not always the most successful or popular writers. This is not merely a temporary disadvantage; but many great philosophers have not only been scouted while they were living, but forgotten as soon as they were dead. The name of Hobbes is perhaps sufficient to explain this assertion. But I do not wish to go farther into this part of the subject, which is obvious in itself. I have said, I believe, enough to take off the air of paradox which hangs over the title of this Essay.

ON THE KNOWLEDGE OF CHARACTER

IT is astonishing, with all our opportunities and practice, how little we know of this subject. For myself, I feel that the more I learn, the less I understand it.

I remember, several years ago, a conversation in the *diligence* coming from Paris, in which, on its being mentioned that a man had married his wife after thirteen years' courtship, a fellow-countryman of mine observed, that "then, at least, he would be acquainted with her character;" when a Monsieur P——, inventor and proprietor of the *Invisible Girl*, made answer, "No, not at all; for that the very next day she might turn out the very reverse of the character that she had appeared in during all the preceding time."[1] I could not help admiring the superior sagacity of the French juggler, and it struck me then that we could never be sure when we had got at the bottom of this riddle.

There are various ways of getting at a knowledge of character — by looks, words, actions. The first of these, which seems the most superficial, is perhaps the safest, and least liable to deceive; nay, it is that which mankind, in spite of their pretending to the contrary, most generally go by. Professions pass for nothing, and actions may be counterfeited; but a man cannot help his looks. "Speech," said a celebrated wit, "was given to man to conceal his thoughts." Yet I do not know that the greatest hypocrites are the least silent. The mouth of Cromwell is pursed up in the portraits of him, as if he was afraid to trust himself with words. Lord Chesterfield advises us, if we wish to know the real sentiments of the person we are conversing with, to look in his face, for he can more easily command his words than his features. A man's whole life may be a lie to himself and others; and yet a picture painted of him by a great artist would probably

[1] "It is not a year or two shows us a man." — Æmilia, in *Othello.*

121

stamp his true character on the canvas, and betray the secret to posterity. Men's opinions were divided, in their life-times, about such prominent personages as Charles V and Ignatius Loyola, partly, no doubt, from passion and interest, but partly from contradictory evidence in their ostensible conduct; the spectator, who has ever seen their pictures by Titian, judges of them at once, and truly. I had rather leave a good portrait of myself behind me than have a fine epitaph. The face, for the most part, tells what we have thought and felt — the rest is nothing. I have a higher idea of Donne from a rude, half-effaced outline of him prefixed to his poems than from anything he ever wrote. Cæsar's *Commentaries* would not have redeemed him in my opinion, if the bust of him had resembled the Duke of W——. My old friend, Fawcett, used to say, that if Sir Isaac Newton himself had lisped, he could not have thought anything of him. So I cannot persuade myself that anyone is a great man, who looks like a fool. In this I may be wrong.

First impressions are often the truest, as we find (not unfrequently) to our cost, when we have been wheedled out of them by plausible professions or actions. A man's look is the work of years, it is stamped on his countenance by the events of his whole life, nay, more, by the hand of nature, and it is not to be got rid of easily. There is, as it has been remarked repeatedly, something in a person's appearance at first sight which we do not like, and that gives us an odd twinge, but which is overlooked in a multiplicity of other circumstances, till the mask is taken off, and we see this lurking character verified in the plainest manner in the sequel. We are struck at first, and by chance, with what is peculiar and characteristic; also with permanent *traits* and general effect; this afterwards goes off in a set of unmeaning, commonplace details. This sort of *prima facie* evidence then, shows what a man is, better than what he says or does; for it shows us the habit of his mind, which is the same under all circumstances and disguises. You will say, on the other hand, that there is no judging by appearances, as a general rule. No one, for instance, would take such a person for a very clever man,

without knowing who he was. Then, ten to one, he is not;
he may have got the reputation, but it is a mistake. You
say, there is Mr. ——, undoubtedly a person of great genius:
yet, except when excited by something extraordinary, he
seems half dead. He has wit at will, yet wants life and
spirit. He is capable of the most generous acts, yet meanness
seems to cling to every motion. He looks like a poor creature
— and in truth he is one! The first impression he gives you
of him answers nearly to the feeling he has of his personal
identity; and this image of himself, rising from his thoughts,
and shrouding his faculties, is that which sits with him in the
house, walks out with him into the street, and haunts his
bedside. The best part of his existence is dull, cloudy,
leaden: the flashes of light that proceed from it, or streak it
here and there, may dazzle others, but do not deceive himself. Modesty is the lowest of the virtues, and is a real confession of the deficiency it indicates. He who undervalues
himself is justly undervalued by others. Whatever good
properties he may possess are, in fact, neutralised by a
"cold rheum" running through his veins, and taking away
the zest of his pretensions, the pith and marrow of his performances. What is it to me that I can write these TABLE-
TALKS? It is true I can, by a reluctant effort, rake up a
parcel of half-forgotten observations, but they do not float
on the surface of my mind, nor stir it with any sense of pleasure, nor even of pride. Others have more property in them
than I have: *they* may reap the benefit, *I* have only had the
pain. Otherwise, they are to me as if they had never existed;
nor should I know that I had ever thought at all, but that
I am reminded of it by the strangeness of my appearance,
and my unfitness for everything else. Look in C——'s face
while he is talking. His words are such as might "create a
soul under the ribs of death." His face is a blank. Which
are we to consider as the true index of his mind? Pain,
languor, shadowy remembrances, are the uneasy inmates
there: his lips move mechanically!

There are people that we do not like, though we may have
known them long, and have no fault to find with them,

k

"their appearance, as we say, is so much against them."
That is not all, if we could find it out. There is, generally,
a reason for this prejudice; for nature is true to itself. They
may be very good sort of people, too, in their way, but still
something is the matter. There is a coldness, a selfishness,
a levity, an insincerity, which we cannot fix upon any particular phrase or action, but we see it in their whole persons
and deportment. One reason that we do not see it in any
other way may be, that they are all the time trying to conceal
this defect by every means in their power. There is, luckily,
a sort of *second sight* in morals: we discern the lurking indi-
cations of temper and habit a long while before their palpable
effects appear. I once used to meet with a person at an
ordinary, a very civil, good-looking man in other respects,
but with an odd look about his eyes, which I could not
explain, as if he saw you under their fringed lids, and you could
not see him again: this man was a common sharper. The
greatest hypocrite I ever knew was a little, demure, pretty,
modest-looking girl, with eyes timidly cast upon the ground,
and an air soft as enchantment; the only circumstance that
could lead to a suspicion of her true character was a cold,
sullen, watery, glazed look about the eyes, which she bent on
vacancy, as if determined to avoid all explanation with yours.
I might have spied in their glittering, motionless surface, the
rocks and quicksands that awaited me below! We do not feel
quite at ease in the company or friendship of those who have
any natural obliquity or imperfection of person. The reason
is, they are not on the best terms with themselves, and are
sometimes apt to play off on others the tricks that nature
has played them. This, however, is a remark that, perhaps,
ought not to have been made. I know a person to whom it
has been objected as a disqualification for friendship, that
he never shakes you cordially by the hand. I own this is a
damper to sanguine and florid temperaments, who abound
in these practical demonstrations and "compliments extern."
The same person, who testifies the least pleasure at meeting
you, is the last to quit his seat in your company, grapples with
a subject in conversation right earnestly, and is, I take it,

backward to give up a cause or a friend. Cold and distant
in appearance, he piques himself on being the king of *good
haters*, and a no less zealous partisan. The most phlegmatic
constitutions often contain the most inflammable spirits —
as fire is struck from the hardest flints.

And this is another reason that makes it difficult to judge
of character. Extremes meet; and qualities display themselves by the most contradictory appearances. Any inclination, in consequence of being generally suppressed, vents
itself the more violently when an opportunity presents itself;
the greatest grossness sometimes accompanies the greatest
refinement, as a natural relief, one to the other; and we find
the most reserved and indifferent tempers at the beginning of
an entertainment, or an acquaintance, turn out the most
communicative and cordial at the end of it. Some spirits
exhaust themselves at first: others gain strength by pro-
gression. Some minds have a greater facility of throwing
off impressions, are, as it were, more transparent or porous
than others. Thus the French present a marked contrast
to the English in this respect. A Frenchman addresses you
at once with a sort of lively indifference: an Englishman is
more on his guard, feels his way, and is either exceedingly
reserved, or lets you into his whole confidence, which he
cannot so well impart to an entire stranger. Again, a Frenchman is naturally humane: an Englishman is, I should say,
only friendly by habit. His virtues and his vices cost him
more than they do his more gay and volatile neighbours.
An Englishman is said to speak his mind more plainly than
others: — yes, if it will give you pain to hear it. He does not
care whom he offends by his discourse: a foreigner generally
strives to oblige in what he says. The French are accused of
promising more than they perform. That may be, and yet
they may perform as many good-natured acts as the English,
if the latter are as averse to perform as they are to promise.
Even the professions of the French may be sincere at the time,
or arise out of the impulse of the moment; though their
desire to serve you may be neither very violent nor very
lasting. I cannot think, notwithstanding, that the French

are not a serious people; nay, that they are not a more reflecting people than the common run of the English. Let
those who think them merely light and mercurial, explain that
enigma, their everlasting prosing tragedy. The English are
considered as comparatively a slow, plodding people. If the
French are quicker, they are also more plodding. See, for
example, how highly finished and elaborate their works of art
are! How systematic and correct they aim at being in all their
productions of a graver cast! "If the French have a fault,"
as Yorick said, "it is that they are too grave." With wit,
sense, cheerfulness, patience, good-nature and refinement of
manners, all they want is imagination and sturdiness of moral
principle! Such are some of the contradictions in the character of the two nations, and so little does the character of
either appear to have been understood! Nothing can be
more ridiculous indeed than the way in which we exaggerate
each other's vices and extenuate our own. The whole is an
affair of prejudice on one side of the question, and of partiality on the other. Travellers who set out to carry back a
true report of the case appear to lose not only the use of their
understandings, but of their senses, the instant they set
foot in a foreign land. The commonest facts and appearances
are distorted and discoloured. They go abroad with certain
preconceived notions on the subject, and they make every
thing answer, in reason's spite, to their favourite theory.
In addition to the difficulty of explaining customs and manners foreign to our own, there are all the obstacles of wilful
prepossession thrown in the way. It is not, therefore, much
to be wondered at that nations have arrived at so little
knowledge of one another's characters; and that, where the
object has been to widen the breach between them, any slight
differences that occur are easily blown into a blaze of fury by
repeated misrepresentations, and all the exaggerations that
malice or folly can invent!

This ignorance of character is not confined to foreign
nations: we are ignorant of that of our own countrymen in a
class a little below or above ourselves. We shall hardly
pretend to pronounce magisterially on the good or bad quali-

ties of strangers; and, at the same time, we are ignorant of those of our friends, of our kindred, and of our own. We are in all these cases either too near or too far off the object to judge of it properly.

Persons, for instance, in a higher or middle rank of life know little or nothing of the characters of those below them, as servants, country people, etc. I would lay it down in the first place as a general rule on this subject, that all uneducated people are hypocrites. Their sole business is to deceive. They conceive themselves in a state of hostility with others, and stratagems are fair in war. The inmates of the kitchen and the parlour are always (as far as respects their feeling and intentions towards each other) in Hobbes's "state of nature." Servants and others in that line of life have nothing to exercise their spare talents for invention upon but those about them. Their superfluous electrical particles of wit and fancy are not carried off by those established and fashionable conductors, novels and romances. Their faculties are not buried in books, but all alive and stirring, erect and bristling like a cat's back. Their coarse conversation sparkles with "wild wit, invention ever new." Their betters try all they can to set themselves up above them, and they try all they can to pull them down to their own level. They do this by getting up a little comic interlude, a daily, domestic, homely drama out of the odds and ends of the family failings, of which there is in general a pretty plentiful supply, or make up the deficiency of materials out of their own heads. They turn the qualities of their masters and mistresses inside out, and any real kindness or condescension only sets them the more against you. They are not to be taken in that way — they will not be balked in the spite they have to you. They only set to work with redoubled alacrity, to lessen the favour or to blacken your character. They feel themselves like a degraded *caste*, and cannot understand how the obligations can be all on one side, and the advantages all on the other. You cannot come to equal terms with them — they reject all such overtures as insidious and hollow — nor can you ever calculate upon their gratitude or good will, any more than if

they were so many strolling Gipsies or wild Indians. They
have no fellow-feeling, they keep no faith with the more
privileged classes. They are in your power, and they endeavour to be even with you by trick and cunning, by lying
and chicanery. In this they have nothing to restrain them.
Their whole life is a succession of shifts, excuses, and expedients. The love of truth is a principle with those only who
have made it their study, who have applied themselves to the
pursuit of some art or science where the intellect is severely
tasked, and learns by habit to take a pride in, and to set a
just value on, the correctness of its conclusions. To have a
disinterested regard to truth, the mind must have contemplated it in abstract and remote questions; whereas the ignorant and vulgar are only conversant with those things in
which their own interest is concerned. All their notions are
local, personal, and consequently gross and selfish. They say
whatever comes uppermost — turn whatever happens to
their own account — and invent any story, or give any answer that suits their purposes. Instead of being bigoted to
general principles, they trump up any lie for the occasion,
and the more of a *thumper* it is, the better they like it; the
more unlooked-for it is, why, so much the more of a *God-send!*
They have no conscience about the matter; and if you find
them out in any of their manœuvres, are not ashamed of
themselves, but angry with you. If you remonstrate with
them, they laugh in your face. The only hold you have of
them is their interest — you can but dismiss them from your
employment; and *service is no inheritance.* If they affect
anything like decent remorse, and hope you will pass it over,
all the while they are probably trying to recover the wind of
you. Persons of liberal knowledge or sentiments have no
kind of chance in this sort of mixed intercourse with these
barbarians in civilised life. You cannot tell, by any signs or
principles, what is passing in their minds. There is no common point of view between you. You have not the same
topics to refer to, the same language to express yourself.
Your interests, your feelings are quite distinct. You take
certain things for granted as rules of action: they take nothing

for granted but their own ends, pick up all their knowledge out of their own occasions, are on the watch only for what they can catch — are

> "Subtle as the fox for prey:
> Like warlike as the wolf, for what they eat."

They have indeed a regard to their character, as this last may affect their livelihood or advancement, none as it is connected with a sense of propriety; and this sets their mother-wits and native talents at work upon a double file of expedients, to bilk their consciences and salve their reputation. In short, you never know where to have them, any more than if they were of a different species of animals; and in trusting to them, you are sure to be betrayed and over-reached. You have other things to mind, they are thinking only of you, and how to turn you to advantage. *Give and take* is no maxim here. You can build nothing on your own moderation or on their false delicacy. After a familiar conversation with a waiter at a tavern, you over-hear him calling you by some provoking nickname. If you make a present to the daughter of the house where you lodge, the mother is sure to recollect some addition to her bill. It is a running fight. In fact, there is a principle in human nature not willingly to endure the idea of a superior, a sour jacobinical disposition to wipe out the score of obligation, or efface the tinsel of external advantages — and where others have the opportunity of coming in contact with us, they generally find the means to establish a sufficiently marked degree of degrading equality. No man is a hero to his *valet-de-chambre*, is an old maxim. A new illustration of this principle occurred the other day. While Mrs. Siddons was giving her readings of Shakespeare to a brilliant and admiring drawing-room, one of the servants in the hall below was saying, "What, I find the old lady is making as much noise as ever!" So little is there in common between the different classes of society, and so impossible is it ever to unite the diversities of custom and knowledge which separate them.

Women, according to Mrs. Peachum, are "bitter bad judges" of the characters of men; and the men are not much better of theirs, if we can form any guess from their choice in marriage. Love is proverbially blind. The whole is an affair of whim and fancy. Certain it is, that the greatest favourites with the other sex are not those who are most liked or respected among their own. I never knew but one clever man who was what is called a *lady's man;* and he (unfortunately for the argument) happened to be a considerable coxcomb. It was by this irresistible quality, and not by the force of his genius, that he vanquished. Women seem to doubt their own judgments in love, and to take the opinion which a man entertains of his own prowess and accomplishments for granted. The wives of poets are (for the most part) mere pieces of furniture in the room. If you speak to them of their husbands' talents or reputation in the world, it is as if you made mention of some office that they held. It can hardly be otherwise, when the instant any subject is started or conversation arises in which men are interested or try one another's strength, the women leave the room, or attend to something else. The qualities then in which men are ambitious to excel, and which ensure the applause of the world, eloquence, genius, learning, integrity, are not those which gain the favour of the fair. I must not deny, however, that wit and courage have this effect. Neither is youth or beauty the sole passport to their affections.

> "The way of woman's will is hard to find,
>   Harder to hit."

Yet there is some clue to this mystery, some determining cause; for we find that the same men are universal favourites with women, as others are uniformly disliked by them. Is not the load-stone that attracts so powerfully, and in all circumstances, a strong and undisguised bias towards them, a marked attention, a conscious preference of them to every other passing object or topic? I am not sure, but I incline to think so. The successful lover is the *cavalier servente* of all nations. The man of gallantry behaves as if he had made an assignation with every woman he addresses. An argument immediately draws off my attention from the prettiest woman in the room. I accordingly succeed better in argument — than in love! — I do not think that what is called *Love at first sight* is so great an absurdity as it is sometimes imagined to be. We generally make up our minds beforehand to the sort of person we should like, grave or gay, black, brown, or fair; with golden tresses or with raven locks; — and when we meet with a complete example of the qualities we admire, the bargain is soon struck. We have never seen anything to come up to our newly discovered goddess before, but she is what we have been all our lives looking for. The idol we fall down and worship is an image familiar to our minds. It has been present to our waking thoughts, it has haunted us in our dreams, like some fairy vision. Oh! thou, who, the first time I ever beheld thee, didst draw my soul into the circle of thy heavenly looks, and wave enchantment round me, do not think thy conquest less complete because it was instantaneous; for in that gentle form (as if another Imogen had entered) I saw all that I had ever loved of female grace, modesty, and sweetness!

I shall not say much of friendship as giving an insight into character, because it is often founded on mutual infirmities and prejudices. Friendships are frequently taken up on some sudden sympathy, and we see only as much as we please of one another's characters afterwards. Intimate friends are not fair witnesses to character, any more than professed enemies. They cool, indeed, in time, part, and retain only a rankling grudge at past errors and oversights. Their testimony in the latter case is not quite free from suspicion.

One would think that near relations, who live constantly together, and always have done so, must be pretty well acquainted with one another's characters. They are nearly in the dark about it. Familiarity confounds all traits of distinction: interest and prejudice take away the power of judging. We have no opinion on the subject, any more than of one another's faces. The Penates, the household gods, are veiled. We do not see the features of those we love, nor do we clearly distinguish their virtues or their vices. We take them as they are found in the lump: — by weight, and not

by measure. We know all about the individuals, their sentiments, history, manners, words, actions, everything: but we
know all these too much as facts, as inveterate, habitual
impressions, as clothed with too many associations, as sanc-
tified with too many affections, as woven too much into the
web of our hearts, to be able to pick out the different threads,
to cast up the items of the debtor and creditor account, or
to refer them to any general standard of right and wrong.
Our impressions with respect to them are too strong, too real,
too much *sui generis*, to be capable of a comparison with anything but themselves. We hardly inquire whether those for
whom we are thus interested, and to whom we are thus knit,
are *better* or *worse* than others — the question is a kind of
profanation — all we know is, they are *more* to us than anyone else can be. Our sentiments of this kind are rooted and
grow in us, and we cannot eradicate them by voluntary means.
Besides, our judgments are bespoke, our interests take part
with our blood. If any doubt arises, if the veil of our implicit confidence is drawn aside by any accident for a moment,
the shock is too great, like that of a dislocated limb, and we
recoil on our habitual impressions again. Let not that veil
ever be rent entirely asunder, so that those images may be left
bare of reverential awe, and lose their religion: for nothing
can ever support the desolation of the heart afterwards.

The greatest misfortune that can happen among relations
is a different way of bringing up, so as to set one another's
opinions and characters in an entirely new point of view.
This often lets in an unwelcome daylight on the subject, and
breeds schisms, coldness, and incurable heart-burnings in
families. I have sometimes thought whether the progress
of society and march of knowledge does not do more harm in
this respect, by loosening the ties of domestic attachment,
and preventing those who are most interested in, and anxious
to think well of one another, from feeling a cordial sympathy
and approbation of each other's sentiments, manners, views,
etc., than it does good by any real advantage to the com-
munity at large. The son, for instance, is brought up to the
church, and nothing can exceed the pride and pleasure the

father takes in him, while all goes on well in this favourite
direction. His notions change, and he imbibes a taste for
the Fine Arts. From this moment there is an end of anything like the same unreserved communication between them.
The young man may talk with enthusiasm of his "Rembrandts, Correggios, and stuff:" it is all *Hebrew* to the elder;
and whatever satisfaction he may feel in hearing of his son's
progress, or good wishes for his success, he is never reconciled
to the new pursuit, he still hankers after the first object that
he had set his mind upon. Again, the grandfather is a Cal-
vinist, who never gets the better of his disappointment at his
son's going over to the Unitarian side of the question. The
matter rests here, till the grandson, some years after, in the
fashion of the day and "infinite agitation of men's wit,"
comes to doubt certain points in the creed in which he has
been brought up, and the affair is all abroad again. Here are
three generations made uncomfortable and in a manner set
at variance, by a veering point of theology, and the officious,
meddling, biblical critics! Nothing, on the other hand, can
be more wretched or common than that upstart pride and
insolent good fortune which is ashamed of its origin; nor are
there many things more awkward than the situation of rich
and poor relations. Happy, much happier, are those tribes
and people who are confined to the same *caste* and way of life
from sire to son, where prejudices are transmitted like in-
stincts, and where the same unvarying standard of opinion
and refinement blends countless generations in its impro-
gressive, everlasing mould!

Not only is there a wilful and habitual blindness in near
kindred to each other's defects, but an incapacity to judge
from the quantity of materials, from the contradictoriness of
the evidence. The chain of particulars is too long and massy
for us to lift it or put it into the most approved ethical scales.
The concrete result does not answer to any abstract theory,
to any logical definition. There is black, and white, and grey,
square and round — there are too many anomalies, too many
redeeming points, in poor human nature, such as it actually
is, for us to arrive at a smart, summary decision on it. We

know too much to come to any hasty or partial conclusion. We do not pronounce upon the present act, because a hundred others rise up to contradict it. We suspend our judgments altogether, because in effect one thing unconsciously balances another; and perhaps this obstinate, pertinacious indecision would be the truest philosophy in other cases, where we dispose of the question of character easily, because we have only the smallest part of the evidence to decide upon. Real character is not one thing, but a thousand things; actual qualities do not conform to any factitious standard in the mind, but rest upon their own truth and nature. The dull stupor under which we labour in respect of those whom we have the greatest opportunities of inspecting nearly, we should do well to imitate, before we give extreme and uncharitable verdicts against those whom we only see in passing, or at a distance. If we knew them better, we should be disposed to say less about them.

In the truth of things, there are none utterly worthless, none without some drawback on their pretensions, or some alloy of imperfection. It has been observed that a familiarity with the worst characters lessens our abhorrence of them; and a wonder is often expressed that the greatest criminals look like other men. The reason is that *they are like other men in many respects.* If a particular individual was merely the wretch we read of, or conceive in the abstract, that is, if he was the mere personified idea of the criminal brought to the bar, he would not disappoint the spectator, but would look like what he would be — a monster! But he has other qualities, ideas, feelings, nay, probably virtues, mixed up with the most profligate habits or desperate acts. This need not lessen our abhorrence of the crime, though it does of the criminal; for it has the latter effect only by showing him to us in different points of view, in which he appears a common mortal, and not the caricature of vice we took him for, or spotted all over with infamy. I do not at the same time think this a lax or dangerous, though it is a charitable view of the subject. In my opinion, no man ever answered in his own mind (except in the agonies of conscience or of repentance,

in which latter case he throws the imputation from himself
in another way) to the abstract idea of a *murderer*. He may
have killed a man in self-defence, or "in the trade of war,"
or to save himself from starving, or in revenge for an injury,
but always "so as with a difference," or from mixed and
questionable motives. The individual, in reckoning with
himself, always takes into the account the consideration of
time, place, and circumstance, and never makes out a case
of unmitigated, unprovoked villany, of "pure defecated evil"
against himself. There are degrees in real crimes: we reason
and moralise only by names and in classes. I should be loth,
indeed, to say, that "whatever is, is right:" but almost every
actual choice inclines to it, with some sort of imperfect,
unconscious bias. This is the reason, besides the ends of
secresy, of the invention of *slang* terms for different acts of
profligacy committed by thieves, pickpockets, etc. The
common names suggest associations of disgust in the minds of
others, which those who live by them do not willingly recog-
nise, and which they wish to sink in a technical phraseology.
So there is a story of a fellow who, as he was writing down his
confession of a murder, stopped to ask how the word *murder*
was spelt; this, if true, was partly because his imagination was
staggered by the recollection of the thing, and partly because
he shrunk from the verbal admission of it. "*Amen* stuck in
his throat!" The defence made by Eugene Aram of himself
against a charge of murder, some years before, shows that he
in imagination completely flung from himself the *nominal*
crime imputed to him; he might indeed, have staggered an
old man with a blow, and buried his body in a cave, and lived
ever since upon the money he found upon him, but there
was "no malice in the case, none at all," as Peachum says.
The very coolness, subtlety, and circumspection of his defence (as masterly a legal document as there is upon record)
prove that he was guilty of the act, as much as they prove
that he was unconscious of the *crime*.[1] In the same spirit,

[1] The bones of the murdered man were dug up in an old hermitage. On this, as one instance of the acuteness which he displayed
all through the occasion, Aram remarks, "Where would you expect

and I conceive with great metaphysical truth, Mr. Coleridge, in his tragedy of *Remorse*, makes Ordonio (his chief character) wave the acknowledgment of his meditated guilt to his own mind, by putting into his mouth that striking soliloquy:

> "Say, I had lay'd a body in the sun!
> Well! in a month there swarm forth from the corse
> A thousand, nay, ten thousand sentient beings
> In place of that one man. Say I had *kill'd* him!
> Yet who shall tell me, that each one and all
> Of these ten thousand lives is not as happy
> As that one life, which being push'd aside,
> Made room for these unnumber'd." — Act ii, sc. ii.

I am not sure, indeed, that I have not got this whole train of speculation from him; but I should not think the worse of it on that account. That gentleman, I recollect, once asked me whether I thought that the different members of a family really like one another so well, or had so much attachment as was generally supposed; and I said that I conceived the regard they had towards each other was expressed by the word *interest*, rather than by any other; which he said was the true answer. I do not know that I could mend it now. Natural affection is not pleasure in one another's company, nor admiration of one another's qualities; but it is an intimate and deep knowledge of the things that affect those to whom we are bound by the nearest ties, with pleasure or pain; it is an anxious, uneasy, fellow-feeling with them, a jealous watchfulness over their good name, a tender and unconquerable yearning for their good. The love, in short, we bear them, is the nearest to that we bear ourselves. *Home*, according to the old saying, *is home, be it never so homely.* We love ourselves, not according to our deserts, but our cravings after good: so we love our immediate relations in the next degree (if not, even sometimes a higher one) because we know best what they have suffered and what sits nearest to their hearts. We are implicated, in fact, in their welfare, by habit and sympathy, as we are in our own.

to find the bones of a man sooner than in a hermit's cell, except you were to look for them in a cemetery?". See *Newgate Calendar* for the year 1758 or 9.

If our devotion to our own interests is much the same as to theirs, we are ignorant of our own characters for the same reason. We are parties too much concerned to return a fair verdict, and are too much in the secret of our own motives or situation not to be able to give a favourable turn to our actions. We exercise a liberal criticism upon ourselves, and put off the final decision to a late day. The field is large and open. Hamlet exclaims, with a noble magnanimity, "I count myself indifferent honest, and yet I accuse me of such things!" If you could prove to a man that he is a knave, it would not make much difference in his opinion, his self-love is stronger than his love of virtue. Hypocrisy is generally used as a mask to deceive the world, not to impose on ourselves: for once detect the delinquent in his knavery, and he laughs in your face or glories in his iniquity. This at least happens except where there is a contradiction in the character and our vices are involuntary, and at variance with our convictions. One great difficulty is to distinguish ostensible motives, or such as we acknowledge to ourselves, from tacit or secret springs of action. A man changes his opinion readily, he thinks it candour: it is levity of mind. For the most part, we are stunned and stupid in judging of ourselves. We are callous by custom to our defects or excellencies, unless where vanity steps in to exaggerate or extenuate them. I cannot conceive how it is that people are in love with their own persons, or astonished at their own performances, which are but a nine days' wonder to every one else. In general it may be laid down that we are liable to this twofold mistake in judging of our own talents: we, in the first place, nurse the rickety bantling, we think much of that which has cost us much pains and labour, and comes against the grain; and we also set little store by what we do with most ease to ourselves, and therefore best. The works of the greatest genius are produced almost unconsciously, with an ignorance on the part of the persons themselves that they have done anything extraordinary. Nature has done it for them. How little Shakespeare seems to have thought of himself or of his fame! Yet, if "to know another well, were to know one's self," he must have been acquainted with his own pretensions and character, "who knew all qualities with a learned spirit." His eye seems never to have been bent upon himself, but outwards upon nature. A man, who thinks highly of himself, may almost set it down that it is without reason. Milton, notwithstanding, appears to have had a high opinion of himself, and to have made it good. He was conscious of his powers, and great by design. Perhaps his tenaciousness, on the score of his own merit, might arise from an early habit of polemical writing, in which his pretensions were continually called to the bar of prejudice and party spirit, and he had to plead not guilty to the indictment. Some men have died unconscious of immortality, as others have almost exhausted the sense of it in their life-times. Correggio might be mentioned as an instance of the one, Voltaire of the other.

There is nothing that helps a man in his conduct through life more than a knowledge of his own characteristic weaknesses (which, guarded against, become his strength), as there is nothing that tends more to the success of a man's talents than his knowing the limits of his faculties, which are thus concentrated on some practicable object. One man can do but one thing. Universal pretensions end in nothing. Or, as Butler has it, too much wit requires

> "As much again to govern it."

There are those who have gone, for want of this self-knowledge, strangely out of their way, and others who have never found it. We find many who succeed in certain departments, and are yet melancholy and dissatisfied, because they failed in the one to which they first devoted themselves, like discarded lovers who pine after their scornful mistress. I will conclude with observing that authors in general overrate the extent and value of posthumous fame: for what (as it has been asked) is the amount even of Shakespeare's fame? That in that very country which boasts his genius and his birth, perhaps, scarce one person in ten has ever heard of his name, or read a syllable of his writings!

ON THE FEAR OF DEATH

"And our little life is rounded with a sleep."

PERHAPS the best cure for the fear of death is to reflect that life has a beginning as well as an end. There was a time when we were not: this gives us no concern — why then should it trouble us that a time will come when we shall cease to be? I have no wish to have been alive a hundred years ago, or in the reign of Queen Anne: why should I regret and lay it so much to heart that I shall not be alive a hundred years hence, in the reign of I cannot tell whom?

When Bickerstaff wrote his Essays, I knew nothing of the subjects of them; nay, much later, and but the other day, as it were, in the beginning of the reign of George III, when Goldsmith, Johnson, Burke, used to meet at the Globe, when Garrick was in his glory, and Reynolds was over head and ears with his portraits, and Sterne brought out the volumes of *Tristram Shandy* year by year, it was without consulting me. I had not the slightest intimation of what was going on: the debates in the House of Commons on the American war, or the firing at Bunker's Hill, disturbed not me: yet I thought this no evil — I neither ate, drank, nor was merry, yet I did not complain: I had not then looked out into this breathing world, yet I was well; and the world did quite as well without me as I did without it! Why then should I make all this out-cry about parting with it, and being no worse off than I was before? There is nothing in the recollection that at a certain time we were not come into the world, that "the gorge rises at" — why should we revolt at the idea that we must one day go out of it? To die is only to be as we were before we were born; yet no one feels any remorse, or regret, or repugnance, in contemplating this last idea. It is rather a relief and dis-burthening of the mind; it seems to have been holiday time with us then; we were not called to appear upon the stage

139   1

of life, to wear robes or tatters, to laugh or cry, be hooted
or applauded; we had lain *perdus* all this while, snug, out
of harm's way; and had slept out our thousands of centuries
without wanting to be waked up; at peace and free from care,
in a long nonage, in a sleep deeper and calmer than that of
infancy, wrapped in the softest and finest dust. And the
worst that we dread is, after a short, fretful, feverish being,
after vain hopes, and idle fears, to sink to final repose again,
and forget the troubled dream of life! . . . Ye armed men,
knights templars, that sleep in the stone aisles of that old
Temple church, where all is silent above, and where a deeper
silence reigns below (not broken by the pealing organ), are ye
not contented where ye lie? Or would you come out of your
long homes to go to the Holy War? Or do ye complain that
pain no longer visits you, that sickness has done its worst,
that you have paid the last debt to nature, that you hear no
more of the thickening phalanx of the foe, or your lady's
waning love; and that while this ball of earth rolls its eternal
round, no sound shall ever pierce through to disturb your
lasting repose, fixed as the marble over your tombs, breathless as the grave that holds you! And thou, oh! thou, to whom
my heart turns, and will turn while it has feeling left, who
didst love in vain, and whose first was thy last sigh, wilt not
thou too rest in peace (or wilt thou cry to me complaining from
thy clay-cold bed) when that sad heart is no longer sad, and
that sorrow is dead which thou wert only called into the world
to feel!

It is certain that there is nothing in the idea of a pre-existent
state that excites our longing like the prospect of a posthumous existence. We are satisfied to have begun life when we
did; we have no ambition to have set out on our journey
sooner; and feel that we have had quite enough to do to
battle our way through since. We cannot say,

> "The wars we well remember of King Nine,
> Of old Assaracus and Inachus divine."

Neither have we any wish: we are contented to read of them
in story, and to stand and gaze at the vast sea of time that

separates us from them. It was early days then: the world was not *well-aired* enough for us; we have no inclination to have been up and stirring. We do not consider the six thousand years of the world before we were born as so much time lost to us: we are perfectly indifferent about the matter. We do not grieve and lament that we did not happen to be in time to see the grand mask and pageant of human life going on in all that period; though we are mortified at being obliged to quit our stand before the rest of the procession passes.

It may be suggested in explanation of this difference, that we know from various records and traditions what happened in the time of Queen Anne, or even in the reigns of the Assyrian monarchs; but that we have no means of ascertaining what is to happen hereafter but by awaiting the event, and that our eagerness and curiosity are sharpened in proportion as we are in the dark about it. This is not at all the case; for at that rate we should be constantly wishing to make a voyage of discovery to Greenland or to the moon, neither of which we have, in general, the least desire to do. Neither, in truth, have we any particular solicitude to pry into the secrets of futurity, but as a pretext for prolonging our own existence. It is not so much that we care to be alive a hundred or a thousand years hence, any more than to have been alive a hundred or a thousand years ago; but the thing lies here, that we would all of us wish the present moment to last for ever. We would be as we are, and would have the world remain just as it is, to please us.

"The present eye catches the present object" —

to have and to hold while it may; and abhors, on any terms, to have it torn from us, and nothing left in its room. It is the pang of parting, the unloosing our grasp, the breaking asunder some strong tie, the leaving some cherished purpose unfulfilled, that creates the repugnance to go, and "makes calamity of so long life," as it often is.

> ——"Oh! thou strong heart!
> There's such a covenant 'twixt the world and thee,
> They're loth to break!"

The love of life, then, is an habitual attachment, not an abstract principle. Simply *to be* does not "content man's natural desire;" we long to be in a certain time, place, and circumstance. We would much rather be now, "on this bank and shoal of time," than have our choice of any future period, than take a slice of fifty or sixty years out of the Millennium, for instance. This shows that our attachment is not confined either to *being* or to *well-being;* but that we have an inveterate prejudice in favour of our immediate existence, such as it is. The mountaineer will not leave his rock, nor the savage his hut; neither are we willing to give up our present mode of life, with all its advantages and disadvantages, for any other that could be substituted for it. No man would, I think, exchange his existence with any other man, however fortunate. We had as lief *not be*, as *not be ourselves*. There are some persons of that reach of soul that they would like to live two hundred and fifty years hence, to see what height of empire America will have grown up in that period, or whether the English constitution will last so long. These are points beyond me. But I confess I should like to live to see the downfall of the Bourbons. That is a vital question with me; and I should like it the better, the sooner it happens!

No young man ever thinks he shall die. He may believe that others will, or assent to the doctrine that "all men are mortal" as an abstract proposition, but he is far enough from bringing it home to himself individually.[1] Youth, buoyant activity, and animal spirits hold absolute antipathy with old age as well as with death; nor have we, in the hey-day of life, any more than in the thoughtlessness of childhood, the remotest conception how

> "This sensible warm motion can become
> A kneaded clod" —

nor how sanguine, florid health and vigour shall "turn to withered, weak, and grey." Or, if in a moment of idle speculation we indulge in this notion of the close of life as a theory, it is amazing at what a distance it seems; what a long,

---

[1] "All men think all men mortal but themselves." — *Young.*

leisurely interval there is between; what a contrast its slow and solemn approach affords to our present gay dreams of existence! We eye the farthest verge of the horizon, and think what a way we shall have to look back upon ere we arrive at our journey's end; and without our in the least suspecting it, the mists are at our feet, and the shadows of age encompass us. The two divisions of our lives have melted into each other; the extreme points close and meet with none of that romantic interval stretching out between them, that we had reckoned upon; and for the rich, melancholy, solemn hues of age, "the sear, the yellow leaf," the deepening shadows of an autumnal evening, we only feel a dank, cold mist, encircling all objects, after the spirit of youth is fled. There is no inducement to look forward; and what is worse, little interest in looking back to what has become so trite and common. The pleasures of our existence have worn themselves out, are "gone into the wastes of time," or have turned their indifferent side to us; the pains by their repeated blows have worn us out, and have left us neither spirit nor inclination to encounter them again in retrospect. We do not want to rip up old grievances, nor to renew our youth like the phœnix, nor to live our lives twice over. Once is enough. As the tree falls, so let it lie. Shut up the book and close the account once for all!

It has been thought by some that life is like the exploring of a passage that grows narrower and darker the farther we advance, without a possibility of ever turning back, and where we are stifled for want of breath at last. For myself, I do not complain of the greater thickness of the atmosphere as I approach the narrow house. I felt it more, formerly,[1] when the idea alone seemed to suppress a thousand rising hopes and weighed upon the pulses of the blood. At present I rather feel a thinness and want of support, I stretch out my hand to some object and find none, I am too much in a world of abstraction; the naked map of life is spread out before me, and

---

[1] I remember once, in particular, having this feeling in reading Schiller's *Don Carlos*, where there is a description of death, in a degree that almost stifled me.

in the emptiness and desolation I see Death coming to meet me. In my youth I could not behold him for the crowd of objects and feelings, and Hope stood always between us, saying, "Never mind that old fellow!" If I had lived indeed, I should not care to die. But I do not like a contract of pleasure broken off unfulfilled, a marriage with joy unconsummated, a promise of happiness rescinded. My public and private hopes have been left a ruin, or remain only to mock me. I would wish them to be re-edified. I should like to see some prospect of good to mankind, such as my life began with. I should like to leave some sterling work behind me. I should like to have some friendly hand to consign me to the grave. On these conditions I am ready, if not willing, to depart. I shall then write on my tomb — *Grateful and Contented!* But I have thought and suffered too much to be willing to have thought and suffered in vain. In looking back, it sometimes appears to me as if I had in a manner slept out my life in a dream or shadow on the side of the hill of knowledge, where I have fed on books, on thoughts, on pictures, and only heard in half-murmurs the trampling of busy feet, or the noises of the throng below. Waked out of this dim, twilight existence, and startled with the passing scene, I have felt a wish to descend to the world of realities, and join in the chase. But I fear too late, and that I had better return to my bookish chimeras and indolence once more! *Zanetto, lascia le donne, et studia la matematica.* I will think of it.

It is not wonderful that the contemplation and fear of death become more familiar to us as we approach nearer to it; that life seems to ebb with the decay of blood and youthful spirits; and that as we find everything about us subject to chance and change, as our strength and beauty die, as our hopes and passions, our friends and our affections leave us, we begin by degrees to feel ourselves mortal!

I have never seen death but once, and that was in an infant. It is years ago. The look was calm and placid, and the face was fair and firm. It was as if a waxen image had been laid out in the coffin, and strewed with innocent flowers. It was not like death, but more like an image of life! No breath moved the lips, no pulse stirred, no sight or sound would enter those eyes or ears more. While I looked at it, I saw no pain was there; it seemed to smile at the short pang of life which was over; but I could not bear the coffin-lid to be closed — it seemed to stifle me; and still as the nettles wave in a corner of the churchyard over his little grave, the welcome breeze helps to refresh me, and ease the tightness at my breast!

An ivory or marble image, like Chantry's monument of the two children, is contemplated with pure delight. Why do we not grieve and fret that the marble is not alive, or fancy that it has a shortness of breath? It never was alive; and it is the difficulty of making the transition from life to death, the struggle between the two in our imagination, that confounds their properties painfully together, and makes us conceive that the infant that is but just dead, still wants to breathe, to enjoy, and look about it, and is prevented by the icy hand of death, locking up its faculties and benumbing its senses; so that, if it could, it would complain of its own hard state. Perhaps religious considerations reconcile the mind to this change sooner than any others, by representing the spirit as fled to another sphere, and leaving the body behind it. So in reflecting on death generally, we mix up the idea of life with it, and thus make it the ghastly monster it is. We think how we should feel, not how the dead feel.

"Still from the tomb the voice of nature cries;
Even in our ashes live their wonted fires!"

There is an admirable passage on this subject in Tucker's *Light of Nature Pursued*, which I shall transcribe, as by much the best illustration I can offer of it.

"The melancholy appearance of a lifeless body, the mansion provided for it to inhabit, dark, cold, close, and solitary, are shocking to the imagination; but it is to the imagination only, not the understanding; for whoever consults this faculty will see at first glance that there is nothing dismal in all these circumstances; if the corpse were kept wrapped up in a warm bed, with a roasting fire in the chamber, it would feel no comfortable warmth therefrom; were store of tapers lighted up as soon as day shuts in, it would see no objects to divert it; were it left at large it would have no liberty, nor if surrounded with company would be cheered thereby; neither are the distorted features expressions of pain, uneasiness, or distress. This everyone knows, and will readily allow upon being suggested, yet still cannot behold, nor even cast a thought upon those objects without shuddering; for knowing that a living person must suffer grievously under such appearances, they become habitually formidable to the mind, and strike a mechanical horror, which is increased by the customs of the world around us."

There is usually one pang added voluntarily and unnecessarily to the fear of death, by our affecting to compassionate the loss which others will have in us. If that were all, we might reasonably set our minds at rest. The pathetic exhortation on country tombstones, "Grieve not for me, my wife and children dear," etc., is for the most part speedily followed to the letter. We do not leave so great a void in society as we are inclined to imagine, partly to magnify our own importance, and partly to console ourselves by sympathy. Even in the same family the gap is not so great; the wound closes up sooner than we should expect. Nay, *our room* is not infrequently thought better than *our company*. People walk along the streets the day after our deaths just as they did before, and the crowd is not diminished. While we were living, the world seemed in a manner to exist only for us, for our delight and amusement, because it contributed to them. But our hearts cease to beat, and it goes on as usual, and thinks no more about us than it did in our lifetime. The million are devoid of sentiment, and care as little for you or me as if we belonged to the moon. We live the week over in the Sunday's paper, or are decently interred in some obituary at the month's end! It is not surprising that we are forgotten so soon after we quit this mortal stage: we are scarcely noticed, while we are on it. It is not merely that our names are not known in China — they have hardly been heard of in the next street. We are hand and glove with the universe, and think the obligation is mutual. This is an evident fallacy. If this, however, does not trouble us now, it will not hereafter. A handful of dust can have no quarrel to pick with its neighbours, or complaint to make against Providence, and might well exclaim, if it had but an understanding and a tongue, "Go thy ways, old world, swing round in blue ether, voluble to every age, you and I shall no more jostle!"

It is amazing how soon the rich and titled, and even some of those who have wielded great political power, are forgotten.

"A little rule, a little sway,
Is all the great and mighty have
Betwixt the cradle and the grave" —

and, after its short date, they hardly leave a name behind them. "A great man's memory may, at the common rate, survive him half a year." His heirs and successors take his titles, his power, and his wealth — all that made him considerable or courted by others; and he has left nothing else behind him either to delight or benefit the world. Posterity are not by any means so disinterested as they are supposed to be. They give their gratitude and admiration only in return for benefits conferred. They cherish the memory of those to whom they are indebted for instruction and delight; and they cherish it just in proportion to the instruction and delight they are conscious they receive. The sentiment of admiration springs immediately from this ground, and cannot be otherwise than well founded.[1]

The effeminate clinging to life as such, as a general or abstract idea, is the effect of a highly civilised and artificial state of society. Men formerly plunged into all the vicis-

---

[1] It has been usual to raise a very unjust clamour against the enormous salaries of public singers, actors, and so on. This matter seems reducible to a *moral equation*. They are paid out of money raised by voluntary contributions in the strictest sense; and if they did not bring certain sums into the treasury, the managers would not engage them. These sums are exactly in proportion to the number of individuals to whom their performance gives an extraordinary degree of pleasure. The talents of a singer, actor, etc., are therefore worth just as much as they will fetch.

situdes and dangers of war, or staked their all upon a single
die, or some one passion, which if they could not have gratified, life became a burthen to them — now our strongest passion is to think, our chief amusement is to read new plays,
new poems, new novels, and this we may do at our leisure,
in perfect security, *ad infinitum*. If we look into the old his-
tories and romances, before the *belles lettres* neutralised
human affairs and reduced passion to a state of mental
equivocation, we find the heroes and heroines not setting
their lives "at a pin's fee," but rather courting opportunities
of throwing them away in very wantonness of spirit. They
raise their fondness for some favourite pursuit to its height,
to a pitch of madness, and think no price too dear to pay for
its full gratification. Everything else is dross. They go to
death as to a bridal bed, and sacrifice themselves or others
without remorse at the shrine of love, of honour, of religion,
or any other prevailing feeling. Romeo runs his "seasick,
weary bark" upon the rocks of death, the instant he finds himself deprived of his Juliet; and she clasps his neck in their last
agonies, and follows him to the same fatal shore. One strong
idea takes possession of the mind and overrules every other;
and even life itself, joyless without that, becomes an object
of indifference or loathing. There is at least more of imagination in such a state of things, more vigour of feeling and
promptitude to act than in our lingering, languid, protracted
attachment to life for its own poor sake. It is, perhaps, also
better, as well as more heroical, to strike at some daring
or darling object, and if we fail in that, to take the consequences manfully, than to renew the lease of a tedious,
spiritless, charmless existence, merely (as Pierre says) "to
lose it afterwards in some vile brawl" for some worthless
object. Was there not a spirit of martyrdom as well as a
spice of the reckless energy of barbarism in this bold defiance
of death? Had not religion something to do with it; the
implicit belief in a future life, which rendered this of less
value, and embodied something beyond it to the imagination;
so that the rough soldier, the infatuated lover, the valorous
knight, etc., could afford to throw away the present venture,

and take a leap into the arms of futurity, which the modern sceptic shrinks back from, with all his boasted reason and vain philosophy, weaker than a woman! I cannot help thinking so myself; but I have endeavoured to explain this point before, and will not enlarge further on it here.

A life of action and danger moderates the dread of death. It not only gives us fortitude to bear pain, but teaches us at every step the precarious tenure on which we hold our present being. Sedentary and studious men are the most apprehensive on this score. Dr. Johnson was an instance in point. A few years seemed to him soon over, compared with those sweeping contemplations on time and infinity with which he had been used to pose himself. In the *still life* of a man of letters, there was no obvious reason for a change. He might sit in an armchair and pour out cups of tea to all eternity. Would it had been possible for him to do so! The most rational cure after all for the inordinate fear of death is to set a just value on life. If we merely wish to continue on the scene to indulge our headstrong humours and tormenting passions, we had better begone at once; and if we only cherish a fondness for existence according to the good we derive from it, the pang we feel at parting with it will not be very severe!

ON THE SPIRIT OF OBLIGATIONS

THE two rarest things to be met with are good sense and good nature. For one man who judges right, there are twenty who can say good things; as there are numbers who will serve you or do friendly actions, for one who really wishes you well. It has been said, and often repeated, that "mere good nature is a fool:" but I think that the dearth of sound sense, for the most part, proceeds from the want of a real, unaffected interest in things, except as they react upon ourselves; or from a neglect of the maxim of that good old philanthropist, who said, "*Nihil humani a me alienum puto.*" The narrowness of the heart warps the understanding, and makes us weigh objects in the scale of our self-love, instead of those of truth and justice. We consider not the merits of the case, or what is due to others, but the manner in which our own credit or consequence will be affected; and adapt our opinions and conduct to the last of these rather than to the first. The judgment is seldom wrong where the feelings are right; and they generally are so, provided they are warm and sincere. He who intends others well, is likely to advise them for the best; he who has any cause at heart, seldom ruins it by his imprudence. Those who play the public or their friends slippery tricks, have in secret no objection to betray them.

One finds out the folly and malice of mankind by the impertinence of friends — by their professions of service and tenders of advice — by their fears for your reputation and anticipation of what the world may say of you; by which means they suggest objections to your enemies, and at the same time absolve themselves from the task of justifying your errors, by having warned you of the consequences — by the care with which they tell ill news, and conceal from you any flattering circumstance — by their dread of your engaging in any creditable attempt, and mortification, if you succeed — by the difficulties and hindrances they throw in your way — by their satisfaction when you happen to make a slip or get into a scrape, and their determination to tie your hands behind you, lest you should get out of it — by their panic-terrors at your entering into a vindication of yourself, lest in the course of it you should call upon them for a certificate to your character — by their luke-warmness in defending, by their readiness in betraying you — by the high standard by which they try you, and to which you can hardly ever come up — by their forwardness to partake your triumphs, by their backwardness to share your disgrace — by their acknowledgment of your errors out of candour, and suppression of your good qualities out of envy — by their not contradicting, or by their joining in the cry against you, lest they too should become objects of the same abuse — by their playing the game into your adversaries' hands, by always letting their imaginations take part with their cowardice, their vanity, and selfishness against you; and thus realising or hastening all the ill consequences they affect to deplore, by spreading that very spirit of distrust, obloquy, and hatred which they predict will be excited against you!

In all these pretended demonstrations of an over-anxiety for our welfare, we may detect a great deal of spite and ill-nature lurking under the disguise of a friendly and officious zeal. It is wonderful how much love of mischief and rankling spleen lies at the bottom of the human heart, and how a constant supply of gall seems as necessary to the health and activity of the mind as of the body. Yet perhaps it ought not to excite much surprise that this gnawing, morbid, acrimonious temper should produce the effects it does, when, if it does not vent itself on others, it preys upon its own comforts, and makes us see the worst side of everything, even as it regards our own prospects and tranquillity. It is the not being comfortable in ourselves, that makes us seek to render other people uncomfortable. A person of this character will advise you against a prosecution for a libel, and shake his head at your attempting to shield yourself from a

shower of calumny — it is not that he is afraid you will be
nonsuited, but that you will gain a verdict! They caution
you against provoking hostility, in order that you may submit
to indignity. They say that "if you publish a certain work
it will be your ruin" — hoping that it will, and by their
tragical denunciations bringing about this very event as far
as it lies in their power, or at any rate, enjoying a premature
triumph over you in the meantime. What I would say to
any friend who may be disposed to foretell a general outcry
against any work of mine, would be to request him to judge
and speak of it for himself, as he thinks it deserves — and not
by his overweening scruples and qualms of conscience on my
account, to afford those very persons whose hostility he dep-
recates the cue they are to give to party prejudice, and which
they may justify by his authority.

Suppose you are to give lectures at a public institution,
these friends and well-wishers hope "you'll be turned out —
if you preserve your principles, they are sure you will." Is
it that your consistency gives them any concern? No, but
they are uneasy at your gaining a chance of a little popularity
— they do not like this new feather in your cap, they wish
to see it struck out, *for the sake of your character* — and when
this was once the case, it would be an additional relief to them
to see your character following the same road the next day.
The exercise of their bile seems to be the sole employment and
gratification of such people. They deal in the miseries of
human life. They are always either hearing or foreboding
some new grievance. They cannot contain their satisfaction,
if you tell them any mortification or cross-accident that has
happened to yourself; and if you complain of their want of
sympathy, they laugh in your face. This would be unaccountable, but for the spirit of perversity and contradiction
implanted in human nature. If things go right, there is
nothing to be done — these active-minded persons grow
restless, dull, vapid, — life is a sleep, a sort of *euthanasia* —
let them go wrong, and all is well again; they are once more
on the alert, have something to pester themselves and other
people about; may wrangle on, and "make mouths at the

invisible event!" Luckily, there is no want of materials for this disposition to work upon, *there is plenty of grist for the mill*. If you fall in love, they tell you (by the way of consolation) it is a pity that you did not fall downstairs and fracture a limb — it would be a relief to your mind, and shew you your folly. So they would reform the world. The class of persons I speak of are almost uniform grumblers and croakers against governments, and it must be confessed, governments are of great service in fostering their humours. "Born for their use, they live but to oblige them." While kings are left free to exercise their proper functions, and poet laureates make out their Mittimus to Heaven without a warrant, they will never stop the mouths of the censorious by changing their dispositions; the juices of faction will ferment, and the secretions of the state be duly performed! I do not mind when a character of this sort meets a Minister of State like an east wind round a corner, and gives him an ague fit; but should he meddle with me? Why should he tell me I write too much, and say that I should gain reputation if I could contrive to starve for a twelvemonth? Or if I apply to him for a loan of fifty pounds for present necessity, send me word back that he has too much regard for me to comply with my request? It is unhandsome irony. It is not friendly, 'tis not pardonable.[1]

I like real good nature and good will better than I do any offers of patronage or plausible rules for my conduct in life. I may suspect the soundness of the last, and I may not be quite sure of the motives of the first. People complain of ingratitude for benefits, and of the neglect of wholesome advice. In the first place, we pay little attention to advice, because we are seldom thought of in it. The person who gives it either contents himself to lay down (*ex cathedrâ*) certain vague, general maxims, and "wise saws," which we knew before; or, instead of considering what we *ought to do*, recommends what he himself *would do*. He merely substitutes his own will, caprice, and prejudices for ours, and expects us to be guided by them. Instead of changing places

---

[1] This circumstance did not happen to me, but to an acquaintance.

with us (to see what is best to be done in the given circumstances), he insists on our looking at the question from his
point of view, and acting in such a manner as to please him.
This is not at all reasonable; for *one man's meat*, according
to the old adage, *is another man's poison*. And it is not
strange, that starting from such opposite premises, we should
seldom jump in a conclusion, and that the art of giving and
taking advice is little better than a game at cross-purposes.
I have observed that those who are the most inclined to
assist others are the least forward or peremptory with their
advice; for having our interest really at heart, they consider
what can, rather than what *cannot* be done, and aid our
views and endeavour to avert ill consequences by moderating
our impatience and allaying irritations, instead of thwarting
our main design, which only tends to make us more extravagant and violent than ever. In the second place, benefits are
often conferred out of ostentation or pride, rather than from
true regard; and the person obliged is too apt to perceive this.
People who are fond of appearing in the light of patrons will
perhaps go through fire and water to serve you, who yet would
be sorry to find you no longer wanted their assistance, and
whose friendship cools and their good will slackens, as you are
relieved of their active zeal from the necessity of being further
beholden to it. Compassion and generosity are their favorite
virtues; and they countenance you, as you afford them opportunities for exercising them. The instant you can go alone,
you are discarded as unfit for their purpose.

This is something more than mere good nature or humanity.
A thoroughly good-natured man, a real friend, is one who is
pleased at our good fortune, as well as prompt to seize every
occasion of relieving our distress. We apportion our gratitude accordingly. We are thankful for good will rather
than for services, for the motive rather than for the *quantum*
of favour received — a kind word or look is never forgotten,
while we cancel prouder and weightier obligations; and those
who esteem us or evince a partiality to us are those whom we
still consider as our best friends. Nay, so strong is this
feeling, that we extend it even to those counterfeits in friend-

ship, flatterers and sycophants. Our self-love, rather than our self-interest, is the master key to our affections.

I am not convinced that those are always the best-natured or the best-conditioned men, who busy themselves most with the distresses of their fellow creatures. I do not know that those whose names stand at the head of all subscriptions to charitable institutions, and who are perpetual stewards of dinners and meetings to encourage and promote the establishment of asylums for the relief of the blind, the halt, and the orphan poor, are persons fitted with the best tempers or the kindliest feelings. I do not dispute their virtue; I doubt their sensibility. I am not here speaking of those who make a trade of the profession of humanity, or set their names down out of mere idle parade and vanity. I mean those who really enter into the details and drudgery of this sort of service *con amore*, and who delight in surveying and in diminishing the amount of human misery. I conceive it possible that a person who is going to pour oil and balm into the wounds of afflicted humanity, at a meeting of the Western Dispensary, by handsome speeches and by a handsome donation (not grudgingly given) may be thrown into a fit of rage that very morning, by having his toast too much buttered, may quarrel with the innocent prattle and amusements of his children, cry "Pish!" at every observation his wife utters, and scarcely feel a moment's comfort at any period of his life, except when he hears of some case of pressing distress that calls for his immediate interference, and draws off his attention from his own situation and feelings by the act of alleviating it. Those martyrs to the cause of humanity, in short, who run the gauntlet of the whole catalogue of unheard-of crimes and afflicting casualties, who ransack prisons, and plunge into lazar-houses and slave-ships as their daily amusement and highest luxury, must generally, I think, (though not always), be prompted to the arduous task by uneasy feelings of their own, and supported through it by iron nerves. Their fortitude must be equal to their pity. I do not think Mr. Wilberforce a case in point in this argument. He is evidently a delicately framed, nervous, sensi-

tive man. I should suppose him to be a kind and affection-
ately disposed person in all the relations of life. His weakness
is too quick a sense of reputation, a desire to have the good
word of all men, a tendency to truckle to power and fawn on
opinion. But there are some of these philanthropists that a
physiognomist has hard work to believe in. They seem made
of pasteboard, they look like mere machines; their benevolence may be said to go on rollers, and they are screwed to the
sticking-place by the wheels and pulleys of humanity:

> " If to their share some splendid virtues fall,
> Look in their face, and you forget them all."

They appear so much the creatures of the head and so little
of the heart, they are so cold, so lifeless, so mechanical, so
much governed by calculation, and so little by impulse, that
it seems the toss-up of a halfpenny, the mere turn of a feather,
whether such people should become a Granville Sharp, or a
Hubert in *King John*, a Howard, or a Sir Hudson Lowe!

"Charity covers a multitude of sins." Wherever it is,
there nothing can be wanting; wherever it is not, all else is
vain. "The meanest peasant on the bleakest mountain is
not without a portion of it (says Sterne), he finds the lacerated
lamb of another's flock," etc. (See the passage in the
Sentimental Journey.) I do not think education or circumstances can ever entirely eradicate this principle. Some professions may be supposed to blunt it, but it is perhaps more
in appearance than in reality. Butchers are not allowed to
sit on a jury for life and death; but probably this is a prejudice; if they have the *destructive organ* in an unusual degree
of expansion, they vent their sanguinary inclinations on the
brute creation; and besides, they look too jolly, rosy, and in
good case (they and their wives), to harbour much cruelty in
their dispositions. Neither would I swear that a man was
humane, merely for abstaining from animal food. A tiger
would not be a lamb, though it fed on milk. Surgeons are in
general thought to be unfeeling, and steeled by custom to the
sufferings of humanity. They may be so, as far as relates
to broken bones and bruises, but not to other things. Nor

are they necessarily so in their profession; for we find different degrees of callous insensibility in different individuals. Some practitioners have an evident delight in alarming the apprehensions and cutting off the limbs of their patients; these would have been ill-natured men in any situation in life, and merely make an excuse of their profession to indulge their natural ill-humour and brutality of temper. A surgeon who is fond of giving pain to those who consult him will not spare the feelings of his neighbours in other respects; has a tendency to probe other wounds besides those of the body; and is altogether a harsh and disagreeable character. A Jack-Ketch may be known to tie the fatal noose with trembling fingers; or a jailor may have a heart softer than the walls of his prison. There have been instances of highwaymen who were proverbially gentlemen. I have seen a Bow-street officer[1] (not but that the transition is ungracious and unjust) reading Racine, and following the recitation of Talma at the door of a room which he was sent to guard. Police-magistrates, from the scenes they have to witness and the characters they come in contact with, may be supposed to lose the fine edge of delicacy and sensibility; yet they are not all alike, but differ, as one star differs from another in magnitude. One is as remarkable for mildness and lenity, as another is notorious for harshness and severity. The late Mr. Justice Fielding was a member of this profession, which (however little accordant with his own feelings) he made pleasant to those of others. He generally sent away the disputants in that unruly region, where he presided, tolerably satisfied. I have often seen him, escaped from the noisy, repulsive scene, sunning himself in the adjoining walks of St. James's Park, and with mild aspect, and lofty but unwieldy mien, eyeing the verdant glades and lengthening vistas where perhaps his childhood loitered. He had a strong resemblance to his father, the immortal author of *Tom Jones*. I never passéd him that I did not take off my hat to him in spirit. I could not help thinking of Parson Adams, of Booth and Amelia. I seemed to belong, by intel-

[1] Lavender.

lectual adoption, to the same family, and would willingly have acknowledged my obligation to the father to the son. He had something of the air of Colonel Bath. When young, he had very excellent prospects in the law, but neglected a brief sent him by the Attorney-General, in order to attend a glee-club, for which he had engaged to furnish a rondeau. This spoiled his fortune. A man whose object is to please himself, or to keep his word to his friends, is the last man to thrive at court. Yet he looked serene and smiling to his latest breath, conscious of the goodness of his own heart, and of not having sullied a name that had thrown a light upon humanity!

There are different modes of obligation, and different avenues to our gratitude and favour. A man may lend his countenance who will not part with his money, and open his mind to us who will not draw out his purse. How many ways are there, in which our peace may be assailed, besides actual want! How many comforts do we stand in need of, besides meat and drink and clothing! Is it nothing to "administer to a mind diseased" — to heal a wounded spirit? After all other difficulties are removed, we still want some one to bear with our infirmities, to impart our confidence to, to encourage us in our *hobbies* (nay, to get up and ride behind us) and to like us with all our faults. True friendship is self-love at second-hand; where, as in a flaming mirror, we may see our errors softened, and where we may fancy our opinion of ourselves confirmed by an impartial and faithful witness. He (of all the world) creeps the closest in our bosoms, into our favour and esteem, who thinks of us most nearly as we do of ourselves. Such a one is indeed the pattern of a friend, another self — and our gratitude for the blessing is as sincere, as it is hollow in most other cases! This is one reason why entire friendship is scarcely to be found, except in love. There is a hardness and a severity in our judgments of one another; the spirit of competition also intervenes, unless where there is too great an inequality of pretension or difference of taste to admit of mutual sympathy and respect; but a woman's vanity is interested in making the object of her choice the God of her idolatry; and in the intercourse with the sex, there is the finest reflection of opposite and answering excellences imaginable! It is in the highest spirit of the religion of love in the female breast, that Lord Byron has put that beautiful apostrophe into the mouth of Anah, in speaking of her angel-lover (alas! are not the sons of men too, when they are deified in the hearts of women, only "a little lower than the angels?")

> "And when I think that his immortal wings
> Shall one day hover o'er the sepulchre
> Of the poor child of clay, that so adored him,
> As He adored the Highest, death becomes
> Less terrible!"

This is a dangerous string, which I ought never to touch upon; but the shattered chords vibrate of themselves!

The difference of age, of situation in life, and an absence of all consideration of business have, I apprehend, something of the same effect in producing a refined and abstracted friendship. The person whose doors I enter with most pleasure and quit with most regret, never did me the smallest favour. I once did him an uncalled-for service, and we nearly quarrelled about it. If I were in the utmost distress, I should just as soon think of asking his assistance as of stopping a person on the highway. Practical benevolence is not his *forte*. He leaves the profession of that to others. His habits, his theory are against it as idle and vulgar. His hand is closed, but what of that? His eye is ever open, and reflects the universe; his silver accents, beautiful, venerable as his silver hairs, but not scanted, flow as a river. I never ate or drank in his house; nor do I know or care how the flies or spiders fare in it, or whether a mouse can get a living. But I know that I can get there what I can get nowhere else — a welcome, as if one was expected to drop in just at that moment, a total absence of all respect of persons and of airs of self-consequence, endless topics of discourse, refined thoughts, made more striking by ease and simplicity of manner — the husk, the shell of humanity is left at the door, and the spirit, mellowed by time, resides within! All you have to do is to sit and listen; and it is like hearing one of Titian's faces speak. To think of wordly matters is a profanation, like that of the money-changers in the Temple; or it is to regard the bread and wine of the Sacrament with carnal eyes. We enter the enchanter's cell, and converse with the divine inhabitant. To have this privilege always at hand, and to be circled by that spell whenever we choose, with an *"Enter Sessami,"* is better than sitting at the lower end of the tables of the great, than eating awkwardly from gold plate, than drinking fulsome toasts, or being thankful for gross favours, and gross insults!

Few things tend more to alienate friendship than a want of punctuality in our engagements. I have known the breach of a promise to dine or sup break up more than one intimacy. A disappointment of this kind rankles in the mind — it cuts up our pleasures (those rare events in human life, which ought not to be wantonly sported with!) — it not only deprives us of the expected gratification, but it renders us unfit for, and out of humour with, every other; it makes us think our society not worth having, which is not the way to make us delighted with our own thoughts; it lessens our self-esteem, and destroys our confidence in others; and having leisure on our hands (by being thus left alone) and sufficient provocation withal, we employ it in ripping up the faults of the acquaintance who has played us this slippery trick, and in forming resolutions to pick a quarrel with him the very first opportunity we can find. I myself once declined an invitation to meet Talma, who was an admirer of Shakespeare, and who idolised Buonaparte, to keep an appointment with a person who had *forgot* it! One great art of women, who pretend to manage their husbands and keep them to themselves, is to contrive some excuse for breaking engagements with friends for whom they entertain any respect, or who are likely to have any influence over them.

There is, however, a class of persons who have a particular satisfaction in falsifying your expectations of pleasure in their society, who make appointments for no other ostensible purpose than *not to keep them;* who think their ill-behaviour gives them an air of superiority over you, instead of placing them at your mercy; and who, in fact, in all their overtures of condescending kindness towards you, treat you exactly as if there was no such person in the world. Friendship is with them a *mono-drama*, in which they play the principal and sole part. They must needs be very imposing or amusing characters to surround themselves with a circle of friends, who find that they are to be mere cyphers. The egotism would in such instances be offensive and intolerable, if its very excess did not render it entertaining. Some individuals carry this hard, unprincipled, reckless unconsciousness of everything but themselves and their own purposes to such a pitch, that they may be compared to *automata*, whom you never expect to consult your feelings or alter their movements out of complaisance to others. They are wound up to a certain point, by an internal machinery which you do not very well comprehend; but if they perform their accustomed evolutions so as to excite your wonder or laughter, it is all very well, you do not quarrel with them, but look on at the *pantomine* of friendship while it lasts or is agreeable.

There are (I may add here) a happy few, whose manner is so engaging and delightful, that injure you how they will, they cannot offend you. They rob, ruin, ridicule you, and you cannot find in your heart to say a word against them. The late Mr. Sheridan was a man of this kind. He *could not* make enemies. If anyone came to request the repayment of a loan from him, he borrowed more. A cordial shake of his hand was a receipt in full for all d mands. He could "coin his *smile* for drachma ," cancelled bonds with *bon mots*, and gave jokes in discharge of a bill. A friend of his said, "If I pull off my hat to him in the street, it costs me fifty pounds, and if he speaks to me, it's a hundred!"

Only one other reflection occurs to me on this subject. I used to think better of the world than I do. I thought its great fault, its original sin, was barbarous ignorance and want, which would be cured by the diffusion of civilisation and letters. But I find (or fancy I do) that as selfishness is the vice of unlettered periods and nations, envy is the bane of more refined and intellectual ones. Vanity springs out of

the grave of sordid self-interest. Men were formerly ready
to cut one another's throats about the gross means of sub-
sistence, and now they are ready to do it about reputation.
The worst is, you are no better off if you fail than if you
succeed. You are despised if you do not excel others, and
hated if you do. Abuse or praise equally weans your friends
from you. We cannot bear eminence in our own department
or pursuit, and think it an impertinence in any other. Instead of being delighted with the proofs of excellence and the
admiration paid to it, we are mortified with it, thrive only by
the defeat of others, and live on the carcass of mangled reputation. By being tried by an *ideal* standard of vanity and affectation, real objects and common people become odious or
insipid. Instead of being raised, all is prostituted, degraded,
vile. Everything is reduced to this feverish, importunate,
harassing state. I'm heartily sick of it, and I'm sure I have
reason if anyone has.

ON THE FEELING OF IMMORTALITY
IN YOUTH

"Life is a pure flame, and we live by an invisible sun within us."
—Sir Thomas Browne.

No young man believes he shall ever die. It was a saying of my brother's, and a fine one. There is a feeling of Eternity in youth, which makes us amends for everything. To be young is to be as one of the Immortal Gods. One half of time indeed is flown — the other half remains in store for us with all its countless treasures; for there is no line drawn, and we see no limit to our hopes and wishes. We make the coming age our own.

"The vast, the unbounded prospect lies before us."

Death, old age, are words without a meaning, that pass by us like the idle air which we regard not. Others may have undergone, or may still be liable to them — we "bear a charmed life," which laughs to scorn all such sickly fancies. As in setting out on a delightful journey, we strain our eager gaze forward —

"Bidding the lovely scenes at distance hail,"

and see no end to the landscape, new objects presenting themselves as we advance; so, in the commencement of life, we set no bounds to our inclinations, nor to the unrestricted opportunities of gratifying them. We have as yet found no obstacle, no disposition to flag; and it seems that we can go on so forever. We look round in a new world, full of life, and motion, and ceaseless progress; and feel in ourselves all the vigour and spirit to keep pace with it, and do not foresee from any present symptoms how we shall be left behind in the natural course of things, decline into old age, and drop into the grave. It is the simplicity, and as it were *abstracted-*
163

ness of our feelings in youth, that (so to speak) identifies us with nature, and (our experience being slight and our passions strong) deludes us into a belief of being immortal like it. Our short-lived connection with existence, we fondly flatter ourselves, is an indissoluble and lasting union — a honeymoon that knows neither coldness, jar, nor separation. As infants smile and sleep, we are rocked in the cradle of our wayward fancies, and lulled into security by the roar of the universe around us — we quaff the cup of life with eager haste without draining it, instead of which it only overflows the more — objects press around us, filling the mind with their magnitude and with the throng of desires that wait upon them, so that we have no room for the thoughts of death. From the plenitude of our being we cannot change all at once to dust and ashes, we cannot imagine "this sensible, warm motion, to become a kneaded clod" — we are too much dazzled by the brightness of the waking dream around us to look into the darkness of the tomb. We no more see our end than our beginning: the one is lost in oblivion and vacancy, as the other is hid from us by the crowd and hurry of approaching events. Or the grim shadow is seen lingering in the horizon, which we are doomed never to overtake, or whose last, faint, glimmering outline touches upon Heaven and translates us to the skies! Nor would the hold that life has taken of us permit us to detach our thoughts from the present objects and pursuits, even if we would. What is there more opposed to health, than sickness; to strength and beauty, than decay and dissolution; to the active search of knowledge, than mere oblivion? Or is there none of the usual advantage to bar the approach of Death, and mock his idle threats; Hope supplies their place, and draws a veil over the abrupt termination of all our cherished schemes. While the spirit of youth remains unimpaired, ere the "wine of life is drank up," we are like people intoxicated or in a fever, who are hurried away by the violence of their own sensations; it is only as present objects begin to pall upon the sense, as we have been disappointed in our favourite pursuits, cut off from our closest ties, that passion loosens its hold upon the breast, that we by degrees become weaned from the world, and allow ourselves to contemplate, "as in a glass, darkly," the possibility of parting with it for good. The example of others, the voice of experience, has no effect upon us whatever. Casualties we must avoid: the slow and deliberate advances of age we can play at *hide-and-seek* with. We think ourselves too lusty and too nimble for that blear-eyed decrepid old gentleman to catch us. Like the foolish fat scullion, in Sterne, when she hears that Master Bobby is dead, our only reflection is, "So am not I!" The idea of death, instead of staggering our confidence, rather seems to strengthen and enhance our possession and our enjoyment of life. Others may fall around like leaves, or be mowed down like flowers by the scythe of Time: these are but tropes and figures to the unreflecting ears and overweening presumption of youth. It is not till we see the flowers of Love, Hope, and Joy, withering around us, and our own pleasures cut up by the roots, that we bring the moral home to ourselves, that we abate something of the wanton extravagance of our pretensions, or that the emptiness and dreariness of the prospect before us reconciles us to the stillness of the grave!

> "Life! thou strange thing, thou hast a power to feel
> Thou art, and to perceive that others are."[1]

Well might the poet begin his indignant invective against an art, whose professed object is its destruction, with this animated apostrophe to life. Life is indeed a strange gift, and its privileges are most miraculous. Nor is it singular that when the splendid boon is first granted us, our gratitude, our admiration, and our delight should prevent us from reflecting on our own nothingness, or from thinking it will ever be recalled. Our first and strongest impressions are taken from the mighty scene that is opened to us, and we very innocently transfer its durability as well as magnificence to ourselves. So newly found, we cannot make up our minds to parting with it yet and at least put off that consideration to an indefinite term. Like a clown at a fair, we are full of amaze-

[1] Fawcett's *Art of War*, a poem, 1794.

ment and rapture, and have no thoughts of going home, or that it will soon be night. We know our existence only from external objects, and we measure it by them. We can never be satisfied with gazing; and nature will still want us to look on and applaud. Otherwise, the sumptuous entertainment, "the feast of reason and the flow of soul," to which they were invited, seems little better than mockery and a cruel insult. We do not go from a play till the scene is ended, and the lights are ready to be extinguished. But the fair face of things still shines on; shall we be called away before the curtain falls, or ere we have scarce had a glimpse of what is going on? Like children, our step-mother Nature holds us up to see the raree-show of the universe; and then, as if life were a burthen to support, lets us instantly down again. Yet in that short interval, what "brave sublunary things" does not the spectacle unfold; like a bubble, at one minute reflecting the universe, and the next, shook to air! — To see the golden sun and the azure sky, the outstretched ocean, to walk upon the green earth, and to be lord of a thousand creatures, to look down the giddy precipices or over the distant flowery vales, to see the world spread out under one's finger in a map, to bring the stars near, to view the smallest insects in a microscope, to read history, and witness the revolutions of empires and the succession of generations, to hear of the glory of Sidon and Tyre, of Babylon and Susa, as of a faded pageant, and to say all these were, and are now nothing, to think that we exist in such a point of time, and in such a corner of space, to be at once spectators and a part of the moving scene, to watch the return of the seasons, of spring and autumn, to hear

> " The stockdove plain amid the forest deep,
> That drowsy rustles to the sighing gale" —

to traverse desert wilderness, to listen to the midnight choir, to visit lighted halls, or plunge into the dungeon's gloom, or sit in crowded theatres and see life itself mocked, to feel heat and cold, pleasure and pain, right and wrong, truth and falsehood, to study the works of art and refine the sense of beauty

to agony, to worship fame and to dream of immortality, to
have read Shakspeare and belong to the same species as
Sir Isaac Newton;[1] to be and to do all this, and then in a

[1] Lady Wortley Montague says, in one of her letters, that "she
would much rather be a rich *effendi*, with all his ignorance, than Sir
Isaac Newton, with all his knowledge." This was not perhaps an
impolitic choice, as she had a better chance of becoming one than the
other, there being many rich effendis to one Sir Isaac Newton.
The wish was not a very intellectual one. The same petulance of
rank and sex breaks out everywhere in these *Letters*. She is constantly reducing the poets or philosophers who have the misfortune
of her acquaintance, to the figure they might make at her lady-
ship's levee or toilette, not considering that the public mind does
not sympathise with this process of a fastidious imagination. In
the same spirit, she declares of Pope and Swift, that "had it not been
for the *good-nature* of mankind, these two superior beings were entitled, by their birth and hereditary fortune, to be only a couple of
link-boys." Gulliver's *Travels*, and the *Rape of the Lock*, go for
nothing in this critical estimate, and the world raised the authors
to the rank of superior beings, in spite of their disadvantages of birth
and fortune, *out of pure good nature!* So again, she says of Richardson, that he had never got beyond the servant's hall, and was utterly
unfit to describe the manners of people of quality; till in the capricious workings of her vanity, she persuades herself that Clarissa is
very like what she was at her age, and that Sir Thomas and Lady
Grandison strongly resembled what she had heard of her mother
and remembered of her father. It is one of the beauties and advantages of literature, that it is the means of abstracting the mind from
the narrowness of local and personal prejudices, and of enabling us
to judge of truth and excellence by their inherent merits alone. Woe
be to the pen that would undo this fine illusion (the only reality),
and teach us to regulate our notions of genius and virtue by the circumstances in which they happen to be placed! You would not expect a person whom you saw in a servant's hall, or behind a counter,
to write Clarissa; but after he had written the work, to *pre-judge* it
from the situation of the writer, is an unpardonable piece of injustice
and folly. His merit could only be the greater from the contrast.
If literature is an elegant accomplishment, which none but persons
of birth and fashion should be allowed to excel in, or to exercise with
advantage to the public, let them by all means take upon them the
task of enlightening and refining mankind: if they decline this re-
sponsibility as too heavy for their shoulders, let those who do the
drudgery in their stead, however inadequately, for want of their
polite example, receive the meed that is their due, and not be treated
as low pretenders who have encroached upon the provinces of their
betters. Suppose Richardson to have been acquainted with the

moment to be nothing, to have it all snatched from one like
a juggler's ball or a phantasmagoria; there is something

great man's steward, or valet, instead of the great man himself, I
will venture to say that there was more difference between him who
lived in an *ideal world*, and had the genius and felicity to open that
world to others, and his friend the steward, than between the lacquey
and the mere lord, or between those who lived in different rooms of
the same house, who dined on the same luxuries at different tables,
who rode outside or inside of the same coach, and were proud of
wearing or of bestowing the same tawdry livery. If the lord is
distinguished from his valet by anything else, it is by education and
talent, which he has in common with the author. But if the latter
shows these in the highest degree, it is asked what are his pretensions?
Not birth or fortune, for neither of these would enable him to write
Clarissa. One man is born with a title and estate, another with
genius. That is sufficient; and we have no right to question the
genius for want of the *gentility*, unless the former ran in families, or
could be bequeathed with a fortune, which is not the case. Were it
so, the flowers of literature, like jewels and embroidery, would be
confined to the fashionable circles; and there would be no pretenders
to taste or elegance but those whose names were found in the court
list. No one objects to Claude's landscapes as the work of a pastry-
cook, or withholds from Raphael the epithet of *divine*, because his
parents were not rich. This impertinence is confined to men of
letters; the evidence of the senses baffles the envy and foppery of
mankind. No quarter ought to be given to this *aristocratic* tone of
criticism whenever it appears. People of quality are not contented
with carrying all the external advantages for their own share, but
would persuade you that all the intellectual ones are packed up in
the same bundle. Lord Byron was a later instance of this double
and unwarrantable style of pretension — *monstrum ingens, biforme*.
He could not endure a lord who was not a wit, nor a poet who was
not a lord. Nobody but himself answered to his own standard of
perfection. Mr. Moore carries a proxy in his pocket from some noble
persons to estimate literary merit by the same rule. Lady Mary
calls Fielding names, but she afterwards makes atonement by doing
justice to his frank, free, hearty nature, where he says "his spirits
gave him raptures with his cook-maid, and cheerfulness when he was
starving in a garret, and his happy constitution made him forget
everything when he was placed before a venison-pasty or over a flask
of champagne." She does not want shrewdness and spirit when
her petulance and conceit do not get the better of her, and she has
done ample and merited execution on Lord Bolingbroke. She is,
however, very angry at the freedoms taken with the Great; *smells
a rat* in this indiscriminate scribbling, and the familiarity of writers
with the reading public; and inspired by her Turkish costume, fore-
tells a French and English revolution as the consequences of transfer-

revolting and incredible to sense in the transition, and no wonder that, aided by youth and warm blood, and the flush of enthusiasm, the mind contrives for a long time to reject it with disdain and loathing as a monstrous and improbable fiction, like a monkey on a house-top, that is loath, amidst its fine discoveries and specious antics, to be tumbled headlong into the street, and crushed to atoms, the sport and laughter of the multitude!

The change, from the commencement to the close of life, appears like a fable, after it had taken place; how should we treat it otherwise than as a chimera before it has come to pass? There are some things that happened so long ago, places or persons we have formerly seen, of which such dim traces remain, we hardly know whether it was sleeping or waking they occurred; they are like dreams within the dream of life, a mist, a film before the eye of memory, which, as we try to recall them more distinctly, elude our notice altogether. It is but natural that the lone interval that we thus look back upon should have appeared long and endless in prospect. There are others so distinct and fresh, they seem but of yesterday — their very vividness might be deemed a pledge of their permanence. Then, however far back our impressions may go, we find others still older (for our years are multiplied in youth) descriptions of scenes that we had read, and people before our time, Priam and the Trojan war; and even then, Nestor was old and dwelt delighted on his youth, and spoke of the race of heroes that were no more; — what wonder that, seeing this long line of being pictured in our minds, and reviving as it were in us, we should give ourselves involuntary credit for an indeterminate existence? In the cathedral at Peterborough there is a monument to Mary, Queen of Scots, at which I used to gaze when a boy, while the events of the period, all that had happened since, passed in review before me. If all this mass of feeling and imagination could be crowded into a moment's compass, what might not the whole

ring the patronage of letters from the *quality* to the mob, and of supposing that ordinary writers or readers can have any notions in common with their superiors.

of life be supposed to contain? We are heirs of the past, we count on the future as our natural reversion. Besides, there are some of our early impressions so exquisitely tempered, it appears that they must always last — nothing can add to or take away from their sweetness and purity — the first breath of spring, the hyacinth dipped in the dew, the mild lustre of the evening-star, the rainbow after a storm — while we have the full enjoyment of these, we must be young; and what can ever alter us in this respect? Truth, friend-- ship, love, books, are also proof against the canker of time; and while we live but for them, we can never grow old. We take out a new lease of existence from the objects on which we set our affections, and become abstracted, impassive, immortal in them. We cannot conceive how certain sentiments should ever decay or grow cold in our breasts; and, consequently to maintain them in their first youthful glow and vigour, the flame of life must continue to burn as bright as ever, or rather, they are the fuel that feed the sacred lamp, that kindle "the purple light of love," and spread a golden cloud around our heads! Again, we not only flourish and survive in our affections (in which we will not listen to the possibility of a change, any more than we foresee the wrinkles on the brow of a mistress), but we have a further guarantee against the thoughts of death in our favourite studies and pursuits and in their continual advance. Art we know is long; life, we feel, should be so too. We see no end of the difficulties we have to encounter: perfection is slow of attainment, and we must have time to accomplish it in. Rubens complained that when he had just learned his art, he was snatched away from it: we trust we shall be more fortunate! A wrinkle in an old head takes whole days to finish it properly: but to catch "the Raphael grace, the Guido air," no limit should be put to our endeavours. What a prospect for the future! What a task we have entered upon! and shall we be arrested in the middle of it? We do not reckon our time thus employed lost, or our pains thrown away, or our progress slow — we do not droop or grow tired, but "gain a new vigour at our endless task;" — and shall Time grudge us the opportunity to finish what we have auspiciously begun, and have formed a sort of compact with nature to achieve? The fame of the great names we look up to is also imperishable; and shall not we, who contemplate it with such intense yearnings, imbibe a portion of ethereal fire, the *divinæ particula auræ*, which nothing can extinguish? I remember to have looked at a print of Rembrandt for hours together, without being conscious of the flight of time, trying to resolve it into its component parts, to connect its strong and sharp gradations, to learn the secret of its reflected lights, and found neither satiety nor pause in the prosecution of my studies. The print over which I was poring would last long enough; why should the idea in my mind, which was finer, more impalpable, perish before it? At this, I redoubled the ardour of my pursuit, and by the very subtlety and refinement of my inquiries, seemed to bespeak for them an exemption from corruption and the rude grasp of Death.[1]

Objects, on our first acquaintance with them, have that singleness and integrity of impression that it seems as if nothing could destroy or obliterate them, so firmly are they stamped and rivetted on the brain. We repose on them with a sort of voluptuous indolence, in full faith and boundless confidence. We are absorbed in the present moment, or return to the same point — idling away a great deal of time in youth, thinking we have enough to spare. There is often a local feeling in the air, which is as fixed as if it were marble; we loiter in dim cloisters, losing ourselves in thought and in their glimmering arches; a winding road before us seems as long as the journey of life, and as full of events. Time and experience dissipate this illusion; and by reducing them to detail, circumscribe the limits of our expectations. It is only as the pageant of life passes by and the masques turn their backs upon us, that we see through the deception, or believe that the train will have an end. In many cases, the slow progress and monotonous texture of our lives, before we

---

[1] Is it not this that frequently keeps artists alive so long, *viz.* the constant occupation of their minds with vivid images, with little of the *wear and tear* of the body?

mingle with the world and are embroiled in its affairs, has a tendency to aid the same feeling. We have a difficulty, when left to ourselves, and without the resource of books or some more lively pursuit, to "beguile the slow and creeping hours of time," and argue that if it moves on always at this tedious snail's-pace, it can never come to an end. We are willing to skip over certain portions of it that separate us from favourite objects, that irritate ourselves at the unnecessary delay. The young are prodigal of life from a superabundance of it; the old are tenacious on the same score, because they have little left, and cannot enjoy even what remains of it.

For my part, I set out in life with the French Revolution, and that event had considerable influence on my early feelings, as on those of others. Youth was then doubly such. It was the dawn of a new era, a new impulse had been given to men's minds, and the sun of Liberty rose upon the sun of Life in the same day, and both were proud to run their race together. Little did I dream, while my first hopes and wishes went hand in hand with those of the human race, that long before my eyes should close, that dawn would be overcast, and set once more in the night of despotism — "total eclipse!" Happy that I did not. I felt for years, and during the best part of my existence, *heart-whole* in that cause, and triumphed in the triumphs over the enemies of man! At that time, while the fairest aspirations of the human mind seemed about to be realised, ere the image of man was defaced and his breast mangled in scorn, philosophy took a higher, poetry could afford a deeper range. At that time, to read *The Robbers* was indeed delicious, and to hear

> "From the dungeon of the tower time-rent,
> That fearful voice, a famish'd father's cry,"

could be borne only amidst the fulness of hope, the crash of the fall of the strongholds of power, and the exulting sounds of the march of human freedom. What feelings the death-scene in *Don Carlos* sent into the soul! In that headlong career of lofty enthusiasm, and the joyous opening of the

prospects of the world and our own, the thought of death
crossing it, smote doubly cold upon the mind; there was a
stifling sense of oppression and confinement, an impatience
of our present knowledge, a desire to grasp the whole of our
existence in one strong embrace, to sound the mystery of life
and death, and in order to put an end to the agony of doubt
and dread, to burst through our prison-house, and confront
the King of Terrors in his grisly palace! . . . As I was writing
out this passage, my miniature-picture when a child lay on
the mantle-piece, and I took it out of the case to look at it.
I could perceive few traces of myself in it; but there was the
same placid brow, the dimpled mouth, the same timid, inquisitive glance as ever.   But its careless smile did not seem
to reproach me with having become recreant to the sentiments that were then sown in my mind, or with having written
a sentence that could call up a blush in this image of ingenuous
youth!

"That time is past with all its giddy raptures."   Since the
future was barred to my progress, I have turned for consolation to the past, gathering up the fragments of my early recollections, and putting them into form that might live.   It is
thus, that when we find our personal and substantial identity
vanishing from us, we strive to gain a reflected and sustituted
one in our thoughts; we do not like to perish wholly, and wish
to bequeath our names at least to posterity.   As long as we
can keep alive our cherished thoughts and nearest interests
in the minds of others, we do not appear to have retired altogether from the stage, we still occupy a place in the estimation of mankind, exercise a powerful influence over them, and
it is only our bodies that are trampled into dust or dispersed
to air.   Our darling speculations still find favour and en-
couragement, and we make as good a figure in the eyes of
our descendants, nay, perhaps, a better than we did in our
life-time.   This is one point gained; the demands of our
self-love are so far satisfied.   Besides, if by the proofs of
intellectual superiority we survive ourselves in this world, by
exemplary virtue or unblemished faith, we are taught to
ensure an interest in another and a higher state of being, and

to anticipate at the same time the applauses of men and angels.

"Even from the tomb the voice of nature cries;
Even in our ashes live their wonted fires."

As we advance in life, we acquire a keener sense of the value of time. Nothing else, indeed, seems of any consequence; and we become misers in this respect. We try to arrest its few last tottering steps, and to make it linger on the brink of the grave. We can never leave off wondering how that which has ever been should cease to be, and would still live on, that we may wonder at our own shadow, and when "all the life of life is flown," dwell on the retrospect of the past. This is accompanied by a mechanical tenaciousness of whatever we possess, by a distrust and a sense of fallacious hollowness in all we see. Instead of the full, pulpy feeling of youth, every thing is flat and insipid. The world is a painted witch, that puts us off with false shews and tempting appearances. The ease, the jocund gaiety, the unsuspecting security of youth are fled: nor can we, without flying in the face of common sense,

"From the last dregs of life, hope to receive
What its first sprightly runnings could not give."

If we can slip out of the world without notice or mischance, can tamper with bodily infirmity, and frame our minds to the becoming composure of *still-life*, before we sink into total insensibility, it is as much as we ought to expect. We do not in the regular course of nature die all at once: we have mouldered away gradually long before; faculty after faculty, attachment after attachment, we are torn from ourselves piece-meal while living; year after year takes something from us; and death only consigns the last remnant of what we were to the grave. The revulsion is not so great, and a quiet *euthanasia* is a winding-up of the plot, that is not out of reason or nature.

That we should thus in a manner outlive ourselves, and dwindle imperceptibly into nothing, is not surprising, when even in our prime the strongest impressions leave so little traces of themselves behind, and the last object is driven out by the succeeding one. How little effect is produced on us at any time by the books we have read, the scenes we have witnessed, the sufferings we have gone through! Think only of the variety of feelings we experience in reading an interesting romance, or being present at a fine play — what beauty, what sublimity, what soothing, what heart-rending emotions! You would suppose these would last for ever, or at least subdue the mind to a correspondent tone and harmony — while we turn over the page, while the scene is passing before us, it seems as if nothing could ever after shake our resolution, that "treason domestic, foreign levy, nothing could touch us farther!" The first splash of mud we get, on entering the street, the first pettifogging shopkeeper that cheats us out of two-pence, and the whole vanishes clean out of our remembrance, and we become the idle prey of the most petty and annoying circumstances. The mind soars by an effort to the grand and lofty; it is at home in the grovelling, the disagreeable, and the little. This happens in the height and hey-day of our existence, when novelty gives a stronger impulse to the blood and takes a faster hold of the brain (I have known the impression on coming out of a gallery of pictures then last half a day) — as we grow old, we become more feeble and querulous, every object "reverbs its own hollowness," and both worlds are not enough to satisfy the peevish importunity and extravagant presumption of our desires! There are a few superior, happy beings, who are born with a temper exempt from every trifling annoyance. This spirit sits serene and smiling as in its native skies, and a divine harmony (whether heard or not) plays around them. This is to be at peace. Without this, it is in vain to fly into deserts, or to build a hermitage on the top of rocks, if regret and ill-humour follow us there; and with this, it is needless to make the experiment. The only true retirement is that of the heart; the only true leisure is the repose of the passions. To such persons it makes little difference whether they are young or old; and they die as they have lived, with graceful resignation.

MERRY ENGLAND

THIS old-fashioned epithet might be supposed to have been bestowed ironically, or on the old principle — *Ut lucus a non lucendo*. Yet there is something in the sound that hits the fancy, and a sort of truth beyond appearances. To be sure, it is from a dull, homely ground that the gleams of mirth and jollity break out; but the streaks of light that tinge the evening sky are not the less striking on that account. The beams of the morning sun shining on the lonely glades, or through the idle branches of the tangled forest, the leisure, the freedom, "the pleasure of going and coming without knowing where," the troops of wild deer, the sports of the chase, and other rustic gambols were sufficient to justify the well-known appellation of "Merry Sherwood," and in like manner we may apply the phrase to *Merry England*. The smile is not the less sincere because it does not always play upon the cheek; and the jest is not the less welcome, nor the laugh less hearty, because they happen to be a relief from care or leaden-eyed melancholy. The instances are the more precious as they are rare; and we look forward to them with the greater good will, or back upon them with the greater gratitude, as we drain the last drop in the cup with particular relish. If not always gay or in good spirits, we are glad when any occasion draws us out of our natural gloom, and disposed to make the most of it. We may say with Silence in the play, "I have been merry ere now," — and this once was to serve him all his life; for he was a person of wonderful silence and gravity, though "he chirped over his cups," and announced with characteristic glee that "there were pippins and cheese to come." Silence was in this sense a merry man, that is, he would be merry if he could, and a very great economy of wit,

176

like a very slender fare, was a banquet to him, from the simplicity of his taste and habits. "Continents," says Hobbes, "have most of what they contain" — and in this view it may be contended that the English are the merriest people in the world, since they only show it on high-days and holidays. They are then like a school-boy let loose from school, or like a dog that has slipped his collar. They are not gay like the French, who are one eternal smile of self-complacency, tortured into affectation, or spun out into languid indifference, nor are they voluptuous and immersed in sensual indolence, like the Italians; but they have that sort of intermittent, fitful, irregular gaiety, which is neither worn out by habit, nor deadened by passion, but is sought with avidity as it takes the mind by surprise, is startled by a sense of oddity and incongruity, indulges its wayward humours or lively impulses, with perfect freedom and lightness of heart, and seizes occasion by the forelock, that it may return to serious business with more cheerfulness, and have something to beguile the hours of thought or sadness. I do not see how there can be high spirits without low ones; and everything has its price according to circumstances. Perhaps we have to pay a heavier tax on pleasure, than some others: what skills it, so long as our good spirits and good hearts enable us to bear it?

"They" (the English), says Froissart, "amused themselves sadly after the fashion of their country" — *ils se rejouissoient tristement selon la coutume de leur pays.* They have indeed a way of their own. Their mirth is a relaxation from gravity, a challenge to dull care to be gone; and one is not always clear at first, whether the appeal is successful. The cloud may still hang on the brow; the ice may not thaw at once. To help them out in their new character is an act of charity. Anything short of hanging or drowning is something to begin with. They do not enter into their amusements the less doggedly because they may plague others. They like a thing the better for hitting them a rap on the knuckles, for making their blood tingle. They do not dance or sing, but they make good cheer — "eat, drink, and are merry."

No people are fonder of field-sports, Christmas gambols, or practical jests. Blindman's buff, hunt-the-slipper, hot-cockles, and snap-dragon are all approved English games, full of laughable surprises and "hairbreadth 'scapes," and serve to amuse the winter fireside after the roast beef and plum pudding, the spiced ale and roasted crab, thrown (hissing-hot) into the foaming tankard. Punch (not the liquor, but the puppet) is not, I fear, of English origin; but there is no place, I take it, where he finds himself more at home or meets a more joyous welcome, where he collects greater crowds at the corners of streets, where he opens the eyes or distends the cheeks wider, or where the bangs and blows, the uncouth gestures, ridiculous anger and screaming voice of the chief performer excite more boundless merriment or louder bursts of laughter among all ranks and sorts of people. An English theatre is the very throne of pantomime; nor do I believe that the gallery and boxes of Drury-lane or Covent-garden filled on the proper occasion with holiday folks (big or little) yield the palm for undisguised, tumultuous, inextinguishable laughter to any spot in Europe. I do not speak of the refinement of the mirth (this is no fastidious speculation) but of its cordiality, on the return of these long looked-for and licensed periods; and I may add here, by way of illustration, that the English common people are a sort of grown children, spoiled and sulky perhaps, but full of glee and merriment, when their attention is drawn off by some sudden and striking object. The May-pole is almost gone out of fashion among us: but May-day, besides its flowering hawthorns and its pearly dews, has still its boasted exhibition of painted chimney-sweepers and their Jack-o'-the-Green, whose tawdry finery, bedizened faces, unwonted gestures, and short-liyed pleasures call forth good-humoured smiles and looks of sympathy in the spectators. There is no place where trap-ball, fives, prison-base, foot-ball, quoits, bowls are better understood or more successfully practiced; and the very names of a cricket bat and ball make English fingers tingle. What happy days must "Long Robinson" have passed in getting ready his wickets and mending his

bats, who when two of the fingers of his right hand were
struck off by the violence of a ball, had a screw fastened to it
to hold the bat, and with the other hand still sent the ball
thundering against the boards that bounded *Old Lord's
cricket ground!* What delightful hours must have been his
in looking forward to the matches that were to come, in re-
counting the feats he had performed in those that were past!
I have myself whiled away whole mornings in seeing him
strike the ball (like a countryman mowing with a scythe)
to the farthest extremity of the smooth, level, sun-burnt
ground, and with long, awkward strides count the notches
that made victory sure! Then again, cudgel-playing, quarter-
staff, bull and badger-baiting, cock-fighting are almost the
peculiar diversions of this island, and often objected to us
as barbarous and cruel; horse-racing is the delight and the
ruin of numbers; and the noble science of boxing is all our
own. Foreigners can scarcely understand how we can
squeeze pleasure out of this pastime; the luxury of hard
blows given or received; the joy of the ring; nor the perseverance of the combatants.[1] The English also excel, or are
not excelled in wiring a hare, in stalking a deer, in shooting,
fishing, and hunting. England to this day boasts her Robin
Hood and his merry men, that stout archer and outlaw, and
patron saint of the sporting calendar. What a cheerful

---

[1] "The gentle and free passage of arms at Ashby" was, we are told,
so called by the Chroniclers of the time, on account of the feats of
horsemanship and the quantity of knightly blood that was shed.
This last circumstance was perhaps necessary to qualify it with the
epithet of "gentle," in the opinion of some of these historians. I
think the reason why the English are the bravest nation on earth, is
that the thought of blood or a delight in cruelty is not the chief
excitement with them. Where it is, there is necessarily a *reaction;*
for though it may add to our eagerness and savage ferocity in in-
flicting wounds, it does not enable us to endure them with greater
patience. The English are led to the attack or sustain it equally well,
because they fight as they box, not out of malice, but to show *pluck*
and manhood. *Fair play and old England forever!* This is the only
bravery that will stand the test. There is the same determination
and spirit shown in resistance as in attack; but not the same pleasure
in getting a cut with a sabre as in giving one. There is, therefore,
always a certain degree of effeminacy mixed up with any approach

sound is that of the hunters, issuing from the autumnal wood
and sweeping over hill and dale!

> — " A cry more tuneable
> Was never halloo'd to by hound or horn."

What sparkling richness in the scarlet coats of the riders,
what a glittering confusion in the pack, what spirit in the
horses, what eagerness in the followers on foot, as they dis-
perse over the plain, or force their way over hedge and ditch!
Surely, the coloured prints and pictures of these, hung up in
gentlemen's halls and village alehouses, however humble as
works of art, have more life and health and spirit in them,
and mark the pith and nerve of the national character more
creditably than the mawkish, sentimental, affected designs
of Theseus and Pirithous, and Æneas and Dido, pasted on
foreign *salons à manger*, and the interior of country houses.
If our tastes are not epic, nor our pretensions lofty, they are
simple and our own; and we may possibly enjoy our native
rural sports, and the rude remembrances of them, with the
truer relish on this account, that they are suited to us and we
to them. The English nation, too, are naturally "brothers
of the angle." This pursuit implies just that mixture of
patience and pastime, of vacancy and thoughtfulness, of
idleness and business, of pleasure and of pain, which is suited
to the genius of an Englishman, and as I suspect, of no one
else in the same degree. He is eminently gifted to stand in
the situation assigned by Dr. Johnson to the angler, "at one
end of a rod with a worm at the other." I should suppose no

to cruelty, since both have their source in the same principle, viz. an
over-valuing of pain (a). This was the reason the French (having
the best cause and the best general in the world) ran away at Waterloo, because they were inflamed, furious, drunk with the blood of
their enemies, but when it came to their turn, wanting the same
stimulus, they were panic-struck, and their hearts and their senses
failed them all at once.

(a) Vanity is the same half-witted principle, compared with pride.
It leaves men in the lurch when it is most needed; is mortified at
being reduced to stand on the defensive, and relinquishes the field
to its more surly antagonist.

other language can show such a book as an often-mentioned one, Walton's *Complete Angler*, — so full of *naïveté*, of unaffected sprightliness, of busy trifling, of dainty songs, of refreshing brooks, of shady arbours, of happy thoughts and of the herb called *Heart's Ease!* Some persons can see neither the wit nor wisdom of this genuine volume, as if a book as well as a man might not have a personal character belonging to it, amiable, venerable from the spirit of joy and thorough goodness it manifests, independently of acute remarks or scientific discoveries; others object to the cruelty of Walton's theory and practice of trout-fishing — for my part, I should as soon charge an infant with cruelty for killing a fly, and I feel the same sort of pleasure in reading his book as I should have done in the company of this happy, childlike old man, watching his ruddy cheek, his laughing eye, the kindness of his heart, and the dexterity of his hand in seizing his finny prey! It must be confessed, there is often an odd sort of *materiality* in English sports and recreations. I have known several persons whose existence consisted wholly in manual exercises, and all whose enjoyments lay at their fingerends. Their greatest happiness was in cutting a stick, in mending a cabbage-net, in digging a hole in the ground, in hitting a mark, turning a lathe, or in something else of the same kind, at which they had a certain *knack*. Well is it when we can amuse ourselves with such trifles and without injury to others! This class of character, which the *Spectator* has immortalised in the person of Will Wimble, is still common among younger brothers and retired gentlemen of small incomes in town or country. The *cockney* character is of our English growth, as this intimates a feverish, fidgety delight in rural sights and sounds, and a longing wish, after the turmoil and confinement of a city-life, to transport one's-self to the freedom and breathing sweetness of a country retreat. London is half suburbs. The suburbs of Paris are a desert, and you see nothing but crazy windmills, stone walls, and a few straggling visitants in spots where in England you would find a thousand villas, a thousand terraces crowned with their own delights, or be stunned with the noise of

bowling-greens and tea-gardens, or stifled with the fumes of
tobacco mingling with fragrant shrubs, or the clouds of dust
raised by half the population of the metropolis panting and
toiling in search of a mouthful of fresh air.   The Parisian is,
perhaps, as well (or better) contented with himself wherever
he is, stewed in his shop or his garret;   the Londoner is miserable in these circumstances, and glad to escape from them.[1]
Let no one object to the gloomy appearance of a London
Sunday, compared with a Parisian one.   It is a part of our
politics and our religion;   we would not have James the
First's *Book of Sports* thrust down our throats;   and besides,
it is a part of our character to do one thing at a time, and not
to be dancing a jig and on our knees in the same breath.   It
is true the Englishman spends his Sunday evening at the alehouse —

> "And e'en on Sunday
> Drank with Kirton Jean till Monday". —

but he only unbends and waxes mellow by degrees, and sits
soaking till he can neither sit, stand, nor go;   it is his vice, and
a beastly one it is, but not a proof of any inherent distaste to
mirth or good-fellowship.   Neither can foreigners throw the
carnival in our teeth with any effect: those who have seen
it (at Florence, for example) will say that it is duller than
anything in England.   Our Bartholomew Fair is Queen Mab
herself to it!   What can be duller than a parcel of masks
moving about the streets and looking as grave and monotonous as possible from day to day, and with the same lifeless
formality in their limbs and gestures as in their features?
One might as well expect variety and spirit in a procession of
waxwork.   We must be hard run indeed, when we have re-
course to a pasteboard proxy to set off our mirth;   a mask may
be a very good cover for licentiousness (though of that I saw
no signs), but is a very bad exponent of wit and humour.   I
should suppose there is more drollery and unction in the

---

[1] The English are fond of change of scene;   the French of change
of posture;   the Italians like to sit still and do nothing.

caricatures in Gilray's shop-window, than in all the masks
in Italy, without exception.[1]

The humour of English writing and description has often
been wondered at; and it flows from the same source as the
merry *traits* of our character. A degree of barbarism and
rusticity seems necessary to the perfection of humour. The
droll and laughable depend on peculiarity and incongruity
of character. But with the progress of refinement, the peculiarities of individuals and of classes wear out or lose their
sharp, abrupt edges; nay, a certain slowness and dullness of
understanding is required to be struck with odd and unaccountable appearances, for which a greater facility of apprehension can sooner assign an explanation that breaks the
force of the seeming absurdity, and to which a wider scope of
imagination is more easily reconciled. Clowns and country
people are more amused, are more disposed to laugh and make
sport of the dress of strangers, because from their ignorance
the surprise is greater, and they cannot conceive anything to
be natural or proper to which they are unused. Without a
given portion of hardness and repulsiveness of feeling the
ludicrous cannot well exist. Wonder and curiosity, the
attributes of inexperience, enter greatly into its composition.
Now it appears to me that the English are (or were) just at
that mean point between intelligence and obtuseness, which
must produce the most abundant and happiest crop of
humour. Absurdity and singularity glide over the French
mind without jarring or jostling with it; or they evaporate
in levity; — with the Italians they are lost in indolence or
pleasure. The ludicrous takes hold of the English imagination, and clings to it with all its ramifications. We
resent any difference or peculiarity of appearance at first,
and yet, having not much malice at our hearts, we are glad to

[1] Bells are peculiar to England. They jingle them in Italy during
the carnival as boys do with us at Shrovetide; but they have no notion of ringing them. The sound of village bells never cheers you
in travelling, nor have you the lute or cittern in their stead. Yet
the expression of "Merry Bells" is a favourite, and not one of the
least appropriate in our language.

turn it into a jest — we are liable to be offended, and as
willing to be pleased — struck with oddity from not knowing
what to make of it, we wonder and burst out a-laughing at
the eccentricity of others, while we follow our own bent from
wilfulness or simplicity, and thus afford them, in our turn,
matter for the indulgence of the comic vein. It is possible
that a greater refinement of manners may give birth to finer
distinctions of satire and a nicer tact for the ridiculous; but
our insular situation and character are, I should say, most
likely to foster, as they have in fact fostered, the greatest
quantity of natural and striking humour, in spite of our
plodding tenaciousness, and want both of gaiety and quickness of perception. A set of raw recruits with their awkward
movements and unbending joints are laughable enough:
but they cease to be so, when they have once been drilled into
discipline and uniformity. So it is with nations that lose
their angular points and grotesque qualities with education
and intercourse: but it is in a mixed state of manners that
comic humour chiefly flourishes, for, in order that the drollery may not be lost, we must have spectators of the passing
scene who are able to appreciate and embody its most remarkable features, — wits as well as *butts* for ridicule. I
shall mention two names in this department which may
serve to redeem the national character from absolute dullness
and solemn pretence, — Fielding and Hogarth. These were
thorough specimens of true English humour; yet both were
grave men. In reality, too high a pitch of animal spirits
runs away with the imagination, instead of helping it to reach
the goal; is inclined to take the jest for granted when it
ought to work it out with patient and marked touches, and
it ends in vapid flippancy and impertinence. Among our
neighbours on the Continent, Moliere and Rabelais carried
the freedom of wit and humour to an almost incredible height;
but they rather belonged to the old French school, and even
approach and exceed the English license and extravagance of
conception. I do not consider Congreve's wit (though it
belongs to us) as coming under the article here spoken of; for
his genius is any thing but *merry*. Lord Byron was in the

habit of railing at the spirit of our good old comedy, and of abusing Shakspeare's clowns and fools, which he said the refinement of the French and Italian stage would not endure and which only our grossness and puerile taste could tolerate. In this I agree with him; and it is *pat* to my purpose. I flatter myself that we are almost the only people who understand and relish *nonsense*. We are not "merry and wise," but indulge our mirth to excess and folly. When we trifle, we trifle in good earnest; and having once relaxed our hold of the helm, drift idly down the stream, and delighted with the change, are tossed about "by every little breath" of whim or caprice,

"That under Heaven is blown.".

All we then want is to proclaim a truce with reason, and to be pleased with as little expense of thought or pretension to wisdom as possible. This licensed fooling is carried to its very utmost length in Shakespeare, and in some other of our elder dramatists, without, perhaps, sufficient warrant or the same excuse. Nothing can justify this extreme relaxation but extreme tension. Shakspeare's trifling does indeed tread upon the very borders of vacancy: his meaning often hangs by the very slenderest threads. For this he might be blamed if it did not take away our breath to follow his eagle flights, or if he did not at other times make the cordage of our hearts crack. After our heads ache with thinking, it is fair to play the fool. The clowns were as proper an appendage to the gravity of our antique literature, as fools and dwarfs were to the stately dignity of courts and noble houses in former days. Of all people, they have the best right to claim a total exemption from rules and rigid formality, who, when they have anything of importance to do, set about it with the greatest earnestness and perseverance, and are generally grave and sober to a proverb.[1] Poor Swift, who wrote more idle or *nonsense* verses than any man, was the severest of moralists; and his feelings and observations morbidly acute. Did not

[1] The strict formality of French serious writing is resorted to as a foil to the natural levity of their character.

Lord Byron himself follow up his *Childe Harold* with his *Don Juan?* — not that I insist on what he did as any illustration of the English character. He was one of the English Nobility, not one of the English People; and his occasional ease and familiarity were in my mind equally constrained and affected, whether in relation to the pretensions of his rank or the efforts of his genius.

They ask you in France, how you pass your time in England without amusements; and can with difficulty believe that there are theatres in London, still less that they are larger and handsomer than those in Paris. That we should have comic actors, "they own, surprises them." They judge of the English character in the lump as one great jolter-head, containing all the stupidity of the country, as the large ball at the top of the Dispensary in Warwick-lane, from its resemblance to a gilded pill, has been made to represent the whole pharmacopœia and professional quackery of the ˙kingdom. They have no more notion, for instance, how we should have such an actor as Liston on our stage, than if we were to tell them we have parts performed by a sea-otter; nor if they were to see him, would they be much the wiser, or know what to think of his unaccountable twitches of countenance or nondescript gestures, of his teeth chattering in his head, his eyes that seem dropping from their sockets, his nose that is tickled by a jest as by a feather, and shining with self-complacency as if oiled, his ignorant conceit, his gaping stupor, his lumpish vivacity in Lubin Log or Tony Lumpkin; for as our rivals do not wind up the machine to such a determined intensity of purpose, neither have they any idea of its running down to such degrees of imbecility and folly, or coming to an absolute *standstill* and lack of meaning, nor can they enter into or be amused with the contrast. No people ever laugh heartily who can give a reason for their doing so; and I believe the English in general are not yet in this predicament. They are not metaphysical, but very much in a state of nature; and this is one main ground why I give them credit for being merry, notwithstanding appearances. Their mirth is not the mirth of vice or desperation, but of innocence and a native wildness. They do not cavil or boggle at niceties, or merely come to the edge of a joke, but break their necks over it with a wanton "Here goes," where others make a *pirouette* and stand upon decorum. The French cannot, however, be persuaded of the excellence of our comic stage, nor of the store we set by it. When they ask what amusements we have, it is plain they can never have heard of Mrs. Jordan, nor King, nor Bannister, nor Suett, nor Munden, nor Lewis, nor little Simmons, nor Dode, and Parsons, and Emery, and Miss Pope, and Miss Farren, and all those who even in my time have gladdened a nation and "made life's business like a summer's dream." Can I think of them, and of their names that glittered in the playbills when I was young, exciting all the flutter of hope and expectation of seeing them in their favourite parts of Nell, or Little Pickle, or Touchstone, or Sir Peter Teazle, or Lenitive in *The Prize*, or Lingo, or Crabtree, or Nipperkin, or old Dornton, or Ranger, or the Copper Captain, or Lord Sands, or Filch, or Moses, or Sir Andrew Aguecheek, or Acres, or Elbow, or Hodge, or Flora, or the Duenna, or Lady Teazle, or Lady Grace, or of the gaiety that sparkled in all eyes, and the delight that overflowed all hearts, as they glanced before us in these parts,

"Throwing a gaudy shadow upon life," —

and not feel my heart yearn within me, or couple the thoughts of England and the spleen together? Our cloud has at least its rainbow tints: ours is not one long polar night of cold and dullness, but we have the gleaming lights of fancy to amuse us, the household fires of truth and genius to warm us. We can go to a play and see Liston; or stay at home and read *Roderick Random;* or have Hogarth's prints of *Marriage à la Mode* hanging round our room. "Tut! there's livers even in England," as well as "out of it." We are not quite the *forlorn hope* of humanity, the last of nations. The French look at us across the Channel, and seeing nothing but water and a cloudy mist, think that this is England.

——"What's our Britain
In the world's volume? In a great pool a swan's nest."

If they have any farther idea of us, it is of George III and our Jack tars, the House of Lords and House of Commons, and this is no great addition to us. To go beyond this, to talk of arts and elegances as having taken up their abode here, or to say that Mrs. Abington was equal to Mademoiselle Mars, and that we at one time got up the *School for Scandal*, as they do the *Misanthrope*, is to persuade them that Iceland is a pleasant summer retreat, or to recommend the whale fishery as a classical amusement. The French are the *cockneys* of Europe, and have no idea how anyone can exist out of Paris, or be alive without incessant grimace and *jabber*. Yet what imports it? What! though the joyous train I have just enumerated were, perhaps, never heard of in the precincts of the Palais-Royal, is it not enough that they gave pleasure where they were, to those who saw and heard them? Must our laugh, to be sincere, have its echo on the other side of the water? Had not the French their favourites and their enjoyments at the time, that we knew nothing of? Why then should we not have ours (and boast of them too) without their leave? A monopoly of self-conceit is not a monopoly of all other advantages. The English, when they go abroad, do not take away the prejudice against them by their looks. We seem duller and sadder than we are. As I write this, I am sitting in the open air in a beautiful valley near Vevey: Clarens is on my left, the Dent de Jamant is behind me, the rocks of Meillerie opposite: under my feet is a green bank, enamelled with white and purple flowers, in which a dewdrop here and there still glitters with pearly light —

"And gaudy butterflies flutter around."

Intent upon the scene and upon the thoughts that stir within me, I conjure up the cheerful passages of my life, and a crowd of happy images appear before me. No one would see it in my looks — my eyes grow dull and fixed, and I seem rooted to the spot, as all this phantasmagoria passes in review before me, glancing a reflex lustre on the face of the world and nature. But the traces of pleasure, in my case, sink into an absorbent ground of thoughtful melancholy, and require to be brought out by time and circumstances, or (as the critics tell you) by the *varnish* of style!

The *comfort*, on which the English lay so much stress, is of the same character, and arises from the same source as their mirth. Both exist by contrast and a sort of contradiction. The English are certainly the most uncomfortable of all people in themselves, and therefore it is that they stand in need of every kind of comfort and accommodation. The least thing puts them out of their way, and therefore everything must be in its place. They are mightily offended at disagreeable tastes and smells, and therefore they exact the utmost neatness and nicety. They are sensible of heat and cold, and therefore they cannot exist, unless everything is snug and warm, or else open and airy, where they are. They must have "all appliances and means to boot." They are afraid of interruption and intrusion, and therefore they shut themselves up in in-door enjoyments and by their own firesides. It is not that they require luxuries (for that implies a high degree of epicurean indulgence and gratification), but they cannot do without *their comforts;* that is, whatever tends to supply their physical wants, and ward off physical pain and annoyance. As they have not a fund of animal spirits and enjoyments in themselves, they cling to external objects for support, and derive solid satisfaction from the ideas of order, cleanliness, plenty, property, and domestic quiet, as they seek for diversion from odd accidents and grotesque surprises, and have the highest possible relish not of voluptuous softness, but of hard knocks and dry blows, as one means of ascertaining their personal identity.

ON DISAGREEABLE PEOPLE

THOSE people who are uncomfortable in themselves are disagreeable to others. I do not here mean to speak of persons who offend intentionally, or are obnoxious to dislike from some palpable defect of mind or body, ugliness, pride, ill-humour, etc., — but of those who are disagreeable in spite of themselves, and, as it might appear, with almost every qualification to recommend them to others. This want of success is owing chiefly to something in what is called their *manner;* and this again has its foundation in a certain cross-grained and unsociable state of feeling on their part, which influences us, perhaps, without our distinctly adverting to it. The mind is a finer instrument than we sometimes suppose it, and is not only swayed by overt acts and tangible proofs, but has an instinctive feeling of the air of truth. We find many individuals in whose company we pass our time, and have no particular fault to find with their understandings or character, and yet we are never thoroughly satisfied with them: the reason will turn out to be, upon examination, that they are never thoroughly satisfied with themselves, but uneasy and out of sorts all the time; and this makes us uneasy with them, without our reflecting on, or being able to discover the cause.

Thus, for instance, we meet with persons who do us a number of kindnesses, who show us every mark of respect and good will, who are friendly and serviceable, — and yet we do not feel grateful to them, after all. We reproach ourselves with this as caprice or insensibility, and try to get the better of it; but there is something in their way of doing things that prevents us from feeling cordial or sincerely obliged to them. We think them very worthy people, and would be glad of an opportunity to do them a good turn if it were in our power; but we cannot get beyond this; the utmost we can do is to save appearances, and not come to an open rupture with

them. The truth is, in all such cases, we do not sympathise
(as we ought) with them, because they do not sympathise
(as they ought) with us. They have done what they did from
a sense of duty, in a cold, dry manner, or from a meddlesome
busybody humour; or to shew their superiority over us, or to
patronise our infirmity; or they have dropped some hint by
the way, or blundered upon some topic they should not, and
have shown, by one means or other, that they were occupied
with anything but the pleasure they were affording us, or a
delicate attention to our feelings. Such persons may be
styled *friendly grievances*. They are commonly people of
low spirits and disappointed views, who see the discouraging
side of human life, and, with the best intentions in the world,
contrive to make everything they have to do with uncomfortable. They are alive to your distress, and take pains to
remove it; but they have no satisfaction in the gaiety and
ease they have communicated, and are on the *look-out* for
some new occasion of signalising their zeal; nor are they backward to insinuate that you will soon have need of their assistance, to guard you against running into fresh difficulties,
or to extricate you from them. From large benevolence of
soul and "discourse of reason, looking before and after,"
they are continually reminding you of something that has
gone wrong in time past, or that may do so in that which is
to come, and are surprised that their awkward hints, sly in-
nuendos, blunt questions, and solemn features do not excite
all the complacency and mutual good understanding in you
which it is intended that they should. When they make
themselves miserable on your account, it is hard that you will
not lend them your countenance and support. This de-
plorable humour of theirs does not hit anyone else. They
are useful, but not agreeable people; they may assist you in
your affairs, but they depress and tyrannise over your feelings.
When they have made you happy, they will not let you be so
— have no enjoyment of the good they have done — will on
no account part with their melancholy and desponding tone
— and, by their mawkish insensibility and doleful grimaces,
throw a damp over the triumph they are called upon to

celebrate. They would keep you in hot water, that they may
help you out of it. They will nurse you in a fit of sickness
(congenial sufferers!) — arbitrate a law-suit for you, and
embroil you deeper — procure you a loan of money; — but
all the while they are only delighted with rubbing the sore
place, and casting the colour of your mental or other disorders.
"The whole need not a physician;" and, being once placed
at ease and comfort, they have no farther use for you as
subjects for their singular beneficence, and you are not sorry
to be quit of their tiresome interference. The old proverb,
A friend in need is a friend indeed, is not verified in them.
The class of persons here spoken of are the very reverse of
summer-friends, who court you in prosperity, flatter your
vanity, are the humble servants of your follies, never see or
allude to anything wrong, minister to your gaiety, smooth
over every difficulty, and, with the slightest approach of misfortune or of anything unpleasant, take French leave: —

> " As when, in prime of June, a burnished fly,
> Sprung from the meads, o'er which he sweeps along,
> Cheered by the breathing bloom and vital sky,
> Tunes up amid these airy halls his song,
> Soothing at first the gay reposing throng;
> And oft he sips their bowl, or nearly drowned,
> He thence recovering drives their beds among,
> And scares their tender sleep with trump profound;
> Then out again he flies to wing his mazy round."
> Thomson's *Castle of Indolence.*

However we may despise such triflers, yet we regret them more
than those well-meaning friends on whom a dull melancholy
vapour hangs, that drags them and everyone about them to
the ground.

Again, there are those who might be very agreeable people,
if they had but spirit to be so; but there is a narrow, unaspir-
ing, under-bred tone in all they say or do. They have great
sense and information — abound in a knowledge of character
— have a fund of anecdote — are unexceptionable in manners and appearance — and yet we cannot make up our minds
to like them: we are not glad to see them, nor sorry when they
go away. Our familiarity with them, however great, wants the

principle of cement, which is a certain appearance of frank
cordiality and social enjoyment. They have no pleasure in
the subjects of their own thoughts, and therefore can communicate none to others. There is a dry, husky, grating
manner — a pettiness of detail — a tenaciousness of particulars, however trifling or unpleasant — a disposition to
cavil — an aversion to enlarged and liberal views of things —
in short, a hard, painful, unbending *matter-of-factness*, from
which the spirit and effect are banished, and the letter only is
attended to, which makes it impossible to sympathise with
their discourse. To make conversation interesting or agreeable, there is required either the habitual tone of good company, which gives a favourable colouring to every thing —
or the warmth and enthusiasm of genius, which, though
it may occasionally offend or be thrown off its guard, makes
amends by its rapturous flights, and flings a glancing light
upon all things. The literal and *dogged* style of conversation
resembles that of a French picture, or its mechanical fidelity
is like evidence given in a court of justice, or a police report.
From the literal to the plain-spoken, the transition is easy.
The most efficient weapon of offense is truth. Those who
deal in dry and repulsive matters-of-fact, tire out their friends;
those who blurt out hard and home truths, make themselves
mortal enemies wherever they come. There are your blunt,
honest creatures, who omit no opportunity of letting you know
their minds, and are sure to tell you all the ill, and conceal all
the good they hear of you. They would not flatter you for
the world, and to caution you against the malice of others,
they think the province of a friend. This is not candour, but
impudence; and yet they think it odd you are not charmed
with their unreserved communicativeness of disposition.
Gossips and tale-bearers, on the contrary, who supply the
tittle-tattle of the neighborhood, flatter you to your face, and
laugh at you behind your back, are welcome and agreeable
guests in all companies. Though you know it will be your
turn next, yet for the sake of the immediate gratification,
you are contented to pay your share of the public tax upon
character, and are better pleased with the falsehoods that

never reach your ears, than with the truths that others (less complaisant and more sincere) utter to your face — so short-sighted and willing to be imposed upon is our self-love! There is a man who has the air of not being convinced without an argument: you avoid him as if he were a lion in your path. There is another, who asks you fifty questions as to the commonest things you advance: you would sooner pardon a fellow who held a pistol to your breast and demanded your money. No one regards a turnpike-keeper, or a custom-house officer, with a friendly eye: he who stops you in an excursion of fancy, or ransacks the articles of your belief obstinately and churlishly, to distinguish the spurious from the genuine, is still more your foe. These inquisitors and cross-examiners upon system make ten enemies for every controversy in which they engage. The world dread nothing so much as being convinced of their errors. In doing them this piece of service, you make war equally on their prejudices, their interests, their pride, and indolence. You not only set up for a superiority of understanding over them, which they hate, but you deprive them of their ordinary grounds of action, their topics of discourse, of their confidence in themselves, and those to whom they have been accustomed to look up for instruction and advice. It is making children of them. You unhinge all their established opinions and trains of thought; and after leaving them in this listless, vacant, unsettled state — dissatisfied with their own notions and shocked at yours — you expect them to court and be delighted with your company, because, forsooth, you have only expressed your sincere and conscientious convictions. Mankind are not deceived by professions, unless they choose. They think that this pill of true doctrine, however it may be gilded over, is full of gall and bitterness to them; and, again, it is a maxim of which the vulgar are firmly persuaded, that plain-speaking (as it is called) is, nine parts in ten, spleen and self-opinion; and the other part, perhaps, honesty. Those who will not abate an inch in argument, and are always seeking to recover the wind of you, are, in the eye of the world, disagreeable, unconscionable people, who ought to be *sent to Coventry*, or left to wrangle by themselves. No persons, however, are more averse to contradiction than these same dogmatists. What shows our susceptibility on this point is, that there is no flattery so adroit or effectual as that of implicit assent. Anyone, however mean his capacity or ill-qualified to judge, who gives way to all our sentiments, and never seems to think but as we do, is indeed an *alter idem* — another self; and we admit him without scruple into our entire confidence, "yea, into our heart of hearts."

It is the same in books. Those which, under the disguise of plain-speaking, vent paradoxes, and set their faces against the common sense of mankind, are neither "the volumes

> ——"that enrich the shops,
> That pass with approbation through the land;"

nor, I fear, can it be added —

> "That bring their authors an immortal fame."

They excite a clamour and opposition at first, and are in general soon consigned to oblivion. Even if the opinions are in the end adopted, the authors gain little by it, and their names remain in their original obloquy; for the public will own no obligations to such ungracious benefactors. In like manner, there are many books written in a very delightful vein, though with little in them, and that are accordingly popular. Their principle is to please, and not to offend; and they succeed in both objects. We are contented with the deference shown to our feelings for the time, and grant a truce both to wit and wisdom. The "courteous reader" and the good-natured author are well matched in this instance, and find their account in mutual tenderness and forbearance to each other's infirmities. I am not sure that Walton's *Angler* is not a book of this last description —

> "That dallies with the innocence of thought,
> Like the old age."

Hobbes and Mandeville are in the opposite extreme, and have met with a correspondent fate. The *Tatler* and *Spectator* are in the golden mean, carry instruction as far as it can go without shocking, and give the most exquisite pleasure without one particle of pain. *"Desire to please, and you will infallibly please,"* is a maxim equally applicable to the study or the drawing-room. Thus also we see actors of very small pretensions, and who have scarce any other merit than that of being on good terms with themselves, and in high good humour with their parts (though they hardly understand a word of them), who are universal favourites with the audience. Others, who are masters of their art, and in whom no slip or flaw can be detected, you have no pleasure in seeing, from something dry, repulsive, and unconciliating in their manner; and you almost hate the very mention of their names, as an unavailing appeal to your candid decision in their favour, and as taxing you with injustice for refusing it.

We may observe persons who seem to take a peculiar delight in the *disagreeable*. They catch all sorts of uncouth tones and gestures, the manners and dialect of clowns and hoydens, and aim at vulgarity as desperately as others ape gentility. [This is what is often understood by a *love of low life*.] They say the most unwarrantable things, without meaning or feeling what they say. What startles or shocks other people is to them a sport — an amusing excitement — a fillip to their constitutions; and from the bluntness of their perceptions, and a certain wilfulness of spirit, not being able to enter into the refined and agreeable, they make a merit of despising everything of the kind. Masculine women, for example, are those who, not being distinguished by the charms and delicacy of the sex, affect a superiority over it by throwing aside all decorum. We also find another class, who continually do and say what they ought not, and what they do not intend, and who are governed almost entirely by an instinct of absurdity. Owing to a perversity of imagination or irritability of nerve, the idea that a thing is improper acts as a provocation to it: the fear of committing a blunder is so strong, that in their agitation they *bolt* out whatever is uppermost in their minds, before they are aware of the consequence. The dread of something wrong haunts and rivets their attention to it; and an uneasy, morbid apprehensiveness of temper takes away their self-possession, and hurries them into the very mistakes they are most anxious to avoid.

If we look about us, and ask who are the agreeable and disagreeable people in the world, we shall see that it does not depend on their virtues or vices — their understanding or stupidity — but as much on the degree of pleasure or pain they seem to feel in ordinary social intercourse. What signify all the good qualities anyone possesses, if he is none the better for them himself? If the cause is so delightful, the effect ought to be so too. We enjoy a friend's society only in proportion as he is satisfied with ours. Even wit, however it may startle, is only agreeable as it is sheathed in good-humour. There are a kind of *intellectual stammerers*, who are delivered of their good things with pain and effort; and consequently what costs them such evident uneasiness does not impart unmixed delight to the bystanders. There are those, on the contrary, whose sallies cost them nothing — who abound in a flow of pleasantry and good-humour; and who float down the stream with them carelessly and triumphantly,

"Wit at the helm, and Pleasure at the prow."

Perhaps it may be said of English wit in general, that it too much resembles pointed lead; after all, there is something heavy and dull in it! The race of small wits are not the least agreeable people in the world. They have their little joke to themselves, enjoy it, and do not set up any preposterous pretensions to thwart the current of our self-love. Toad-eating is accounted a thriving professior; and a *butt*, according to the *Spectator*, is a highly useful member of society — as one who takes whatever is said of him in good part, and as necessary to conduct off the spleen and superfluous petulance of the company. Opposed to these are the swaggering bullies — the licensed wits — the free-thinkers — the loud talkers, who, in the jockey phrase, have *lost their mouths*, and cannot be reined in by any regard to decency or common sense. The more obnoxious the subject, the more are they charmed with it, converting their want of feeling into a proof of superiority to vulgar prejudice and squeamish affectation.

But there is an unseemly exposure of the mind, as well as of the body. There are some objects that shock the sense, and cannot with propriety be mentioned: there are naked truths that offend the mind, and ought to be kept out of sight as much as possible. For human nature cannot bear to be too hardly pressed upon. One of these cynical truisms, when brought forward to the world, may be forgiven as a slip of the pen; a succession of them, denoting a deliberate purpose and *malice prepense*, must ruin any writer. Lord Byron had got into an irregular course of these a little before his death — seemed desirous, in imitation of Mr. Shelley, to run the gauntlet of public obloquy — and, at the same time, wishing to screen himself from the censure he defied, dedicated his *Cain* to Sir Walter Scott — a pretty godfather to such a bantling!

Some persons are of so teazing and fidgetty a turn of mind, that they do not give you a moment's rest. Everything goes wrong with them. They complain of a headache or the weather. They take up a book, and lay it down again — venture an opinion, and retract it before they have half done — offer to serve you, and prevent someone else from doing it. If you dine with them at a tavern, in order to be more at your ease, the fish is too little done — the sauce is not the right one; they ask for a sort of wine which they think is not to be had, or if it is, after some trouble, procured, do not touch it; they give the waiter fifty contradictory orders, and are restless and sit on thorns the whole of dinner-time. All this is owing to a want of robust health, and of a strong spirit of enjoyment; it is a fastidious habit of mind, produced by a valetudinary habit of body: they are out of sorts with every thing, and of course their ill-humour and captiousness communicates itself to you, who are as little delighted with them as they are with other things. Another sort of people, equally objectionable with this helpless class, who are disconcerted by a shower of rain or stopped by an insect's wing, are those who, in the opposite spirit, will have everything their own way, and carry all before them — who cannot brook the slightest shadow of opposition — who are always in the heat of an argument — who knit their brows and clench their teeth in some speculative discussion, as if they were engaged in a personal quarrel — and who, though successful over almost every competitor, seem still to resent the very offer of resistance to their supposed authority, and are as angry as if they had sustained some premeditated injury. There is an impatience of temper and an intolerance of opinion in this that conciliates neither our affection nor esteem. To such persons nothing appears of any moment but the indulgence of a domineering intellectual superiority to the disregard and discomfiture of their own and everybody else's comfort. Mounted on an abstract proposition, they trample on every courtesy and decency of behaviour; and though, perhaps, they do not intend the gross personalities they are guilty of, yet they cannot be acquitted of a want of due consideration for others, and of an intolerable egotism in the support of truth and justice. You may hear one of these Quixotic declaimers pleading the cause of humanity in a voice of thunder, or expatiating on the beauty of a Guido with features distorted with rage and scorn. This is not a very amiable or edifying spectacle.

There are persons who cannot make friends. Who are they? Those who cannot be friends. It is not the want of understanding or good nature, of entertaining or useful qualities, that you complain of: on the contrary, they have probably many points of attraction; but they have one that neutralises all these — they care nothing about you, and are neither the better nor worse for what you think of them. They manifest no joy at your approach; and when you leave them, it is with a feeling that they can do just as well without you. This is not sullenness, nor indifference, nor absence of mind; but they are intent solely on their own thoughts, and you are merely one of the subjects they exercise them upon. They live in society as in a solitude; and, however their brain works, their pulse beats neither faster nor slower for the common accidents of life. There is, therefore, something cold and repulsive in the air that is about them — like that of marble. In a word, they are *modern philosophers;* and the modern philosopher is what the pedant was of old — a being

200 PHILOSOPHY AND REFLECTION

who lives in a world of his own, and has no correspondence
with this. It is not that such persons have not done you
services — you acknowledge it; it is not that they have said
severe things of you — you submit to it as a necessary evil;
but it is the cool manner in which the whole is done that
annoys you — the speculating upon you, as if you were
nobody — the regarding you, with a view to an experiment
in corpore vili — the principle of dissection — the determination to spare no blemishes — to cut you down to your real
standard; — in short, the utter absence of the partiality of
friendship, the blind enthusiasm of affection, or the delicacy of
common decency, that whether they "hew you as a carcass
fit for hounds, or carve you as a dish fit for the gods," the
operation on your feelings and your sense of obligation is
just the same; and, whether they are demons or angels in
themselves, you wish them equally *at the devil!*

Other persons of worth and sense give way to mere violence
of temperament (with which the understanding has nothing to
do) — are burnt up with a perpetual fury — repel and throw
you to a distance by their restless, whirling motion — so that
you dare not go near them, or feel as uneasy in their company
as if you stood on the edge of a volcano. They have their
tempora mollia fandi; but then what a stir may you not expect
the next moment! Nothing is less inviting or less comfortable
than this state of uncertainty and apprehension. Then there
are those who never approach you without the most alarming
advice or information, telling you that you are in a dying
way, or that your affairs are on the point of ruin, by way of
disburthening their consciences; and others, who give you
to understand much the same thing as a good joke, out of
sheer impertinence, constitutional vivacity, and want of
something to say. All these, it must be confessed, are disagreeable people; and you repay their over-anxiety or total
forgetfulness of you, by a determination to cut them as
speedily as possible. We meet with instances of persons
who overpower you by a sort of boisterous mirth and rude
animal spirits, with whose ordinary state of excitement it is as
impossible to keep up as with that of anyone really intoxi-

cated; and with others who seem scarce alive — who take
no pleasure or interest in anything — who are born to ex-
emplify the maxim,

> "Not to admire is all the art I know
> To make men happy, or to keep them so," —

and whose mawkish insensibility or sullen scorn are equally
annoying. In general, all people brought up in remote country
places, where life is crude and harsh —all sectaries — all partisans of a losing cause, are discontented and disagreeable.
Commend me above all to the Westminster School of Reform,
whose blood runs as cold in their veins as the torpedo's, and
whose touch jars like it. Catholics are, upon the whole,
more amiable than Protestants — foreigners than English
people. Among ourselves, the Scotch, as a nation, are particularly disagreeable. They hate every appearance of comfort themselves, and refuse it to others. Their climate,
their religion, and their habits are equally averse to pleasure.
Their manners are either distinguished by a fawning sycoph-
ancy (to gain their own ends, and conceal their natural defects)
that makes one sick; or by a morose, unbending callousness,
that makes one shudder. I had forgot to mention two other
descriptions of persons who fall under the scope of this essay:
— those who take up a subject and run on with it intermin-
ably, without knowing whether their hearers care one word
about it, or in the least minding what reception their oratory
meets with — these are pretty generally voted *bores* (mostly
German ones); — and others, who may be designated as
practical paradox-mongers — who discard the "milk of human
kindness," and an attention to common observances, from all
their actions, as effeminate and puling — who wear a white hat
as a mark of superior understanding, and carry home a handkerchief full of mushrooms in the top of it as an original discovery — who give you crawfish for supper instead of lobsters;
seek their company in a garret, and over a gin-bottle, to
avoid the imputation of affecting genteel society; and discard
them after a term of years, and warn others against them,
as being *honest fellows*, which is thought a vulgar prejudice,

This is carrying the harsh and repulsive even beyond the disagreeable — to the hateful. Such persons are generally people of commonplace understandings, obtuse feelings, and inordinate vanity. They are formidable if they get you in their power — otherwise, they are only to be laughed at.

There are a vast number who are disagreeable from meanness of spirit, downright insolence, from slovenliness of dress or disgusting tricks, from folly or ignorance: but these causes are positive moral or physical defects, and I only meant to speak of that repulsiveness of manners which arises from want of tact and sympathy with others. So far of friendship; a word, if I durst, of love. Gallantry to women (the sure road to their favour) is nothing but the appearance of extreme devotion to all their wants and wishes — a delight in their satisfaction, and a confidence in yourself, as being able to contribute towards it. The slightest indifference with regard to them, or distrust of yourself, are equally fatal. The amiable is the voluptuous in looks, manner, or words. No face that exhibits this kind of expression — whether lively or serious, obvious or suppressed, will be thought ugly — no address, awkward — no lover who approaches every woman he meets as his mistress, will be unsuccessful. Diffidence and awkwardness are the two antidotes to love.

To please universally, we must be pleased with ourselves and others. There should be a tinge of the coxcomb, an oil of self-complacency, an anticipation of success — there should be no gloom, no moroseness, no shyness — in short, there should be very little of an Englishman, and a good deal of a Frenchman. But though, I believe, this is the receipt, we are none the nearer making use of it. It is impossible for those who are naturally disagreeable ever to become otherwise. This is some consolation, as it may save a world of useless pains and anxiety. *"Desire to please, and you will infallibly please,"* is a true maxim; but it does not follow that it is in the power of all to practice it. A vain man, who thinks he is endeavouring to please, is only endeavouring to shine, and is still farther from the mark. An irritable man, who puts a check upon himself, only grows dull, and loses spirit to be anything. Good temper and a happy spirit (which are the indispensable requisites) can no more be commanded than good health or good looks; and though the plain and sickly need not distort their features, and may abstain from excess, this is all they can do. The utmost a disagreeable person can do is to hope to be less disagreeable than with care and study he might become, and to pass unnoticed in society. With this negative character he should be contented, and may build his fame and happiness on other things.

I will conclude with a character of men who neither please nor aspire to please anybody, and who can come in nowhere so properly as at the fag-end of an essay: — I mean that class of discontented but amusing persons, who are infatuated with their own ill success, and reduced to despair by a lucky turn in their favour. While all goes well, they are *like fish out of water*. They have no reliance on or sympathy with their good fortune, and look upon it as a momentary delusion. Let a doubt be thrown on the question, and they begin to be full of lively apprehensions again; let all their hopes vanish, and they feel themselves on firm ground once more. From want of spirit or of habit, their imaginations cannot rise above the low ground of humility — cannot reflect the gay, flaunting tints of the fancy — flag and droop into despondency — and can neither indulge the expectation, nor employ the means of success. Even when it is within their reach, they dare not lay hands upon it; and shrink from unlooked-for bursts of prosperity, as something of which they are both ashamed and unworthy. The class of *croakers* here spoken of are less delighted at other people's misfortunes than their own. Their neighbours may have some pretensions — they have none. Querulous complaints and anticipations of pleasure are the food on which they live; and they at last acquire a passion for that which is the favourite theme of their thoughts, and can no more do without it than without the pinch of snuff with which they season their conversation, and enliven the pauses of their daily prognostics.

P

ON FAMILIAR STYLE~

IT is not easy to write a familiar style. Many people mistake a familiar for a vulgar style, and suppose that to write without affectation is to write at random. On the contrary, there is nothing that requires more precision, and, if I may so say, purity of expression, than the style I am speaking of. It utterly rejects not only all unmeaning pomp, but all low, cant phrases, and loose, unconnected, *slipshod* allusions. It is not to take the first word that offers, but the best word in common use; it is not to throw words together in any combinations we please, but to follow and avail ourselves of the true idiom of the language. To write a genuine familiar or truly English style, is to write as anyone would speak in common conversation, who had a thorough command and choice of words, or who could discourse with ease, force, and perspicuity, setting aside all pedantic and oratorical flourishes. Or to give another illustration, to write naturally is the same thing in regard to common conversation, as to read naturally is in regard to common speech. It does not follow that it is an easy thing to give the true accent and inflection to the words you utter, because you do not attempt to rise above the level of ordinary life and colloquial speaking. You do not assume indeed the solemnity of the pulpit, or the tone of stage-declamation: neither are you at liberty to gabble on at a venture, without emphasis or discretion, or to resort to vulgar dialect or clownish pronunciation. You must steer a middle course. You are tied down to a given and appropriate articulation, which is determined by the habitual associations between sense and sound, and which you can only hit by entering into the author's meaning, as you must find the proper words and style to express yourself by fixing your thoughts on the subject you have to write about. Anyone may mouth out a passage with a theatrical cadence, or get upon stilts to tell his thoughts: but to write or speak with propriety and simplicity is a more difficult task. Thus it is easy to affect a pompous style, to use a word twice as big as the thing you want to express: it is not so easy to pitch upon the very word that exactly fits it. Out of eight or ten words equally common, equally intelligible, with nearly equal pretensions, it is a matter of some nicety and discrimination to pick out the very one, the preferableness of which is scarcely perceptible, but decisive. The reason why I object to Dr. Johnson's style is, that there is no discrimination, no selection, no variety in it. He uses none but "tall, opaque words," taken from the "first row of the rubric:" — words with the greatest number of syllables, or Latin phrases with merely English terminations. If a fine style depended on this sort of arbitrary pretension, it would be fair to judge of an author's elegance by the measurement of his words, and the substitution of foreign circumlocutions (with no precise associations) for the mother-tongue.[1] How simple is it to be dignified without ease, to be pompous without meaning! Surely, it is but a mechanical rule for avoiding what is low to be always pedantic and affected. It is clear you cannot use a vulgar English word, if you never use a common English word at all. A fine tact is shown in adhering to those which are perfectly common, and yet never falling into any expressions which are debased by disgusting circumstances, or which owe their signification and point to technical or professional allusions. A truly natural or familiar style can never be quaint or vulgar, for this reason, that it is of universal force and applicability, and that quaintness and vulgarity arise out of the immediate connection of certain words with coarse and disagreeable, or with confined ideas. The last form what we understand by *cant* or *slang* phrases. To give an example of what is not very clear in the general statement. I should say that the

---

[1] I have heard of such a thing as an author who makes it a rule never to admit a monosyllable into his vapid verse. Yet the charm and sweetness of Marlowe's lines depended often on their being made up almost entirely of monosyllables.

phrase *To cut with a knife,* or *To cut a piece of wood,* is perfectly free from vulgarity, because it is perfectly common;
but to *cut an acquaintance* is not quite unexceptionable, because it is not perfectly common or intelligible, and has
hardly yet escaped out of the limits of slang phraseology.
I should hardly therefore use the word in this sense without
putting it in italics as a license of expression, to be received
cum grano salis. All provincial or bye-phrases come under
the same mark of reprobation — all such as the writer trans-
fers to the page from his fireside or a particular *coterie,* or
that he invents for his own sole use and convenience. I conceive that words are like money, not the worse for being common, but that it is the stamp of custom alone that gives them
circulation or value. I am fastidious in this respect, and
would almost as soon coin the currency of the realm as
counterfeit the King's English. I never invented or gave a
new and unauthorised meaning to any word but one single
one (the term *impersonal* applied to feelings) and that was in
an abstruse metaphysical discussion to express a very difficult
distinction. I have been (I know) loudly accused of revel-
ling in vulgarisms and broken English. I cannot speak to
that point: but so far I plead guilty to the determined use of
acknowledged idioms and common elliptical expressions. I
am not sure that the critics in question know the one from the
other, that is, can distinguish any medium between formal
pedantry and the most barbarous solecism. As an author, I
endeavour to employ plain words and popular modes of construction, as were I a chapman and dealer, I should common weights and measures.

The proper force of words lies not in the words themselves,
but in their application. A word may be a fine-sounding
word, of an unusual length, and very imposing from its learning and novelty, and yet in the connection in which it is introduced, may be quite pointless and irrelevant. It is not
pomp or pretension, but the adaptation of the expression to
the idea that clenches a writer's meaning: — as it is not the
size or glossiness of the materials, but their being fitted each
to its place, that gives strength to the arch; or as the pegs and

nails are as necessary to the support of the building as the larger timbers, and more so than the mere showy, unsubstantial ornaments. I hate anything that occupies more space than it is worth. I hate to see a load of band-boxes go along the street, and I hate to see a parcel of big words without anything in them. A person who does not deliberately dispose of all his thoughts alike in cumbrous draperies and flimsy disguises, may strike out twenty varieties of familiar everyday language, each coming somewhat nearer to the feeling he wants to convey, and at last not hit upon that particular and only one, which may be said to be identical with the exact impression in his mind. This would seem to show that Mr. Cobbett is hardly right in saying that the first word that occurs is always the best. It may be a very good one; and yet a better may present itself on reflection or from time to time. It should be suggested naturally, however, and spontaneously, from a fresh and lively conception of the subject. We seldom succeed by trying at improvement, or by merely substituting one word for another that we are not satisfied with, as we cannot recollect the name of a place or person by merely plaguing ourselves about it. We wander farther from the point by persisting in a wrong scent; but it starts up accidentally in the memory when we least expected it, by touching some link in the chain of previous association.

There are those who hoard up and make a cautious display of nothing but rich and rare phraseology; — ancient medals, obscure coins, and Spanish pieces of eight. They are very curious to inspect; but I myself would neither offer nor take them in the course of exchange. A sprinkling of archaisms is not amiss; but a tissue of obsolete expressions is more fit *for keep than wear*. I do not say I would not use any phrase that had been brought into fashion before the middle or the end of the last century; but I should be shy of using any that had not been employed by any approved author during the whole of that time. Words, like clothes, get old-fashioned, or mean and ridiculous, when they have been for some time laid aside. Mr. Lamb is the only imitator of old English style I can read with pleasure; and he is so thoroughly imbued with the spirit

of his authors, that the idea of imitation is almost done away.
There is an inward unction, a marrowy vein both in the
thought and feeling, an intuition, deep and lively, of his subject, that carries off any quaintness or awkwardness arising
from an antiquated style and dress. The matter is completely
his own, though the manner is assumed. Perhaps his ideas
are altogether so marked and individual, as to require their
point and pungency to be neutralised by the affectation of a
singular but traditional form of conveyance. Tricked out
in the prevailing costume, they would probably seem more
startling and out of the way. The old English authors,
Burton, Fuller, Coryate, Sir Thomas Browne, are a kind of
mediators between us and the more eccentric and whimsical
modern, reconciling us to his peculiarities. I do not however
know how far this is the case or not, till he condescends to
write like one of us. I must confess that what I like best of
his papers under the signature of Elia (still I do not presume,
amidst such excellence, to decide what is most excellent) is the
account of *Mrs. Battle's Opinions on Whist*, which is also the
most free from obsolete allusions and turns of expression —

"A well of native English undefiled."

To those acquainted with his admired prototypes, these
Essays of the ingenious and highly gifted author have the
same sort of charm and relish, that Erasmus's *Colloquies* or a
fine piece of modern Latin have to the classical scholar.
Certainly, I do not know any borrowed pencil that has more
power or felicity of execution than the one of which I have
here been speaking.

It is as easy to write a gaudy style without ideas, as it is to
spread a pallet of showy colours, or to smear in a flaunting
transparency. "What do you read?" — "Words, words,
words." — "What is the matter?" — "*Nothing*," it might
be answered. The florid style is the reverse of the familiar.
The last is employed as an unvarnished medium to convey
ideas; the first is resorted to as a spangled veil to conceal the
want of them. When there is nothing to be set down but
words, it costs little to have them fine. Look through the

dictionary, and cull out a *florilegium*, rival the *tulipomania*. *Rouge* high enough, and never mind the natural complexion. The vulgar, who are not in the secret, will admire the look of preternatural health and vigour; and the fashionable, who regard only appearances, will be delighted with the imposition. Keep to your sounding generalities, your tinkling phrases, and all will be well. Swell out an unmeaning truism to a perfect tympany of style. A thought, a distinction is the rock on which all this brittle cargo of verbiage splits at once. Such writers have merely *verbal* imaginations, that retain nothing but words. Or their puny thoughts have dragon-wings, all green and gold. They soar far above the vulgar failing of the *sermo humi obrepens* — their most ordinary speech is never short of an hyperbole, splendid, imposing, vague, incomprehensible, magniloquent, a cento of sounding commonplaces. If some of us, whose "ambition is more lowly," pry a little too narrowly into nooks and corners to pick up a number of "unconsidered trifles," they never once direct their eyes or lift their hands to seize on any but the most gorgeous, tarnished, threadbare patchwork set of phrases, the left-off finery of poetic extravagance, transmitted down through successive generations of barren pretenders. If they criticise actors and actresses, a huddled phantasmagoria of feathers, spangles, floods of light, and oceans of sound float before their morbid sense, which they paint in the style of Ancient Pistol. Not a glimpse can you get of the merits or defects of the performers: they are hidden in a profusion of barbarous epithets and wilful rhodomontade. Our hypercritics are not thinking of these little *fantoccini* beings —

"That strut and fret their hour upon the stage"—

but of tall phantoms of words, abstractions, *genera* and *species*, sweeping clauses, periods that unite the Poles, forced alliterations, astounding antitheses —

"And on their pens *Fustian* sits plumed."

If they describe kings and queens, it is an Eastern pageant. The Coronation at either House is nothing to it. We get at four repeated images — a curtain, a throne, a sceptre, and a foot-stool. These are with them the wardrobe of a lofty imagination; and they turn their servile strains to servile uses. Do we read a description of pictures? It is not a reflection of tones and hues which "nature's own sweet and cunning hand laid on," but piles of precious stones, rubies, pearls, emeralds, Golconda's mines, and all the blazonry of art. Such persons are in fact besotted with words, and their brains are turned with the glittering, but empty and sterile phantoms of things. Personifications, capital letters, seas of sunbeams, visions of glory, shining inscriptions, the figures of a transparency, Britannia with her shield, or Hope leaning on an anchor, make up their stock in trade. They may be considered as *hieroglyphical* writers. Images stand out in their minds isolated and important merely in themselves, without any ground-work of feeling — there is no context in their imaginations. Words affect them in the same way, by the mere sound, that is, by their possible, not by their actual application to the subject in hand. They are fascinated by first appearances, and have no sense of consequences. Nothing more is meant by them than meets the ear: they understand or feel nothing more than meets their eye. The web and texture of the universe, and of the heart of man, is a mystery to them: they have no faculty that strikes a chord in unison with it. They cannot get beyond the daubings of fancy, the varnish of sentiment. Objects are not linked to feelings, words to things, but images revolve in splendid mockery, words represent themselves in their strange rhapsodies. The categories of such a mind are pride and ignorance — pride in outside show, to which they sacrifice everything, and ignorance of the true worth and hidden structure both of words and things. With a sovereign contempt for what is familiar and natural, they are the slaves of vulgar affectation — of a routine of high-flown phrases. Scorning to imitate realities, they are unable to invent anything, to strike out one original idea. They are not copyists of nature, it is true: but they are the poorest of all plagiarists, the plagiarists of words. All is far-fetched, dear-bought, artificial, oriental in subject and allusion: all is mechanical, conventional, vapid, formal, pedantic in style and execution. They startle and confound the understanding of the reader, by the remoteness and obscurity of their illustrations: they soothe the ear by the monotony of the same everlasting round of circuitous metaphors. They are the *mock-school* in poetry and prose. They flounder about between fustian in expression, and bathos in sentiment. They tantalise the fancy, but never reach the head nor touch the heart. Their Temple of Fame is like a shadowy structure raised by Dullness to Vanity, or like Cowper's description of the Empress of Russia's palace of ice, as "worthless as in show 'twas glittering" —

"It smiled, and it was cold!"

ON THE PROSE–STYLE OF POETS

"Do you read or sing?   If you sing, you sing very ill."

I HAVE but an indifferent opinion of the prose-style of poets: not that it is not sometimes good, nay, excellent; but it is never the better, and generally the worse, from the habit of writing verse.   Poets are winged animals, and can cleave the air, like birds, with ease to themselves and delight to the beholders; but like those "feathered, two-legged things," when they light upon the ground of prose and matter-of-fact, they seem not to have the same use of their feet.

What is a little extraordinary, there is a want of *rhythmus* and cadence in what they write without the help of metrical rules.   Like persons who have been accustomed to sing to music, they are at a loss in the absence of the habitual accompaniment and guide to their judgment.   Their style halts, totters, is loose, disjointed, and without expressive pauses or rapid movements.   The measured cadence and regular *singsong* of rhyme or blank verse have destroyed, as it were, their natural ear for the mere characteristic harmony which ought to subsist between the sound and the sense.   I should almost guess the Author of *Waverley* to be a writer of ambling verses from the desultory vacillation and want of firmness in the march of his style.   There is neither *momentum* nor elasticity in it; I mean as to the *score*, or effect upon the ear.   He has improved since in his other works: to be sure, he has had practice enough.[1]   Poets either get into this incoherent, undermined, shuffling style, made up of "unpleasing flats and sharps," of unaccountable starts and pauses, of doubtful

---

[1] Is it not a collateral proof that Sir Walter Scott is the Author of *Waverley*, that ever since these novels began to appear, his Muse has been silent, till the publication of Halidon-Hill?

odds and ends, flirted about like straws in a gust of wind; or, to avoid it and steady themselves, mount into a sustained and measured prose (like the translation of Ossian's *Poems*, or some parts of Shaftesbury's *Characteristics*) which is more odious still, and as bad as being at sea in a calm. Dr. Johnson's style (particularly in his *Rambler*) is not free from the last objection. There is a tune in it, a mechanical recurrence of the same rise and fall in the clauses of his sentences, independent of any reference to the meaning of the text, or progress or inflection of the sense. There is the alternate roll of his cumbrous cargo of words; his periods complete their revolutions at certain stated intervals, let the matter be longer or shorter, rough or smooth, round or square, different or the same. This monotonous and balanced mode of composition may be compared to that species of portrait-painting which prevailed about a century ago, in which each face was cast in a regular and preconceived mould. The eyebrows were arched mathematically as if with a pair of compasses, and the distances between the nose and mouth, the forehead and chin, determined according to a "foregone conclusion," and the features of the identical individual were afterwards accommodated to them, how they could![1]

Horne Tooke used to maintain that no one could write a good prose style who was not accustomed to express himself *vivâ voce*, or to talk in company. He argued that this was the fault of Addison's prose, and that its smooth, equable uniformity, and want of sharpness and spirit, arose from his not having familiarised his ear to the sound of his own voice, or at least only among his friends and admirers, where there was but little collision, dramatic fluctuation, or sudden contrariety of opinion to provoke animated discussion, and give birth to different intonations and lively transitions of speech. His style (in this view of it) was not indented, nor did it project from the surface. There was no stress laid on one word more than another — it did not hurry on or stop short, or sink or swell with the occasion: it was throughout equally

[1] See the portraits of Kneller, Richardson, and others.

insipid, flowing, and harmonious, and had the effect of a studied recitation rather than of a natural discourse. This would not have happened (so the Member for Old Sarum contended) had Addison laid himself out to argue at his club, or to speak in public; for then his ear would have caught the necessary modulations of sound arising out of the feeling of the moment, and he would have transferred them unconsciously to paper. Much might be said on both sides of this question:[1] but Mr. Tooke was himself an unintentional confirmation of his own argument; for the tone of his written compositions is as flat and un aised as his manner of speaking was hard and dry. Of the poet it is said by some one, that

> "He murmurs by the running brooks
> A music sweeter than their own."

On the contrary, the celebrated person just alluded to might be said to grind the sentences between his teeth which he afterwards committed to paper, and threw out crusts to the critics, *bon-mots* to the Electors of Westminster (as we throw bones to the dogs) without altering a muscle, and without the smallest tremulousness of voice or eye![2] I certainly so far agree with the above theory as to conceive that no style is worth a farthing that is not calculated to be read out, or that is not allied to spirited conversation: but I at the same time think the process of modulation and inflection may be quite as complete, or more so, without the external enunciation; and that an author had better try the effect of his sentences on his stomach than on his ear. He may be deceived by the last, not by the first. No person, I imagine, can dictate a

[1] Goldsmith was not a talker, though he blurted out his good things now and then: yet his style is gay and voluble enough. Pope was also a silent man; and his prose is timid and constrained, and his verse inclining to the monotonous.

[2] As a singular example of steadiness of nerves, Mr. Tooke on one occasion had got upon the table at a public dinner to return thanks for his health having been drunk. He held a bumper of wine in his hand, but he was received with considerable opposition by one party, and at the end of the disturbance, which lasted for a quarter of an hour, he found the wine glass still full to the brim.

good style, or spout his own compositions with impunity. In the former case, he will flounder on before the sense or words are ready, sooner than suspend his voice in air; and in the latter, he can supply what intonation he pleases, without consulting his readers. Parliamentary speeches sometimes read well aloud; but we do not find, when such persons sit down to write, that the prose-style of public speakers and great orators is the best, most natural, or varied of all others. It has almost always either a professional twang, a mechanical rounding off, or else is stunted and unequal. Charles Fox was the most rapid and even *hurried* of speakers; but his written style halts and creeps slowly along the ground.[1] A speaker is necessarily kept within bounds in expressing certain things, or in pronouncing a certain number of words, by the limits of the breath or power of respiration: certain sounds are observed to join in harmoniously or happily with others: an emphatic phrase must not be placed where the power of utterance is enfeebled or exhausted, etc. All this must be attended to in writing (and will be so unconsciously by a practised hand), or there will be *hiatus in manuscriptis*. The words must be so arranged, in order to make an efficient readable style, as "to come trippingly off the tongue." Hence it seems that there is a natural measure of prose in the feeling of the subject and the power of expression in the voice, as there is an artificial one of verse in the number and

[1] I have been told, that when Sheridan was first introduced to Mr. Fox, what cemented an immediate intimacy between them was the following circumstance. Mr. Sheridan had been the night before to the House of Commons; and being asked what his impression was, said he had been principally struck with the difference of manner between Mr. Fox and Lord Stormont. The latter began by declaring in a slow, solemn, drawling, nasal tone that "when he considered the enormity and the unconstitutional tendency of the measures just proposed, he was hurried away in a torrent of passion and a whirlwind of impetuosity," pausing between every word and syllable; while the first said (speaking with the rapidity of lightning, and with breathless anxiety and impatience), that "such was the magnitude, such the importance, such the vital interest of this question, that he could not help imploring, he could not help adjuring the House to come to it with the utmost calmness, the utmost coolness, the utmost deliberation." This trait of discrimination instantly won Mr. Fox's heart.

co-ordination of the syllables; and I conceive that the trammels of the last do not (where they have been long worn) greatly assist the freedom or the exactness of the first.

Again, in poetry, from the restraints in many respects, a greater number of inversions, or a latitude in the transposition of words is allowed, which is not conformable to the strict laws of prose. Consequently, a poet will be at a loss, and flounder about for the common or (as we understand it) *natural* order of words in prose-composition. Dr. Johnson endeavoured to give an air of dignity and novelty to his diction by affecting the order of words usual in poetry. Milton's prose has not only this drawback, but it has also the disadvantage of being formed on a classic model. It is like a fine translation from the Latin; and indeed, he wrote originally in Latin. The frequency of epithets and ornaments, too, is a resource for which the poet finds it difficult to obtain an equivalent. A direct, or simple prose-style seems to him bald and flat; and instead of forcing an interest in the subject by severity of description and reasoning, he is repelled from it altogether by the absence of those obvious and meretricious allurements by which his senses and his imagination have been hitherto stimulated and dazzled. Thus there is often at the same time a want of splendour and a want of energy in what he writes, without the invocation of the Muse — *invita Minervâ.* It is like setting a rope-dancer to perform a tumbler's tricks — the hardness of the ground jars his nerves; or it is the same thing as a painter's attempting to carve a block of marble for the first time — the coldness chills him, the colourless uniformity distracts him, the precision of form demanded disheartens him. So in prose writing, the severity of composition required damps the enthusiasm, and cuts off the resources of the poet. He is looking for beauty when he should be seeking for truth; and aims at pleasure, which he can only communicate by increasing the sense of power in the reader. The poet spreads the colours of fancy, the illusions of his own mind, round every object, *ad libitum;* the prose-writer is compelled to extract his materials patiently, and bit by bit, from his subject. What he adds of ornament, what he borrows from the pencil, must be sparing, and judiciously inserted. The first pretends to nothing but the immediate indulgence of his feelings: the last has a remote practical purpose. The one strolls out into the adjoining fields or grooves to gather flowers: the other has a journey to go, sometimes through dirty roads, and at others through untrodden and difficult ways. It is this effeminacy, this immersion in sensual ideas, or craving after continual excitement, that spoils the poet for his prose-tasks. He cannot wait till the effect comes of itself, or arises out of the occasion: he must force it upon all occasions, or his spirit droops and flags under a supposed imputation of dullness. He can never drift with the current, but is always hoisting sail, and has his streamers flying. He has got a striking simile on hand; he *lugs* it in with the first opportunity, and with little connexion, and so defeats his object. He has a story to tell: he tells it in the first page, and where it would come in well, has nothing to say; like Goldsmith, who having to wait upon a Noble Lord, was so full of himself and of the figure he should make, that he addressed a set speech, which he had studied for the occasion, to his Lordship's butler, and had just ended as the nobleman made his appearance. The prose-ornaments of the poet are frequently beautiful in themselves, but do not assist the subject. They are pleasing excrescences — hindrances, not helps in an argument. The reason is, his embellishments in his own walk grow out of the subject by natural association; that is, beauty gives birth to kindred beauty, grandeur leads the mind on to greater grandeur. But in treating a common subject, the link is truth, force of illustration, weight of argument, not a graceful harmony in the immediate ideas; and hence the obvious and habitual clue which before guided him is gone, and he hangs on his patchwork, tinsel finery at random, in despair, without propriety, and without effect. The poetical prose-writer stops to describe an object, if he admires it, or thinks it will bear to be dwelt on: the genuine prose-writer only alludes to or characterises it in passing, and with reference to his subject. The prose-writer is master of his materials: the poet is the slave of his style. Everything showy, everything extraneous tempts him, and he reposes idly on it: he is bent on pleasure, not on business. He aims at effect, at captivating the reader, and yet is contented with commonplace ornaments, rather than none. Indeed, this last result must necessarily follow, where there is an ambition to shine, without the effort to dig for jewels in the mine of truth. The habits of a poet's mind are not those of industry or research: his images come to him, he does not go to them; and in prose-subjects, and dry matters-of-fact and close reasoning, the natural stimulus that at other times warms and rouses, deserts him altogether. He sees no unhallowed visions, he is inspired by no day-dreams. All is tame, literal, and barren, without the Nine. Nor does he collect his strength to strike fire from the flint by the sharpness of collision, by the eager-ness of his blows. He gathers roses, he steals colours from the rainbow. He lives on nectar and ambrosia. He "treads the primrose path of dalliance," or ascends "the highest heaven of invention," or falls flat to the ground. *He is nothing, if not fanciful!*

I shall proceed to explain these remarks, as well as I can, by a few instances in point.

It has always appeared to me that the most perfect prose-style, the most powerful, the most dazzling, the most daring, that which went the nearest to the verge of poetry, and yet never fell over, was Burke's. It has the solidity and sparkling effect of the diamond: all other *fine writing* is like French paste or Bristol-stones in the comparison. Burke's style is airy, flighty, adventurous, but it never loses sight of the subject; nay, is always in contact with, and derives its increased or varying impulse from it. It may be said to pass yawning gulfs "on the unsteadfast footing of a spear;" still it has an actual resting-place and tangible support under it — it is not suspended on nothing. It differs from poetry, as I conceive, like the chamois from the eagle; it climbs to an almost equal height, touches upon a cloud, overlooks a precipice, is picturesque, sublime — but all the while, instead of soaring through the air, it stands upon a rocky cliff, clambers up by abrupt and intricate ways, and browses on the roughest bark, or crops the tender flower. The principle which guides his pen is truth, not beauty — not pleasure, but power. He has no choice, no selection of subject to flatter the reader's idle taste, or assist his own fancy: he must take what comes, and make the most of it. He works the most striking effects out of the most unpromising materials, by the mere activity of his mind. He rises with the lofty, descends with the mean, luxuriates in beauty, gloats over deformity. It is all the same to him, so that he loses no particle of the exact, characteristic, extreme impression of the thing he writes about and that he communicates this to the reader, after exhausting every possible mode of illustration, plain or abstracted, figurative or literal. Whatever stamps the original image more distinctly on the mind is welcome. The nature of his task precludes continual beauty; but it does not preclude continual ingenuity, force, originality. He had to treat of political questions, mixed modes, abstract ideas, and his fancy (or poetry, if you will) was ingrafted on these artificially, and as it might sometimes be thought, violently, instead of growing naturally out of them, as it would spring of its own accord from individual objects and feelings. There is a resistance in the *matter* to the illustration applied to it — the concrete and abstract are hardly co-ordinate; and therefore it is that, when the first difficulty is overcome, they must agree more closely in the essential qualities, in order that the coincidence may be complete. Otherwise, it is good for nothing; and you justly charge the author's style with being loose, vague, flaccid, and imbecile. The poet has been said

> "To make us heirs
> Of truth and pure delight in endless lays."

Not so the prose-writer, who always mingles clay with his gold, and often separates truth from mere pleasure. He can only arrive at the last through the first. In poetry, one pleasing or striking image obviously suggests another: the increasing the sense of beauty or grandeur is the principle of composition: in prose, the professed object is to impart conviction, and nothing can be admitted by way of ornament or relief that does not add new force or clearness to the original conception. The two classes of ideas brought together by the orator or impassioned prose-writer, to wit, the general subject and the particular image, are so far incompatible, and the identity must be more strict, more marked, more determinate, to make them coalesce to any practical purpose. Every word should be a blow: every thought should instantly grapple with its fellow. There must be a weight, a precision, a conformity from association in the tropes and figures of animated prose to fit them to their place in the argument, and make them *tell*, which may be dispensed with in poetry, where there is something much more congenial between the subject-matter and the illustration —

"Like beauty making beautiful old rime!"

What can be more remote, for instance, and at the same time more apposite, more *the same*, than the following comparison of the English Constitution to "the proud Keep of Windsor," in the celebrated *Letter to a Noble Lord?*

"Such are *their* ideas; such *their* religion, and such *their* law. But as to *our* country and *our* race, as long as the well-compacted structure of our Church and State, the sanctuary, the holy of holies of that ancient law, defended by reverence, defended by power — a fortress at once and a temple [1] — shall stand inviolate on the brow of the British Zion; as long as the British Monarchy — not more limited than fenced by the orders of the State — shall, like the proud Keep of Windsor, rising in the majesty of proportion, and girt with the double belt of its kindred and coeval towers; as long as this awful structure shall oversee and guard the subjected land, so long the mounds and dykes of the low, fat, Bedford level will have nothing to fear from all the pickaxes of all the levellers of France. As long as our Sovereign Lord the King, and his faithful subjects, the Lords and Commons of this realm — the triple cord which no man can break; the solemn, sworn, constitutional frank-pledge of this nation; the firm guarantees of

[1] "Templum in modum arcis."
— Tacitus, *Of the Temple of Jerusalem.*

each other's being, and each other's rights; the joint and several securities, each in its place and order, for every kind, and every quality of property and of dignity — as long as these endure, so long the Duke of Bedford is safe: and we are all safe together — the high from the blights of envy and the spoliations of rapacity; the low from the iron hand of oppression and the insolent spurn of contempt. Amen! and so be it: and so it will be,

'Dum domus Æneæ Capitoli immobile saxum
Accolet; imperiumque pater Romanus habebit.'"

Nothing can well be more impracticable to a simile than the vague and complicated idea which is here embodied in one; yet how finely, how nobly it stands out, in natural grandeur, in royal state, with double barriers round it to answer for its identity, with "buttress, frieze, and coigne of 'vantage" for the imagination to "make its pendant bed and procreant cradle," till the idea is confounded with the object representing it — the wonder of a kingdom; and then how striking, how determined the descent, "at one fell swoop," to the "low, fat, Bedford level!" Poetry would have been bound to maintain a certain decorum, a regular balance between these two ideas; sterling prose throws aside all such idle respect to appearances, and with its pen, like a sword, "sharp and sweet," lays open the naked truth! The poet's Muse is like a mistress, whom we keep only while she is young and beautiful, *durante bene placito;* the Muse of prose is like a wife, whom we take during life, *for better for worse.* Burke's execution, like that of all good prose, savours of the texture of what he describes, and his pen slides or drags over the ground of his subject, like the painter's pencil. The most rigid fidelity and the most fanciful extravagance meet, and are reconciled in his pages. I never pass Windsor but I think of this passage in Burke, and hardly know to which I am indebted most for enriching my moral sense, that, or the fine picturesque stanza in Gray,

"From Windsor's heights the expanse below
Of mead, of lawn, of wood survey," etc.

I might mention that the so-much-admired description, in one of the India speeches, of Hyder Ally's army (I think it is) which "now hung like a cloud upon the mountain, and now burst upon the plain like a thunderbolt," would do equally well for poetry or prose. It is a bold and striking illustration of a naturally impressive object. This is not the case with the Abbe Sieyes's far-famed "pigeon-holes," nor with the comparison of the Duke of Bedford to "the Leviathan, tumbling about his unwieldy bulk in the ocean of royal bounty." Nothing here saves the description but the force of the invective; the startling truth, the vehemence, the remoteness, the aptitude, the perfect peculiarity and coincidence of the allusion. No writer would ever have thought of it but himself; no reader can ever forget it. What is there in common, one might say, between a Peer of the Realm, and "that sea-beast," of those

"Created hugest that swim the ocean-stream?"

Yet Burke has knit the two ideas together, and no man can put them asunder. No matter how slight and precarious the connection, the length of line it is necessary for the fancy to give out in keeping hold of the object on which it has fastened, he seems to have "put his hook in the nostrils" of this enormous creature of the crown, that empurples all its track through the glittering expanse of a profound and restless imagination!

In looking into the *Iris* of last week, I find the following passages, in an article on the death of Lord Castlereagh.

"The splendour of Majesty leaving the British metropolis, careering along the ocean, and landing in the capital of the North, is distinguished only by glimpses through the dense array of clouds in which Death hid himself, while he struck down to the dust the stateliest courtier near the throne, and the broken train of which pursues and crosses the Royal progress wherever its glories are presented to the eye of imagination. . . .

"The same indefatigable mind — a mind of all work — which thus ruled the Continent with a rod of iron, the sword

— within the walls of the House of Commons ruled a more distracted region with a more subtle and finely-tempered weapon, the tongue; and truly, if this *was* the only weapon his Lordship wielded there, where he had daily to encounter, and frequently almost alone, enemies more formidable than Buonaparte, it must be acknowledged that he achieved greater victories than Demosthenes or Cicero ever gained in far more easy fields of strife; nay, he wrought miracles of speech, outvying those miracles of song, which Orpheus is said to have performed, when not only men and brutes, but rocks, woods, and mountains, followed the sound of his voice and lyre. . . .

"But there was a worm at the root of the gourd that flourished over his head in the brightest sunshine of a court; both perished in a night, and in the morning, that which had been his glory and his shadow, covered him like a shroud; while the corpse, notwithstanding all his honours, and titles, and offices, lay uncovered in the place where it fell, till a judgment had been passed upon him — which the poorest peasant escapes when he dies in the ordinary course of nature." — *Sheffield Advertiser*, Aug. 20, 1822.

This, it must be confessed, is very unlike Burke: yet Mr. Montgomery is a very pleasing poet, and a strenuous politician. The whole is *travelling out of the record*, and to no sort of purpose. The author is constantly getting away from the impression of his subject, to envelop himself in a cloud of images, which weaken and perplex, instead of adding force and clearness to it. Provided he is figurative, he does not care how commonplace or irrelevant the figures are, and wanders on, delighted in a labyrinth of words, like a truant schoolboy, who is only glad to escape from his task. He has a very slight hold of his subject, and is tempted to let it go for any fallacious ornament of style. How obscure and circuitous is the allusion to "the clouds in which Death hid himself, to strike down the stateliest courtier near the throne!" How hackneyed is the reference to Demosthenes and Cicero, and how utterly quaint and unmeaning is the ringing the changes upon Orpheus and his train of men, beasts, woods,

rocks, and mountains in connection with Lord Castlereagh!
But he is better pleased with his classical fable than with
the death of the Noble Peer, and delights to dwell upon it, to
however little use. So he is glad to take advantage of the
scriptural idea of a gourd; not to enforce, but as a relief to his
reflections; and points his conclusion with a puling sort
of commonplace, that a person who dies a natural death, has
no coroner's inquest to sit upon him. All these are the
faults of the ordinary poetical style. Poets think they are
bound, by the tenour of their indenture to the Muses, to
."elevate and surprise" in every line; and not having the
usual resources at hand in common or abstracted subjects,
aspire to the end without the means. They make, or pretend,
an extraordinary interest where there is none. They are
ambitious, vain, and indolent — more busy in preparing idle
ornaments which they take their chance of bringing in somehow or other, than intent on eliciting truths by fair and honest
inquiry. It should seem as if they considered prose as a sort
of waiting-maid to poetry, that could only be expected to
wear her mistress's cast-off finery. Poets have been said to
succeed best in fiction; and the account here given may in
part explain the reason. That is to say, they must choose
their own subject, in such a manner as to afford them continual
opportunities of appealing to the senses and exciting the
fancy. Dry details, abstruse speculations, do not give scope
to vividness of description; and, as they cannot bear to be
considered dull, they become too often affected, extravagant,
and insipid.

I am indebted to Mr. Coleridge for the comparison of
poetic prose to the second-hand finery of a lady's maid (just
made use of). He himself is an instance of his own observation, and (what is even worse) of the opposite fault — an
affectation of quaintness and originality. With bits of
tarnished lace and worthless frippery, he assumes a sweeping
oriental costume, or borrows the stiff dresses of our ancestors,
or starts an eccentric fashion of his own. He is swelling
and turgid — everlastingly aiming to be greater than his subject; filling his fancy with fumes and vapours in the pangs and

throes of miraculous parturition and bringing forth only *still births*. He has an incessant craving, as it were, to exalt every idea into a metaphor, to expand every sentiment into a lengthened mystery, voluminous and vast, confused and cloudy. His style is not succinct, but incumbered with a train of words and images that have no practical, and only a possible relation to one another — that add to its stateliness, but impede its march. One of his sentences winds its "forlorn way obscure" over the page like a patriarchal procession with camels laden, wreathed turbans, household wealth, the whole riches of the author's mind poured out upon the barren wastes of his subject. The palm-tree spreads its sterile branches overhead, and the land of promise is seen in the distance. All this is owing to his wishing to overdo everything — to make something more out of everything than it is, or than it is worth. The simple truth does not satisfy him — no direct proposition fills up the moulds of his understanding. All is foreign, far-fetched, irrelevant, laboured, and unproductive. To read one of his disquisitions is like hearing the variation to a piece of music without the score. Or, to vary the simile, he is not like a man going a journey by the stage-coach along the high-road, but is always getting into a balloon, and mounting into the air, above the plain of prose. Whether he soars to the empyrean, or dives to the centre (as he sometimes does), it is equally to get away from the question before him, and to prove that he owes everything to his own mind. His object is to invent; he scorns to imitate. The business of prose is the contrary. But Mr. Coleridge is a poet, and his thoughts are free.

I think the poet-laureate is a much better prose writer. His style has an antique quaintness, with a modern familiarity. He has just a sufficient sprinkling of *archaisms*, of allusions to old Fuller, and Burton, and Latimer, to set off or qualify the smart flippant tone of his apologies for existing abuses, or the ready, galling virulence of his personal invectives. Mr. Southey is a faithful historian, and no inefficient partisan. In the former character, his mind is tenacious of facts; and in the latter, his spleen and jealousy prevent the "extravagant and erring spirit" of the poet from losing itself in Fancy's endless maze. He "stoops to earth," at least, and prostitutes his pen to some purpose (not at the same time losing his own soul, and gaining nothing by it) — and he vilifies Reform, and praises the reign of George III in good set terms, in a straightforward, intelligible, practical, pointed way. He is not buoyed up by conscious power out of the reach of common apprehensions, but makes the most of the obvious advantages he possesses. You may complain of a pettiness and petulance of manner, but certainly there is no want of spirit or facility of execution. He does not waste powder and shoot in the air, but loads his piece, takes a level aim, and hits his mark. One would say (though his Muse is ambidexter) that he wrote prose with his right hand; there is nothing awkward, circuitous, or feeble in it. "The words of Mercury are harsh after the songs of Apollo:" but this would not apply to him. His prose-lucubrations are pleasanter reading than his poetry. Indeed, he is equally practised and voluminous in both; and it is no improbable conjecture, that Mr. Southey may have had some idea of rivalling the reputation of Voltaire in the extent, the spirit, and the versatility of his productions in prose and verse, except that he has written no tragedies but *Wat Tyler!*

To my taste, the Author of *Rimini*, and Editor of the *Examiner*, is among the best and least corrupted of our poetical prose-writers. In his light but well-supported columns we find the raciness, the sharpness, and sparkling effect of poetry, with little that is extravagant or far-fetched, and no turgidity or pompous pretension. Perhaps there is too much the appearance of relaxation and trifling (as if he had escaped the shackles of rhyme), a caprice, a levity, and a disposition to innovate in words and ideas. Still the genuine master-spirit of the prose-writer is there; the tone of lively, sensible conversation; and this may in part arise from the author's being himself an animated talker. Mr. Hunt wants something of the heat and earnestness of the political partisan; but his familiar and miscellaneous papers have all the ease, grace, and point of the best style of essay-writing. Many of his effusions in the *Indicator* show, that if he had devoted himself exclusively to that mode of writing, he inherits more of the spirit of Steele than any man since his time.

Lord Byron's prose is bad; that is to say, heavy, laboured, and coarse: he tries to knock someone down with the butt-end of every line, which defeats his object — and the style of the Author of *Waverley* (if he comes fairly into this discussion) as mere style is villainous. It is pretty plain he is a poet; for the sound of names runs mechanically in his ears, and he rings the changes unconsciously on the same words in a sentence, like the same rhymes in a couplet.

Not to spin out this discussion too much, I would conclude by observing, that some of the old English prose-writers (who were not poets) are the best, and, at the same time, the most *poetical* in the favourable sense. Among these we may reckon some of the old divines, and Jeremy Taylor at the head of them. There is a flush like the dawn over his writings; the sweetness of the rose, the freshness of the morning dew. There is a softness in his style, proceeding from the tenderness of his heart: but his head is firm, and his hand is free. His materials are as finely wrought up as they are original and attractive in themselves. Milton's prose-style savours too much of poetry, and, as I have already hinted, of an imitation of the Latin. Dryden's is perfectly unexceptionable, and a model, in simplicity, strength, and perspicuity, for the subjects he treated of.

ON A LANDSCAPE OF NICOLAS POUSSIN

"And blind Orion hungry for the morn."

ORION, the subject of this landscape, was the classical Nimrod; and is called by Homer, "a hunter of shadows, himself a shade." He was the son of Neptune; and having lost an eye in some affray between the gods and men, was told that if he would go to meet the rising sun, he would recover his sight. He is represented setting out on his journey, with men on his shoulders to guide him, a bow in his hand, and Diana in the clouds greeting him. He stalks along, a giant upon earth, and reels and falters in his gait, as if just awaked out of sleep, or uncertain of his way; — you see his blindness, though his back is turned. Mists rise around him, and veil the sides of the green forests; earth is dank and fresh with dews, the "grey dawn and the Pleiades before him dance," and in the distance are seen the blue hills and sullen ocean. Nothing was ever more finely conceived or done. It breathes the spirit of the morning; its moisture, its repose, its obscurity, waiting the miracle of light to kindle it into smiles: the whole is, like the principal figure in it, "a forerunner of the dawn." The same atmosphere tinges and imbues every object, the same dull light "shadowy sets off" the face of nature: one feeling of vastness, of strangeness, and of primeval forms pervades the painter's canvas, and we are thrown back upon the first integrity of things. This great and learned man might be said to see nature through the glass of time: he alone has a right to be considered as the painter of classical antiquity. Sir Joshua has done him justice in this respect. He could give to the scenery of his heroic fables that unimpaired look of original nature, full, solid, large, luxuriant, teeming with life and power; or deck it with all the pomp of art, with temples and towers, and mythologic groves. His pictures

"denote a foregone conclusion." He applies nature to his
purposes, works out her images according to the standard
of his thoughts, embodies high fictions; and the first conception being given, all the rest seems to grow out of, and be
assimilated to it, by the unfailing process of a studious imagination. Like his own Orion, he overlooks the surrounding
scene, appears to "take up the isles as a very little thing, and
to lay the earth in a balance." With a laborious and mighty
grasp, he put nature into the mould of the ideal and antique;
and was among painters (more than any one else) what Milton
was among poets. There is both something of the same
pedantry, the same stiffness, the same elevation, the same
grandeur, the same mixture of art and nature, the same
richness of borrowed materials, the same unity of character.
Neither the poet nor the painter lowered the subjects they
treated, but filled up the outline in the fancy, and added
strength and reality to it; and thus not only satisfied, but
surpassed the expectations of the spectator and the reader.
This is held for the triumph and the perfection of works of
art. To give us nature, such as we see it, is well and deserving
of praise; to give us nature, such as we have never seen, but
have often wished to see it, is better, and deserving of higher
praise. He who can show the world in its first naked glory,
with the hues of fancy spread over it, or in its high and palmy
state, with the gravity of history stamped on the proud monuments of vanished empire, — who, by his "so potent art,"
can recall time past, transport us to distant places, and join
the regions of imagination (a new conquest) to those of
reality, — who shows us not only what nature is, but what
she has been, and is capable of, — he who does this, and does
it with simplicity, with truth, and grandeur, is lord of nature
and her powers; and his mind is universal, and his art the
master-art!

There is nothing in this "more than natural," if criticism
could be persuaded to think so. The historic painter does not
neglect or contravene nature, but follows her more closely
up into her fantastic heights, or hidden recesses. He demon-
strates what she would be in conceivable circumstances, and

under implied conditions. He "gives to airy nothing a local
habitation," not "a name." At his touch, words start up
into images, thoughts become things. He clothes a dream, a
phantom with form and colour and the wholesome attributes
of reality. *His* art is a second nature; not a different one.
There are those, indeed, who think that not to copy nature
is the rule for attaining perfection. Because they cannot
paint the objects which they have seen, they fancy themselves
qualified to paint the ideas which they have not seen. But
it is possible to fail in this latter and more difficult style of
imitation, as well as in the former humbler one. The de-
tection, it is true, is not so easy, because the objects are not
so nigh at hand to compare, and therefore there is more room
both for false pretension and for self-deceit. They take an
epic motto or subject, and conclude that the spirit is implied as
a thing of course. They paint inferior portraits, maudlin,
lifeless faces, without ordinary expression, or one look, feature,
or particle of nature in them, and think that this is to rise to
the truth of history. They vulgarise and degrade whatever
is interesting or sacred to the mind, and suppose that they
thus add to the dignity of their profession. They represent
a face that seems as if no thought or feeling of any kind had
ever passed through it, and would have you believe that this
is the very sublime of expression, such as it would appear in
heroes, or demi-gods of old, when rapture or agony was raised
to its height. They show you a landscape that looks as if the
sun never shone upon it, and tell you that it is not modern
— that so earth looked when Titan first kissed it with his
rays. This is not the true *ideal*. It is not to fill the moulds
of the imagination, but to deface and injure them: it is not
to come up to, but to fall short of the poorest conception in
the public mind. Such pictures should not be hung in the
same room with that of Orion.[1]

[1] Everything tends to show the manner in which a great artist is
formed. If any person could claim an exemption from the careful
imitation of individual objects, it was Nicolas Poussin. He studied
the antique, but he also studied nature. "I have often admired,"
says Vignuel de Marville, who knew him at a late period of his life,
"the love he had for his art. Old as he was, I frequently saw him

Poussin was, of all painters, the most poetical. He was the painter of ideas. No one ever told a story half so well, nor so well knew what was capable of being told by the pencil. He seized on, and struck off with grace and precision, just that point of view which would be likely to catch the reader's fancy. There is a significance, a consciousness in whatever he does (sometimes a vice, but oftener a virtue) beyond any other painter. His Giants sitting on the tops of craggy mountains, as huge themselves, and playing idly on their Pan's-pipes, seem to have been seated there these three thousand years, and to know the beginning and the end of their own story. An infant Bacchus or Jupiter is big with his future destiny. Even inanimate and dumb things speak a language of their own. His snakes, the messengers of fate, are inspired with human intellect. His trees grow and expand their leaves in the air, glad of the rain, proud of the sun, awake to the winds of heaven. In his Plague of Athens, the very buildings seem stiff with horror. His picture of the Deluge is, perhaps, the finest historical landscape in the world. You see a waste of waters, wide, interminable: the sun is labouring, wan and weary, up the sky; the clouds, dull and leaden, lie like a load upon the eye, and heaven and earth

among the ruins of ancient Rome, out in the Campagna, or along the banks of the Tiber, sketching a scene that had pleased him; and I often met him with his handkerchief full of stones, moss, or flowers, which he carried home, that he might copy them exactly from nature. One day I asked him how he had attained to such a degree of perfection, as to have gained so high a rank among the great painters of Italy? He answered, *I have neglected nothing.*" — *See his Life lately published.* It appears from this account that he had not fallen into a recent error, that Nature puts the man of genius out. As a contrast to the foregoing description, I might mention, that I remember an old gentleman once asking Mr. West in the British Gallery, if he had ever been at Athens? To which the President made answer, No; nor did he feel any great desire to go; for that he thought he had as good an idea of the place from the catalogue, as he could get by living there for any number of years. What would he have said, if any one had told him, he could get as good an idea of the subject of one of his great works from reading the catalogue of it, as from seeing the picture itself! Yet the answer was characteristic of the genius of the painter.

seem commingling into one confused mass! His human figures
are sometimes "o'er-informed" with this kind of feeling.
Their actions have too much gesticulation, and the set expression of the features borders too much on the mechanical
and caricatured style. In this respect, they form a contrast
to Raphael's, whose figures never appear to be sitting for
their pictures, or to be conscious of a spectator, or to have
come from the painter's hand. In Nicolas Poussin, on the
contrary, everything seems to have a distinct understanding
with the artist; "the very stones prate of their whereabout:"
each object has its part and place assigned, and is in a sort of
compact with the rest of the picture. It is this conscious
keeping, and, as it were, *internal* design, that gives their
peculiar character to the works of this artist. There was a
picture of Aurora in the British Gallery a year or two ago. It
was a suffusion of golden light. The Goddess wore her saf-
fron-coloured robes, and appeared just risen from the gloomy
bed of old Tithonus. Her very steeds, milk-white, were
tinged with the yellow dawn. It was a personification of the
morning. — Poussin succeeded better in classic than in sacred
subjects. The latter are comparatively heavy, forced, full of
violent contrasts of colour, of red, blue, and black, and without
the true prophetic inspiration of the characters. But in his
Pagan allegories and fables he was quite at home. The
native gravity and native levity of the Frenchman were com-
bined with Italian scenery and an antique gusto, and gave
even to his colouring an air of learned indifference. He wants,
in one respect, grace, form, expression; but he has everywhere
sense and meaning, perfect costume and propriety. His
personages always belong to the class and time represented,
and are strictly versed in the business in hand. His grotesque
compositions in particular, his Nymphs and Fauns, are superior (at least, as far as style is concerned) even to those of
Rubens. They are taken more immediately out of fabulous
history. Rubens's Satyrs and Bacchantes have a more
jovial and voluptuous aspect, are more drunk with pleasure,
more full of animal spirits and riotous impulses; they laugh
and bound along —

" Leaping like wanton kids in pleasant spring:"

but those of Poussin have more of the intellectual part of the character, and seem vicious on reflection, and of set purpose. Rubens's are noble specimens of a class; Poussin's are allegorical abstractions of the same class, with bodies less pampered, but with minds more secretly depraved. The Bacchanalian groups of the Flemish painter were, however, his masterpieces in composition. Witness those prodigies of colour, character, and expression at Blenheim. In the more chaste and refined delineation of classic fable, Poussin was without a rival. Rubens, who was a match for him in the wild and picturesque, could not pretend to vie with the elegance and purity of thought in his picture of Apollo giving a poet a cup of water to drink, nor with the gracefulness of design in the figure of a nymph squeezing the juice of a bunch of grapes from her fingers (a rosy wine-press) which falls into the mouth of a chubby infant below. But, above all, who shall celebrate, in terms of fit praise, his picture of the shepherds in the Vale of Tempe going out in a fine morning of the spring, and coming to a tomb with this inscription: — ET EGO IN ARCADIA VIXI! The eager curiosity of some, the expression of others who start back with fear and surprise, the clear breeze playing with the branches of the shadowing trees, "the valleys low, where the mild zephyrs use," the distant, uninterrupted, sunny prospects speak (and forever will speak on) of ages past to ages yet to come![1]

Pictures are a set of chosen images, a stream of pleasant thoughts passing through the mind. It is a luxury to have the walls of our rooms hung round with them, and no less so to have such a gallery in the mind, to con over the relics of ancient art bound up "within the book and volume of the brain, unmixed (if it were possible) with baser matter!" A life passed among pictures, in the study and the love of art, is a

[1] Poussin has repeated this subject more than once, and appears to have revelled in its witcheries. I have before alluded to it, and may again. It is hard that we should not be allowed to dwell as often as we please on what delights us, when things that are disagreeable recur so often against our will.

happy, noiseless dream: or rather, it is to dream and to be
awake at the same time; for it has all "the sober certainty of
waking bliss," with the romantic voluptuousness of a visionary and abstracted being. They are the bright consummate
essences of things, and "he who knows of these delights to
taste and interpose them oft, is not unwise!" — The Orion,
which I have here taken occasion to descant upon, is one of a
collection of excellent pictures, as this collection is itself one
of a series from the old masters, which have for some years
back embrowned the walls of the British Gallery, and enriched
the public eye. What hues (those of nature mellowed by
time) breathe around, as we enter! What forms are there,
woven into the memory! What looks, which only the answering looks of the spectator can express! What intellectual stores have been yearly poured forth from the shrine
of ancient art! The works are various, but the names the
same — heaps of Rembrandts frowning from the darkened
walls, Rubens's glad, gorgeous groups, Titians more rich and
rare, Claudes always exquisite, sometimes beyond compare,
Guido's endless cloying sweetness, the learning of Poussin
and the Caracci, and Raphael's princely magnificence,
crowning all. We read certain letters and syllables in the
catalogue, and at the well-known magic sound, a miracle of
skill and beauty starts to view. One might think that one
year's prodigal display of such perfection would exhaust the
labours of one man's life; but the next year, and the next to
that, we find another harvest reaped and gathered in to the
great garner of art, by the same immortal hands —

> " Old Genius the porter of them was;
> He letteth in,. he letteth out to wend." —

Their works seem endless as their reputation — to be many
as they are complete — to multiply with the desire of the
mind to see more and more of them; as if there were a living
power in the breath of Fame, and in the very names of the
great heirs of glory "there were propagation too!" It is
something to have a collection of this sort to count upon once
a year; to have. one last, lingering look yet to come. Pic-

tures are scattered like stray gifts through the world; and
while they remain, earth has yet a little gilding left, not quite
rubbed off, dishonoured, and defaced. There are plenty of
standard works still to be found in this country, in the collections at Blenheim, at Burleigh, and in those belonging to
Mr. Angerstein, Lord Grosvenor, the Marquis of Stafford,
and others, to keep up this treat to the lovers of art for many
years: and it is the more desirable to reserve a privileged
sanctuary of this sort, where the eye may dote, and the
heart take its fill of such pictures as Poussin's Orion, since the
Louvre is stripped of its triumphant spoils, and since he who
collected it, and wore it as a rich jewel in his Iron Crown, the
hunter of greatness and of glory, is himself a shade!

MR. COLERIDGE

THE present is an age of talkers, and not of doers; and the reason is, that the world is growing old. We are so far advanced in the Arts and Sciences, that we live in retrospect, and doat on past achievements. The accumulation of knowledge has been so great, that we are lost in wonder at the height it has reached, instead of attempting to climb or add to it; while the variety of objects distracts and dazzles the looker-on. What *niche* remains unoccupied? What path untried? What is the use of doing anything, unless we could do better than all those who have gone before us? What hope is there of this? We are like those who have been to see some noble monument of art, who are content to admire without thinking of rivalling it; or like the guests after a feast, who praise the hospitality of the donor "and thank the bounteous Pan" — perhaps carrying away some trifling fragments; or like the spectators of a mighty battle, who still hear its sound afar off, and the clashing of armour and the neighing of the war-horse and the shout of victory is in their ears, like the rushing of innumerable waters!

Mr. Coleridge has "a mind reflecting ages past;" his voice is like the echo of the congregated roar of the "dark rearward and abyss" of thought. He who has seen a mouldering tower by the side of a crystal lake, hid by the mist, but glittering in the wave below, may conceive the dim, gleaming, uncertain intelligence of his eye; he who has marked the evening clouds uprolled (a world of vapours) has seen the picture of his mind, unearthly, unsubstantial, with gorgeous tints and ever-varying forms —

> "That which was now a horse, even with a thought
> The rack dislimns, and makes it indistinct
> As water is in water."

Our author's mind is (as he himself might express it) *tangential*. There is no subject on which he has not touched, none on which he has rested. With an understanding fertile, subtle, expansive, "quick, forgetive, apprehensive," beyond all living precedent, few traces of it perhaps remain. He lends himself to all impressions alike; he gives up his mind and liberty of thought to none. He is a general lover of art and science, and wedded to no one in particular. He pursues knowledge as a mistress, with outstretched hands and winged speed; but as he is about to embrace her, his Daphne turns — alas! not to a laurel! Hardly a speculation has been left on record from the earliest time, but it is loosely folded up in Mr. Coleridge's memory, like a rich, but somewhat tattered piece of tapestry: we might add (with more seeming than real extravagance)·that scarce a thought can pass through the mind of man, but its sound has at some time or other passed over his head with rustling pinions.

On whatever question or author you speak, he is prepared to take up the theme with advantage — from Peter Abelard down to Thomas Moore, from the subtlest metaphysics to the politics of the *Courier*. There is no man of genius in whose praise he descants, but the critic seems to stand above the author, and "what in him is weak, to strengthen, what is low, to raise and support:" nor is there any work of genius that does not come out of his hands like an illuminated Missal, sparkling even in its defects. If Mr. Coleridge had not been the most impressive talker of his age, he would probably have been the finest writer; but he lays down his pen to make sure of an auditor, and mortgages the admiration of posterity for the stare of an idler. If he had not been a poet, he would have been a powerful logician; if he had not dipped his wing in the Unitarian controversy, he might have soared to the very summit of fancy. But, in writing verse, he is trying to subject the Muse to *transcendental* theories: in his abstract reasoning, he misses his way by strewing it with flowers.

All that he has done of moment, he had done twenty years ago: since then, he may be said to have lived on the sound of his own voice. Mr. Coleridge is too rich in intellectual

wealth, to need to task himself to any drudgery: he has only
to draw the sliders of his imagination, and a thousand subjects expand before him, startling him with their brilliancy,
or losing themselves in endless obscurity —

> "And by the force of blear illusion,
> They draw him on to his confusion."

What is the little he could add to the stock, compared with
the countless stores that lie about him, that he should stoop
to pick up a name, or to polish an idle fancy? He walks
abroad in the majesty of an universal understanding, eyeing
the "rich strond" or golden sky above him, and "goes sounding on his way," in eloquent accents, uncompelled and free!

Persons of the greatest capacity are often those who for
this reason do the least; for surveying themselves from the
highest point of view, amidst the infinite variety of the universe, their own share in it seems trifling, and scarce worth a
thought; and they prefer the contemplation of all that is, or
has been, or can be, to the making a coil about doing what,
when done, is no better than vanity. It is hard to concen-
trate all our attention and efforts on one pursuit, except from
ignorance of others; and without this concentration of our
faculties no great progress can be made in any one thing. It
is not merely that the mind is not capable of the effort; it
does not think the effort worth making. Action is one; but
thought is manifold. He whose restless eye glances through
the wide compass of nature and art, will not consent to have
"his own nothings monstered," but he must do this before
he can give his whole soul to them. The mind, after "letting contemplation have its fill," or

> " Sailing with supreme dominion
> Through the azure deep of air,"

sinks down on the ground, breathless, exhausted, powerless,
inactive; or if it must have some vent to its feelings, seeks the
most easy and obvious; is soothed by friendly flattery, lulled
by the murmur of immediate applause; thinks, as it were,
aloud, and babbles in its dreams!

A scholar (so to speak) is a more disinterested and abstracted character than a mere author. The first looks at the numberless volumes of a library, and says, "All these are mine:" the other points to a single volume (perhaps it may be an immortal one) and says, "My name is written on the back of it." This is a puny and grovelling ambition, beneath the lofty amplitude of Mr. Coleridge's mind. No, he revolves in his wayward soul, or utters to the passing wind, or discourses to his own shadow, things mightier and more various! — Let us draw the curtain, and unlock the shrine. Learning rocked him in his cradle, and while yet a child,

"He lisped in numbers, for the numbers came."

At sixteen he wrote his *Ode on Chatterton*, and he still reverts to that period with delight, not so much as it relates to himself (for that string of his own early promise of fame rather jars than otherwise) but as exemplifying the youth of a poet. Mr. Coleridge talks of himself without being an egotist; for in him the individual is always merged in the abstract and general. He distinguished himself at school and at the University by his knowledge of the classics, and gained several prizes for Greek epigrams. How many men are there (great scholars, celebrated names in literature) who, having done the same thing in their youth, have no other idea all the rest of their lives but of this achievement, of a fellowship and dinner, and who, installed in academic honours, would look down on our author as a mere strolling bard! At Christ's Hospital, where he was brought up, he was the idol of those among his schoolfellows who mingled with their bookish studies the music of thought and of humanity; and he was usually attended round the cloisters by a group of these (inspiring and inspired) whose hearts even then burnt within them as he talked, and where the sounds yet linger to mock Elia on his way, still turning pensive to the past!

One of the finest and rarest parts of Mr. Coleridge's conversation is, when he expatiates on the Greek tragedians (not that he is not well acquainted, when he pleases, with the epic poets, or the philosophers, or orators, or historians of antiquity) — on the subtle reasonings and melting pathos of Euripides, on the harmonious gracefulness of Sophocles, tuning his love-laboured song, like sweetest warblings from a sacred grove; on the high-wrought, trumpet-tongued eloquence of Æschylus, whose *Prometheus*, above all, is like an Ode to Fatè and a pleading with Providence, his thoughts being let loose as his body is chained on his solitary rock, and his afflicted will (the emblem of mortality)

"Struggling in vain with ruthless destiny."

As the impassioned critic speaks and rises in his theme, you would think you heard the voice of the Man hated by the Gods, contending with the wild winds as they roar; and his eye glitters with the spirit of Antiquity!

Next, he was engaged with Hartley's tribes of mind, "etherial braid, thought-woven," — and he busied himself for a year or two with vibrations and vibratiuncles, and the great law of association that binds all things in its mystic chain, and the doctrine of Necessity (the mild teacher of Charity) and the Millennium, anticipative of a life to come; and he plunged deep into the controversy on Matter and Spirit, and, as an escape from Dr. Priestley's Materialism, where he felt himself imprisoned by the logician's spell, like Ariel in the cloven pine-tree, he became suddenly enamoured of Bishop Berkeley's fairy-world,[1] and used in all companies to build the universe, like a brave poetical fiction, of fine words. And he was deep-read in Malebranche, and in Cudworth's *Intellectual System* (a huge pile of learning, unwieldy, enormous) and in Lord Brooke's hieroglyphic theories, and in Bishop Butler's *Sermons*, and in the Duchess of Newcastle's fantastic folios, and in Clarke and South, and

---

[1] Mr. Coleridge named his eldest son (the writer of some beautiful sonnets) after Hartley, and the second after Berkeley. The third was called Derwent, after the river of that name. Nothing can be more characteristic of his mind than this circumstance. All his ideas indeed are like a river, flowing on for ever, and still murmuring as it flows, discharging its waters and still replenished —

"And so by many winding nooks it strays,
With willing sport to the wild ocean!"

Tillotson, and all the fine thinkers and masculine reasoners of that age; and Leibnitz's *Pre-established Harmony* reared its arch above his head, like the rainbow in the cloud, covenanting with the hopes of man.

And then he fell plump, ten thousand fathoms down (but his wings saved him harmless) into the *hortus siccus* of Dissent, where he pared religion down to the standard of reason, and stripped faith of mystery, and preached Christ crucified and the Unity of the Godhead, and so dwelt for a while in the spirit with John Huss and Jerome of Prague and Socinus and old John Zisca, and ran through Neal's *History of the Puritans* and Calamy's *Non-Conformists' Memorial*, having like thoughts and passions with them. But then Spinoza became his God, and he took up the vast chain of being in his hand, and the round world became the centre and the soul of all things in some shadowy sense, forlorn of meaning, and around him he beheld the living traces and the sky-pointing proportions of the mighty Pan; but poetry redeemed him from this spectral philosophy, and he bathed his heart in beauty, and gazed at the golden light of heaven, and drank of the spirit of the universe, and wandered at eve by fairy-stream or fountain,

> " —— When he saw nought but beauty,
> When he heard the voice of that Almighty One
> In every breeze that blew, or wave that murmured" —

and wedded with truth in Plato's shade, and in the writings of Proclus and Plotinus saw the ideas of things in the eternal mind, and unfolded all mysteries with the Schoolmen and fathomed the depths of Duns Scotus and Thomas Aquinas, and entered the third heaven with Jacob Behmen, and walked hand in hand with Swedenborg through the pavilions of the New Jerusalem, and sang his faith in the promise and in the word in his *Religious Musings* — and lowering himself from that dizzy height poised himself on Milton's wings, and spread out his thoughts in charity with the glad prose of Jeremy Taylor, and wept over Bowles's *Sonnets*, and studied Cowper's blank verse, and betook himself to Thomson's *Castle of Indolence*, and sported with the wits of Charles the Second's

days and of Queen Anne, and relished Swift's style and that
of the John Bull (Arbuthnot's we mean, not Mr. Croker's),
and dallied with the British Essayists and Novelists, and
knew all qualities of more modern writers with a learned spirit:
Johnson, and Goldsmith, and Junius, and Burke, and Godwin,
and the *Sorrows of Werter*, and Jean Jacques Rousseau, and
Voltaire, and Marivaux, and Crébillon, and thousands more
— now "laughed with Rabelais in his easy chair" or pointed
to Hogarth, or afterwards dwelt on Claude's classic scenes, or
spoke with rapture of Raphael, and compared the women at
Rome to figures that had walked out of his pictures, or visited
the Oratory of Pisa, and described the works of Giotto and
Ghirlandaio and Massaccio, and gave the moral of the picture of the Triumph of Death, where the beggars and the
wretched invoke his dreadful dart, but the rich and mighty of
the earth quail and shrink before it; and in that land of siren
sights and sounds, saw a dance of peasant girls, and was
charmed with lutes and gondolas, — or wandered into Germany and lost himself in the labyrinths of the Hartz Forest
and of the Kantean philosophy, and amongst the cabalistic
names of Fichte and Schelling and Lessing, and God knows
who. This was long after; but all the former while he had
nerved his heart and filled his eyes with tears, as he hailed the
rising orb of liberty, since quenched in darkness and in blood,
and had kindled his affections at the blaze of the French Revolution, and sang for joy, when the towers of the Bastille and
the proud places of the insolent and the oppressor fell, and
would have floated his bark, freighted with fondest fancies,
across the Atlantic wave with Southey and others to seek for
peace and freedom —

"In Philarmonia's undivided dale!"

Alas! "Frailty, thy name is *Genius!*" — What is become of
all this mighty heap of hope, of thought, of learning and
humanity? It has ended in swallowing doses of oblivion and
in writing paragraphs in the *Courier.* — Such and so little is
the mind of man!

It was not to be supposed that Mr. Coleridge could keep

on at the rate he set off; he could not realize all he knew or thought, and less could not fix his desultory ambition; other stimulants supplied the place, and kept up the intoxicating dream, the fever and the madness of his early impressions. Liberty (the philosopher's and the poet's bride) had fallen a victim, meanwhile, to the murderous practices of the hag, Legitimacy. Proscribed by court-hirelings, too romantic for the herd of vulgar politicians, our enthusiast stood at bay, and at last turned on the pivot of a subtle casuistry to the *unclean side:* but his discursive reason would not let him trammel himself into a poet-laureate or stamp-distributor; and he stopped, ere he had quite passed that well-known "bourne from whence no traveller returns" — and so has sunk into torpid, uneasy repose, tantalized by useless resources, haunted by vain imaginings, his lips idly moving, but his heart forever still, or, as the shattered chords vibrate of themselves, making melancholy music to the ear of memory! Such is the fate of genius in an age when, in the unequal contest with sovereign wrong, every man is ground to powder who is not either a born slave, or who does not willingly and at once offer up the yearnings of humanity and the dictates of reason as a welcome sacrifice to besotted prejudice and loathsome power.

Of all Mr. Coleridge's productions, the *Ancient Mariner* is the only one that we could with confidence put into any person's hands, on whom we wished to impress a favourable idea of his extraordinary powers. Let whatever other objections be made to it, it is unquestionably a work of genius — of wild, irregular, overwhelming imagination, and has that rich, varied movement in the verse, which gives a distant idea of the lofty or changeful tones of Mr. Coleridge's voice. In the *Christabel*, there is one splendid passage on divided friendship. The Translation of Schiller's *Wallenstein* is also a masterly production in its kind, faithful and spirited. Among his smaller pieces there are occasional bursts of pathos and fancy, equal to what we might expect from him; but these form the exception, and not the rule. Such, for instance, is his affecting Sonnet to the author of the *Robbers.*

"Schiller! that hour I would have wish'd to die,
    If through the shudd'ring midnight I had sent
    From the dark dungeon of the tower time-rent,
    That fearful voice, a famish'd father's cry —
    That in no after-moment aught less vast
        Might stamp me mortal! A triumphant shout
        Black horror scream'd, and all her goblin rout
From the more with'ring scene diminish'd pass'd.
"Ah! Bard tremendous in sublimity!
    Could I behold thee in thy loftier mood,
Wand'ring at eve, with finely frenzied eye,
    Beneath some vast old tempest-swinging wood!
    Awhile, with mute awe gazing, I would brood,
Then weep aloud in a wild ecstasy."

His Tragedy, entitled *Remorse*, is full of beautiful and
striking passages; but it does not place the author in the
first rank of dramatic writers. But if Mr. Coleridge's works
do not place him in that rank, they injure instead of conveying
a just idea of the man; for he himself is certainly in the first
class of general intellect.

If our author's poetry is inferior to his conversation, his
prose is utterly abortive. Hardly a gleam is to be found in
it of the brilliancy and richness of those stores of thought
and language that he pours out incessantly, when they are
lost like drops of water in the ground. The principal work,
in which he has attempted to embody his general views of
things, is the FRIEND, of which, though it contains some
noble passages and fine trains of thought, prolixity and obscurity are the most frequent characteristics.

No two persons can be conceived more than opposite in
character or genius than the subject of the present and of
the preceding sketch. Mr. Godwin, with less natural capacity and with fewer acquired advantages, by concentrating
his mind on some given object, and doing what he had to do
with all his might, has accomplished much, and will leave more
than one monument of a powerful intellect behind him; Mr.
Coleridge, by dissipating his, and dallying with every subject
by turns, has done little or nothing to justify to the world or
to posterity the high opinion which all who have ever hear
him converse, or known him intimately, with one accord

entertain of him. Mr. Godwin's faculties have kept at home, and plied their task in the workshop of the brain, diligently and effectually: Mr. Coleridge's have gossiped away their time, and gadded about from house to house, as if life's business were to melt the hours in listless talk. Mr. Godwin is intent on a subject, only as it concerns himself and his reputation; he works it out as a matter of duty, and discards from his mind whatever does not forward his main object as impertinent and vain.

Mr. Coleridge, on the other hand, delights in nothing but episodes and digressions, neglects whatever he undertakes to perform, and can act only on spontaneous impulses without object or method. "He cannot be constrained by mastery." While he should be occupied with a given pursuit, he is thinking of a thousand other things: a thousand tastes, a thousand objects tempt him, and distract his mind, which keeps open house, and entertains all comers; and after being fatigued and amused with morning calls from idle visitors, he finds the day consumed and its business unconcluded. Mr. Godwin, on the contrary, is somewhat exclusive and unsocial in his habits of mind, entertains no company but what he gives his whole time and attention to, and wisely writes over the doors of his understanding, his fancy, and his senses — "No admittance except on business." He has none of that fastidious refinement and false delicacy which might lead him to balance between the endless variety of modern attainments. He does not throw away his life (nor a single half hour of it) in adjusting the claims of different accomplishments, and in choosing between them or making himself master of them all. He sets about his task (whatever it may be), and goes through it with spirit and fortitude. He has the happiness to think an author the greatest character in the world, and himself the greatest author in it.

Mr. Coleridge, in writing an harmonious stanza, would stop to consider whether there was not more grace and beauty in a *Pas de trois*, and would not proceed till he had resolved this question by a chain of metaphysical reasoning without end. Not so Mr. Godwin. That is best to him, which he can do best. He does not waste himself in vain aspirations and effeminate sympathies. He is blind, deaf, insensible, to all but the trump of Fame. Plays, operas, painting, music, ball-rooms, wealth, fashion, titles, lords, ladies, touch him not. All these are no more to him than to the magician in his cell, and he writes on to the end of the chapter through good report and evil report. *Pingo in eternitatem* is his motto. He neither envies nor admires what others are, but is contented to be what he is, and strives to do the utmost he can. Mr. Coleridge has flirted with the Muses as with a set of mistresses: Mr. Godwin has been married twice, to Reason and to Fancy, and has to boast no short-lived progeny by each.

So to speak, he has *valves* belonging to his mind, to regulate the quantity of gas admitted into it, so that like the bare, unsightly, but well-compacted steam-vessel, it cuts its liquid way, and arrives at its promised end: while Mr. Coleridge's bark, "taught with the little nautilus to sail," the sport of every breath, dancing to every wave,

"Youth at its prow, and Pleasure at its helm,".

flutters its gaudy pennons in the air, glitters in the sun, but we wait in vain to hear of its arrival in the destined harbour. Mr. Godwin, with less variety and vividness, with less subtlety and susceptibility both of thought and feeling, has had firmer nerves, a more determined purpose, a more comprehensive grasp of his subject; and the results are as we find them. Each has met with his reward: for justice has, after all, been done to the pretensions of each: and we must, in all cases, use means to ends!

It was a misfortune to any man of talent to be born in the latter end of the last century. Genius stopped the way of Legitimacy, and therefore it was to be abated, crushed, or set aside as a nuisance. The spirit of the monarchy was at variance with the spirit of the age. The flame of liberty, the light of intellect, was to be extinguished with the sword — or with slander, whose edge is sharper than the sword. The war between power and reason was carried on by the first of these abroad, by the last at home. No quarter was given (then or now) by the Government-critics, the authorized censors of the press, to those who followed the dictates of independence, who listened to the voice of the tempter Fancy. Instead of gathering fruits and flowers, immortal fruits and amaranthine flowers, they soon found themselves beset not only by a host of prejudices, but assailed with all the engines of power: by nicknames, by lies, by all the arts of malice, interest and hypocrisy, without the possibility of their defending themselves "from the pelting of the pitiless storm," that poured down upon them from the strongholds of corruption and authority.

The philosophers, the dry abstract reasoners, submitted to this reverse pretty well, and armed themselves with patience "as with triple steel," to bear discomfiture, persecution, and disgrace. But the poets, the creatures of sympathy, could not stand the frowns both of king and people. They did not like to be shut out when places and pensions, when the critic's praises, and the laurel wreath were about to be distributed. They did not stomach being *sent to Coventry,* and Mr. Coleridge sounded a retreat for them by the help of casuistry and a musical voice. — "His words were hollow, but they pleased the ear" of his friends of the Lake School, who turned back disgusted and panic-struck from the dry desert of unpopularity, like Hassan the camel-driver,

> "And curs'd the hour, and curs'd the luckless day,
> When first from Shiraz' walls they bent their way."

They are safely inclosed there. But Mr. Coleridge did not enter with them; pitching his tent upon the barren waste without, and having no abiding place nor city of refuge!

MR. WORDSWORTH

MR. WORDSWORTH'S genius is a pure emanation of the
Spirit of the Age. Had he lived in any other period of the
world, he would never have been heard of. As it is, he has
some difficulty to contend with the hebetude of his intellect
and the meanness of his subject. With him "lowliness is
young ambition's ladder:" but he finds it a toil to climb in this
way the steep of Fame. His homely Muse can hardly raise
her wing from the ground, nor spread her hidden glories to
the sun. He has "no figures nor no fantasies which busy
passion draws in the brains of men:" neither the gorgeous
machinery of mythologic lore, nor the splendid colours of
poetic diction. His style is vernacular: he delivers household
truths. He sees nothing loftier than human hopes, nothing
deeper than the human heart. This he probes, this he
tampers with, this he poises, with all its incalculable weight
of thought and feeling, in his hands, and at the same time
calms the throbbing pulses of his own heart by keeping his
eye ever fixed on the face of nature. If he can make the life-
blood flow from the wounded breast, this is the living colouring with which he paints his verse: if he can assuage the pain
or close up the wound with the balm of solitary musing, or the
healing power of plants and herbs and "skyey influences,"
this is the sole triumph of his art. He takes the simplest
elements of nature and of the human mind, the mere abstract
conditions inseparable from our being, and tries to compound
a new system of poetry from them; and has perhaps succeeded
as well as anyone could. "*Nihil humani a me alienum puto*"
— is the motto of his works. He thinks nothing low or indifferent of which this can be affirmed: everything that professes
to be more than this, that is not an absolute essence of truth
and feeling, he holds to be vitiated, false, and spurious. In

a word, his poetry is founded on setting up an opposition
(and pushing it to the utmost length) between the natural
and the artificial, between the spirit of humanity and the
spirit of fashion and of the world.

It is one of the innovations of the time. It partakes of,
and is carried along with, the revolutionary movement of
our age: the political changes of the day were the model on
which he formed and conducted his poetical experiments.
His Muse (it cannot be denied, and without this we cannot
explain its character at all) is a levelling one. It proceeds on
a principle of equality, and strives to reduce all things to the
same standard. It is distinguished by a proud humility. It
relies upon its own resources, and disdains external show and
relief. It takes the commonest events and objects, as a test
to prove that nature is always interesting from its inherent
truth and beauty, without any of the ornaments of dress or
pomp of circumstances to set it off. Hence the unaccountable
mixture of seeming simplicity and real abstruseness in the
Lyrical Ballads. Fools have laughed at, wise men scarcely
understand, them. He takes a subject or a story merely as
pegs or loops to hang thought and feeling on; the incidents
are trifling, in proportion to his contempt for imposing appearances; the reflections are profound, according to the
gravity and aspiring pretensions of his mind.

His popular, inartificial style gets rid (at a blow) of all the
trappings of verse, of all the high places of poetry: "the
cloud-capt towers, the solemn temples, the gorgeous palaces,"
are swept to the ground, and "like the baseless fabric of a
vision, leave not a wreck behind." All the traditions of
learning, all the superstitions of age, are obliterated and
effaced. We begin *de novo* on a *tabula rasa* of poetry. The
purple pall, the nodding plume of tragedy are exploded as
mere pantomime and trick, to return to the simplicity of
truth and nature. Kings, queens, priests, nobles, the altar
and the throne, the distinctions of rank, birth, wealth, power,
"the judge's robe, the marshal's truncheon, the ceremony that
to great ones 'longs," are not to be found here. The author
tramples on the pride of art with greater pride. The Ode and

Epode, the Strophe and the Antistrophe, he laughs to scorn. The harp of Homer, the trump of Pindar and of Alcæus, are still. The decencies of costume, the decorations of vanity are stripped off without mercy as barbarous, idle, and Gothic. The jewels in the crisped hair, the diadem on the polished brow, are thought meretricious, theatrical, vulgar; and nothing contents his fastidious taste beyond a simple garland of flowers. Neither does he avail himself of the advantages which nature or accident holds out to him. He chooses to have his subject a foil to his invention, to owe nothing but to himself.

He gathers manna in the wilderness; he strikes the barren rock for the gushing moisture. He elevates the mean by the strength of his own aspirations; he clothes the naked with beauty and grandeur from the stores of his own recollections. No cypress grove loads his verse with funeral pomp: but his imagination lends "a sense of joy

"To the bare trees and mountains bare,
    And grass in the green field."

No storm, no shipwreck startles us by its horrors: but the rainbow lifts its head in the cloud, and the breeze sighs through the withered fern. No sad vicissitude of fate, no overwhelming catastrophe in nature deforms his page: but the dew-drop glitters on the bending flower, the tear collects in the glistening eye.

"Beneath the hills, along the flowery vales,
    The generations are prepared; the pangs,
    The internal pangs are ready; the dread strife
    Of poor humanity's afflicted will,
    Struggling in vain with ruthless destiny."

As the lark ascends from its low bed on fluttering wing, and salutes the morning skies, so Mr. Wordsworth's unpretending Muse in russet guise scales the summits of reflection, while it makes the round earth its footstool and its home!

Possibly a good deal of this may be regarded as the effect of disappointed views and an inverted ambition. Prevented by native pride and indolence from climbing the ascent of

learning or greatness, taught by political opinions to say to
the vain pomp and glory of the world, "I hate ye," seeing
the path of classical and artificial poetry blocked up by the
cumbrous ornaments of style and turgid *commonplaces*, so
that nothing more could be achieved in that direction but
by the most ridiculous bombast or the tamest servility, he has
turned back, partly from the bias of his mind, partly perhaps
from a judicious policy — has struck into the sequestered
vale of humble life, sought out the Muse among sheep-cotes,
and hamlets, and the peasant's mountain-haunts, has discarded all the tinsel pageantry of verse, and endeavoured
(not in vain) to aggrandise the trivial, and add the charm of
novelty to the familiar. No one has shown the same imagination in raising trifles into importance: no one has displayed
the same pathos in treating of the simplest feelings of the
heart. Reserved, yet haughty, having no unruly or violent
passions (or those passions having been early suppressed),
Mr. Wordsworth has passed his life in solitary musing or in
daily converse with the face of nature. He exemplifies in an
eminent degree the power of *association;* for his poetry has
no other source or character. He has dwelt among pastoral
scenes, till each object has become connected with a thousand
feelings, a link in the chain of thought, a fibre of his own
heart. Everyone is by habit and familiarity strongly attached to the place of his birth, or to objects that recall the
most pleasing and eventful circumstances of his life.

But to the author of the *Lyrical Ballads* nature is a kind of
home; and he may be said to take a personal interest in the
universe. There is no image so insignificant that it has not in
some mood or other found the way into his heart: no sound
that does not awaken the memory of other years.

> "To him the meanest flower that blows can give
> Thoughts that do often lie too deep for tears."

The daisy looks up to him with sparkling eye as an old acquaintance: the cuckoo haunts him with sounds of early youth
not to be expressed: a linnet's nest startles him with boyish
delight: an old withered thorn is weighed down with a heap

s

of recollections: a grey cloak, seen on some wild moor, torn by the wind or drenched in the rain, afterwards becomes an object of imagination to him: even the lichens on the rock have a life and being in his thoughts. He has described all these objects in a way and with an intensity of feeling that no one else had done before him, and has given a new view or aspect of nature. He is in this sense the most original poet now living, and the one whose writings could the least be spared: for they have no substitute elsewhere. The vulgar do not read them; the learned, who see all things through books, do not understand them; the great despise. The fashionable may ridicule them: but the author has created himself an interest in the heart of the retired and lonely student of nature, which can never die.

Persons of this class will still continue to feel what he has felt: he has expressed what they might in vain wish to express, except with glistening eye and faltering tongue! There is a lofty, philosophic tone, a thoughtful humanity, infused into his pastoral vein. Remote from the passions and events of the great world, he has communicated interest and dignity to the primal movements of the heart of man, and ingrafted his own conscious reflections on the casual thoughts of hinds and shepherds. Nursed amidst the grandeur of mountain scenery, he has stooped to have a nearer view of the daisy under his feet, or plucked a branch of white-thorn from the spray: but, in describing it, his mind seems imbued with the majesty and solemnity of the objects around him. The tall rock lifts its head in the erectness of his spirit; the cataract roars in the sound of his verse; and in its dim and mysterious meaning the mists seem to gather in the hollows of Helvellyn, and the forked Skiddaw hovers in the distance. There is little mention of mountainous scenery in Mr. Wordsworth's poetry; but by internal evidence one might be almost sure that it was written in a mountainous country, from its bareness, its simplicity, its loftiness, and its depth!

His later philosophic productions have a somewhat different character. They are a departure from, a dereliction of, his first principles. They are classical and courtly. They are polished in style without being gaudy, dignified in subject without affectation. They seem to have been composed not in a cottage at Grasmere, but among the half-inspired groves and stately recollections of Cole-Orton. We might allude in particular, for examples of what we mean, to the lines on a Picture by Claude Lorraine and to the exquisite poem, entitled *Laodamia*. The last of these breathes the pure spirit of the finest fragments of antiquity — the sweetness, the gravity, the strength, the beauty and the languor of death —

"Calm contemplation and majestic pains."

Its glossy brilliancy arises from the perfection of the finishing like that of a careful sculpture, not from gaudy colouring. The texture of the thoughts has the smoothness and solidity of marble. It is a poem that might be read aloud in Elysium, and the spirits of departed heroes and sages would gather round to listen to it!

Mr. Wordsworth's philosophic poetry, with a less glowing aspect and less tumult in the veins than Lord Byron's on similar occasions, bends a calmer and keener eye on mortality; the impression, if less vivid, is more pleasing and permanent; and we confess it (perhaps it is a want of taste and proper feeling) that there are lines and poems of our author's, that we think of ten times for once that we recur to any of Lord Byron's. Or if there are any of the latter's writings that we can dwell upon in the same way, that is, as lasting and heart-felt sentiments, it is when laying aside his usual pomp and pretension, he descends with Mr. Wordsworth to the common ground of a disinterested humanity. It may be considered as characteristic of our poet's writings, that they either make no impression on the mind at all, seem mere *nonsense-verses*, or that they leave a mark behind them that never wears out. They either

"Fall blunted from the indurated breast,"

without any perceptible result, or they absorb it like a passion. To one class of readers he appears sublime, to another (and we fear the largest) ridiculous. He has probably realised

Milton's wish, — "and fit audience 'found, though few:" but we suspect he is not reconciled to the alternative.

There are delightful passages in *The Excursion*, both of natural description and of inspired reflection (passages of the latter kind that in the sound of the thoughts and of the swelling language resemble heavenly symphonies, mournful *requiems* over the grave of human hopes); but we must add, in justice and in sincerity, that we think it impossible that this work should ever become popular, even in the same degree as the *Lyrical Ballads*. It affects a system without having any intelligible clue to one, and, instead of unfolding a principle in various and striking lights, repeats the same conclusions till they become flat and insipid. Mr. Wordsworth's mind is obtuse, except as it is the organ and the receptacle of accumulated feelings; it is not analytic, but synthetic; it is reflecting, rather than theoretical. The *Excursion*, we believe, fell still-born from the press. There was something abortive, and clumsy, and ill-judged in the attempt. It was long and laboured. The personages, for the most part, were low, the fare rustic; the plan raised expectations which were not fulfilled, and the effect was like being ushered into a stately hall and invited to sit down to a splendid banquet in the company of clowns, and with nothing but successive courses of apple-dumplings served up. It was not even *toujours perdrix!*

Mr. Wordsworth, in his person, is above the middle size, with marked features and an air somewhat stately and quixotic. He reminds one of some of Holbein's heads: grave, saturnine, with a slight indication of sly humour, kept under by the manners of the age or by the pretensions of the person. He has a peculiar sweetness in his smile, and great depth and manliness and a rugged harmony in the tones of his voice. His manner of reading his own poetry is particularly imposing; and in his favourite passages his eye beams with preternatural lustre, and the meaning labours slowly up from his swelling breast. No one who has seen him at these moments could go away with an impression that he was a "man of no mark or likelihood." Perhaps the comment of his face and voice is necessary to convey a full idea of his poetry. His language

may not be intelligible; but his manner is not to be mistaken.
It is clear that he is either mad or inspired. In company,
even in a *tête-à-tête*, Mr. Wordsworth is often silent, indolent,
and reserved. If he is become verbose and oracular of late
years, he was not so in his better days. He threw out a bold
or an indifferent remark without either effort or pretension,
and relapsed into musing again. He shone most (because he
seemed most roused and animated) in reciting his own poetry,
or in talking about it. He sometimes gave striking views of
his feelings and trains of association in composing certain
passages; or if one did not always understand his distinctions,
still there was no want of interest: there was a latent meaning
worth inquiring into, like a vein of ore that one cannot exactly
hit upon at the moment, but of which there are sure indi-
cations. His standard of poetry is high and severe, almost
to exclusiveness. He admits of nothing below, scarcely of
anything above, himself. It is fine to hear him talk of the
way in which certain subjects should have been treated by
eminent poets, according to his notions of the art. Thus he
finds fault with Dryden's description of Bacchus in the *Alexander's Feast,* as if he were a mere good-looking youth or
boon companion —

> "Flushed with a purple grace,
> He shows his honest face" —

instead of representing the god returning from the conquest
of India, crowned with vine-leaves and drawn by panthers,
and followed by troops of satyrs, of wild men and animals
that he had tamed. You would think, in hearing him speak
on this subject, that you saw Titian's picture of the meeting
of *Bacchus and Ariadne* — so classic were his conceptions, so
glowing his style.

Milton is his great idol, and he sometimes dares to compare
himself with him. His Sonnets, indeed, have something of
the same high-raised tone and prophetic spirit. Chaucer is
another prime favourite of his, and he has been at the pains to'
modernize some of the *Canterbury Tales.* Those persons
who look upon Mr. Wordsworth as a merely puerile writer,

must be rather at a loss to account for his strong predilection
for such geniuses as Dante and Michael Angelo. We do not
think our author has any very cordial sympathy with Shakespeare. How should he? Shakespeare was the least of an
egotist of anybody in the world. He does not much relish
the variety and scope of dramatic composition. "He hates
those interlocutions between Lucius and Caius." Yet Mr.
Wordsworth himself wrote a tragedy when he was young;
and we have heard the following energetic lines quoted from
it, as put into the mouth of a person smit with remorse for
some rash crime:

> "——Action is momentary,
> The motion of a muscle this way or that;
> Suffering is long, obscure, and infinite!"

Perhaps for want of light and shade, and the unshackled
spirit of the drama, this performance was never brought
forward. Our critic has a great dislike to Gray, and a fondness for Thomson and Collins. It is mortifying to hear him
speak of Pope and Dryden whom, because they have been
supposed to have all the possible excellences of poetry, he will
allow to have none.

Nothing, however, can be fairer, or more amusing than the
way in which he sometimes exposes the unmeaning verbiage of
modern poetry. Thus in the beginning of Dr. Johnson's
Vanity of Human Wishes —

> "Let observation with extensive view
> Survey mankind from China to Peru" —

he says there is a total want of imagination accompanying
the words; the same idea is repeated three times under the
disguise of a different phraseology. It comes to this: "let
observation with extensive *observation observe* mankind;"
or take away the first line, and the second,

> "Survey mankind from China to Peru,"

literally conveys the whole. Mr. Wordsworth is, we must
say, a perfect Drawcansir as to prose writers. He complains
of the dry reasoners and matter-of-fact people for their want

of *passion;* and he is jealous of the rhetorical declaimers and rhapsodists as trenching on the province of poetry. He condemns all French writers (as well of poetry as prose) in the lump. His list in this way is indeed small. He approves of Walton's *Angler,* Paley, and some other writers of an inoffensive modesty of pretension. He also likes books of voyages and travels, and *Robinson Crusoe.* In art, he greatly esteems Bewick's woodcuts and Waterloo's sylvan etchings. But he sometimes takes a higher tone, and gives his mind fair play. We have known him enlarge with a noble intelligence and enthusiasm on Nicolas Poussin's fine landscape compositions, pointing out the unity of design that pervades them, the superintending mind, the imaginative principle that brings all to bear on the same end; and declaring he would not give a rush for any landscape that did not express the time of day, the climate, the period of the world it was meant to illustrate, or had not this character of *wholeness* in it.

His eye also does justice to Rembrandt's fine and masterly effects. In the way in which that artist works something out of nothing, and transforms the stump of a tree, a common figure, into an *ideal* object by the gorgeous light and shade thrown upon it, he perceives an analogy to his own mode of investing the minute details of nature with an atmosphere of sentiment, and in pronouncing Rembrandt to be a man of genius, feels that he strengthens his own claim to the title. It has been said of Mr. Wordsworth, that "he hates conchology, that he hates the Venus of Medici." But these, we hope, are mere epigrams and *jeux d'esprit,* as far from truth as they are free from malice: a sort of running satire or critical clenches —

> "Where one for sense and one for rhyme
> Is quite sufficient at one time."

We think, however, that if Mr. Wordsworth had been a more liberal and candid critic, he would have been a more sterling writer. If a greater number of sources of pleasure had been open to him, he would have communicated pleasure to the world more frequently. Had he been less fastidious in

pronouncing sentence on the works of others, his own would
have been received more favourably, and treated more le-
niently. The current of his feelings is deep, but narrow; the
range of his understanding is lofty and aspiring rather than
discursive. The force, the originality, the absolute truth
and identity, with which he feels some things, makes him indifferent to so many others. The simplicity and enthusiasm
of his feelings, with respect to nature, render him bigoted and
intolerant in his judgments of men and things. But it happens to him, as to others, that his strength lies in his weakness;
and perhaps we have no right to complain. We might get
rid of the cynic and the egotist, and find in his stead a commonplace man. We should "take the good the gods pro-
vide us:" a fine and original vein of poetry is not one of their
most contemptible gifts; and the rest is scarcely worth thinking of, except as it may be a mortification to those who expect
perfection from human nature, or who have been idle enough
at some period of their lives to deify men of genius as pos-
sessing claims above it. But this is a chord that jars, and
we shall not dwell upon it.

Lord Byron we have called, according to the old proverb,
"the spoiled child of fortune:" Mr. Wordsworth might plead,
in mitigation of some peculiarities, that he is "the spoiled
child of disappointment." We are convinced, if he had been
early a popular poet, he would have borne his honours meekly,
and would have been a person of great *bonhomie* and frank-
ness of disposition. But the sense of injustice and of undeserved ridicule sours the temper and narrows the views.
To have produced works of genius, and to find them neglected
or treated with scorn, is one of the heaviest trials of human
patience. We exaggerate our own merits when they are
denied by others, and are apt to grudge and cavil at every
particle of praise bestowed on those to whom we feel a conscious
superiority. In mere self-defense we turn against the world
when it turns against us, brood over the undeserved slights
we receive; and thus the genial current of the soul is stopped,
or vents itself in effusions of petulance and self-conceit.
Mr. Wordsworth has thought too much of contemporary

critics and criticism, and less than he ought of the award of posterity and of the opinion, we do not say of private friends, but of those who were made so by their admiration of his genius.

He did not court popularity by a conformity to established models, and he ought not to have been surprised that his originality was not understood as a matter of course. He has *gnawed too much on the bridle*, and has often thrown out crusts to the critics, in mere defiance or as a point of honour when he was challenged, which otherwise his own good sense would have withheld. We suspect that Mr. Wordsworth's feelings are a little morbid in this respect, or that he resents censure more than he is gratified by praise. Otherwise, the tide has turned much in his favour of late years. He has a large body of determined partisans, and is at present sufficiently in request with the public to save or relieve him from the last necessity to which a man of genius can be reduced — that of becoming the God of his own idolatry!

HAMLET

This is that Hamlet the Dane, whom we read of in our youth, and whom we may be said almost to remember in our after years; he who made that famous soliloquy on life, who gave the advice to the players, who thought "this goodly frame, the earth, a sterrl promontory, and this brave o'er-hanging firmament, the air, this majestical roof fretted with golden fire, a foul and pestilent congregation of vapours;" whom "man delighted not, nor woman neither;" he who talked with the grave-diggers, and moralised on Yorick's skull; the school-fellow of Rosencrans and Guildenstern at Wittenberg; the friend of Horatio; the lover of Ophelia; he that was mad and sent to England; the slow avenger of his father's death; who lived at the court of Horwendillus five hundred years before we were born, but all whose thoughts we seem to know as well as we do our own, because we have read them in Shakespeare.

Hamlet is a name; his speeches and sayings but the idle coinage of the poet's brain. What then, are they not real? They are as real as our own thoughts. Their reality is in the reader's mind. It is *we* who are Hamlet. This play has a prophetic truth, which is above that of history. Whoever has become thoughtful and melancholy through his own mishaps or those of others; whoever has borne about with him the clouded brow of reflection, and thought himself "too much i' th' sun;" whoever has seen the golden lamp of day dimmed by envious mists rising in his own breast, and could find in the world before him only a dull blank with nothing left remarkable in it; whoever has known "the pangs of despised love, the insolence of office, or the spurns which patient merit of the unworthy takes;" he who has felt his mind sink within him, and sadness cling to his heart like a malady, who has had his hopes blighted and his youth stag-gered by the apparitions of strange things; who cannot be well at ease, while he sees evil hovering near him like a spectre; whose powers of action have been eaten up by thought, he to whom the universe seems infinite, and himself nothing; whose bitterness of soul makes him careless of consequences, and who goes to a play as his best resource to shove off, to a second remove, the evils of life by a mock representation of them — this is the true Hamlet.

We have been so used to this tragedy that we hardly know how to criticise it any more than we should know how to describe our own faces. But we must make such observations as we can. It is one of Shakespeare's plays that we think of the oftenest, because it abounds most in striking reflections on human life, and because the distresses of Hamlet are transferred, by the turn of his mind, to the general account of humanity. Whatever happens to him we apply to ourselves, because he applies it to himself as a means of general reasoning. He is a great moraliser; and what makes him worth attending to is, that he moralises on his own feelings and experience. He is not a commonplace pedant. If *Lear* shews the greatest depth of passion, *Hamlet* is the most remarkable for the ingenuity, originality, and unstudied development of character. Shakespeare had more magnanimity than any other poet, and he has shown more of it in this play than in any other. There is no attempt to force an interest: everything is left for time and circumstances to unfold. The attention is excited without effort, the incidents succeed each other as matters of course, the characters think and speak and act just as they might do, if left entirely to themselves. There is no set purpose, no straining at a point. The observations are suggested by the passing scene — the gusts of passion come and go like sounds of music borne on the wind. The whole play is an exact transcript of what might be supposed to have taken place at the court of Denmark, at the remote period of time fixed upon, before the modern refinements in morals and manners were heard of. It would have been interesting enough to have been admitted as a by-stander in such a scene, at such a time, to have heard and seen something of what was going on. But here we are more than spectators. We have not only "the outward pageants and the signs of grief;" but "we have that within which passes show." We read the thoughts of the heart, we catch the passions living as they rise. Other dramatic writers give us very fine versions and paraphrases of nature: but Shakespeare, together with his own comments, gives us the original text, that we may judge for ourselves. This is a very great advantage.

The character of Hamlet stands quite by itself. It is not a character marked by strength of will or even of passion, but by refinement of thought and sentiment. Hamlet is as little of the hero as a man can well be: but he is a young and princely novice, full of high enthusiasm and quick sensibility — the sport of circumstances, questioning with fortune and refining on his own feelings, and forced from the natural bias of his disposition by the strangeness of his situation. He seems incapable of deliberate action, and is only hurried into extremities on the spur of the occasion, when he has no time to reflect, as in the scene where he kills Polonius, and again, where he alters the letters which Rosencrans and Guildenstern are taking with them to England, purporting his death. At other times, when he is most bound to act, he remains puzzled, undecided, and sceptical, dallies with his purposes, till the occasion is lost, and always finds some pretence to relapse into indolence and thoughtfulness again. For this reason he refuses to kill the King when he is at his prayers, and by a refinement in malice, which is in truth only an excuse for his own want of resolution, defers his revenge to some more fatal opportunity, when he shall be engaged in some act "that has no relish of salvation in it.'"

> " He kneels and prays,
> And now I'll do 't, and so he goes to heaven,
> And so am I reveng'd: *that would be scanned.*
> He kill'd my father, and for that,
> I, his sole son, send him to heaven.
> Why this is reward, not revenge.
> Up sword and know thou a more horrid time;
> When he is drunk, asleep, or in a rage."

He is the prince of philosophical speculators, and because he

cannot have his revenge perfect, according to the most refined idea his wish can form, he misses it altogether. So he
scruples to trust the suggestions of the Ghost, contrives the
scene of the play to have surer proof of his uncle's guilt, and
then rests satisfied with this confirmation of his suspicions, and
the success of his experiment, instead of acting upon it. Yet
he is sensible of his own weakness, taxes himself with it, and
tries to reason himself out of it.

> "How all occasions do inform against me,
> And spur my dull revenge! What is a man,
> If his chief good and market of his time
> Be but to sleep and feed? A beast; no more.
> Sure he that made us with such large discourse,
> Looking before and after, gave us not
> That capability and god-like reason
> To rust in us unus'd: now whether it be
> Bestial oblivion, or some craven scruple
> Of thinking too precisely on th' event, —
> A thought which quarter'd, hath but one part wisdom,
> And ever three parts coward; — I do not know
> Why yet I live to say, this thing's to do;
> Sith I have cause, and will, and strength, and means
> To do it. Examples gross as earth excite me:
> Witness this army of such mass and charge,
> Led by a delicate and tender prince,
> Whose spirit with divine ambition puff'd,
> Makes mouths at the invisible event,
> Exposing what is mortal and unsure
> To all that fortune, death, and danger dare,
> Even for an egg-shell. 'Tis not to be great,
> Never to stir without great argument;
> But greatly to find quarrel in a straw,
> When honour's at the stake. How stand I then,
> That have a father kill'd, a mother stain'd,
> Excitements of my reason and my blood,
> And let all sleep, while to my shame I see
> The imminent death of twenty thousand men,
> That fantasy and trick of fame,
> Go to their graves like beds, fight for a plot
> Whereon the numbers cannot try the cause,
> Which is not tomb enough and continent
> To hide the slain? — O, from this time forth,
> My thoughts be bloody or be nothing worth."

Still he does nothing; and this very speculation on his own infirmity only affords him another occasion for indulging it. It is not for any want of attachment to his father or abhorrence of his murder that Hamlet is thus dilatory, but it is more to his taste to indulge his imagination in reflecting upon the enormity of the crime and refining on his schemes of vengeance, than to put them into immediate practice. His ruling passion is to think, not to act: and any vague pretence that flatters this propensity instantly diverts him from his previous purposes.

The moral perfection of this character has been called in question, we think, by those who did not understand it. It is more interesting than according to rules: amiable, though not faultless. The ethical delineations of "that noble and liberal casuist" (as Shakespeare has been well called) do not exhibit the drab-coloured quakerism of morality. His plays are not copied either from the *Whole Duty of Man* or from *The Academy of Compliments!* We confess, we are a little shocked at the want of refinement in those who are shocked at the want of refinement in Hamlet. The want of punctilious exactness in his behaviour either partakes of the "license of the time," or else belongs to the very excess of intellectual refinement in the character which makes the common rules of life, as well as his own purposes, sit loose upon him. He may be said to be amenable only to the tribunal of his own thoughts, and is too much taken up with the airy world of contemplation to lay as much stress as he ought on the practical consequences of things. His habitual principles of action are unhinged and out of joint with the time. His conduct to Ophelia is quite natural in his circumstances. It is that of assumed severity only. It is the effect of disappointed hope, of bitter regrets, of affection suspended, not obliterated, by the distractions of the scene around him! Amidst the natural and preternatural horrors of his situation, he might be excused in delicacy from carrying on a regular courtship. When "his father's spirit was in arms," it was not a time for the son to make love in. He could neither marry Ophelia, nor wound her mind by explaining the cause of his alienation, which he durst hardly

trust himself to think of. It would have taken him years to
have come to a direct explanation on the point. In the
harassed state of his mind, he could not have done otherwise
than he did. His conduct does not contradict what he says
when he sees her funeral,

> "I loved Ophelia: forty thousand brothers
> Could not with all their quantity of love
> Make up my sum.",

Nothing can be more affecting or beautiful than the Queen's
apostrophe to Ophelia on throwing the flowers into the grave.

> "Sweets to the sweet, farewell.
> I hop'd thou should'st have been my Hamlet's wife:
> I thought thy bride-bed to have deck'd, sweet maid,
> And not have strew'd thy grave.",

Shakespeare was thoroughly a master of the mixed motives
of human character, and he here shews us the Queen, who was
so criminal in some respects, not without sensibility and
affection in other relations of life. — Ophelia is a character
almost too exquisitely touching to be dwelt upon. O rose
of May, O flower too soon faded! Her love, her madness, her
death, are described with the truest touches of tenderness and
pathos. It is a character which nobody but Shakespeare could
have drawn in the way that he has done, and to the conception of which there is not even the smallest approach, except
in some of the old romantic ballads.[1] Her brother, Laertes,
is a character we do not like so well: he is too hot and choleric,
and somewhat rhodomontade. Polonius is a perfect character in its kind; nor is there any foundation for the objections
which have been made to the consistency of this part. It is
said that he acts very foolishly and talks very sensibly.
There is no inconsistency in that. Again, that he talks wisely
at one time and foolishly at another; that his advice to Laertes

---

[1] In the account of her death, a friend has pointed out an instance
of the poet's exact observation of nature: —

> "There is a willow growing o'er a brook,
> That shows its hoary leaves i' th' glassy stream."

The inside of the leaves of the willow, next the water, is of a whitish
colour, and the reflection would therefore be "hoary."

is very sensible, and his advice to the King and Queen on the subject of Hamlet's madness very ridiculous. But he gives the one as a father, and is sincere in it; he gives the other as a mere courtier, a busy-body, and is accordingly officious, garrulous, and impertinent. In short, Shakespeare has been accused of inconsistency in this and other characters, only because he has kept up the distinction which there is in nature, between the understandings and the moral habits of men, between the absurdity of their ideas and the absurdity of their motives. Polonius is not a fool, but he makes himself so. His folly, whether in his actions or speeches, comes under the head of impropriety of intention.

We do not like to see our author's plays acted, and least of all, *Hamlet*. There is no play that suffers so much in being transferred to the stage. Hamlet himself seems hardly capable of being acted. Mr. Kemble unavoidably fails in this character from a want of ease and variety. The character of Hamlet is made up of undulating lines; it has the yielding flexibility of "a wave o' th' sea." Mr. Kemble plays it like a man in armour, with a determined inveteracy of purpose, in one undeviating straight line, which is as remote from the natural grace and refined susceptibility of the character, as the sharp angles and abrupt starts which Mr. Kean introduces into the part. Mr. Kean's Hamlet is as much too splenetic and rash as Mr. Kemble's is too deliberate and formal. His manner is too strong and pointed. He throws a severity, approaching to virulence, into the common observations and answers. There is nothing of this in *Hamlet*. He is, as it were, wrapped up in his reflections, and only *thinks aloud*. There should therefore be no attempt to impress what he says upon others by a studied exaggeration of emphasis or manner; no *talking at* his hearers. There should be as much of the gentleman and scholar as possible infused into the part, and as little of the actor. A pensive air of sadness should sit reluctantly upon his brow, but no appearance of fixed and sullen gloom. He is full of weakness and melancholy, but there is no harshness in his nature. He is the most amiable of misanthropes.

NOTES

MY FIRST ACQUAINTANCE WITH POETS

The first essay in *Winterslow*, 1839. It appeared originally in *The Liberal* in 1823, and was an expansion of a letter in *The Examiner* in 1817.

The essay is an account of his first awakening to poetry through his acquaintance with Coleridge and Wordsworth.

☞ **1, 1. W—m.** Wem, the "obscure village" mentioned later in the essay.

1, 3. dreaded name of Demogorgon. *Paradise Lost*, II, 964–965.

1, 19. *proud Salopians.* Compare *Coriolanus*, v, 6, 115–116. A Salopian is an inhabitant of Salop, or Shropshire.

1, 23. High-born Hoel's harp. Gray, *The Bard*, 1, 28.

2, 5. With Styx. Pope, *Ode on St. Cecilia's Day*, 90–91.

2, 13. I owe to Coleridge. See *On Reading Old Books*, p. 29.

2, 17. Whitchurch. A town about nine miles north of Wem.

2, 21–24. like the fires in the *Agamemnon* **of Æschylus.** Lines 281–317 describe how the fire-beacons sent the news of Troy's fall from Mount Ida to Argos.

2, 36. *Il y a des impressions.* From Rousseau's *Confessions*. When he read this book he was living "the happiest years of our life. . . . There were indeed impressions which neither time nor circumstances can efface." — *On the Character of Rousseau*, in *The Round Table*.

3, 4. his text. *St. John*, vi, 15.

3, 6. rose like a steam. *Comus*, 556.

3, 12. One crying. *St. Matthew*, iii, 3–4.

3, 24–25. as though he should never be old. Sidney, *Arcadia*, Bk. I.

3, 31. Such were the notes. Pope, *Epistle to the Earl of Oxford*, 1.

4, 6. Jus Divinum. Divine Law.

4, 7. Like to that sanguine flower. *Lycidas*, 106.

4, 20. As are the children. Thomson, *Castle of Indolence*, II, xxiii, "Bright as the children of yon azure sheen."

4, 23–24. 'A certain tender bloom. *Ibidem*, I, vii.

4, 26. Murillo and Valesquez. Great Spanish painters, whose dates are 1618–1682 and 1599–1660, respectively.

5, 1. somewhat fat and pursy. *Hamlet*, iii, 4, 153.

5, 13. Adam Smith. The celebrated author of *The Wealth of Nations*, and founder of the science of political economy (1723–1790).

6, 19. judgment to come. Cf. *Acts*, xxiv, 25.

7, 1. Mary Wolstonecraft (1759–1797), the wife of William Godwin and the mother of Shelley's second wife. She is the author of a pioneer work on woman's rights, *Vindication of the Rights of Women*, 1792.

7, 2. Mackintosh, Sir James (1765–1832), the author of one of the many answers to Burke's *Reflections on the Revolution in France* (1790), *Vindiciæ Gallicæ*, 1791.

7, 20. Wedgwood (1771–1805), son of Josiah Wedgwood, the famous potter.

7, 23. Godwin. William Godwin (1756–1836), the author of the *Enquiry Concerning Political Justice*, 1793. The contemporary importance of the man and his books is presented by Hazlitt in *The Spirit of the Age*.

8, 3. Holcroft. Thomas Holcroft (1745–1809), an actor, dramatist, and novelist who enjoys a nebulous immortality in his play, *The Road to Ruin*. Hazlitt edited his diaries, under the title *The Memoirs of Holcroft*, 1816.

8, 21. Deva. The Latin form of Dee, the Welsh river famed in song.

8, 25. Hill of Parnassus. That is, he would be enabled to devote himself to poetry. Parnassus was the Greek mount of poetry and inspiration.

8, 25–26. Delectable Mountains. In *The Pilgrim's Progress*.

9, 11. sounding. Hazlitt mistakes Chaucer here. The scholar is represented not as "sounding on his way," but as "sowning in moral vertu." "Sowning" means not "sounding in," but "tending to," or "inclining toward." Perhaps Hazlitt has confused Chaucer and Wordsworth, Excursion III, 71: "Went sounding on, a dim and perilous way."

9, 23. Hume. David Hume (1711–1776), whose most famous work is the *Treatise on Human Nature*, 1739–1740.

9, 21. South. Robert South (1634–1716), a celebrated English divine, whose *Sermons* are a part of English prose.

9, 21–22. *Credat Judaeus Apella.* Horace, *Satires*, I, 5, 100, "Let the Jew Apella believe it!"

9, 30. Berkeley. George Berkeley (1685–1753). His *Essay on Vision* was published in 1709; the *Theory of Matter and Spirit* in 1733.

9, 34–35. " Thus I confute him." Boswell's *Life of Johnson*, under the year 1763: "I never shall forget the alacrity with which Johnson answered — striking his foot with mighty force against a large stone till he rebounded from it — 'I refute it *thus.*'"

9, 37. Tom Paine (1737–1809), author of *The Rights of Man* (1791–1792), one of the many replies to Burke's *Reflections on the French Revolution*.

10, 4. Bishop Butler. Joseph Butler (1692–1752), an English divine and philosopher, author of the celebrated *Analogy of Religion*, 1736. The *Sermons* were published in 1726.

10, 16. *Natural Disinterestedness.* This treatise was Hazlitt's first original publication, 1805, and developed the characteristic Revolutionary thesis of the inherent excellence of the natural man.

11, 3. Paley. William Paley (1743–1805), a once popular philosopher and theologian. The *Moral and Political Philosophy* was published in 1785.

11, 10–11. "**Kind and affable.**" See *Paradise Lost*, VIII, 648–650.

11, 21. He has somewhere told himself. In *Biographia Literaria*, Chapter x.

11, 28. *Vision of Judgment.* The *Vision of Judgment*, by Southey, a panegyric of George III, called forth the "other." *Vision of Judgment* by Byron, which was published in Leigh Hunt's *Liberal*, 1822.

11, 30. Bridge-street Junto. The Tory [*Quarterly Review* was published by Murray in Bridge Street, London.

12, 13–14. *Ode on the Departing Year.* Written in 1796.

12, 21. Tom Jones. Fielding's *Tom Jones*, Book X, Chapter v.

12, 24. *Paul and Virginia.* By Bernardin de Sainte-Pierre, 1788.

13, 9. *Camilla.* By Fanny Burney, 1796.

13, 22. free use. A mistake. Wordsworth paid £23 a year for the place. Mrs. Sandford, *Tom Poole and his Friends*, I, 225. Hazlitt may have confused Alfoxden with Racedown, the previous home of Wordsworth, which he had occupied rent-free.

13, 26. "**Scales that fence.**" The source of this quotation has never been identified.

13, 29. *Lyrical Ballads.* Published in September, 1798, soon after Hazlitt's visit. None of Wordsworth's poems existed in scattered publications, *i.e.*, in the form of *Sybilline Leaves*. Hazlitt here has reference to Coleridge's use of the term to describe the widely scattered nature of his publication of 1817 — the *Sybilline Leaves*.

13, 37. ."**hear the loud stag speak.**" The source of this quotation has never been identified.

14, 19–23. *Betty Foy, The Mad Mother, Complaint of a Poor Indian Woman.* Poems by Wordsworth published in the *Lyrical Ballads*.

14, 25. "**In spite of pride.**" Pope, *Essay on Man*, I, 293.

14, 30. "**While yet the trembling year.**" James Thomson, *Spring*, 18.

14, 34. Of Providence. *Paradise Lost*, ii, 559–560.

15, 19. Peter Bell. The hero of Wordsworth's poem by that name, which was published in 1819.

15, 26. Chantry's bust. Sir Francis Chantry (1781–1842) executed a bust of Wordsworth in 1821.

15, 27. Haydon. Benjamin Robert Haydon (1786–1846) introduced a portrait of Wordsworth into his painting of Christ's Entrance into Jerusalem.

15, 38. *Castle Spectre.* Mathew Gregory Lewis (1775–1818) was called "Monk" because of his romance, *The Monk*, 1795. *The Castle Spectre*, a dramatic romance, was produced in 1797.

16, 2. *ad captandum* merit, the power of capturing public applause.

16, 15. "his face was as a book." *Macbeth*, i, 5, 63.

16, 37. Tom Poole (1765–1837). A good friend of Coleridge, Wordsworth, and other literary men. He was a wealthy tanner.

17, 6. "followed in the chase." *Othello*, ii, 3, 369–370.

17, 20. Sir Walter Scott's. This fling at the Tory proclivities of Scott may refer to a banquet given to George IV, by the Magistrates of Edinburgh, August 24, 1822 (Waller and Glover).

17, 27. Poussin's or Domenichino's. Gaspar Poussin (1613–1675) changed his name from Dughet to Poussin out of regard for his brother-in-law, Nicolas Poussin. Domenico Zampieri (1581–1641) was a painter of Bologna.

18, 21. prose tale. *The Wanderings of Cain.*

18, 22. *Death of Abel.* By the Swiss idyllic poet, Solomon Gessner (1730–1788), published in 1758.

18, 29 ff. He said the *Lyrical Ballads* . . . Henry II. Hazlitt's version of the aim of Wordsworth and Coleridge to adopt a diction that would be the "neutral style," neither ancient nor modern, but essential English. Hazlitt's own prose is deeply influenced by just such an aim.

Coleridge's statement is found in his criticisms of Wordsworth, especially in Chapters xviii–xx of the *Biographia Literaria.* There is nothing in these chapters which carries the beginning of the English "neutral style" beyond Chaucer.

19, 20. *Caleb Williams.* A famous novel by William Godwin, published in 1794.

19, footnote. Buffamalco or Buffalmacco (1262–1351), a Florentine painter. The jester in Boccaccio's *Decameron.*

19, 24. "ribbed sea-sands." *Ancient Mariner*, 226–227. These two lines are by Wordsworth.

19, 29 ff. This conversation, and others like it, doubtless gave Wordsworth the impression that Hazlitt "was somewhat unreasonably attached to modern books of moral philosophy," and led him to write *Expostulation and Reply* and *The Tables Turned*, calling attention to the importance of first-hand experiences. See Wordsworth's *Advertisement* to the *Lyrical Ballads*, 1798.

20, 27. Remorse. Produced at Drury Lane Theatre, January 23, 1813. It was a re-writing of *Osorio*, which was finished in 1797.

20, 29. Elliston. Robert William Elliston (1774–1831), an admired actor of the period.

21, 8–9. "But there is matter . . . tale." Wordsworth, *Heart-Leap Well*, 95–96.

ON READING OLD BOOKS

Reprinted in *Table Talk*, 1821–1822, from *The London Magazine*, February, 1821.

22, 4–5. *Tales of My Landlord.* A series of Scott's novels, including *Old Mortality*, *Rob Roy*, and *The Bride of Lammermoor*.

22, 7. **Lady Morgan** (1783?–1859), a writer of Irish stories, the best known of which is *The Wild Irish Girl*, 1806.

22, 8. *Anastasius; or Memoirs of a Greek, written at the Close of the Eighteenth Century*, 1819, by Thomas Hope (1770?–1831). The book enjoyed considerable popularity.

22, 11. *Delphine.* A novel by Madame de Staël, 1802.

22, 13. "in their newest gloss." *Macbeth*, i, 7, 34.

22, 18. **Andrew Millar** (1707–1768), famous as the publisher of Fielding, Thomson, and other well-known authors.

22, 20. **Thurloe's** *State Papers.* John Thurloe (1616–1668) published a collection of the State Papers of the Protectorate, 7 vols. folio, 1742.

22, 21. **Sir William Temple** (1628–1699), author of *Essays*, published in 1680 and 1692. Dr. Johnson says he was the first writer to give cadence to English prose.

22, 22. **Sir Godfrey Kneller** (1646–1723), a famous portrait painter.

23, 19. **rifaccimentos**, recasts of old works.

24, 3. "for thoughts and for remembrance." *Hamlet*, iv, 5, 175–177.

24, 4. **Fortunatus's wishing-cap.** Fortunatus is the hero of a widely diffused popular tale.

24, 8. *Bruscambille.* See Sterne, *Tristram Shandy*, III, xxxv.

24, 9. *Peregrine Pickle.* A novel by Tobias Smollett (1721–1771), published in 1751.

24, 10–11. **Memoirs of Lady Vane**, in *Peregrine Pickle.*

24, 11–14. **masquerade**, in *Tom Jones*, XIII, vii; **Thwackum and Square**, III, iii; **Molly Seagrim**, IV, viii; **Sophia and her muff**, V, iv; **her aunt's lecture**, VII, iii.

24, 21. "the puppets dallying." *Hamlet*, iii, 2, 257.

24, 30. **Christian's burthen.** In *The Pilgrim's Progress.*

24, 32. "ignorance was bliss." Cf. Gray, *Ode on a Distant Prospect of Eton College.*

25, 8. **Ballantyne.** James Ballantyne, a publisher who is famous for his relations with Scott.

25, 9. **Minerva press.** A publishing house which issued highly-colored tales.

25, 12. **butter and honey.** Cf. *Isaiah*, vii, 15.

25, 16. **Cooke's pocket-edition.** John Cooke (1731–1820) published a *Select Edition of British Novels*, 1792, in weekly parts.

25, 18–19. **Mrs. Radcliffe's** *Romance of the Forest.* Published in 1791.

25, 20. "sweet in the mouth." *Revelation*, x, 9.

25, 22. "gay creatures." Milton, *Comus*, 299–301.

25, 32. **discovers Square.** V, v.

25, 33–34. **Parson Adams . . . Mrs. Slip-slop.** IV, xiv.

25, 35. *Joseph Andrews.* Fielding's first novel, 1742. Fanny is the heroine.

26, 1. like ————. Probably Sarah Walker of the *Liber Amoris.*

26, 5. Major Bath. In Fielding's *Joseph Andrews.* **Commodore Trunnion.** In Smollett's *Peregrine Pickle.*

26, 5–6. Trim and my Uncle Toby. In Sterne's *Tristram Shandy.*

26, 6. Don Quixote and Sancho and Dapple. Sancho and Dapple are Don Quixote's squire and his steed in *Don Quixote.*

26, 7. Gil Blas and Dame Lorenza Sephora. *Gil Blas* is a satirical novel (1715) by Le Sage. Gil Blas is the main character in the story and Dame Lorenza is one of the principal female characters.

26, 7. Laura. An actress, mistress, and patroness of Gil Blas. See *Gil Blas,* Book III, Chapters 5, 7, 10, 11, 12; Book IV, Chapter 1; Book VII, Chapters 6–11; and Book XII, Chapters 1–3.

26, 8. Lucretia. In *Joseph Andrews.*

26, 16. "O Memory!" The source of this quotation has not been traced.

26, 21–22. Chubb's Tracts. By Thomas Chubb (1697–1747), a deist.

26, 30–31. "fate, free-will." Milton, *Paradise Lost,* II, 560.

26, 35–36. "Would I had never seen Wittenberg." Marlowe, *Dr. Faustus,* Scene xiv.

26, 37. Hartley, Hume, Berkeley. David Hartley (1705–1757), author of *Observations on Man,* 1749; David Hume (1711–1776); George Berkeley (1685–1751).

Locke's *Essay on the Human Understanding,* 1690.

27, 2. Hobbes. Thomas Hobbes (1588–1679). His most famous book is *Leviathan,* 1651.

27, 8. *New Eloise.* By Rousseau, published in 1761.

27, 9–10. St. Preux. *New Eloise,* Part VI, Letters IX–XI.

27, 19–20. *Social Contract.* Rousseau published this work in 1762, and *The Confessions* in 1778.

27, 22. I have spoken elsewhere. In his essay on Rousseau in *The Round Table.*

27, 25. "scattered like stray gifts." Wordsworth, *Stray Pleasures,* 27–28.

27, 26. *Emilius.* By Rousseau, published in 1762.

27, 30. Sir Fopling Flutter. In Sir George Etherege's *The Man of Mode,* 1676.

28, 9–10. leurre de dupe. A phrase from Rousseau's *Confessions,* IV, meaning "a lure for a 'gull.'"

28, 12–13. "a load to sink a navy." *Henry VIII,* iii, 2, 383.

28, 33. Marcian Colonna. Lamb, *Sonnet to . . . Barry Cornwall.*

28, 36. "Come like shadows." *Macbeth,* iv, 1, iii.

28, 37. "tiger-moth's wings." Keats, *Eve of St. Agnes,* 214.

29, 3–4. "blood of queens and kings." *Ibidem,* 217.

29, 9. "Words, words, words." *Hamlet,* ii, 2, 194–197.

29, 13–14. fairy tale. Perrault, *The Fairies.*

29, 14. great preacher. Edward Irving (1792–1834), a friend of Thomas Carlyle and his wife.

29, 18. "**as the hart that panteth.**" Cf. *Psalm* xlii, 1.

29, 20. **Goethe's** *Sorrows of Werter* . . . **Schiller's** *Robbers.* One of many references to the great reputation of these examples of "German sentiment." *Werter* was published in 1774, *The Robbers* in 1781.

29, 21. **Giving my stock.** Cf. *As You Like It*, ii, 1, 48–49.

29, 22–23. **Coleridge's fine sonnet.** Printed in 1796, and probably written as early as 1794.

29, 28–30. **I believe I may date,** etc. Fully expressed in *My First Acquaintance with Poets*.

29, 34. **Valentine, Tattle, Miss Prue.** Characters in Congreve's *Love for Love*, 1695.

30, 3. "**know my cue.**" Cf. *Othello*, I, ii, 84–85.

30, 4. *Intus et in cute, i.e.,* "intimately and in the skin." Persius, *Satires*, III, 30.

30, 9–10. **Sir Humphrey Davy** (1778–1829), a celebrated English scientist, inventor of the safety lamp.

30, 27. **the divine Clementina.** In Richardson's *Sir Charles Grandison*, 1753.

30, 28. "**with every trick and line.**" *All's Well that Ends Well*, i, 1, 106–107.

30, 30. **Mackenzie's** *Julia de Roubigné.* Henry Mackenzie (1745–1831) published this story in 1777. *The Man of Feeling* was published in 1771, and is noted for its sentimentality and profusion of tears.

30, 31. **peace of Amiens.** March, 1802.

30, 35. **Richardson's Romance.** *Clarissa Harlowe.*

31, 5. **Miss ———.** Probably Sarah Walker of the *Liber Amoris.*

31, 5–6. "**that ligament, fine as it was.**" Sterne, *Tristram Shandy*, VI, x (The Story of Le Fever).

31, 11. **story of the hawk.** Commonly called "The Story of the Falcon" (*Decameron*, Day V, Novel IX). This admired story is used by Tennyson in his play, *The Falcon*.

31, 16. *Recruiting Officer.* This drama was written in 1706.

31, 16–17. "**at one proud swoop.**" Cf. *Macbeth*, iv, 3, 219.

31, 21–22. **That time is past** "**with all its giddy raptures.**" Wordsworth, *Lines Composed a Few Miles Above Tintern Abbey*, 84–86.

31, 23. "**embalmed with odours.**" *Paradise Lost*, II, 843.

31, 33. "**His form.**" *Paradise Lost*, I, 591.

31, 37–38. "**falls flat upon the grunsel edge.**" *Paradise Lost*, I, 460.

32, 2–12. Note this passage of noble praise. Hazlitt discriminates between Burke's style, which he admires, and his doctrines, which he detests.

32, 14. **Junius's.** Sir Philip Francis, the author of *Letters of Junius.*

32, 21. **eagle in a dove-cot.** *Coriolanus*, v, 6, 115.

32, 32. *Essay on Marriage.* No such essay by Wordsworth is known. The conjecture of Waller and Glover (in which they are followed by Howe) that Hazlitt may mean the *Letter to the Bishop of Llandoff*, written in 1793, as it was "the only notable prose work which Wordsworth had published" in 1798, is unfounded, as the *Letter* was never published in Wordsworth's lifetime, and was known to very few.

33, 5–11. Note this account by Hazlitt of his own early difficulties in the art of writing.

33, 18–19. "**worthy of all acceptation.**" *I Timothy*, i, 15.

33, 27–28. Clarendon's *History of the Rebellion.* Published in 1704–1707.

33, 34–35. Froissart's *Chronicles.* Jean Froissart (1338–1410?), *Chronicles of France, England, Scotland, and Spain*, 1367–1400. **Ralph Holinshed**, *Chronicles of England, Scotland, and Ireland*, 1377. **John Stow** (1525?–1605), *English Chronicles*, 1561. **Thomas Fuller** (1608–1661), *The History of the Worthies of England*, 1662.

33, 37–38. *A Wife for a Month*, 1623.

33,'38. *Thierry and Theodoret*, 1621.

34, 2. Thucydides. The great Greek historian (B.C. 471–401). **Guicciardini.** Francesco Guicciardini (1483–1540), a well-known Italian historian.

34, 3–4. *Don Quixote*, 1605, *Loves of Persiles and Sigismunda*, 1617, and *Galatea*, 1583, are works by Cervantes, the great Spanish novelist.

34, 6. "another Yarrow." Wordsworth, *Yarrow Unvisited.*

WHETHER GENIUS IS CONSCIOUS OF ITS POWERS

35, 7. Bolingbroke. Henry St. John, Viscount Bolingbroke (1672–1751), to whom Pope addressed his *Essay on Man.*
Sir William Temple. See note on **22, 21.**

35, 13. "**sees not itself.**" Cf. *Julius Cæsar*, i, 2, 52–53.

35, 32. "**a phœnix gazed by all.**" *Paradise Lost*, V, 272.

36, 32–33. *Materiam superabat opus.* Ovid, *Metamorphoses*, II, 5, "the workmanship was more beautiful than the material."

37, 3–4. Correggio (1494–1534), a famous painter of the Lombard school; **Michael Angelo** (1475–1564), famous as sculptor, painter, and poet; **Rembrandt** (1607–1669), the leading Dutch painter.

37, 9. "**Our poesy is as a gum.**" *Timon of Athens*, i, 1, 21–25.

37, 18. Hogarth, William (1697–1764), a celebrated English painter and engraver; known especially for his comic and satiric pictures.

37, 24. Vandyke (1590–1641), the great Flemish portrait painter.

37, 36. *invitâ Minerva.* Horace, *De Arte Poetica*, 385, "against the bent of genius, or nature."

39, 1–2. "**the glory, the intuition, the amenity.**" Charles Lamb, *Lines on "the Virgin of the Rocks."*

39, 13–14. darkness visible. *Paradise Lost*, I, 62. **darkness that could only be felt.** *Exodus*, x, 21.

39, 37. "**through happiness or pains.**" Pope, *Epistle to Mr. Jervas*, 68.

40, 28–29. "**And visions . . . bough.**" This couplet, a favorite quotation of Hazlitt's, occurs in a letter from Gray to Walpole. (Gray's *Letters*, edited by Jovey, Volume I, 7–8.) The lines are apparently a translation (by Gray) of Virgil, *Æneid*, VI, 282–284 (Waller and Glover).

40, 33. "**My mind to me a kingdom is.**" Sir Edward Dyer, in Byrd's *Psalms and Sonnets*, 1588.

41, 4. Millimant. The leading woman character in Congreve's *The Way of the World*, 1700. Hazlitt refers to his *Lectures on the English Comic Writers*, 1819.

41, 9. Friscobaldo. In Thomas Dekker, *The Honest Whore*, Part II. This description is to be found in Hazlitt's *Lectures on the Dramatic Literature of the Age of Elizabeth*, 1820.

41, 10. G . ff . . d. William Gifford (1757–1826) is the subject of a separate publication by Hazlitt, *A Letter to William Gifford, Esq.*, 1819, in which he is very severely handled.

41, 23. Webster or Dekker. John Webster (1602–1624), Thomas Dekker (1570?–1637?). These men are dealt with in *Lectures on the Dramatic Literature of the Age of Elizabeth*, 1820.

41, 25–26. *Characters of Shakespeare's Plays*, 1817.

41, 27. Anti-Jacobin and Anti-Gallican writers. Those who were opposed to the Revolutionary doctrines.

41, 31. *Descent of Liberty.* A masque by Leigh Hunt (1784–1859); published in 1815.

41, 33. sat by the waters of Babylon. *Psalm* cxxxvii, 1–2.

41, 35. the cause of kings or of mankind. This sentence is a terse summary of Hazlitt's consistent belief. His admiration for Napoleon was based on the belief that Napoleon was against the kings.

41, 37. the Mighty. Napoleon.

42, 9. Beast. Cf. *Revelation*, xiii, 4.

42, 16. image and superscription. Cf. *St. Matthew*, xxii, 20; *St. Mark*, xii, 16; *St. Luke*, xx, 24.

42, 22–23. "**Cried out upon in the top of the compass.**" Cf. *Hamlet*, iii, 2, 381–383, and ii, 2, 355.

42, 29. *Characteristics.* Mr. Jerdan reviewed Hazlitt's *Characteristics* (published anonymously in 1823) very favorably in the *Literary Gazette* for July 12, 1823.

43, 5–6. **praised in the** *Examiner, i.e.,* in Leigh Hunt's publication.

43, 9. *Story of Rimini.* Published in 1816.

43, 10–11. "**an Adonis of fifty.**" Words applied by Leigh Hunt to the Prince Regent, for which he and John Hunt were sent to prison.

43, 12–13. "**Return, Alphæus . . . Muse!**" Milton, *Lycidas*, 132–133.

43, 25–26. "**look abroad into universality.**" Bacon, *Advancement of Learning*, Book I.

44, 10. **A. P. E.** Alexander Pope, Esquire.

44, 31. "**They take in vain.**" *Exodus*, xx, 7.

45, 1. "**It is all one as we should love.**" *All's Well that Ends Well*, i, 1, 96–98.

45, 3. "**fast anchored.**" Cf. Cowper, *Retirement*, 84.

45, 11. "**the face of heaven so bright.**" Cf. *Romeo and Juliet*, ii, 2, 20–22.

45, 15. **Bartlemy Fair.** A famous fair held at West Smithfield, London, 1133–1850, about St. Bartholomew's Day, August 24.

45, 21. "**The high endeavour.**" Cf. Cowper, *The Task*, V, 903.

46, 13–14. *bis repetita crambe.* Cf. Juvenal, *Satires*, vii, 154, "twice chewed cabbage."

46, 26. "*Titianus faciebat.*" That is, "Titian was engaged in making [this picture]."

46, 29–30. **Annibal Caracci.** 1560–1609.

47, 27. *Love for Love.* A comedy by Congreve, 1695.

A Farewell to Essay-Writing

Written February 20, 1828, at Winterslow. [Published in the *London Weekly Review* for March 29, 1828. Printed in *Winterslow Essays*, 1850.

48, 1. "**This life is best.**" *Cymbeline*, iii, 3, 29–30.

48, 3. *ultima thule,* "farthest north, *i.e.*, 'most remote' parts of the world."

48, 5. "**a friend in your retreat.**" Cowper, *Retirement*, 741–742.

48, 14. "**done its spiriting gently.**" *The Tempest,* i, 2, 299.

48, 15. **startle the ear of winter.** Cf. Milton, *L'Allegro*, 42, "And singing startle the dull Night."

48, 23. "**credulous hope.**" Cf. Milton, *Paradise Regained*, II, 166, "credulous desire"; and Wordsworth, *To the Clouds*, 88–89, "credulous desire nourish the hope."

48, 27–28. "**the spring comes slowly.**" Coleridge, *Christabel*, 12.

48, 28–29. "**fields are dank and ways are mire.**" Milton, Sonnet, "Laurence, of virtuous father virtuous son."

49, 13. "**left its little life in air.**" Pope, *Windsor Forest*, 134.

49, 24. "**peep through the blanket of the past.**" *Macbeth*, i, 5, 51.

49, 32. **Louvre.** The great Paris gallery of painting and sculpture, where Hazlitt studied painting.

50, 6. "**open all the cells.**" Cowper, *The Task*, VI, 11–12.

50, 14. *Theodore and Honoria.* Dryden's retelling of a story from Boccaccio. The scene referred to is in lines 102–124.

50, 18–19. "**Of all the cities . . . stands.**" *Theodore and Honoria*, 1–2.

50, 28–29. "**Which when Honoria viewed . . . renew'd.**" Lines 342–343.

50, 31–32. "**And made th'** *insult* . . . **tears.**" Dryden, *Sigismonda and Guiscardo*, 668–669.

51, 8. *con amore.* Italian, "with pleasure."

51, 10–11. "**Let honour and preferment . . . sold.**" Dryden, Epilogue to *Mithridates, King of Pontus*, 16–17 (1678).

51, 23–24. "**Fall'n was Glenartny's stately tree . . . more.**" Sir Walter Scott, *Glenfinlas*, final stanza.

52, 29–30. "**admired of all observers.**" Cf. *Hamlet*, iii, 1, 162.

53, 34. "**I know not** *seems.*" *Hamlet*, i, 2, 76.

53, 35. "**Companion.**" Leigh Hunt.

54, 2. *Aut Caesar aut nullus.* "Either Cæsar or no one."

54, 17. **L———.** Charles Lamb.

54, 28. *Antonio.* The play was produced at Drury Lane Theatre, December 13, 1800, and "failed of success" most signally.

55, 4. "**Nor can I think.**" Dryden, *The Hind and the Panther*, I, 315.

55, 16–17. **Chaucer's** *Flower and Leaf.* This poem is now known not to be Chaucer's. The author is unknown.

55, 22. "**And ayen . . . ear.**" *Flower and Leaf*, Stanza 15.

55, 27. **Miss L———.** Mary Lamb.

55, 28. **Claude Lorraine** (1600–1682). A celebrated French landscape painter, much admired by Hazlitt.

56, 1. **Wilson.** Richard Wilson (1714–1782), a noted English landscape painter.

56, 5. **hashed mutton.** See Fielding, *Amelia*, Book X, Chapter v, in which Amelia eats the hashed mutton which she had prepared for her extravagant husband.

56, 26. "**And curtain close . . . view.**" Collins, *Ode on the Poetical Character*, 76.

On Classical Education

This essay was first published in *The Examiner* for February 12, 1815, where it formed the greater part of No. 7 of the Round Table series. The germ of the essay was published in *The Morning Chronicle* for September 25, 1813, as a part of one of Hazlitt's *Common Places*, and consisted of the first three paragraphs. It was republished in revised form in *The Round Table*, 1817.

57, 2. "**a discipline of humanity.**" Sir Francis Bacon, *Essays, Of Marriage and Single Life.*

57, 16. **set on a hill.** *St. Matthew*, v, 14.

57, 19–26. "**Still green with bays . . . flow.**" Pope, *Essay on Criticism*, 181–188.

57, 31–32. **Conversing with the** *mighty dead.* Cf. Thomson, *Winter*, 431, "And hold high converse with the mighty dead."

58, 30. **A celebrated political writer.** No doubt William Cobbett (1762–1835).

59, 1. "**The world is too much with us.**" Freely quoted from Wordsworth's Sonnet.

59, 38. *Falstaff's reasoning.* *1 Henry IV*, v, 1, 138–143.

60, 6. "**They that are whole.**" *St. Matthew*, ix, 12.

ON THE IGNORANCE OF THE LEARNED

This essay was first published in the *Scots' Magazine*, July, 1818. It was reprinted in *Table Talk*, 1821–1822.

61, 1–12. "**For the more languages . . . own.**" Samuel Butler (1612–1680), *Satire upon the Abuse of Human Learning*, 57–68.

61, 30. "**spectacles.**" Speaking of Shakespeare, Dryden says, "He needed not the spectacles of books to read Nature." *Essay of Dramatic Poesy.*

62, 10. "**Leave me to my repose.**" Gray, *The Descent of Odin.* "Leave me, leave me to repose" is the refrain of the poem. It was doubtless given currency by Burke, who quoted it in his *Letter to a Noble Lord*, 1795.

62, 15. "**take up his bed and walk.**" *St. Matthew*, ix, 6.

62, 21. "**enfeebles all internal strength.**" Goldsmith, *The Traveller*, 270.

62, 32. "**sweats in the eye of Phœbus.**" *Henry V*, iv, 1, 290–291.

64, 12. "**Th' enthusiast Fancy.**" Cf. Charles Lamb, *Fancy Employed on Divine Subjects*, 1–2:

> "The truant Fancy was a wanderer ever,
> A lone enthusiast maid."

64, 22–23. **least respectable character.** George Canning.

65, 23. **A person of this class.** Dr. Charles Burney (1757–1827); author of *Remarks on the Greek Verses of Milton*, 1790.

65, 26–27. **Dr. ———.** Dr. Burney and Dr. Samuel Parr.

65, 27. **Porson.** Richard Porson (1759–1808), a famous Greek scholar, professor at the University of Cambridge.

66, 7. "**The mighty world of eye and ear.**" Wordsworth, *Lines Composed a Few Miles Above Tintern Abbey*, 105–106.

66, 8. "**knowledge quite shut out.**" *Paradise Lost*, III, 50.

66, 12–16. "**Of the colouring of Titian.**" Sterne, *Tristram Shandy*, III, 12.

66, 35. "**knows no touch of it.**" *Hamlet*, iii, 2, 371.

67, 6–7. "**the act and practique part of life.**" *Henry V*, i, 1, 51–52.

67, 9–11. "**has no skill in surgery.**" *1 Henry IV*, v, 1, 134.

68, 4. *Anas.* Miscellaneous collections of information about persons or things.

68, 28. **Baxter.** Richard Baxter (1615–1691), author of *The Saints' Everlasting Rest*, 1650.

69, 5–6. "**wink and shut their apprehensions up.**" Marston, *Antonio's Revenge*, Prologue.

69, 21–25. **Laud,** William (1573–1645); **Whitgift,** John (1530?–1604), both Archbishops of Canterbury; **Bull,** George (1634–1740); **Waterland,** Daniel (1683–1740); **Prideaux,** Humphrey (1648–1724); **Beausobre,** Isaac de (1659–1738); **Calmet,** Augustine (1672–1757); **Puffendorf,** Samuel, Baron von (1632–1694); **Vattel,** Eméri de (1714–1767); **Scaliger,** Joseph J. (1540–1609); **Cardan,** Jerome (1503–1576); **Scioppius,** or Schoppe, Kaspar (1576–1649).

69, 28–29. "**gone to the vault of all the Capulets.**" *Romeo and Juliet*, iv, 1, 111–112.

THE INDIAN JUGGLERS

This essay first appeared in *Table Talk*, 1821–1822. The essay is in praise of skill, bodily and mental. A good juggler is better than a mediocre statesman.

74, 35. "**In argument . . . still.**" Goldsmith, *The Deserted Village*, 211–212.

75, 33. "**to allow for the wind.**" Scott, *Ivanhoe*, Chapter xiii.

76, 9. "**human face divine.**" *Paradise Lost*, III, 44.

76, 26. **H———s and H———s.** W. C. Hazlitt in his edition of *Table Talk* prints the first name as "Haydons." Is the second one "Hazlitts"?

76, 27. "**in tones and gestures hit.**" Cf. *Paradise Regained*, IV, 255.

76, 31–32. "**commercing with the skies.**" Milton, *Il Penseroso*, 39.

77, 20–21. "**And visions as poetic . . . bough.**" See note on **40**, 28–29.

77, 30. "**Thrills in each nerve.**" Cf. Addison, *Milton's Style Imitated*, 123–124.

78, 11. "**half flying, half on foot.**" Cf. *Paradise Lost*, II, 941–942.

78, 26–27. **I know an individual.** Leigh Hunt.

78, 35. *Nugæ canoræ.* Horace, *De Arte Poetica*, 322, "nonsense versified."

78, 36. **Rochester,** Earl of (1647–1680), a poet and courtier in the reign of Charles II.

78, 37. **Surrey,** Earl of (1517–1547), who with Sir Thomas Wyatt inaugurated the period of Elizabethan literature.

80, 20–21. **Jedediah Buxton** (1705–1772), a mathematical prodigy, who was unable to obtain an education and so accomplished nothing notable. **Napier,** John (1550–1617), who invented logarithms.

81, 8. **John Hunter** (1728–1793), a noted English surgeon, physiologist, and anatomist.

81, 26–27. "**great scholar's memory** . . . **century.**" Cf. *Hamlet,* iii, 2, 139–140.

82, 2. Wolsey. Cardinal Wolsey (1471–1530).

82, 3. Mendicant Friar. A begging friar.

82, 7. Molière, the great French comic dramatist (1622–1673); **Rabelais** (1495–1553), author of *Pantagruel,* 1553; **Montaigne** (1533–1592), the great French essayist.

82, 30–31. "**Care mounted behind the horseman.**" Horace, *Odes,* III, i, 40.

82, 34. "**in the instant.**" *Macbeth,* i, 5, 59.

82, 35. "**domestic treason.**" Cf. *Macbeth,* iii, 2, 25–26.

83, 32. Cobbett, William (1762–1835), a noted English radical writer and politician.

84, 14–15. Rosemary Branch. A well-known tavern at Peckham.

84, 35. Copenhagen-house. A tavern in the north of London.

85, 38. The Fleet prison and the **King's Bench** prison had well-known courts for the game of fives.

86, 4. "**Who enters here.**" Cf. Pope, *The Dunciad,* IV, 518–519.

86, 12. the present Speaker. Mr. Charles Manners Sutton was elected Speaker of the House on June 2, 1817.

86, 17–18. "**Let no rude hand** . . . *jacet.*" Wordsworth, *Ellen Irwin,* 55–56.

On Going a Journey

This incomparable essay in praise of walking was first published in the *New Monthly Magazine,* 1822, Volume IV, p. 22. It was reprinted in *Table Talk,* 1821–1822.

87, 5. "**The fields his study** . . . **book.**" Robert Bloomfield (1766–1823), *The Farmer's Boy, Spring,* 31.

87, 12–13. "**a friend in my retreat** . . . **sweet.**" Cowper, *Retirement,* 741–742.

87, 22–24. "**May plume her feathers** . . . **impair'd.**" Milton, *Comus,* 378–381.

87, 27. Tilbury. A gig, or two-wheeled carriage, without a top or cover.

88, 5. "**sunken wrack.**" *Henry V,* i, 2, 165.

88, 12–13. "**Leave, oh, leave me.**" Gray, *The Descent of Odin,* refrain. See note on 62, 10.

88, 26–27. "**Out upon such half-faced fellowship.**" *I Henry IV,* I, iii, 208.

89, 37. "**give it an understanding.**" *Hamlet,* i, 2, 250.

89, 38. C———. Coleridge.

90, 3–4. "**He talked far above singing.**" Beaumont and Fletcher, *Philaster,* v, 5.

90, 4. so clothe. *St. Matthew,* vi, 30.

90, 6. swelling theme. Cf. *Henry V,* Prologue to Act i, sc. 4.

90, 8. "**that fine madness.**" Thomas Drayton, *Censure of Poets.*

90, 12–29. "**Here be woods . . . sweetest.**" John Fletcher, *The Faithful Shepherdess*, I, iii, 27–43.

90, 37. **L——.** Charles Lamb.

91, 8–9. **take one's ease at one's inn.**" *1 Henry IV*, iii, 3, 93.

91, 15. "**the cups that cheer.**" Cf. Cowper, *The Task*, IV, 39–40.

91, 19. **cow-heel.** *Don Quixote*, II, xlix.

91, 21. **Shandean.** Like that shown in *Tristram Shandy.*

91, 23. *Procul.* Virgil, *Æneid*, VI, 258, "Away, away, ye initiated!"

92, 5–6. "**unhoused free condition.**" *Othello*, i, 2, 26.

92, 7–8. "**Lord of one's self.**" Cf. John Dryden, *To my Honoured Kinsman, John Driden*, 18.

92, 29–30. **St. Neot's.** A small town near Peterborough. About 1796 Hazlitt made a walking tour into the North, and may have seen the engravings at that time.

92, 30–31. **Gribelin's engravings of the Cartoons.** Made in 1707.

92, 33. **Westall,** Richard (1765–1836), a prominent English historical painter.

93, 1. *Paul and Virginia.* See note on **12,** 24.

93, 2. **at Bridgewater.** When he visited Coleridge and Wordsworth in 1798. See *My First Acquaintance with Poets.*

93, 4. *Camilla.* Published in 1796.

93, 5–6. *New Eloise . . . St. Preux.* Rousseau, *La Nouvelle Heloise*, Part IV, Letter xvii.

93, 10. *bon bouche.* Properly, *bonne bouche*, a choice morsel to top off with.

93, 16–17. "**green upland swells.**" Cf. Coleridge, *Ode to the Departing Year*, 125–126.

93, 19. "**glittered green.**" *Ode to the Departing Year*, 124.

93, 28. **faded into the light of common day.** Wordsworth, *Ode on the Intimations of Immortality*, 76. Cf. also *To a Highland Girl*, 16–17.

93, 30. "**The beautiful is vanished, and returns not.**" Coleridge, *The Death of Wallenstein*, V, i, 68.

94, 3–7. **Yet will I turn,** etc. This sentence is an amalgam of Wordsworth, *Lines Composed a Few Miles Above Tintern Abbey*, 56–58, *Revelation*, xxi, 6, and xxii, 1–2.

94, 18. **bares its bosom.** Cf. Wordsworth, Sonnet, *The world is too much with us*, 5.

94, 26–27. "**Beyond Hyde Park,**" . . . **Fopling Flutter.** Sir George Etherege (1635?–1691), *The Man of Mode*, V, ii. In the text Fopling is misprinted Topling.

95, 28. "**The mind is its own place.**" *Paradise Lost*, I, 254.

95, 33. "**With glistering spires.**" *Paradise Lost*, III, 550.

95, 36. **Bodleian.** The great Library at the University of Oxford. **Blenheim.** The seat of the Duke of Marlborough, near Oxford.

95, 37. **ciceroni,** guides.

96, 19–20. **When I first set my foot on the laughing shores of France.** This was in 1802, and so he writes at a distance of twenty years.

96, 26. **"vine-covered hills."** From William Roscoe, *Lines Written in 1798*. This poem is parodied in Canning and Frere's *Anti-Jacobin*.

97, 3. **"jump,"** risk. Cf. *Macbeth*, i, 7, 7.

97, 5. **Dr. Johnson.** Boswell, *Life of Johnson*, III, 301 (Hill's ed.).

97, 14. **"Out of my country and myself I go."** The source of this quotation has not been discovered.

WHY DISTANT OBJECTS PLEASE

First published in *Table Talk*, 1821–1822.

98, 9. **"descry new lands."** *Paradise Lost*, I, 290–291.

98, 12–13. **Ethereal mould, sky-tinctured.** A good example of Hazlitt's Miltonic echoes. Cf. *Paradise Lost*, II, 139, and V, 285.

98, 19–22. **"But thou, oh Hope!"** William Collins, *The Passions*, 29–32.

98, 27–28. **lord of infinite space.** Cf. *Hamlet*, ii, 2, 261, "king of infinite space." An example of Hazlitt's Shakespearean echoes.

98, 29–30. **"When I was a boy."** At Wem, in Shropshire, he lived within sight of the Welsh hills.

99, 3. **"Yarrow unvisited."** A reference to Wordsworth, *Yarrow Unvisited*, which maintains the thesis that it is best "not idly to disturb a dream of good."

99, 9. **"Unmould their essence."** Cf. "unmoulding reason's mintage" in Milton, *Comus*, 529.

99, 17. **"a mighty stream of tendency."** Wordsworth, *The Excursion*, IX, 87.

99, 21. **"a tide in the affairs of men."** *Julius Cæsar*, iv, 3, 218.

99, 22–23. **"with sails and tackle torn."** Cf. *Paradise Lost*, II, 1044, "though shrouds and tackle torn."

100, 2. **"Such tricks hath strong imagination."** *A Midsummer Night's Dream*, v, 1, 18.

100, 7. **"hangs upon the beatings of our hearts."** Cf. Wordsworth, *Lines Composed a Few Miles Above Tintern Abbey*, 54.

100, 10–11. **"come thronging soft desires."** Cf. *Much Ado About Nothing*, i, 1, 305.

100, 25–26. **"bring back the hour."** Wordsworth, *Ode on the Intimations of Immortality*, 190–191.

101, 9–10. **"that first garden of my innocence."** Cf. Samuel Daniel, *Hymen's Triumph*.

101, 14–16. **"Like the sweet south . . . odour."** Cf. *Twelfth Night*, i, 1, 5–8.

101, 21. **W—m.** Wem, in Shropshire.

101, 24–25. "thing of life." Byron, *The Corsair*, Canto I, iii.

101, 30. "Like some gay creature." Milton, *Comus*, 299.

101, 33. Leigh Hunt . . . in a paper. In his essay, *A Nearer View of Some of the Shops*.

103, 16. "How silver-sweet." *Romeo and Juliet*, ii, 2, 166.

103, 22. "To angels 'twas most like." Cf. *The Flower and the Leaf*, a poem formerly attributed to Chaucer, Stanza 19.

103, footnote. Wilkie's *Blind Fiddler*. David Wilkie (1775–1841), a noted Scottish painter. *The Blind Fiddler* is now in the National Gallery.

104, 5–6. "like an exhalation." Cf. *Comus*, 556, "Rose like a steam of rich distilled perfumes"; and *Paradise Lost*, I, 711, "Rose like an exhalation." This is a good example of the way in which Hazlitt blends quotations to his own taste so that they become part and parcel of his own expression.

104, 15. Mr. Fearn's *Essay*. John Fearn, *An Essay on Consciousness*, 2nd edition, 1812.

107, 33–34. "There's sympathy!" *The Merry Wives of Windsor*, ii, 1, 7.

108, 17–18. ———, the editor of a Scotch magazine. Hazlitt refers to James Gibson Lockhart, who was suspected to be the Editor of *Blackwood's Magazine*.

108, 30. "Those faultless monsters." John Sheffield, Duke of Buckingham, *Essay on Poetry*.

108, 31. "The web of our lives." *All's Well that Ends Well*, iv, 3, 84–87.

On the Disadvantages of Intellectual Superiority

This essay was first published in *Table Talk*, 1821–1822.

109, 9. Petrarch. In *Morte di Laura*, Sonnet xxiv.

109, 16–17. "To be honest . . . thousand." *Hamlet*, ii, 2, 177–179.

110, 1–4. "Stand all astonied . . . fears." Spenser, *The Faerie Queene*, VII, vi, 28.

110, 24. C———. Coleridge.

113, 7. fate, free-will. Cf. *Paradise Lost*, II, 559–560.

113, 12. *otium cum dignitate*. Cicero, *Pro Publio Sextio*, xlv, "ease with dignity."

113, 17. "I am nothing if not critical." *Othello*, ii, 1, 120.

114, 29–30. in the ———. *Quarterly Review*.

114, 37–38. *This is the unkindest cut of all*. Cf. *Julius Cæsar*, iii, 2, 187.

115, 8. *Prince Maurice's Parrot* and an *Essay on the Regal Character*. These papers were published by Hazlitt in *The Examiner*, July 10, 1814, and in *The Yellow Dwarf*, May 16, 1818, respectively.

115, 10–11. a great personage. Gifford, the editor of the *Quarterly Review*.

116, 16. L——. Charles Lamb.

116, 17. L. H. Leigh Hunt.

116, 25. Count Stendhal. Marie-Henri Beyle, a celebrated French writer (1783–1842).

116, 27. S——. Probably Shelley.

116, 28. "germane to the matter." *Hamlet*, v, 2, 165.

G——dw——n. William Godwin.

116, 30. Vetus. Contributed to the *Morning Chronicle*, 1813.

116, 36. *digito monstrari.* Cf. Horace, *Odes*, IV, iii, 22.

116, 37. Mr. Powell's Court. In St. Martin's Street, London.

117, 14–15. Mr. Knight's performance of Filch. Edward Knight (1774–1826), an actor in the Drury Lane Company. Filch is in John Gay's *The Beggar's Opera*, 1728.

117, 15. little Simmons. Samuel Simmons (1777?–1819), a member of the Covent Garden Company.

117, 23. Cavanagh. The great fives player, celebrated in *The Indian Jugglers*.

118, 9–10. "lively, audible, and full of vent." Cf. *Coriolanus*, iv, 5, 237–238.

118, 27–28. Angelica and Foresight, in *Love for Love*. By John Dryden, II, iii.

118, 36–37. "So shalt thou find me . . . bo." *Sardanapalus*, IV, i.

119, 24. sworn at Highgate. See Brand's *Popular Antiquities*, II, 195. The oath in part is "never to kiss the maid when he could kiss the mistress."

120, 3. "not pierceable by power of any star." Spenser, *Faerie Queene*, I, i, 7.

120, 6. "to succeed at the gaming-table." Cf. John Gay, *The Beggar's Opera*, I, iv. The words are Mr. Peachum's.

120, 14–16. "to have a good face . . . nature." Cf. *Much Ado about Nothing*, iii, 3, 14–16.

120, 33. Hobbes, Thomas (1588–1679), the celebrated English philosopher. His best known book is *Leviathan*, 1651.

ON THE KNOWLEDGE OF CHARACTER

This essay was first published in *Table Talk*, 1821–1822.

121, 23. a celebrated wit. Either Voltaire or Talleyrand. The idea has often been expressed.

121, 26–27. Lord Chesterfield. In *Letters to his Son*, cxxx.

121, 32. "It is not a year or two shows us a man." *Othello*, iii, 4, 103.

122, 3. **Charles V** (1500–1558), Emperor of the Holy Roman Empire.

122, 3–4. **Ignatius Loyola** (1491–1556), founder of the Society of Jesus.

122, 10. **Donne**, John (1573–1631), an English poet. The **rude half effaced outline** is by W. Marshall, from a painting of Donne at the age of 18.

122, 14. **W——**. Wellington.

122, 33. *prima facie*. At first view or appearance.

123, 3. **Mr. ——**. Hazlitt?

123, 31. **C——'s**. Coleridge's.

123, 32–33. "**Create a soul**." Milton, *Comus*, 562.

124, 17–18. "**The greatest hypocrite**." Sarah Walker, heroine of *Liber Amoris*.

124, 31. **I know a person**. Hazlitt.

124, 35. "**compliments extern**." *Othello*, i, 1, 63.

126, 9–10. "**If the French have a fault**." Sterne, *A Sentimental Journey*, Versailles.

127, 21. "**wild wit**." Gray, *Ode on A Distant Prospect of Eton College*, 46.

128, 28. *service is no inheritance*. Cf. *All's Well that Ends Well*, i, 3, 25–26, "Service is no heritage.";

129, 4–5. "**Subtle as the fox . . . eat**." *Cymbeline*, iii, 3, 40–41.

129, 37–38. "**bitter bad judges**." Gay, *The Beggar's Opera*, I, iv.

130, 5–6. **I never knew but one clever man**. Probably Leigh Hunt.

130, 25–26. "**The way of woman's will . . . hit**." Cf. Milton, *Samson Agonistes*, 1011–1013.

130, 34. *Cavalier servente*. Literally, "cavalier lover", "handy man."

131, 13. **Oh! thou**. Sarah Walker.

131, 17. **Imogen**. In *Cymbeline*.

132, 10. *sui generis*, unique.

132, 37. "**The son**." Here Hazlitt is giving his personal experience.

133, 5. "**Rembrandts**." Cf. Goldsmith, *Retaliation*, 145, "Raphaels, Correggios, and stuff."

133, 14. "**infinite agitation of men's wit**." Bacon, *Advancement of Learning*, I, iv, 5.

135, 3. "**in the trade of war**." *Othello*, i, 2, 1.

135, 5. "**so as with a difference**." *Hamlet*, iv, 5, 83, "You must wear your rue with a difference."

135, 9. "**pure defecated evil**." Burke, *Letter to a Noble Lord*.

135, 12. "**whatever is, is right**." Pope, *Essay on Man*, I, 294.

135, 24–25. "*Amen* **stuck in his throat**." Cf. *Macbeth*, ii, 2, 32–33.

135, 31. "**no malice in the case**." Gay, *The Beggar's Opera*, I, x.

136, 5–12. **Say, I had lay'd a body in the sun**. In *Osorio*, the original form of *Remorse*, III, 224–231.

137, 8–9. "**I count myself indifferent honest.**" *Hamlet*, iii, 1, 123–125.

138, 2. "**who knew all qualities.**" Cf. *Othcllo*, iii, 3, 259.

138, 24. "**as much again to govern it.**" Pope, *Essay on Criticism*, ll. 80–81, a reading rejected in the quarto of 1743:

> ".' There are whom Heav'n has blest with store of wit,
> Yet want as much again to manage it.'.'

ON THE FEAR OF DEATH

This essay originally appeared in *Table Talk*, 1821–1822.

139, 1. "**And our little life . . . sleep.**" *The Tempest*, iv, 1, 156.

139, 10. **Bickerstaff.** In *The Tatler*, 1709–11. The author is Richard Steele.

139, 13. **the Globe.** A tavern in Fleet Street.

139, 16. *Tristram Shandy.* Volumes I and II in 1760; III and IV in 1761; V and VI in 1762; VII and VIII in 1765; IX in 1767.

139, 26–27. "**the gorge rises at.**" *Hamlet*, v, 1, 206.

140, 2. *perdus,* lost.

140, 9–11. "**Ye armed men . . . Temple church.**" The Temple Church, London, contains tombs of the Knights Templars.

140, 34–35. "**The wars we well remember . . . divine.**" Spenser, *Faerie Queene*, II, ix, 56.

141, 28. "**The present eye.**" *Troilus and Cressida*, iii, 3, 180.

141, 33–34. "**makes calamity of so long life.**" *Hamlet*, iii, 1, 69.

141, 35–37. "**Oh! thou strong heart!**" John Webster, *The White Devil*, V, iii, 96.

142, 2–3. "**Content man's natural desire.**" Pope, *Essay on Man*, I, 109.

142, 4–5. "**on this bank and shoal of time.**" *Macbeth*, i, 7, 6.

142, 23. **No young man ever thinks he shall die.** This is the opening sentence of *On the Feeling of Immortality in Youth*, and is there attributed to Hazlitt's brother John.

142, 24–25. "**all men are mortal.**" A reference to the stock example of the logical syllogism: "All men are mortal; Socrates is a man; therefore Socrates is mortal."

142, 31–32. "**This sensible warm motion . . . clod.**" *Measure for Measure*, iii, 1, 120.

142, 33–34. "**turn to withered, weak, and grey.**" *Paradise Lost*, XI, 540.

142, 37. **All men . . . themselves.** Edward Young, *Night Thoughts*, I, 424.

143, 11. "**the sear, the yellow leaf.**" *Macbeth*, v, 3, 23.

143, 17. "**gone into the wastes of time.**" Cf. Shakespeare, Sonnet xii, 10,

143, 23. **As the tree falls**. Cf. *Ecclesiastes*, xi, 3, "In the place where the tree falleth, there it shall be."

143, 37. *Don Carlos*. Hazlitt refers to the death of the Marquis in Act V.

144, 26. *Zanetto . . . matematica*. Rousseau, *Confessions*, Part II, Book 7, "Zanetto, leave women and study mathematics."

144, 35. **I have never seen death but once**. He probably refers to the death of his son William at the age of less than six months.

145, 9. **"like Chantry's monument."** The famous "Sleeping Children," in Lichfield Cathedral, by Francis Legatt Chantry (1781–1842), a noted English sculptor.

145, 26–27. **"Still from the tomb . . . fires."** Gray, *Elegy in a Country Churchyard*, 91–92.

145, 28–29. **Tucker's** *Light of Nature Pursued*. By Abraham Tucker (1705–1774). Hazlitt abridged the work in 1807.

147, 10–12. **"A little rule . . . grave."** John Dyer (1700–1758), *Grongar Hill* (1727).

147, 14–15. **"A great man's memory . . . year."** *Hamlet*, iii, 2, 139–140.

148, 6. *ad infinitum*. To infinity.

148, 10. **"at a pin's fee."** Cf. *Hamlet*, i, 4, 65.

148, 17–18. **"seasick, weary bark."** *Romeo and Juliet*, v, 3, 118.

148, 30–31. **"to lose it afterwards . . . brawl."** Cf. Thomas Olway, *Venice Preserved*, IV, ii, "To lose it, it may be, at last in a lewd quarrel."

149, 10. **Dr. Johnson.** Johnson often expressed fear of death. See Boswell's *Life of Johnson*.

On the Spirit of Obligations

This essay was first published in the *New Monthly Magazine, Table Talk*, xi, No. 37, Vol. X, 1824. It was republished in *The Plain Speaker*, 2 vols., 1826.

Of this essay Robert Louis Stevenson says in his essay on *Books which have Influenced Me:* ". . . Hazlitt, whose paper *On the Spirit of Obligations* was a turning-point in my life."

150, 10. *Nihil humani*. Terence, *Heauton-timoroumenos*, I, i.

152, 38. **"Make mouths at the invisible event."** *Hamlet*, iv, 4, 50.

153, 9–10. **Born for their use.** Edward Young, *The Revenge*, V, ii.

153, 32. *ex cathedra*. With authority.

153, 33. **"wise saws."** *As You Like It*, ii, 7, 156.

154, 7. **jump.** Agree.

154, 33. *quantum*. Due amount.

155, 16. *con amore*. With pleasure.

155, 18. **pour oil and balm.** Cf. *St. Luke*, x, 34.

155, 37. Mr. Wilberforce. William Wilberforce (1759–1833), a prominent anti-slavery leader.

156, 8–9. screwed to the sticking-place. Cf. *Macbeth*, i, 7, 60.

156, 10–11. "If to their share . . . all." Cf. Pope, *The Rape of the Lock*, II, 17–18.

156, 16. Granville Sharp. An advocate of anti-slavery (1735–1813).

156, 17. Hubert. A murderer in *King John*.

Howard, John (1726–1790), the great reformer of prisons.

Sir Hudson Lowe (1769–1844), the overseer of Napoleon at St. Helena, and maligned by all worshippers of Napoleon.

156, 18. "Charity covers a multitude of sins." *1 Peter*, iv, 8.

156, 20–22. "The meanest peasant . . . flock." Sterne, *A Sentimental Journey*, The Bourbonnais.

157, 17. Talma, François Joseph (1763–1826), a great French tragic actor.

157, 22. As one star differs from another. Cf. *1 Corinthians*, xv, 41.

157, 24–25. Mr. Justice Fielding. William, eldest son of Henry Fielding, the novelist (1748–1820).

157, 37. Booth. In *Amelia*.

158, 3. Colonel Bath. In *Amelia*.

158, 18–19. "administer to a mind diseased." Cf. *Macbeth*, v, 3, 40.

159, 6–7. "a little lower than the angels." *Psalms*, viii, 5.

159, 8–12. "And when I think . . . terrible." Byron's *Heaven and Earth*, Part I, scene i.

159, 18. The person, whose doors I enter with most pleasure. James Northcote, the painter, whose *Conversations* he edited and published in 1830.

160, 6. "Enter Sessami." Cf. "Open Sesame," the magic word which opened the cave door in *Ali Baba and the Forty Thieves*.

161, 24. The late Mr. Sheridan. Richard Brindsley Butler Sheridan, the dramatist, who died in 1816.

161, 28. "Coin his smile for drachmas." Cf. *Julius Cæsar*, iv, 3, 72–73.

On the Feeling of Immortality in Youth

This essay appeared first in the *New Monthly Magazine*, March, 1827. Republished in *Literary Remains* and *Winterslow*.

163, 1. "Life is a pure flame." Sir Thomas Browne (1605–1682), *Hydriotaphia: Urn Burial*, Chapter V.

163, 3. my brother's. John Hazlitt (1767–1837), the painter of miniatures. This saying is quoted in the essay *On the Fear of Death*, **142**, 23.

163, 10. **The vast, the unbounded prospect lies before us.**" Cf. Joseph Addison, *Cato*, V, i, 13, "The wide, unbounded prospect lies before me."

163, 13–14. "**bear a charmed life.**" *Macbeth*, v, 8, 12.

163, 17. "**Bidding the lovely scenes . . . hail.**" Collins, *The Passions*, 32.

164, 15–16. "**this sensible, warm motion . . . clod.**" *Measure for Measure*, iii, 1, 120.

164, 33. "**wine of life.**" *Macbeth*, ii, 3, 100.

165, 2. "**as in a glass, darkly.**" *1 Corinthians*, xiii, 12.

165, 9. "**So am not I!**" *Tristram Shandy*, Book V, Chapter vii.

165, 22–23. "**Life! thou strange thing . . . are.**" Joseph Fawcett, *The Art of War*, 1795, not 1794. An early and influential friend of Hazlitt, as well as of Wordsworth. Hazlitt characterizes him with deep appreciation in the essay *On Criticism*, in *Table Talk*.

166, 6. "**the feast of reason.**" Pope, *Imitations of Horace*, Satire I, 128.

166, 15. "**brave sublunary things.**" Cf. Michael Drayton, *To Henry Reynolds*, "Those brave translunary things."

166, 31–32. "**The stockdove plain . . . gale.**" James Thomson, *The Castle of Indolence*, I, iv.

167, 4. **Lady Wortley Montagu** (1690–1762), famed for her letters. She is usually called Lady Mary Wortley Montagu. *effendi*, a Turkish term of respect. This passage occurs in the Letter of May 17, 1717.

167, 15–18. "**had it not been . . . link-boys.**" In *Works*, II, 254.

167, 21–22. **She says of Richardson.** In *Works*, II, 285 ff., and 222.

168, 31. *monstrum ingens, biforme.* Cf. Virgil, *Æneid*, III, 658. Virgil reads *informe,* — a monster, shapeless, huge.

168, 34. **Mr. Moore.** Thomas Moore (1779–1852).

168, 37. "**his spirits.**" *Works*, II, 283.

170, 19. "**purple light of love.**" Gray, *Progress of Poesy*, 14.

170, 32. "**the Raphael grace, the Guido air.**" Pope, *Epistles*, III, 36, "Match Raphael's grace with thy lov'd Guido's air."

170, 37. "**gain a new vigour.**" William Cowper, *Charity*, 104.

172, 4–5. "**beguile the slow and creeping hours.**" Cf. *As You Like It*, ii, 7, 112, "Lose and neglect the creeping hours of time."

172, 13–**173**, 17. "**For my part . . . youth.**" This is a notable passage, for it expresses with noble eloquence the feelings of Hazlitt, Coleridge, and Wordsworth regarding the French Revolution, while youth was still upon them. Wordsworth exclaims in *The Prelude*, XI, 108–109:

> "Bliss was it in that dawn to be alive,
> But to be young was very Heaven."

In many passages Hazlitt states, with the absolute understanding of a contemporary, the motives of the English revolutionary poets.

172, 30–31. "From the dungeon . . . cry." Coleridge, *Sonnet to Schiller.* See note on *On Reading Old Books*, 29, 22–25.

172, 35. *Don Carlos.* See note on *On the Fear of Death*, 143, 37.

173, 16. "That time is past . . . raptures." Wordsworth, *Lines Composed a Few Miles Above Tintern Abbey*, 84–86.

174, 1–2. "Even from the tomb . . . fires." Gray, *Elegy Written in a Country Churchyard*, 91–92.

174, 9–10. "All the life of life is flown." Cf. Robert Burns, *Lament for James, Earl of Glencairn*, stanza vi.

174, 18–19. "From the last dregs . . . give." John Dryden, *Aurengzebe*, IV, i.

175, 9. "treason domestic." Cf. *Macbeth*, iii, 2, 24–26.

175, 21–22. "reverbs its own hollowness." *King Lear*, i, 1, 145.

MERRY ENGLAND

This essay was first published in the *New Monthly Magazine* for December, 1822. It was republished in *Sketches and Essays*, 1839.

176, 1. ' St. George for Merry England." St. George displaced Saint Edward as patron saint of England in 1349. His name soon became a rallying cry. The epithet "Merry" was early applied to places and is a ballad commonplace, as "Merry Carlisle," "Merry Lincoln," etc. "Merry England" occurs in the *Cursor Mundi*, c. 1310.

176, 3–4. *ut lucus a non lucendo.* The usual form is *lucus a non lucendo*, "light from its not shining," hence, "an absurdity."

176, 11. "The pleasure of going and coming." The source of this quotation has not been identified.

176, 26. "I have been merry." *2 Henry IV*, v, 3, 42.

176, 28. "Chirped over his cups." The title of one of the chapters in *Rabelais*.

176, 29–30. "there were pippins and cheese to come." *The Merry Wives of Windsor*, i, 2, 12.

177, 2–3. "Continents . . . contain." Thomas Hobbes, *Human Nature*.

177, 25–26. "amused themselves sadly." Waller and Glover draw attention to the fact that this famous saying is wrongly attributed to Froissart. The source of the idea is in dispute. See *Notes and Queries*, 1863 ff.

177, 38. "eat, drink, and are merry." Cf. *St. Luke*, xii, 19.

178, 4. "hairbreadth 'scapes." *Othello*, i, 3, 136.

178, 7. Punch. From Italian Punchinello, the popular puppet in the puppet play, *Punch and Judy*.

178, 30–31. **Jack-o'-the-Green.** Strutt, in *English Sports and Pastimes:*

"The Jack in the Green is a piece of pageantry consisting of a hollow frame of wood or wicker-work, made in the form of a sugar loaf, but open at the bottom and sufficiently large and high to receive a man. The frame is covered with green leaves and bunches of flowers interwoven with each other, so that the man within may be completely concealed, who dances with his companions, and the populace are mightily pleased with the oddity of the moving pyramid."

179, 4–5. *Old Lord's.* Lord's is still the famous cricket-ground of London.

179, 25. "**passage of arms at Ashby.**" Described by Sir Walter Scott, *Ivanhoe*, Chapter viii.

180, 3–4. "**A cry more tuneable . . . horn.**" *A Midsummer Night's Dream*, iv, 1, 121–122.

180, 20–21. "**brothers of the angle.**" Isaac Walton, *The Compleat Angler*, Part I, Chapter i. The date of the first edition of this famous book is 1653.

182, 11. *Book of Sports.* The *King's Majesties Declaration to his Subjects concerning lawfull Sports to be Used*, by James I, 1618, re-issued by Charles I, 1633.

182, 16–17. "**And e'en on Sunday . . . Monday.**" Robert Burns, *Tam O'Shanter*, 27–28.

182, 24. **Bartholomew Fair.** A famous fair held at West Smithfield, London, 1133–1850, about St. Bartholomew's Day, August 24.

Queen Mab. The Fairy Queen of English folklore.

183, 1. **Gilray.** James Gilray (1757–1813), the well-known caricaturist, displayed his prints in the window of Miss Humphrey's shop, 29 St. James Street.

184, 38. **Lord Byron.** Byron's *Letters and Journals*, V, 528, 533–535, 539 ff. (Prothero's edition.)

185, 7. "**merry and wise.**" The English popular proverb, "'Tis good to be merry and wise."

185, 13. "**That under Heaven is blown.**" Spenser, *Faerie Queene*, Book I, Canto vii, stanza 32. Cf. also, Marlowe, *Tamburlaine*, Part II, Act iv, scene 3.

186, 27. **Lubin Log.** In James Kennedy (1780–1849), *Love, Law and Physic.*

Tony Lumpkin. In Goldsmith's *She Stoops to Conquer.*

187, 15–20. **Nell** in *The Devil to Pay*, by Coffey; **Little Pickle** in *The Spoil'd Child*, a part created by Mrs. Jordan; **Touchstone** in *As You Like It*; **Sir Peter Teazle** in *The School for Scandal*, by Sheridan; **Lenitive** in *The Prize*, by Prince Hoare; **Lingo** in *The Agreeable Surprise*, by O'Keefe; **Crabtree** in *The School for Scandal*; **Nipperkin** in *Sprigs of Laurel*, a part created by Munden; **old Dornton** in *The Road to Ruin*, by Thomas Holcroft; **Ranger** in *The Suspicious Husband*, by Hoadly; **the Copper Captain** in *Rule a Wife and Have a Wife*, by John Fletcher, one of Lewis's great parts; **Lord Sands** in Shake-speare's *King Henry VIII*, **Filch** in Gay's *The Beggar's Opera;* **Moses** in *The School for Scandal;* **Sir Andrew Aguecheek** in *Twelfth Night;* **Acres** in Sheridan's *The Rivals;* **Elbow** in *Measure for Measure;* **Hodge** in the comic opera *Love in a Village,* by Isaac Bickerstaff; **Flora** in *The Wonder,* by Mrs. Centlivre; the **Duenna** in Sheridan's *Duenna;* **Lady Teazle** in Sheridan's *The School for Scandal;* **Lady Grace** in *The Provoked Husband,* by Vanbrugh and Cibber.

187, 23. "**Throwing a gaudy shadow upon life.**" The source of this quotation has not been discovered.

187, 29. Liston, John (1776?-1846), a comic actor.

187, 29-30. *Roderick Random.* A novel by Tobias Smollett, 1748.

187, 30. Hogarth, William (1697-1764). *Marriage à la Mode,* a series of plates dealing with social satire, 1745.

187, 31. "**Tut! there's livers.**" Cf. *Cymbeline,* iii, 4, 143, "There's livers out of Britain."

187, 36-37. "**What's our Britain . . . nest.**" Cf. *Cymbeline,* iii, 4, 140-142.

188, 5. Mrs. Abington, Frances (1737-1815), a famous actress. Hazlitt wrote, in *Lectures on the Comic Writers:* "I would rather have seen Mrs. Abington's Millamant than any Rosalind that ever appeared on the stage."

Mademoiselle Mars (1779-1847), a clever actress in the plays of Molière at the Théâtre Français, Paris.

188, 7. *Misanthrope.* One of Molière's greatest plays, 1666.

188, 23. As I write this. During the journey from August, 1824, to October, 1825.

188, 29. "**And gaudy butterflies.**" Gay, *The Beggar's Opera,* I (Polly's Song).

189, 15. "**all appliances.**" *2 Henry IV,* iii, 1, 29.

ON DISAGREEABLE PEOPLE

First published in the *New Monthly Magazine,* August, 1827. Re-published in *Sketches and Essays,* 1839.

191, 22. "**discourse of reason.**" Cf. *Hamlet,* i, 2, 150, and iv, 4, 36-37.

192, 7. "**The whole need not a physician.**" *St. Matthew,* ix, 12.

192, 18-26. "**As when . . . round.**" Thomson, *Castle of Indolence,* I, Stanza lxiv.

194, 38. *sent to Coventry.* Ostracised, refused the privileges of association.

195, 7. *alter idem,* another exactly similar.

195, 8-9. "**yea, into our heart of hearts.**" *Hamlet,* iii, 2, 78.

195, 12–13. "the volumes that enrich the shops." Earl of Roscommon, *Horace's Art of Poetry* (1680).

195, 16. "That bring their authors." Cf. The Earl of Roscommon, *Horace's Art of Poetry*, "That bring their authors to eternal fame."

195, 31. Walton's *Angler. The Compleat Angler*, 1653.

195, 32–33. "That dallies . . . old age." *Twelfth Night*, ii, 4, 48–49.

195, 34. Mandeville, Bernard (1670–1723), author of the famous *Fable of the Bees; or Private Vices Public Benefits*, 1714.

197, 20. "Wit at the helm . . . prow. Cf. Gray, *The Bard*, 74. "Youth on the prow, and Pleasure at the helm."

197, 27–28. a butt, according to the *Spectator. Spectator*, No. 47.

198, 13. *Cain; a Mystery*, published in 1821.

200, 8. *in corpore vili*, "on a worthless body."

200, 12. "hew you . . . gods." Cf. *Julius Cæsar*, ii, 1, 173–174.

200, 23. *tempora mollia fandi*. Cf. Virgil, *Æneid*, IV, 293–294, "the happiest moments for speech."

201, 4–5. "Not to admire . . . them so." Pope, *Imitations of Horace*, Book I, Epistle vi, 1–2.

201, 10. Westminster School of Reform. The group of reformers around the *Westminster Review*, founded in 1823 by Jeremy Bentham. James Mill and John Stuart Mill were also associated with the group.

201, 28–29. "the milk of human kindness." *Macbeth*, i, 5, 15.

ON FAMILIAR STYLE

This essay first appeared in *Table Talk*, 1821–1822. It should be studied by anyone who wishes to appreciate what English style is, as it is one of the wisest essays ever written on this important theme.

205, 12. "tall, opaque words." Sterne, *Tristram Shandy*, Book III, Chapter xx (Author's Preface).

205, 13. "first row of the rubric." Cf. *Hamlet*, ii, 2, 437, "the first row of the pious chanson." The rubrics are the headings or directions, so called because they were originally written in red.

205, 35–38. With true instinct for style in English, Hazlitt pitches upon the verse of Marlowe.

206, 16–20. I never invented . . . distinction. The truth of these words becomes more apparent and more remarkable as one studies the various prose of Hazlitt. His diction is remarkably free from all the faults that come from a striving after modernity or antiquity.

208, 12. Burton, Robert (1577–1640), the author of *The Anatomy of Melancholy;* Fuller, Thomas (1608–1661), author of *History of the Worthies of England*, 1662; Coryate, or Coryat, Thomas (1577–1617), an English traveller, author of *Coryat's Crudities*, 1611; Browne, or

Brown, Sir Thomas (1605–1682), author of *Religio Medici*, 1643, and *Hydriotaphia*, 1658. These authors were influential in the formation of Lamb's style.

208, 17. Elia. The name under which Lamb first contributed to *The London Magazine* in 1820, and which he retained.

208, 19. *Mrs. Battle's Opinions on Whist.* This famous essay first appeared in *The London Magazine*, February, 1821.

208, 21. "A well of native English undefiled." Spenser, *Faerie Queene*, IV, ii, 32:

> "Dan Chaucer, well of English undefyled,
> On Fame's eternall beadroll worthie to be fyled."

208, 24. Erasmus's *Colloquies.* Erasmus (1466–1536) wrote the *Colloquies* in 1524.

208, 31. "What do you read?" *Hamlet*, ii, 2, 193–195.

209, 13. *sermo humi obrepens.* Cf. Horace, *Epistles*, II, i, 250–251, "that crawls in prose along the ground."

209, 16. "ambition is more lowly." Cf. *The Tempest*, i, 2, 480–481:

> "My affections
> Are then most humble."

209, 18. "unconsidered trifles." *The Winter's Tale*, iv, 3, 25–26.

209, 25. Ancient Pistol. In *Henry IV*, *Henry V*, and *The Merry Wives of Windsor*.

209, 30. "That strut . . . stage." *Macbeth*, v, 5, 25.

209, 34. "And on their pens . . . plumed." Cf. *Paradise Lost*, IV, 988–989:

> "And on his crest
> Sat Horror plumed."

210, 5–6. "Nature's own sweet . . . laid on." *Twelfth Night*, i, 5, 258.

211, 10. Cowper's description. Cowper, *The Task*, 173–176.

On the Prose-Style of Poets

This essay appeared in *The Plain Speaker; Opinions on Books, Men, and Things*, 1826.

212, 1. "Do you read or sing?" Hazlitt attributes this to Cæsar, who put this question to a certain speaker.

212, 7. "feathered, two-legged things." Cf. Dryden, *Absalom and Achitophel*, i, 170.

212, 26–27. "unpleasing flats and sharps. Cf. *Romeo and Juliet*, iii, 5, 28, "Straining harsh discords and unpleasing sharps."

213, 3. **Ossian's** *Poems*. The so-called translations by *James Macpherson* (1736–1796), published 1761–1763.

213, 4. **Shaftesbury's** *Characteristics*. *Characteristics of Men, Manners, Opinions, and Times*, by Anthony Ashley Cooper, third Earl of Shaftesbury (1671–1713). The book was published in 1711, and was one of the most influential philosophical works of the eighteenth century.

213, 20–21. "**foregone conclusion.**" *Othello*, iii, 3, 426.

213, 23. **Horne Tooke** (1736–1812), author of *The Diversions of Purley*, and Member of Parliament for Old Sarum.

214, 3. **Old Sarum.** See previous note. He was defeated for Westminster.

214, 13–14. "**He murmurs . . . own.**" Wordsworth, *A Poet's Epitaph*, 39–40.

215, 22. "**come trippingly off the tongue.**" Cf. *Hamlet*, iii, 2, 2.

216, 25. *invita Minervâ*. Horace, *De Arte Poetica*, 385, "against the bent of genius, or nature."

216, 37. *ad libitum*, at his pleasure.

218, 14. **Nine.** That is, the Nine Muses; poetry.

218, 18. "**treads the primrose path of dalliance.**" *Hamlet*, i, 3, 50.

218, 18–19. "**the highest heaven of invention.**" *King Henry V*, Prologue, 2.

218, 19–20. *He is nothing if not fancifull* Cf. *Othello*, ii, 1, 120.

218, 28. **Bristol-stones.** Colorless quartz crystals found near Bristol. They are called Bristol diamonds.

218, 32. "**On the unsteadfast footing.**" *1 Henry IV*, i, 3, 193.

219, 30–31. "**To make us heirs . . . lays.**" Wordsworth, *Personal Talk*, 53–54.

220, 14. "**Like beauty . . . rime.**" Shakespeare, *Sonnet* cvi.

220, 18. *Letter to a Noble Lord.* Burke published this famous pamphlet in 1796.

221, 9–10. "**Dum domus . . . habebit.**" Virgil, *Æneid*, ix, 448–449: "So long as the house of Æneas dwells hard by the immoveable rock of the Capitol, and the father of Rome holds his imperial sway."

221, 15. "**buttress, frieze . . . 'vantage.**" Cf. *Macbeth*, i, 6, 6–8.

221, 19. "**at one fell swoop.**" *Macbeth*, iv, 3, 119.

221, 20. "**low, fat Bedford level.**" From the passage quoted from Burke's *Letter to a Noble Lord* on page 220. The Duke of Bedford was one of the persons attacked in the pamphlet.

221, 23–24. "**sharp and sweet.**" Cf. *All's Well that Ends Well*, iv, 4, 33, "as sweet as sharp."

221, 26. *durante bene placito*, "during his good pleasure."

221, 27. *for better for worse*. Words from the usual marriage ceremony.

221, 36–37. "**From Windsor's heights . . . survey.**" Cf. Gray, *Ode on a Distant Prospect of Eton College*, 6–7.

222, 1. the so-much-admired description. In the *Speech on the Revenues of the Carnatic*, February 28, 1785.

222, 7. Abbé Sieyès's far-famed "pigeon-holes." In Burke's *Letter to a Noble Lord*.

222, 8. "the Leviathan." In Burke's *Letter to a Noble Lord*.

222, 17. "Created hugest . . . stream." *Paradise Lost*, I, 200–202.

222, 22. "put his hook in the nostrils." *Job*, xli, 1–2.

222, 27. Lord Castlereagh. Viscount Castlereagh and Marquis of Londonderry (1769–1822). He committed suicide; hence the reference to the corpse "lying uncovered in the place where it fell". (**223, 18**), and to the "coroner's inquest" (**224**, 8).

223, 22–23. Mr. Montgomery. James Montgomery (1771–1854), editor of the Sheffield *Iris*, 1794–1825.

223, 24. *travelling out of the record*, wandering from the point at issue.

224, 11. "elevate and surprise." Buckingham, *The Rehearsal*, I, 1.

224, 20–21. Poets have been said to succeed best in fiction. Edmund Waller is said to have made this reply to Charles II when the King complained of the poor qualities of the poet's verses on the Restoration as compared with his panegyric on Cromwell.

225, 8–9. "forlorn way obscure." Cf. *Paradise Lost*, II, 615.

225, 30. the poet laureate. Robert Southey.

225, 33. Fuller, Thomas (1608–1661), author of *The Worthies of England;* **Burton,** Robert (1577–1640), author of *The Anatomy of Melancholy;* **Latimer,** Hugh (1491–1555), author of *Sermons*.

226, 2. "stoops to earth." Cf. Pope, *Epistle to Dr. Arbuthnot*, 341.

226, 15–16. "the words of Mercury." *Love's Labour's Lost*, v, 2, 939–940.

226, 23. *Wat Tyler*. Written in 1794, published in 1817.

226, 24. The author of *Rimini*. Leigh Hunt published *Rimini* in 1816. His *Examiner* began to appear January 3, 1808.

227, 1. his effusions in the *Indicator*. From October 13, 1819, to March 21, 1821, and from March 28, 1821, to October 13, 1821.

On a Landscape of Nicolas Poussin

This essay was first published in the *London Magazine* for August, 1821. It was republished in *Table Talk*, 1821–1822.

Nicolas Poussin (1594–1665) was a celebrated French painter.

228, 1. "And blind Orion . . . morn." Cf. John Keats, *Endymion*, II, 198.

228, 3. "a hunter of shadows." Homer's *Odyssey*, XI, 572–575.

228, 4–5. having lost an eye. He offered violence to Merope, and was blinded by her father Œnopion with the help of Dionysus.

228, 13-14. "**grey dawn and the Pleiades.**" *Paradise Lost*, VII, 373-374.

228, 21. "**shadowy sets off.**" *Paradise Lost*, V, 43.

228, 27. **Sir Joshua has done him justice in this respect.** See Sir Joshua Reynolds, *Dicourses*, V.

229, 1. "**denote a foregone conclusion.**" *Othello*, iii, 3, 428.

229, 7. "**take up the isles.**" *Isaiah*, xl, 15.

229, 26. "**so potent art.**" *The Tempest*, v, 1, 50.

229, 34. "**more than natural.**" *Hamlet*, ii, 2, 385.

230, 1. "**gives to airy nothing.**" *A Midsummer Night's Dream*, v, 1, 16-17.

232, 2. "**o'er-informed.**" Dryden, *Absalom and Achitophel*, I, 158.

232, 10. "**the very stones prate.**" *Macbeth*, ii, 1, 58.

233, 1. "**Leaping like . . . spring.**" Spenser, *The Faerie Queene*, I, vi, 14.

233, 18. "**his picture of the shepherds.**" A favorite with Hazlitt. It is in the Louvre.

233, 20. "**Et ego in Arcadia vixi.**" The source of this quotation has never been definitely determined. See *Notes and Queries*, Series VI, Volume VI, 396.

233, 23. "**the valleys low.**" Cf. *Lycidas*, 136.

233, 31-32. "**within the book . . . matter.**" *Hamlet*, i, 5, 103-104.

234, 2-3. "**the sober certainty . . . bliss.**" Milton, *Comus*, 263.

234, 5. "**he who knows of these delights.**" Milton, *Sonnet to Mr. Lawrence*.

234, 21. **the Caracci.** The Caracci were three: Agostino (1558-1602), his brother Annibale (1560-1609), and their cousin Lodovico (1555-1619). They founded the Bolognese school of painting.

234, 29-30. "**Old Genius . . . wend.**" Spenser, *Faerie Queene*, III, vi, 31-32.

234, 35. "**there were propagation too:**' Cf. *Measure for Measure*, i, 2, 154, "Only propagation of a dower."

235, 1. "**scattered like stray gifts.**" Cf. Wordsworth, *Stray Pleasures*, 27-28.

235, 5. **Blenheim.** The seat of the Duke of Marlborough, about ten miles from Oxford.

Burleigh. Burleigh House, the seat of Lord Burleigh, near Stamford in Lincolnshire.

235, 6. **Mr. Angerstein.** John Julius Angerstein (1735-1823), a merchant and patron of the arts, whose collection forms the basis of the present National Gallery.

235, 6. **Lord Grosvenor.** In Grosvenor House, London, founded by Richard, first Earl of Grosvenor.

The Marquis of Stafford. In London.

235, 10-11. **the Louvre is stripped.** The paintings and other treasures of Art which Napoleon had carried to the Louvre were restored in 1815.

235, 12. Iron Crown. The Iron Crown of Charlemagne was offered Napoleon when he was crowned in Paris, December 2, 1804.
235, 13. the hunter of greatness and glory. Napoleon died on May 5, 1821, at St. Helena.

MR. COLERIDGE

This essay was first published in *The Spirit of the Age or Contemporary Portraits*, 1825. This essay should be compared with *My First Acquaintance with Poets*, as the expression of Hazlitt's disillusionment. A good deal of the essay is based on conversations with Coleridge, and a number of the references to Coleridge's activities cannot be found in his published writings.

In the lecture on *The Living Poets*, in his *Lectures on the English Poets*, delivered and published in 1818, Hazlitt paid the following tribute to Coleridge, which should be compared with the present essay and with *My First Acquaintance with Poets*. The passage is, moreover, one of the great passages in English prose.

" But I may say of him here, that he is the only person I ever knew who answered to the idea of a man of genius. He is the only person from whom I ever learnt anything. There is only one thing he could learn from me in return, but *that* he has not. He was the first poet I ever knew. His genius at that time had angelic wings, and fed on manna. He talked on forever; and you wished him to talk on forever. His thoughts did not seem to come with labour and effort; but as if borne on the gusts of genius, and as if the wings of his imagination lifted him from off his feet. His voice rolled on the ear like the pealing organ, and its sound alone was the music of thought. His mind was clothed with wings; and raised on them, he lifted philosophy to heaven. In his descriptions, you then saw the progress of human happiness and liberty in bright and never-ending succession, like the steps of Jacob's ladder, with airy shapes ascending and descending, and with the voice of God at the top of the ladder. And shall I, who heard him then, listen to him now? Not I! . . . That spell is broke; that time is gone forever; that voice is heard no more: but still the recollection comes rushing by with thoughts of long-past years, and rings in my ears with never-dying sound.",

236, 14–15. and thank the bounteous Pan. Cf. Milton, *Comus*, 176.
236, 20. ' a mind reflecting ages past." In the first line of a commendatory poem signed "J. M. S." in the Second Folio (1632). Coleridge conjectured that J. M. S. indicated "John Milton, Student."
236, 21–22. " dark rearward and abyss." Cf. *The Tempest*, i, 2, 50, "In the dark backward and abysm of time."

236, 29–31. "**That which was . . . water.**" *Antony and Cleopatra*, iv, 14, 9–11.

237, 4. "**quick, forgetive.**" Cf. *2 Henry IV*, iv, 3, 106–107.

237, 19. **Peter Abelard** (1079–1142), the famous scholar and lover of Eloisa.

237, 21. *Courier.* A newspaper to which Coleridge contributed at various periods from before 1809 to the close of his active life.

237, 23. "**what in him is weak.**" Cf. *Paradise Lost*, I, 22–23.

238, 5–6. "**and by the force . . . confusion.**" Cf. *Macbeth*, iii, 5, 28–29.

238, 11. "**rich strond.**" Spencer's *Faerie Queene*, III, iv, 18, 29, 34.

238, 11–12. "**goes sounding on his way.**" See the note on **9**, 6.

238, 27 "**his own things monstered.**" Cf. *Coriolanus*, ii, 1, 81, "To hear my nothings monster'd."

238, 28–29 **letting contemplation have its fill.** George Dyer, *Grongar Hill*, 26.

238, 30–31. "**Sailing with supreme . . . air.**" Gray, *The Progress of Poesy*, 115–116.

239, 12. "**He lisped in numbers . . . came.**" Pope, *Prologue to the Satires*, 128

239, 13. *Ode on Chatterton. Monody on the Death of Chatterton.* Composed in 1790, when Coleridge was only eighteen.

239, 20–21. **gained several prizes.** He won the Browne Gold Medal for a Greek Ode in 1792.

239, 26–27. **Christ's Hospital.** A famous boys' school in London which was attended by Coleridge and Lamb. Hazlitt here has reference to the famous passage on Coleridge in the well-known essay by Lamb (ELIA) on *Christ's Hospital Five and Twenty Years Ago* (1820): "Samuel Taylor Coleridge — Logician, Metaphysician, Bard! — How have I seen the casual passer through the Cloisters stand still, intranced with admiration (while he weighed the disproportion between the *speech* and the *garb* of the young Mirandula), to hear thee unfold, in thy deep and sweet intonations, the mysteries of Jamblichus, or Plotinus (for even in those years thou waxedst not pale at such philosophic draughts), or reciting Homer in his Greek, or Pindar — while the walls of the old Grey Friars re-echoed to the accents of the *inspired charity boy!*"

240, 9. "**Struggling in vain . . . destiny.**" Wordsworth, *The Excursion*, VI, 557.

240, 14. **Hartley's tribes of mind.** David Hartley (1705–1757), author of *Observations on Man, his Frame, his Duty, and his Expectations*, 1749. "Tribes of the mind" is reminiscent of Coleridge's own words describing Hartley's system, *Religious Musings*, 369, "he first who marked the ideal tribes." Cf. Collins, *Ode on the Poetical Character*, 47, "All the shadowy tribes of mind."

240, 15. **etherial braid, thought-woven.** Cf. Collins, *Ode to Evening*, 7, "With brede ethereal wove."

240, 16. vibratiuncles. Theoretical fine movements in the brain, refinements of external and nervous vibrations, by which sensations were produced. This is an important aspect of Hartley's system.

240, 16–17. the great law of association. In Hartley's system, this law expressed the process by which sensation changed from sensation to ideas of sensation and hence to ideas of thought and the more ideal forms of thought.

240, 21. Priestley's Materialism. Dr. Priestley identified matter and spirit in his philosophy.

241, 22–23. like Ariel. *The Tempest*, I, ii.

240, 24. Bishop Berkeley's fairy-world. This refers to the idealistic nature of Berkeley's philosophy, as contrasted with the materialism of Hartley's and Priestley's.

240, 26. Malebranche (1638–1715), a French metaphysician who is best known in English criticism as the great enemy of Imagination in his *Recherche de la Vérité*, 1674.

240, 27. Cudworth's *Intellectual System.* Published in 1678, by Ralph Cudworth (1617–1688).

240, 28. Lord Brooke. Fulke Greville, Lord Brooke (1554–1628), the friend and biographer of Sir Philip Sidney.

240, 29. Bishop Butler. Joseph Butler (1692–1752), author of the famous *Analogy of Religion*, 1736.

240, 29–30. the Duchess of Newcastle (1624–1674) published poems, plays, and philosophical works, 1653–1668.

240, 30. Clarke, Samuel (1675–1729), a noted divine and metaphysician. His most famous contribution to philosophic thought is his argument for the existence of God. **South,** Robert (1633–1716), a famous English divine. He began the notable controversy on the Trinity, 1693.

241, 1. Tillotson, John (1630–1694), became Archbishop of Canterbury in 1691.

241, 2. Leibnitz's *Pre-established Harmony.* Liebnitz (1646–1716) was a celebrated German philosopher. His system was that of a pre-established harmony between matter and spirit.

241, 6. *hortus siccus,* collection of dried botanical specimens.

Dissent. A dissenter is one who dissents from the doctrines of the established Church.

241, 10. John Huss (1369–1415), the great Bohemian religious reformer and martyr; **Jerome of Prague** (1365–1416), an associate and follower of Huss; **Socinus** (1530–1604), an Italian Unitarian theologian (1360–1424), a noted follower of Huss.

241, 11. Neal, Daniel (1648–1743), *History of the Puritans*, 1732–1738.

241, 12. Calamy, Edmund (1671–1732), *Account of the Ministers, Lecturers, Masters, and Fellows of Colleges and Schoolmasters who were Ejected or Silenced after the Restoration of 1660*, 1702.

241, 12–13. **like thoughts and passions.** Cf. *Acts*, xiv, 15, "like passions."

241, 13. **Spinoza,** Baruch de (1632–1677), the most eminent expounder of pantheism.

241, 23–25. "**When he saw nought but beauty . . . murmured.**" The source of this quotation has not been discovered.

241, 27. **Proclus** (A.D. 412–485), the most famous of the Athenian Neo-Platonists; **Plotinus** (A.D. 204–270), a Neo-Platonic philosopher.

241, 29. **Duns Scotus** (1265?–1308), one of the founders of scholasticism; **Aquinas,** Thomas (1225 or 1227–1274), a celebrated theologian and scholastic philosopher.

241, 30. **Jacob Behmen** (1575–1624), a celebrated German mystic.

241, 31. **Swedenborg,** Emanuel (1688–1772), a celebrated Swedish Theosophist, founder of the Swedenborgian church; author of *Arcana Cælestia*, 1749–1756.

241, 33. *Religious Musings.* Written by Coleridge "on the Christmas Eve of 1794."

241, 36. **Bowles's** *Sonnets.* Coleridge has left a notable account of this in his *Biographia Literaria*, Chapter I.

242, 2. **Arbuthnot,** John (1667–1735). He published *Life in a Bottomless Pit; or History of John Bull*, 1712.

242, 7. **Marivaux,** Pierre (1688–1763), a French dramatist and novelist. **Crébillon,** Prosper de (1674–1762), a noted French tragic poet.

242, 8. "**laughed with Rabelais.**" Cf. Pope, *The Dunciad*, I, 22.

242, 9–18. Coleridge visited Rome in 1806. Some idea of what his conversations were may be gathered from his *Table Talk*, issued by H. N. Coleridge in 1835.

242, 14. **Triumph of Death.** A fresco in the Campo Santo, Pisa, now ascribed to the Lorenzetti.

242, 20. **Kantean philosophy.** Coleridge gives an account of this stage of his development in his *Biographia Literaria*, Chapter IX.

242, 26. **sang for joy.** In *Destruction of the Bastille* written in 1789.

242, 31. "**In Philharmonia's undivided dale.**" Coleridge, *Monody on the Death of Chatterton*, version of 1794, line 151, "Freedom's undivided dale," and *To Rev. W. J. Hort*, 15, "In Freedom's undivided dell." This refers to the scheme of Pantisocracy, a communal settlement in America, planned by Coleridge, Southey, and others.

242, 32. "**Frailty, thy name is** *Genius.*" Cf. *Hamlet*, i, 2, 146.

242, 35. *Courier.* See note on **237**, 21.

243, 11. **Poet laureate or stamp-distributor.** A palpable hit at Southey and Wordsworth respectively.

243, 13. "**bourne from whence no traveller returns.**" *Hamlet*, iii, 1, 79–80.

243, 32. **one splendid passage.** Lines 408–426.

244, 27. *Friend.* Coleridge began *The Friend* as a weekly paper which continued more or less irregularly from June 1, 1809, to March 15, 1810. It appeared in three volumes in 1818.

244, 32. **Mr. Godwin.** William Godwin, the author of *Political Justice*, 1793.

245, 13. "He cannot be constrained by mastery." Cf. Wordsworth, *The Excursion*, VI, 163–164:

"That Love will not submit to be controlled
By mastery."

246, 7. *Pingo in eternitatem,* "I paint for eternity."

246, 17. "taught with the little nautilus." Pope, *Essay on Man*, III, 177.

246, 19. "Youth at its prow . . . helm." Cf. Gray, *The Bard*, II, 2.

247, 9. "from the pelting . . . storm." *King Lear*, iii, 4, 29.

247, 14. "as with triple steel." *Paradise Lost*, II, 569.

247, 21. "His words were hollow." Cf. *Paradise Lost*, II, 112–17.

247, 25–26. "And curs'd the hour . . . way." Cf. William Collins, *Oriental Eclogues*, II, *refrain.*

MR. WORDSWORTH

This essay first appeared in *The Spirit of the Age; or Contemporary Portraits*, 1825. It should be compared with *My First Acquaintance with Poets.* As in the case of the essay on Mr. Coleridge, a considerable number of the acts and opinions attributed to Wordsworth are from conversations which Hazlitt had with the poet. The essay is full of noble appreciation of Wordsworth, in spite of the acid of disparagement. In many ways, resulting from unusual opportunities and kindred aims, Hazlitt is one of the "best knowers" of Wordsworth, second only to Coleridge — *par nobile fratrum.* The following passage from his lecture on *The Living Poets*, in his *Lectures on the English Poets*, delivered and published in 1818, is at once an illustration of this and a fine example of concentrated criticism.

"Mr. Wordsworth is the most original poet now living. He is the reverse of Walter Scott in his defects and excellences. He has nearly all that the other wants, and wants all that the other possesses. His poetry is not external, but internal; it does not depend upon tradition or story, or old song; he furnishes it from his own mind, and is his own subject. He is the poet of mere sentiment. Of many of the *Lyrical Ballads* it is not possible to speak in terms of too high praise, such as *Heart-leap Well, The Banks of the Wye, Poor Susan,* parts of *The Leech-gatherer,* the *Lines to a Cuckoo, To a Daisy, The Complaint,* several of the *Sonnets,* and a hundred others of inconceivable beauty, of perfect originality and pathos. They open a finer and deeper vein of thought and feeling than any poet in modern times has done, or attempted."

248, 5-6. "**lowliness is young ambition's ladder**." *Julius Cæsar*, ii, 1, 22.

248, 9. "**no figures . . . men**." Cf. *Julius Cæsar*, ii, 1, 231-232.

248, 22. "**skyey influences**." *Measure for Measure*, iii, 1, 9.

248, 27. "*Nihil humani . . . puto.*" Terence, *Heauton-timoroumenos*, I, i, 25.

249, 19. *Lyrical Ballads*. Published in 1798.

249, 26-27. "**the cloud-capt towers**." Cf. *The Tempest*, iv, 1, 151-156.

249, 31. *de novo*, anew; *tabula rasa*, a white sheet.

249, 36. "**the judge's robe**." Cf. *Measure for Measure*, ii, 2, 59-61.

249, 38-**250**, 1. **The Ode and Epode . . . scorn**. That is, he defied the classic tradition in English literature, and wrote simply.

250, 3. **decencies**. Probably a reminiscence of that famous passage in Burke, *Reflections on the Revolution in France*, "All the decent drapery of life is to be rudely torn off," etc.

250, 12. **gathers manna**. *Numbers*, xi, 7-8.

250, 12-13. **strikes the barren rock**. *Numbers*, xx, 11; *Psalm* lxxviii, 20. The Biblical word is "smote."

250, 17-19. "**a sense of joy . . . field**." Wordsworth, *Lines Written at a Small Distance from my House*, 6-8.

250, 26-30. "**Beneath the hills . . . destiny**. Cf. Wordsworth, *The Excursion*, VI, 553-557.

251, 2. **vain pomp and glory**. *Henry VIII*, iii, 2, 365.

251, 20. *association*. Doubtless referring to Wordsworth's own doctrine of poetry as expressed in the Preface to the *Lyrical Ballads*, 1800:

"The principal object, then, which I proposed to myself in these poems was to make the incidents of common life interesting by tracing in them, truly though not ostentatiously, the primary laws of our nature: chiefly as far as regards the manner in which we associate ideas in a state of excitement."

251, 32-33. "**To him the meanest flower . . . tears**." Cf. *Ode on the Intimations of Immortality*, 206-207.

253, 4. **Cole-Orton**. The residence of Sir George Beaumont, a friend and admirer of Wordsworth. Wordsworth frequently expressed his indebtedness to Sir George and Lady Beaumont. He dedicated the 1815 edition of his poems to him.

253, 7. *Laodamia*. Published in 1815.

253, 10. "**Calm contemplation . . . pains**." Cf. *Laodamia*, 72.

253, 33. "**Fall blunted . . . breast**." Cf. Goldsmith, *The Traveller*, 232.

254, 1. "**and fit audience found, though few.**" Cf. *Paradise Lost*, VII, 31. Quoted by Wordsworth in *The Home at Grasmere, The Recluse*, 776–778:

"—— 'Fit audience let me find though few,'
So prayed, more gaining than he asked, the Bard —
In holiest mood.".

254, 3. *The Excursion*. Published in 1814.

254, 24. *toujours perdrix, i.e.*, "always partridges." An allusion to a French king who illustrated the advantages of variety by serving partridges day after day to his confessor, without any change of diet.

254, 36. "**man of no mark or likelihood.**" Cf. *1 Henry IV*, iii, 2, 45.

255, 23–24. "**Flushed with a purple grace . . . face.**" Dryden, *Alexander's Feast*, 51–52.

255, 29. **Titian** (1477–1576), a famous Venetian painter.

255, 30. *Bacchus and Ariadne*, now in the National Gallery, London.

255, 35–36. **modernize some of the** *Canterbury Tales*. *The Prioress' Tale*, 1820; *Troilus and Cressida*, 1841.

256, 6–7. "**He hates those interlocutions.**" Hazlitt says of Wordsworth in *The English Poets*, "He hates the dialogues in Shakespeare."

256, 12–14. "**Action is momentary . . . infinite.**" Cf. Wordsworth, *The Borderers* (written 1795–6, published 1842), lines 1539–1544. In a note to *The White Doe of Rylstone*, published in 1815, he says: "This and the five lines which follow were either read or recited by me, more than thirty years ago, to the late Mr. Hazlitt, who quoted some expressions in them (imperfectly remembered) in a work of his published several years ago."

256, 17. **has a great dislike to Gray.** See the Preface to the *Lyrical Ballads*, 1800. The basis of his dislike is Gray's "poetic diction" and artificiality.

256, 26–27. "**Let observation . . . Peru.**" *The Vanity of Human Wishes*, 1–2.

256, 35. **Drawcansir.** A character in the Duke of Buckingham's *The Rehearsal* (1671); a boasting bully.

257, 8. **Bewick**, Thomas (1753–1828), a famous engraver on wood; **Waterloo**, Antoine (1609?–1676?), a French engraver and etcher.

257, 26–27. "**he hates conchology.**" Hazlitt said this, in his *Lecture on the Living Poets*, in his *Lectures on the English Poets*.

257, 31–32. "**Where one for sense . . . time.**" Samuel Butler, *Hudibras*, II, 29–30.

258, 13–14. "**take the good . . . us.**" Plautus, *Rudens*, IV, vii.

258, 21. "**Lord Byron we have called.**" In the chapter on Lord Byron in *The Spirit of the Age:* "His lordship, as a poet, is a little headstrong and self-willed, a spoiled child of nature and fortune."

HAMLET

This essay in its first form appeared in the *Morning Chronicle* of March 14, 1814, and was called forth by the presentation of Hamlet by Edmund Kean. It was reprinted in *Characters of Shakespeare's Plays*, 1817.

260, 3. that famous soliloquy. *Hamlet*, iii, 1, 56–88.

260, 4. gave the advice to the players. iii, 2, 1–50.

260, 4–5. this goodly frame. ii, 2, 304–323.

260, 9. grave-diggers. v, 1, 1–240.

260, 12. he that was mad. v, i, 103–104.

260, 25. "too much i' th' sun." i, 2, 67.

260, 28–29. "the pangs of despised love." iii, 1, 72.

262, 1–2. "the outward pageants." Cf. i, 2, 86.

262, 2. "we have that within." i, 2, 85.

262, 19–20. where he kills Polonius. iii, 4.

262, 20. alters the letters. iv, 6; v, 2, 49–53.

262, 30. "that has no relish of salvation in it." iii, 3, 92.

263, 9–43. How all occasions . . . worth." iv, 4, 32–66.

264, 13–14. "that noble and liberal casuist." This appears to be an imperfect recollection of Charles Lamb's reference to the old English dramatists as "those noble and liberal casuists," in *Characters of Dramatic Writers Contemporary with Shakespeare* (*Thomas Middleton and William Rowley*).

264, 16. *Whole Duty of Man*, 1659. An ethical treatise of unknown authorship. It is among Lydia Languish's books in Sheridan's *The Rivals*.

264, 17. *The Academy of Compliments; or, the whole Art of Courtship, being the rarest and most exact way of wooing a Maid or Widow, by the way of Dialogue or complimental Expression*. London, no date. Later editions appeared in 1655 and 1669.

264, 21. "license of the time." Cf. *Timon of Athens*, v, 4, 4–5,

> "You have gone and filled the time
> With all licentious measures."

264, 35–36. "his father's spirit . . . arms." i, 2, 255.

265, 6–8. "I loved Ophelia." v, 1, 292–294.

265, 11–14. "Sweets to the sweet . . . grave." v, 1, 266.

265, 19–20. "O rose of May." iv, 5, 157.

265, 32. his advice to Laertes. i, 3, 55–81.

265, 35–36. "There is a willow . . . stream." iv, 7, 167.

266, 1. his advice to the King and Queen. ii, 2, 86–169.

266, 16. Mr. Kemble. John Philip Kemble (1757–1823), a celebrated tragedian, popular as Hamlet, Brutus, and Coriolanus.

266, 19. "a wave o' th' sea." *The Winter's Tale*, iv, 4, 141.

266, 24. Kean, Edmund (1787–1833), a celebrated actor, noted for his brilliant presentation of Shakespeare's characters. He was deeply admired by Hazlitt.

1812260R0021

Printed in Great Britain
by Amazon.co.uk, Ltd.,
Marston Gate.